PENGUIN CANADA

THE BOOK OF DREAMS

O.R. Melling was born in Ireland and grew up in Toronto with her seven sisters and two brothers. At eighteen, she hitchhiked across Canada. While at Trinity College, she joined the Naval Reserve and was stationed on the east and west coasts. In more recent years she has visited Labrador, the Yukon and the Northwest Territories. At present, she lives in Ireland with her daughter, Findabhair, but like a bird in the evening, she's on her way home.

Also by O.R. Melling

The Druid's Tune
The Singing Stone
My Blue Country

The Chronicles of Faerie
The Hunter's Moon
The Summer King
The Light-Bearer's Daughter

Adult Fiction
Falling Out of Time

The Book of Dreams

The Chronicles of Faerie

O. R. Melling

PENGUIN CANADA

Published by the Penguin Group

Penguin Group (Canada), 90 Eglinton Avenue East, Suite 700, Toronto, Ontario, Canada
M4P 2Y3 (a division of Pearson Penguin Canada Inc.)

Penguin Group (USA) Inc., 375 Hudson Street, New York, New York 10014, U.S.A.
Penguin Books Ltd, 80 Strand, London WC2R 0RL, England
Penguin Ireland, 25 St Stephen's Green, Dublin 2, Ireland (a division of Penguin Books Ltd)
Penguin Group (Australia), 250 Camberwell Road, Camberwell, Victoria 3124, Australia
   (a division of Pearson Australia Group Pty Ltd)
Penguin Books India Pvt Ltd, 11 Community Centre, Panchsheel Park, New Delhi – 110 017,
   India
Penguin Group (NZ), cnr Airborne and Rosedale Roads, Albany, Auckland 1310, New Zealand
   (a division of Pearson New Zealand Ltd)
Penguin Books (South Africa) (Pty) Ltd, 24 Sturdee Avenue, Rosebank, Johannesburg 2196,
   South Africa

Penguin Books Ltd, Registered Offices: 80 Strand, London WC2R 0RL, England

First published 2003

(WEB)   10 9 8 7 6 5 4

*Publisher's note: This book is a work of fiction. Names, characters, places and incidents
either are the product of the author's imagination or are used fictitiously, and any
resemblance to actual persons living or dead, events, or locales is entirely coincidental.*

Manufactured in Canada.

NATIONAL LIBRARY OF CANADA CATALOGUING IN PUBLICATION

Melling, O. R.
   The book of dreams / O.R. Melling.

(The chronicles of Faerie ; 4)
ISBN 0-14-100434-7

I. Title. II. Series: Melling, O. R. Chronicles of Faerie ; 4.

PS8576.E463B66 2003   jC813'.54   C2003-905108-0

For Michael Scott
— dear friend, extraordinaire — —

The Book
of Dreams

Melling O.R.

ACKNOWLEDGMENTS

GO RAIBH MILE MAITH AGAIBH TO ALL in Ireland: Findabhair of the laughing fairies, Georgie Whelan for her unending support, Frank Golden and Eve Golden-Woods, Martha and John O'Grady, Kate Thompson, Roy and Martina and the Arbuckle-Brady gang, Kate and Marcus McCabe of the Ark, Carrie Eddison, Tony Hall, Sheila Pratschke and the wonderful staff of the Tyrone Guthrie Centre at Annaghmakerrig—Doreen and Teddy Burns, Theresa Rudden, Lavinia McAdoo, Ann McGuirk, Ingrid Adams; all my guardian angels, Liam Kelly (car), Joe Murray (computer), Billy Duffin (house); Ger McGrath, solicitor and friend; Professor Dáibhí Ó Cróinín for last-minute checks on the Irish; Victor/Victoria's Way in Roundwood Co. Wicklow, the Arts Council of Ireland for a travel grant, the Cultural Relations Committee of the Department of Arts, Sport & Tourism (Ireland), Bray Urban District Council and Wicklow County Council for arts awards.

In Scotland and Spain, thanks Dr Liz and Graham for health, hospitality and friendship. Thank you to those in India for friendship and hospitality—Tapas Bhatt in Auroville and in Delhi, Manam and Joyita Bhatt and Suresh and Aradhana Vaswani and their families. Till we meet again!

Merci beaucoup in Canada: Nena Hardie dearest friend in Toronto and Mulmur, the Creemore Durnfords bagpipes and all, Yvonne and Deirdre Whelan for being themselves, Jean-Francois

Pinsonneault *et sa fille* Mélissa, Bette George for teachings and a bed "in the bush," the Michon-Weir family in NWT for fun and hospitality, Hamu Famu, Debbie and PJ McDonagh, all at CANSCAIP *(we are all family)*, Michael Mesure for his wonderful work with FLAP (Fatal Light Awareness Program), Ross McKee and Wilma Alexander, Commander Fraser McKee for photos of Grosse Île, the Native Canadian Centre of Toronto, Stormwolf of Cherokee Corners for finding my cover artist, editor and friend Meg Masters, Jason Masters for an early opinion, agents Lynn and David Bennett of Transatlantic Inc., Senior Editor Barb Berson for continuing support of my work, former editor and publisher Cynthia Good who was there from the beginning, Cathy MacLean for her wonderful design work (and patience!), Karen Alliston, Tracy Bordian and Jennifer Handel for all the last stuff, and *Prairie Ceilidh* who whooped me through the final lap.

In memoriam, Paddy, Mae and June Butler, my Irish dancing teachers in Toronto throughout my childhood.

Last but not least, my heartfelt thanks to *Na Daoine Maithe* and all the *Man-i-tou* who so kindly gave their inspiration and assistance.

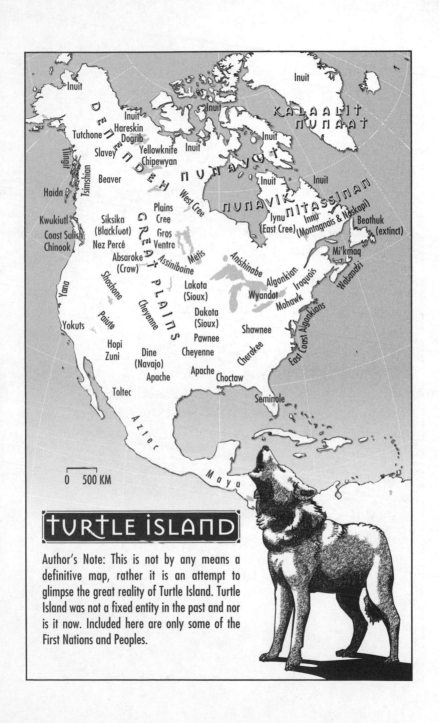

Inuit

Inuit

Inuit

Inuit

KALAALIT ΠUΠAAT

Inuit
Tutchone Hareskin
Dogrib
Slavey Yellowknife Inuit
Chipewyan

ΠUΠAVUT

Tlingit

Beaver

Haida

West Cree

ΠUΠAVIK

Inuit

Inuit

ΠITASSIΠAΠ

Kwakiutl
Coast Salish
Chinook

Siksika
(Blackfoot)
Nez Percé Gros
Ventre

Plains
Cree

Iynu
(East Cree)

Innu
(Montagnais & Naskapi)

Beothuk
(extinct)

Absaroke
(Crow)

Métis

Assiniboine

Anishinabe

Mi'kmaq

Yana

Shoshone

Lakota
(Sioux)

Algonkian

Iroquois

Wabanaki

Wyandot

Yokuts

Paiute

Cheyenne

Dakota
(Sioux)

Mohawk

Shawnee

East Coast Algonkians

Hopi
Zuni

Dine
(Navajo)

Cheyenne

Pawnee

Cherokee

Apache

Apache

Choctaw

Toltec

Seminole

0   500 KM

Aztec

Maya

TURTLE ISLAND

Author's Note: This is not by any means a
definitive map, rather it is an attempt to
glimpse the great reality of Turtle Island. Turtle
Island was not a fixed entity in the past and nor
is it now. Included here are only some of the
First Nations and Peoples.

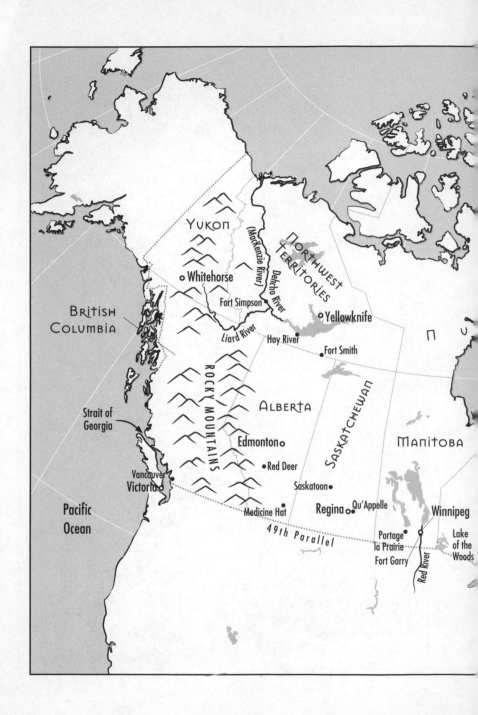

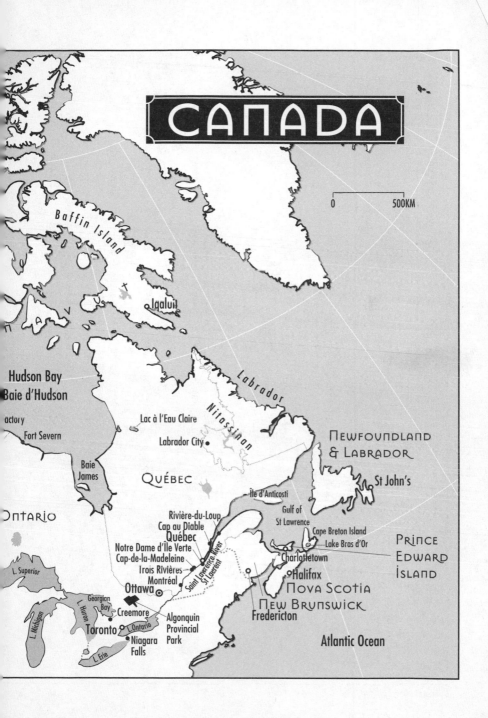

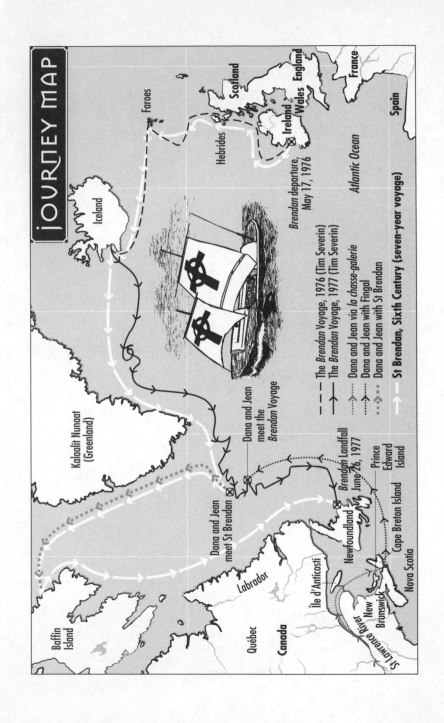

JOURNEY MAP

Faroes

Iceland

Scotland

England

Wales

Ireland ⊗

Hebrides

France

Spain

Brendan departure,
May 17, 1976

Atlantic Ocean

Kalaalit Nunaat
(Greenland)

Dana and Jean
meet the
Brendan Voyage

Brendan Landfall
June 26, 1977

Prince
Edward
Island

Dana and Jean
meet St Brendan ⊗

Baffin
Island

Labrador

Île d'Anticosti

Québec

Canada

Newfoundland ⊗

Cape Breton Island

New
Brunswick

Nova Scotia

St Lawrence River

- – – – The *Brendan* Voyage, 1976 (Tim Severin)
- ——→ The *Brendan* Voyage, 1977 (Tim Severin)
- ········› Dana and Jean via *la chasse-galerie*
- ········› Dana and Jean with Fingal
- ▪▪▪▪▪‹ Dana and Jean with St Brendan
- ——→ **St Brendan, Sixth Century (seven-year voyage)**

The Book of Dreams

CHAPTER ONE

IT WAS THE EARLY HOURS
before dawn. A cool mist hung over the waters of the great lake
that lay still and luminous in the moonlight. The sandy beach was
deserted except for the wolf. He was a big animal, black-haired,
with a white star across his chest. His eyes glowed like gold coins.
Having explored the bluffs overlooking the lake, he padded softly
along the boardwalk. He stopped suddenly to sniff at the air. On
the edges of the wind came a stench that repelled him. *What was
it?* It emanated from the city beyond.

There was a moment's hesitation. He had only recently come
down from the North and he was not yet at home in this territory. For the short time he had lived there, he had kept to the
nature trails and the marshes bordering the river that ran into the
lake. Still, he was no ordinary wolf. He wasn't afraid of urban
streets. Tonight he felt called to the heart of the city.

It was easy to travel in the dark. Traffic was sporadic and few
pedestrians were abroad. Anyone who spotted him assumed he was
a stray dog too big to approach. As he crossed the lawns of Riverdale
Park, he caught the scent of coyote before he met her. *You're a long
way from home, cousin,* she barked. He didn't stop to reply. They were
a mangy and flea-bitten lot, those prairie dogs, moving into the
cities like dishevelled tramps. On he ran, through the inner city
farm, where the horses snorted nervously when he passed by.

As he neared the city centre, the silhouettes of office blocks, hotels and apartments loomed up. Miles of concrete. The streets were almost empty except for night-shift workers and the homeless who made their beds in doorways or bus shelters.

The wolf nosed the air with distaste. What couldn't be seen could be sensed: the sewers under the sidewalks, the smell of overcrowding, the fear and entrapment, bad dreams, failed hopes.

With relief, he reached the green circle of Queen's Park. Avoiding the pools of light shed by lamps on the walkways, he inhaled the night perfume of trees and flowers. Though the park was empty, it spoke to him of the day's events. Here, the evidence of two dogs who had scuffled together in play. There, a popcorn kernel dropped from a hand-pushed wagon and overlooked by squirrels. Further ahead, the track of an electronic wheelchair crossed bicycle treads. The odour of humans was everywhere: an old man who fed pigeons, their white droppings splattered around his bench; students from the university weighed down with books; Sufi dancers inscribing the grass with prints as light as those of sparrows.

He paused at the bronze statue of King Edward on horseback. The monument had come a long way to dominate the park. Wafting around it was the hint of hot breezes scented with jasmine and frangipani. Once upon a time this royal figure had stood in another green park, in the capital of India.

The wolf loped to a small fountain nearby and lowered his head to drink. The ground was littered with hard green nuts, the false drupes of the ginkgo tree planted for ornament amidst native pine and ash. He raised his head to listen. A song floated on the currents of night air. It came from the shadows of the government buildings beyond. A sorrowful song. He moved to investigate.

The Legislative Building of the Province of Ontario was an impressive fortress of rose-coloured sandstone. The walls were arched and carved with friezes. Lion heads and gargoyles grimaced above the wide steps. The wolf peered upward at the vaulted roof. Night owls were gathering to hold their own parliament. He could hear the concern in their low hootings. He was not the only one disturbed that night.

The song he was tracing grew louder now as if calling to him. It didn't come from the galleries inside, dim with thick carpets and polished mahogany. Around the corner of the building, he found the singer.

The memorial was an old rock from a blood-soaked battle-field in Spain. *Candesa.* Its voice was husky and dark-red like pomegranates. *Qué yo no vuelva jamás a sentirme el dolor.* It sang of what it knew, what it had seen. Young Canadians dying in Candesa, far far from home. A lost battalion fighting the shadow of the Enemy. *May I never know the pain again.* They had been named after those who led rebellions in Canada one hundred years before their own battle with fate. *Mackenzie. Papineau.* 1837. *The Mac-Pap Battalion of the International Brigade.* 1937. Battles won, battles lost. Always the light had to fight against the darkness. Would this war never end?

The wolf was overcome with a sense of futility.

He turned at the sound of cloth rustling like wings. Behind him was a statue of a tall angelic figure with shoulder-length hair and a long robe to his feet. The figure strode across a low stone wall with a book in his hand. His head was bowed as he read.

"What are you reading?" the wolf wondered out loud.

"A book of dreams."

The voice seemed to come from a great distance.

"Whose dreams?"

"Ah, that is the question."

Riddles. It was a night of mystery. The wolf accepted the obvious. Magic had come to the city.

3

"Strange times," he said, "when statues talk."

"And wolves listen."

The wolf barked a laugh, but he was uneasy. He couldn't shake the feeling that something was wrong.

"Why does the rock sing?" he asked. "That's old history. Long done and gone."

"History goes and history comes again. The shadow of the Enemy hangs over the city. The rock remembers."

"I knew it. I could smell the badness."

"A servant has come to do its master's work. Will you fight against it?"

"It's not my business. I don't belong here."

"The Enemy hates all life wherever it is found. There is no neutral ground in this war."

The wolf raised his head. He could detect it clearly. Malodorous. Malignant. The dark presence in the city. The maggot at its core. He made up his mind. He knew to which side he belonged.

Racing away, nose to the ground, he followed the trail easily. It stank like a charnel house. As the buildings around him grew taller, pressed closer, he began to feel anxious. He had reached the financial heart of the city. All around him were the head offices of banks, insurance companies and law firms. He skulked through the shadows, on guard. When the sound came overhead, he flattened himself against the pavement.

Like an onrush of wind, it filled the air with rich sibilance. A feathery, whispering, sighing sound. The susurration of wings surging like the sea.

Relieved, the wolf looked skywards. Of course. The season had begun. The Great Fall Migration. Through the darkness they flew, immense flocks of birds. For millennia they had followed this route, foraging for food by day, travelling by night. Each spring they set out for their breeding grounds in the north and each autumn they returned to warmer climes. It was a journey bred into their being.

A yearning for home came over the wolf. How he missed the northern lands of the taiga! How he longed for the dark forests and the deep lakes!

He was so caught up in the beauty of the birds' flight that the new sound came like a blow to his ears. The thud of a small body falling to earth. It came again. And again. And again. Like hard rain. Like bullets. The wolf searched the darkness with keen eyes. Now he saw them, scattered at the base of the office towers, on the steps, in the doorways. Tiny bodies, stunned or lifeless.

For millennia they had followed this route but suddenly, in so short a time, everything had changed. Before they could cross the great lake of Ontario, they faced a murderous test that many would fail. Buildings and towers stood directly in their path, a niagara of glass and blinding light. In the dark, the combination of glass and light was deadly. In rain or fog it was worse. Hundreds even thousands could be killed in one night, at one building. *Death by impact due to high velocity*. If they survived the collision they were trapped in a maze of reflections. Lost and disoriented, reluctant to leave the light, they would flap hopelessly until they dropped to the ground.

Where do we record the passing of wildlife? Who mourns the silent deaths of the small?

The wolf's lips peeled back in a snarl. The guard hairs rose on his body from top to tail. He growled low in his throat. There was something nearby. Some dark thing leaned casually against a wall. It was watching the birds die, enjoying the sight, feeding on the misery as a vampire drinks blood.

As soon as it saw the wolf, the creature attacked. Hazy and ragged, barely formed, it smelled of rotting seaweed and the salt ocean it had crossed. Though weak from its long journey, it could still do harm. It had already killed that night to begin its mission. *He was a murderer from the beginning.* And it was ready to kill again.

Too late, the wolf sensed the latent power of the monster. Tentacles of grey mist snaked through the air and caught him in a death grip. Still he fought back. This was his inheritance. A fierceness that was proud and lonely. A tearing, a howling, a hunger and thirst. *Blessed are they who hunger and thirst.* A wild strength that would die fighting, kicking, screaming, that wouldn't stop till the last breath had been wrung from his body.

His eyes began to close as the darkness gathered round him.

Then the sound of human voices broke the air. Three people turned the corner, bundled up in sweaters and scarves against the chill of pre-dawn. Two were women, a shy and pretty college student and a grey-haired matron with strong good-natured features. They were accompanied by a man in his early thirties, lean-jawed and determined. All carried brown paper bags and butterfly nets. In hushed tones they joked about dragging themselves out of bed for early patrols. Holy quests in the dark. None of them were morning people. All of them were bird people.

Quietly, sadly, they stooped to retrieve the small bodies. Gently, reverently, they handled the slain. Each was named and the cause of death ascertained. The older woman repeated the information into a hand-held recorder.

White-throated sparrow. Female. Head injuries. Broken wings. Death by impact.

Black-and-white warbler. Young male. Crushed skull. Death by impact.

Hermit thrush. Male. Internal injuries. Broken beak. Bloodied eyes. Death by impact.

As the roll call continued, the dead were gathered and placed in bags.

"This one's alive!" the student cried. Her voice quavered with relief. Then a half sob. "Just barely."

The tiny body of a hummingbird rested in her palm, not much bigger than a dragonfly and as delicate and fragile. It was stunned, moving feebly.

She hurried to the others who were more experienced and offered her find.

Under her breath she repeated her mantra. *I will not cry. I will not cry.*

With the quiet efficiency of a nurse, the older woman removed her gloves to inspect the bird.

"Broken beak. Wing damage, see how it droops? The eyes are swollen. Collision injuries. Michael—"

The team leader had already blown air into a paper bag and lined it with tissue. Softly, softly he placed the bird inside.

"I hate bagging them," the student murmured.

"Much better than a box," Michael told her. "If they panic, the paper has give and is less likely to hurt them. We'll look for the living now, bag them and get them to the Centre. Then we'll return for the dead."

"There's a lot more dead than alive," the student said bitterly.

She glared at the buildings, lit up like Christmas trees, creating the fatal light that attracted its victims. She knew the statistics. Hundreds of millions died every year due to collisions with human structures. Why keep the lights on? It was neither cheap nor efficient. Some firms liked the prestige—*look at me on the skyline!*—others were simply too lazy to make the arrangements to turn them off. Old habits die hard.

So do small birds.

She returned to her work, face streaked with tears. The two older volunteers exchanged a look. Unless the girl hardened she wouldn't be able to continue. It happened to many. Like the birds on the sidewalk, they broke inside.

Hidden from sight, in an alcove where he had dragged himself, the wolf watched the three work. They had revived his spirits. He was already recovering from the creature's attack. The creature itself was long gone, having fled a power much greater than itself. Banished by love.

CHAPTER TWO

Gwen woods hurried through Queen's Park wishing she had time to stop and enjoy it. On a sunny afternoon in the last week of August, the park was green and leafy and full of life. Squirrels foraged in the grass, stocking their dreys for the winter. Pigeons flocked to the old man on the bench who tossed them breadcrumbs. A woman in an electric wheelchair stopped to watch a troupe of Sufis at their sacred ballet. As the popcorn man bumped his handcart over the kerb of the road, the coloured toys whirled madly.

At twenty-two, Gwen was plump and pretty with golden-brown hair cut in a short bob. She had just come from a job interview and was formally dressed in a beige suit and pink blouse. The high heels made it difficult for her to run, but she tried to anyway. A quick glance at her watch told her she was late as usual.

Leaving the park, she dashed across the road and on to Massey College. The wrought-iron gates at the entrance were open. Inside was a quadrangle of grass and trees. A clock tower rose above a fountain pool where goldfish swam amongst reeds and lilies. Surrounding the quad was the orange brick building that was residence to professors and post-graduate students. Each room looked down on the square through long narrow windows. She could see some of the students working at their desks, illumined by lamps and computer screens.

Gwen gave her name to the porter and the room she wanted him to ring, then sat on a bench near the fountain to wait. Soothed by the plash of water and the stillness of the place, she felt a pang for her own student days. She wasn't long out of teacher's college and had yet to find a post. A permanent one was unlikely that late in the year, but she still hoped for part-time or substitute work. Failing that, she was looking at a stint in an office or wait-ressing. There were bills to pay and the rent on her apartment. Even as she grimaced at the thought, she couldn't help wonder-ing. Would the trouble ahead affect her work? Her life?

How could it not!

The worried look on Gwen's face was the first thing Laurel noticed when she stepped into the quadrangle. It wasn't reas-suring. She was already unhappy about the meeting. She had only just settled into her rooms at Massey and was about to begin her studies for a Master's degree. Following in the foot-steps of her paternal grandfather, she planned to be a professor of Irish Folklore. This meeting had, of course, to do with folklore. Not the kind found in books, but rather the kind that was alive and kicking.

The telephone call, when it came out of the blue, had been awkward for both of them.

"Laurel Blackburn? Hi. Sorry to bother you but this is impor-tant. Very important. I've been told . . . I mean . . . mutual friends . . . in the other place—"

"Who told you?"

"What?"

"Who told you about me?"

"Oh. Uh. Granny. Grania Harte. She's an old lady. Irish."

There was a pause. Gwen was having difficulty bringing up the subject. Bad enough she had to broach it with a stranger, but it was never easy to talk about Faerie. She knew there was a spell woven around that magic land to obscure and protect it. The Irish always said it was unlucky to talk about "the Good People." Nevertheless, she had a job to do. She rushed out her words.

"Granny's a fairy doctress. A white witch you could call her. She lived in Faerie for seven years where she gained her knowledge. She says she met you a few years ago?"

Laurel spoke guardedly.

"Yes, I remember. It was on a train crossing Ireland. She gave me some good advice."

"She's very wise," Gwen said. She took a deep breath. "She wants us to take a mission together."

Laurel's response was quick and unequivocal.

"I asked to be left alone."

"I know. I understand. I think. But . . . please, could we meet? Just once? It's hard enough talking about this stuff and even harder on the phone."

Laurel heard the desperation and relented a little. "The nature of the beast. They don't like being talked about." Against her own judgement, she could feel herself softening. "All right. I'll meet you, but that's all I'm agreeing to. Can you come here?"

They were both around the same age, but there the similarities ended. Where Gwen was open and easy going, Laurel was diffident and reserved. A tall young woman of lean and athletic build, she wore tight jeans, a dark sweater and high-heeled boots. Her fair hair was pulled back in a French plait to reveal finely honed features and hazel eyes. Though she looked striking, there was an air of vulnerability about her and her manner was defensive.

They sat together on the bench.

Gwen had already guessed why Laurel was wary. She had heard the story as it was told in Faerie: how Laurel's twin sister had died in this world to become High Queen of the other. It underscored a truth she knew from her own experience, something that Granny often repeated in warning.

There has always been commerce between the Earthworld and Faerie, but while the rewards are enchanting the dangers are real.

"I'm sorry about your sister," Gwen said gently now. "For your loss, I mean. I know she's happy where she is."

Laurel nodded. She didn't discuss personal matters with strangers, but she appreciated the sentiment.

"Have you met her?"

"Not yet," Gwen explained. "I heard about her from my friends. To be honest, I don't visit Faerie that often. I only go when I'm on holidays in Ireland. I haven't returned since Honor became queen. I guess you visit often? Faerie, I mean?"

"No. I don't. My sister comes to me in dreams and sometimes in person, but I don't go there."

Though they were sitting beside each other, Gwen sensed the great divide between them. She needed to build a bridge.

"I understand," she said quickly. "Or at least I think I do. We were born into this world. This is where we're meant to live. Faerie is so incredibly beautiful, so magical, it can make being here too pale. That's not right. This is where we belong."

"Yes," Laurel agreed with sudden vehemence. "Faerie can be like a drug. Alluring. Dangerous. Best avoided."

The bitterness echoed in her voice. She had said more than she intended.

"Is that why you asked that no one contact you?" Gwen asked. "Are you afraid of being drawn back in?"

It was a tricky moment but Gwen had to grasp the nettle. She needed Laurel's help.

The last of the summer breezes blew through the quadrangle. The ivy on the walls fidgeted nervously.

They were two young women just out of home and newly launched upon the world, yet they were more, much more. Both had travelled far, not only across the Atlantic to the green isle of Ireland, but also across the ocean of infinity to the land of Faerie. Both had undertaken quests, faced danger and death. Both were heroines of song and story.

When Laurel didn't answer, Gwen cleared her throat. It was time.

"Something terrible is coming. A great attack against Faerie. Against all our hopes and dreams."

A tremor ran through Laurel, but she wasn't surprised. She had already been warned.

"My sister spoke of a 'dark hour' some time ago." Laurel's tone was wry. "But of course the warnings were couched in the usual cryptic premonitions. How they expect to get a clear picture of the future from the flight of birds or the movement of clouds beats me. Did you get the message from a dream?"

"No. Email." Gwen grinned. "Granny has taken to computers. She talks about the World Wide Web like it's a new form of magic. But she does the old stuff too. She saw the attack in a scrying glass even before the High King contacted her. She can also predict things from the movement of clouds—*nephelmancy* it's called—which is close to *austromancy,* divining the wind." She pointed to the spray of water in the fountain. "*Pegomancy* interprets the pattern of water as it falls in a fountain."

Laurel was amused.

"You should be in Folklore Studies. How do you know these things?"

Gwen started to laugh.

"Granny taught me. Maybe if I can't get a job as a teacher I should try being a witch. *Ornithomancy* is my favourite. Can you guess?"

"Something to do with birds?"

"Yep. Reading the flight of birds."

The air was lighter between them.

"I know your story," Laurel admitted. "My sister's harper sang it one night when I still dined in the halls of Faerie. How you led the Company of Seven against the Great Worm to rescue Fairyland. It's a heroic tale."

"We just did what we had to."

Gwen was embarrassed by the praise. She would never be able to see herself as heroic. In books and movies the heroines were always tall and beautiful as well as fearless. Not only did she not look the part, she remembered being scared out of her wits most of the time. That was the difference, of course, between reality and fiction.

"Faerie is really important to me," she said quietly. "Something worth fighting for. Plus my cousin Findabhair was in danger at the time. Truth is, I was in over my head before I knew what was happening. And I couldn't have done it without the others, Katie, Matt, Dara . . ."

Her modesty was disarming. Laurel was beginning to like her. However, she had said too much. Laurel saw the way out and took it immediately.

"You should call up the Company of Seven," she told Gwen. "You've worked with them before and for something this big, you're better off with a team."

Gwen tried not to panic. The bridge she had forged between them was beginning to sway.

"I can't! The Company is scattered. My cousin and her husband, Finvarra, are on tour in the States. They're musicians. The others volunteered but Granny says no. All her auguries have told her that the battle will be fought in Canada. It's up to Canadians to do the job."

Laurel frowned as she remembered. "Honor said the same thing. It has to do with the girl, Dana Faolan? *The light that can bridge the darkness*. She's here in Toronto?"

"She's the key," Gwen nodded. "Our mission is to protect her. Granny was adamant about it. Her exact words were 'You must stand between the child and the quernstones of the Enemy even if you be crushed yourselves.'"

Despite the sunshine, they both shivered. A gloom fell over them.

"To be honest," Gwen said, "I'm not sure why we've been asked to do this. The girl has abilities beyond anything we've got. If you've heard my story, then I guess you know hers too? She's half-fairy. Light flows in her veins. I've been told she's still growing into her powers, but she quested for Faerie when she was only a kid. Why would she need us?"

"Honor's worried about her," Laurel said. "Apparently Dana is not the same girl we know from the story. She's become moody and withdrawn. It makes me wonder if she might have fallen under the influence of the Enemy?"

Gwen was shocked by Laurel's suggestion. But it made her think. Even before she had decided to teach, Gwen was involved with youth groups and summer camps. She had a special affinity for the young, particularly ones with problems. She liked them and understood them.

"Dana was only eleven in her Faerie tale," Gwen pointed out. "That was two years ago. The change in her personality could be due to something less sinister." Gwen grinned. "She's a teenager now."

"Then she's old enough to work with." Laurel glanced at the clock tower. She had arranged to meet one of her professors before the evening meal. "I'm sorry, but I don't want to be involved. You'll have to do this without me."

She stood up quickly.

"But," Gwen stuttered, "you know that only humanity can fight the Enemy. The rescue of Fairyland is up to us! It's always been that way."

"I'm sorry," Laurel repeated and her tone was final. "I'm telling you what I told my sister. I'm no longer a Companion of Faerie. I won't fight their battles."

Laurel hurried away from the look in Gwen's eyes, the same hurt and disappointment she had seen in her sister's.

Gwen sat stunned. What had happened?! She was sure she had been getting through to Laurel. She had felt the first inklings of friendship between them. Yet somehow she had failed. Disheartened to the point of tears, she stared blindly into the fountain.

The water was splashing in a lively dance as it played with the sunlight. Slowly Gwen grew aware of a pattern in the falling, a liquid logic and language. Pegomancy was not her forte, but she saw enough to make her blanch. Something bad was coming. Things could only get worse.

CHAPTER THREE

Brunswick avenue was an old Toronto street lined with leafy trees and big brick houses. The houses were elegant and old-fashioned with bay windows, gables and stained-glass transoms. Most had gardens or landscaped rockeries and verandahs hung with wickerwork planters and wind chimes. Halfway up the street, an abandoned convent stood nailed and boarded. The nuns were long gone and the school they had founded had moved. At the top of the road was a small park with flowerbeds and rosebushes. Overlooking the park was the rambling brownstone where Dana Faolan had lived for the past two years.

The house was a maze of winding stairs, gloomy corridors and rooms with high ceilings. It was divided into generous flats leased out to professors and artists. Dana's family had the third floor with a spacious living room, wide kitchen for dining, and studies for both her father and stepmother. The master bedroom was at the front of the house. Dana's small room was at the back. Once a large balcony, it had windows on three sides.

The glass bedroom was Dana's haven. Like an eagle's eyrie, it overlooked tree tops and the park below. Its one solid wall was covered with pictures of Ireland and posters of animals, particularly wolves. The floor was covered with a gold-and-brown rug that looked like a fall of autumn leaves. There was a cluttered bookcase, a wooden bed with cushions, and a desk for her computer.

When Dana wasn't in her room, she could be found in the back yard. Shunned by the other tenants, it was a lonely place overgrown with weeds and briars. Washing lines hung limp and grey like abandoned streamers. There was a glasshouse with broken panes inhabited by a clan of stray cats. At the foot of an old apple tree was the broken bench where Dana liked to read.

On that warm and sunny Labour Day, she found it hard to concentrate. Tomorrow she would begin high school, her first day in grade nine. The idea was horrifying. A new school. New faces. As if junior high hadn't been bad enough. She flicked through the pages of the book in her lap. It was one her aunts had given her, by their favourite author. He wrote about urban magic and fairies in North America.

I wish.

Dana's thought was bitter. There was no magic here and she knew it. She leaned back against the apple tree and stared up into the branches. Her dark hair was lank on her shoulders, her face was pale, and blue shadows rimmed her eyes. Under the bulky pants and sweater, she was thin and gangly. She let out a sigh. A great longing came over her. She couldn't have imagined being so homesick. The past two years had dragged on like a nightmare. Not a day passed by that she didn't miss Ireland.

She had found it impossible to settle in her new country. For one thing, she had no friends. And though she pretended she didn't care, she was aware of what she was missing that day. Most kids her age had gone in droves to the Exhibition to celebrate their last day of summer freedom. Her father had offered to take her, but at thirteen you went with your peers not your parents.

A tear trickled down her face.

"I'm such a loser," she muttered.

The cat dozing on the bench beside her reached out to claw her hand.

"Ow!" she yelped. "Hey you!"

He was a big tabby, sleek and strong, the king of the cats who lived in the glasshouse. He stared at her coolly.

She had to grin back.

"You're right. Stop feeling sorry for myself."

She tickled his ears and scratched his chin till he purred like a motor.

"It's just hard sometimes," she said softly.

There were other problems that she wouldn't admit to. A tomboy and adventurer when she was younger, Dana hadn't welcomed the changes that came with getting older. She didn't want to think about clothes or make-up or boys. From the way her life had gone so far, it was obvious that the older you got the more you lost. Like Peter Pan, she didn't want to grow up.

When she heard her father calling her to lunch, she ignored him at first. Then the rumblings in her stomach forced her inside. The house was filled with the aromatic scents of cumin, coriander, ginger and cloves. All had been crushed together in a mortar and pestle before going into a pan of melted butter. Yum. Lunch would be spiced dahl and rice.

When Dana reached the kitchen door, she could hear her father and stepmother preparing the meal together. Though neither had raised their voices, it was obvious they were arguing. When her name was mentioned, she stopped to listen.

"I am only saying it is a shame she will not wear brighter clothes. I was sad that she chose only black. And such drab things as well!"

Her stepmother, Aradhana, was referring to their shopping expedition that weekend. New clothes for the new school year.

"We should be glad she isn't into fashion," Gabriel countered, though he sounded uneasy. "It's a good thing she isn't fanatical about her looks. There's too much of that with young girls nowadays. That's how anorexia starts."

"This is true, but also not true. It is important that young people take some pride in their appearance. It is part of their self-esteem. Dana dresses to hide herself. That cannot be good."

Dana was unsettled by her stepmother's words. They were too close for comfort. She cleared her throat loudly before more could be said and entered the kitchen.

The two adults went immediately silent, looking guilty. Dana avoided their eyes and sat down at the table. This threesome had first come together in Ireland where Aradhana owned an Indian restaurant with her brother, Suresh. She was a beautiful young woman, as graceful as a gazelle, with long black hair and dark gentle eyes. Sometimes she wore saris but mostly she wore jeans. When Gabriel fell in love with her, Dana had encouraged the marriage. She knew her parents would never be reunited and she liked Aradhana.

"All set for the big day tomorrow?" Gabriel asked with false heartiness.

Dana ignored him. He tried again.

"We'll go out for dinner to celebrate the occasion. That's a promise."

"And we all know what your promises mean," she said coldly.

Gabriel opened his mouth to retort, but caught a look from his wife, and closed it again. He began to fiddle with the gold ring in his ear, then he rubbed his bald head, the two things he did whenever he was upset. In his early thirties, he was a professional musician and also taught at the university.

"Will you dish out the rice, please, Dana?" her stepmother asked.

The white fluffy basmati was cooked with coconut milk. Dana's mouth watered but she wasn't to be distracted. As she emptied the rice into a large bowl and passed it around the table, she continued her attack.

"If we were in Ireland, I'd already be in secondary school," she pointed out, "with all my friends."

Gabriel sighed but kept silent.

"And you promised me if I didn't like it here, we could go home. Well, I hate it! What kind of promise-keeping is that?"

Gabriel frowned. He had to answer.

"Sometimes parents break their promises. It's impossible to keep them all. You'll discover that yourself one day."

Now the argument began in earnest, continuing through their lunch, till Gabriel finally lost his temper.

"That's it!" he exploded, "I'm fed up with this. You're like a dog at a bone. Go to your room!"

"As if I have anywhere else to go."

She stormed out of the kitchen, slamming the door behind her.

Aradhana stood up to clear the table and patted her husband on the shoulder. While she did her best at times to play the mediator she couldn't intervene every time the two fought. Sooner or later father and daughter would have to make their peace.

Gabriel shook his head with chagrin. He had lost it once again. He knew his daughter was unhappy but there was nothing he could do. He had a good job and so did Radhi and they both loved being in Canada. In fact, except for Dana, everything in Gabriel's life was going great. Though his friends and workmates assured him that it was natural—their teenagers hated them too— he wasn't convinced. Did it really have to be this way? He was dismayed by the loss of her affection. Once upon a time they had been so close. A little family of two. When his first wife, Edane,

ran away and left him to raise their toddler alone, he had taken on
the task with love and enthusiasm. Dana was his princess. He was
her hero. Alas, the fairy tale was not ending happily.

When she reached her room, Dana flung herself across the bed
not knowing if she wanted to scream or cry. Miserable, she stared
at her posters. The images of Ireland reminded her of everything
she had lost: the little terraced house where she and Gabe had
lived together, her best friend Emer with the fiery red hair, the
sea-swept strand of Bray, the Wicklow Mountains. As always when
her unhappiness grew too hard to bear, she made her escape.

It was easy to do, as natural as breathing. Dana closed her eyes
and let her thoughts drift. In the darkness behind her eyelids, the
motes of light gathered. Slowly they began to dance together,
weaving a vision.

A high hill of dappled grass. A shining green slope. The pale mist of
morning mingles with light spilling from the clouds. On the crown of the
hill, a megalith takes shape. Two great standing stones with a capstone
overhead. It forms a dolmen, a great stone archway. Green grass, grey stone,
pale mist and light. The ancient magic of Faerie. A portal to beyond.

No longer an image in her mind, it was there before her.

Dana ran up the hill towards the dolmen. Golden light
issued forth to touch her face like the sun. Faint sounds of
revelry echoed from within. Her heart lifted. This was what
sustained her in her life of exile. Two homelands were hers,
Ireland and Faerie. If she could not have one, at least she had the
other. Half-human, half-fairy, this was her birthright, to walk
between the worlds.

Dana had no sooner stepped through the portal than she
found herself facing a great wall covered in ivy. She grinned to
herself. There was often a trick or a test to undergo. The world of
Faerie was like Chinese boxes, an elaborate puzzle of riddles and
secrets, a maze of dimensions wrapped inside each other. She

inspected the wall. It seemed to go on forever both upwards and sideways. She attempted to climb but her foot found no purchase and she immediately slipped back. She stood there, stumped. Then she heard the giggles. They came from behind the ivy. She giggled herself as she pulled at the leafage.

After a few tugs, the creepers obligingly gave way like green curtains on a stage. There in the stonework was an exquisite frieze that told a tale in multicoloured mosaic.

Fado, fado. Once upon a time . . .

. . . one bright spring day, a fairy queen went a-maying with her ladies in the woods. Through a forest of old oak and ash, they chased two butterflies, a holly blue and a silver fritillary. When her companions sat down to picnic on seedcakes and honey, the queen ran on. Her fair hair flew behind her like wings. Her dress shimmered like sunlight. Suddenly she stopped when she heard a sound. She cocked her head to listen. It was a bewitching melody, so strange, so beguiling. She tread softly to a clearing and there she found him, a dark-haired musician playing a flute.

They stared long at each other, fairy and mortal. Each did not really know what the other was. Both were lost in a spell of love and forgetting.

She left the forest that day, the fairy queen, and she wed her mortal lover. Who and what she was had gone from her memory. She forgot her husband, the fairy king of the mountain, and she became a human bride. Happy in her new life, she bore a child.

The baby grew to three years old, a mischievous toddler with bunches of dark curls. One day the little girl cupped her hands together and let out a glad cry. A pool of golden light had welled in her palms. When her mother saw the mark, her own sign of the Light-Bearer, she backed away in horror. For now she remembered who she was and the king she had forsaken.

As her mind and spirit broke, the fairy queen ran away from her new family and was lost for many years in grief and darkness.

As for the little girl, she grew up with no memory of that tragic day nor of the reason for her mother's disappearance. Raised by her mortal father, she knew nothing of her own fairy blood or her magical gifts.

Then Faerie came a-calling when she was eleven years old. On behalf of the Summer Land she undertook a quest, a sacred mission in the mountains that led her to the truth.

The final scene in the mosaic showed a deep green glen at dusk. There on a high ridge stood the girl with her hands outstretched. Across the glen, on another height, stood the fairy queen, her mother. Between them an arc of light streaked over the valley like a golden rainbow.

Dana smiled at the happy end to the tale, at the reunion of mother and daughter. Of course she recognized all the characters in the story: her fairy mother Edane, her human father Gabriel and herself, half of each. As she applauded the spectacle, the image of her mother in the mural burst into laughter and turned around to greet her.

The wall disappeared and there stood Edane, her golden hair wreathed in holly and ivy, her eyes like blue stars.

"Welcome home, daughter," she said in her melodious voice. "Welcome to the Fair Flowering Place where there is no grief or sorrow nor sickness or death."

"Just what I need," said Dana as they hugged hello.

They were more like friends than mother and daughter. Forever young and forever beautiful, Edane appeared no older than a girl of eighteen. At thirteen years old and the same height as her mother, Dana was quickly catching up. A fleeting concern crossed her mind. What would happen when she grew older than Edane? Dana pushed the thought away. She had come to escape her worries, not to add to them. After all, she didn't have to age either, at least not at the same rate as full mortals. Her fairy blood was strong. She could control how she looked, especially in Faerie.

Remembering that, Dana looked down at her clothing. With a single thought she transformed the baggy pants and sweater into a flowing gown with a silken mantle. As she touched her head lightly, her hair was swept up with a crespine of pearls. In Faerie, she was beautiful.

Edane clapped her hands with delight.

"Come dance with me!"

The shining kingdom was their playground. *Tír Tairngire*. Land of Promise. *Magh Abhlach*. The Plain of the Apple Trees. It was a country that revived the spirits of all who journeyed there, delighting the mind and nourishing the soul. The greensward of meadow was speckled with red poppies and bluebells. Streams overflowed with milk and honey. Sweet music chimed from the gold-leafed trees and the "nobles of the wood," the birds of bright plumage, sang from the branches in the evernew tongue.

> *What is the number of the hosts which the noble wave*
> *of the clear sea reveals?*
>
> *What are the multitudes which dwell there*
> *on the other side of the solid earth?*
>
> *And the bright sun, whither does it go?*

On a summer lawn, they danced a roundelay with many creatures. Wood mice and foxes, hares and hawks, ladybirds and damselflies, all footed lightly, singing and hooting and humming together. When the dancing stopped, they dined in a house of white stone with a roof of peacock feathers and a floor of spangled glass. A feast of fruits and sweet wine was served in dishes of gold and silver.

After the meal, they lounged on silken cushions as music wafted on the air like perfume.

Edane cupped her palms together and smiled to herself as golden light spilled out. She caught her daughter's hands.

"Do you make light?"

Dana was surprised. Truth to tell, she couldn't remember the last time she had tried.

"There's no need to here," she said defensively.

Her mother laughed and shook her head gently.

"What of the other place? You belong to two worlds. Are you not yourself in both?"

Edane flung a stream of light into the air.

"You come from a noble line, Dana. You are the daughter of a *spéirbhean,* a skywoman. You belong to that tribe who herd the stars across the heavens, whose veins flow with light. We are descended from the White Lady of the Waters. That is your legacy."

The more Edane spoke the more suspicious Dana grew. It was not like her mother to ask questions or give lectures.

"Who told you to say this?" she asked indignantly. "Has someone been spying on me?"

"We see everyone on every side and no one sees us," Edane said blithely.

Then her eyes flashed with mischief and she threw up her hands.

"I cannot do this! I cannot be like a human mother. I cannot tell you what to do. Remind you of your duties. *Be good. Behave.* It is against my nature!"

Edane burst into such wild peals of laughter that Dana couldn't help but join in. Here was another reason she loved Faerie. No one expected her to be responsible or mature. Indeed the opposite was encouraged.

Dana stayed for many days and nights. Days spent sailing in a glass-bottomed boat on warm green seas where mermaids dwelled. Nights spent sleeping in a hammock high in the tree tops under stars that sang. Eventually, however, though she tried hard to ignore it, she felt the pull of the Earthworld drawing her back. No matter how much she enjoyed herself in Faerie, her human side inevitably wanted to go home. If it weren't for that pull she might never have returned.

It was twilight. A hush had fallen over the sage-green fields. Dana strolled along arm in arm with her mother. On the road ahead, the portal was taking shape. In flashes of mist and fire the great gateway rose up to span the worlds.

Edane reminded her daughter that no time had passed on the other side.

"I willed it so," she said lightly. "The order of things is ours to play with. We can open time like a fruit and spill out its seeds. For there is ordinary time and there is the Great Time of eternity. Humanity dwells in fallen time. We live in the Dreaming."

With regret and resignation, Dana hugged her mother goodbye.

"I'll be back soon," she murmured.

As soon as Dana stepped through the dolmen, she was back in her bedroom on that sunny Labour Day afternoon. A pang of dread struck her.

Tomorrow she would begin her first day in grade nine.

CHAPTER FOUR

NOT LONG AFTER DANA LEFT Faerie, a young woman appeared beside Edane in a flash of light. Her skin was golden, her eyes sky-blue and her fair hair was crowned with a wreath of white blossoms. She wore the shining raiment of Faerie, yet she seemed a little more solid somehow.

"Your Majesty," Edane greeted her, bowing her head slightly.

Though Edane was a queen in her own right and formal *courteisie* was usually reserved for the Court or grand occasions, still this was Honor, the High Queen of all Faerie.

"Hi," said Honor. "At ease or whatever."

The two giggled. Honor was not long the High Queen and rarely said or did things properly. This made her very popular with her subjects.

"So, your daughter was here again? And she still won't visit me?"

Edane shrugged.

"We spend our days in revelry, then she takes her leave. Her mortality pulls her back to the Earthworld. If I mention going to the Court she always suggests some other diversion. I tried to speak of the matters you mentioned, but to no avail. I do not fathom her at times and when this happens I think to myself, 'This must be her human side.'"

"Thirteen is a difficult age," Honor observed.

Edane looked perplexed a moment, then her features cleared. "Ah, you would know this, being once mortal yourself."

Honor sighed. "I'm beginning to forget, but I do remember *that*. Puberty. What a nightmare."

"She is happy when she is here," Edane pointed out.

A slight frown crossed Honor's face.

"That's what we need to talk about, dear heart. I fear Dana is using Faerie to escape reality."

"And what better place to do it!" Edane agreed. "How fortunate she is that she may claim her inheritance."

Honor paused. She would have to tread carefully. She knew that what she had to say went against the grain, the fairy perspective.

"I'm worried, Edane, that coming here so often is not good for her. It makes it hard for her to live in the world where she was born."

"She is of my blood and my world too," the other responded. "She is doubly in exile now that she lives *i n-ailithre,* in another country. She longs to return home. Both to Ireland and Faerie."

"Life is a journey through a foreign land," Honor said softly. Like a shining mantle, she donned her sovereignty and the wisdom it brought. "All are exiled from their true Home and must travel towards it."

In the sky, the fairy constellations had begun their evening dance. Like golden tops and spiral galaxies they pirouetted across the heavens.

Honor linked her arm in Edane's as they crossed a wide sea, treading the path of moonlight that bridged the water. Her voice was low and musical.

"Because you are a *spéirbhean,* full silver-blooded, you cannot know how these visits weaken your daughter. The High King and I are very concerned. She comes here to avoid her troubles. She is

29

running away. Even as each act of bravery builds our store of courage, so too does each act of cowardice diminish us. It is important that she is strong in both worlds."

Edane was trying hard to listen, but the sky distracted her. A cluster of stars had spun into view like a whirling dervish. Trailing in its wake were two of her sisters, skywomen like herself. They rode the lunar wind as if it were a racehorse and the night a dark sward. As soon as they spied her, they waved wildly.

Honor could see that Edane was only half-listening. That was the frustrating part of dealing with the Fey Folk. Notoriously flighty, they couldn't hold the moment especially if it were a serious one. Only the High King could maintain any gravity for long. Edane was worse than most, not being an earth fairy but a Light-Bearer who fell from the sky. Utterly unrooted. Totally airy-fairy.

But Honor had to get her message through somehow. Someone had to influence Dana, to make her see sense. The High Queen herself had once been a good friend to the girl, but Dana avoided her now. The one time Honor confronted her, the girl had closed up like a clam. Honor could only guess at the problem. The trials of growing up? The move to Canada which the High King had endorsed? Somehow, somewhere, Dana had taken a wrong turn, gone down the wrong road and it was not good, not good at all. Her time was coming and she wasn't ready.

"All the portents are strong," Honor said to Edane. "Soon the Enemy will strike a great blow against Faerie. Worse than any in the past. We are unable to see how or from where it will come, but we do know this. Dana is the key. Her destiny calls."

Even as Honor tried to impress the seriousness of the situation upon Dana's mother, she could see she had already lost.

Edane was gazing skywards, waving back at her sisters. Now they detoured the night wind in her direction. Elegant arms reached down to catch her.

"I must away!" cried Edane.

Corybantic laughter filled the air as Edane climbed onto the lunar current. The skywomen reached for Honor too, but she smiled and shook her head. She didn't need a mad dash through the cosmos right now, however tempting. Ruefully she watched as Edane disappeared into the folds of night, along with any hope of helping Dana directly. The High Queen was running out of options.

Stepping off the moonlit path, Honor crossed the waters of the fairy sea and walked into the west. She walked through the night and the next day and the next, towards a land where the sun never set. The light grew brighter, the sea grew warm and the air breathed a sweet scent. On the edge of the horizon hung the great golden orb of Faerie's sun. She could see the fiery plains where drakes and salamanders basked like red jewels. Golden peaks spilled hot lava. Solar winds ruffled her hair. She did not have to journey to that burning country, but the place she sought was near.

The small island floated like a lily on the waves. It was no more than a green hillock with a single tall tree. The tree appeared to be in bloom with a profusion of white flowers, but as Honor drew near she saw the truth. The branches bore neither fruit nor flower but a great flock of birds. With their heads tucked under their wings, they were all fast asleep, hushed and white like a fall of new snow.

The soul-birds of Faerie.

Honor knew that what she was contemplating was a perilous risk. To waken the soul-birds was to waken Old Magic, an ancient and mysterious force that existed before the worlds came into being, before the great division of good and evil. There was no telling what might happen if she woke that power. It could not be controlled. It was unpredictable. The only thing Honor knew for certain was that it guaranteed change.

And things had to change. So much was wrong and about to get worse. All the prophecies and predictions were clear. Faerie's doom was upon them. Dana should have been the one to counter their fate but she was too weak for the mission. Honor could see that even if her beloved, the High King, could not.

"The rescue of Fairyland is a mortal task," he had assured his wife. "Since the two worlds were born, it has always been that way. Only humanity can fight the Enemy. They have never let us down."

"There's a first time for everything," she tried to tell him.

And that was another exasperating thing about the fairies. Their absolute faith in tradition and old laws. Had no one considered the possibility that humans could fail? Then what would happen! The Earthworld would lose a source of its hopes and dreams and Faerie might lose its very existence.

As if to confirm her worst fears, Honor's own twin sister had rejected her plea for help. While she accepted that Laurel had the right to refuse, the wound had cut deep, further convincing her that the tide was against them.

Honor couldn't sit still while trouble threatened her reign. Having failed to influence events through Laurel or Dana, she was ready to act on her own.

The High Queen of Faerie stood at the bottom of the tree and gazed upwards. There was a light rustling sound in the branches above as the birds sensed her presence. But though the feathery bodies quivered, they remained asleep.

Despite her determination, Honor's fairy soul trembled. Who was she to dare such a thing? To tamper with Old Magic?

"Desperate times call for desperate measures," she muttered to herself.

Before she could change her mind, Honor raised her arms and cried out in full voice.

"Sleepers awake!"

Her cry had the same effect as the report of a shotgun. The birds rose up in a frenzy. The sky throbbed with the flurry of wings. In a great white swell they banked above her, a united arabesque of whispering flight. They hovered there for one pure second of infinity, brooding over the land *with ah! bright wings.* Then in a whirr of wings and wind, they were gone.

Honor stared at the empty tree, the barren branches, the sky without birds. The deed was done. Only time would tell if she had helped or harmed.

CHAPTER FIVE

From ACROSS THE ROAD, Dana regarded her new school with a cold eye. The collegiate was huge, twice the size of her last school. Everything about it filled her with dread: the hostile glint of the tall windows, the prison-grey stone, the interminable number of steps that led into the building. The front doors were open like a maw to swallow the steady stream of youth. Judging by the noisy greetings and laughter, most were willing victims.

Slowly, reluctantly, Dana joined the stream. Her steps were leaden. The knapsack on her back seemed weighted with rocks, not books. In a loose-fitting jacket and black baggy pants that trailed over her running shoes, she blended with the crowd. Her hair fell lankly over her face. A small gold ring shone in her left nostril.

"Out of the question," was Gabriel's decree on body piercing of any kind.

"You wear an earring," she had pointed out hotly.

The dispute had been unexpectedly settled by Aradhana.

"There is a Western prejudice, husband, against piercing the nose. In India it is common for girls and women to wear a jewel or a ring in this manner. As she will wear no other ornament, I think you should allow her this."

Though she would deny it if challenged, Dana's appearance was another protest against her life. Muffled in dark and bulky clothes, she hid from the world around her. On the other side, in Faerie, she emerged like a butterfly resplendent with fairy *glamour,* but as soon as she returned to the Earthworld she re-entered her cocoon.

Head down, shoulders slumped, Dana shuffled through the corridors. Lockers clanged open and shut, friends hailed each other over the crowd, squeals of excitement punctured the mayhem. Forcing herself to stay calm, resisting the urge to flee, she located the classroom assigned to her on orientation day. There were already a number of students there, most of them seated and talking quietly. Some were strangers, enrolled from other neighbourhoods. With a sinking heart, Dana recognized the small group of girls who stood in the aisle, hoping to be noticed. Fashionably dressed, loud and pretty, they were a notorious clique from her old school. One of them nodded to her briefly while the others ignored her.

As she passed by, she couldn't help overhearing the remarks and snickers.

"The black widow spider."

"Maybe she's a witch?"

"Hardly. That would make her interesting."

Dana cringed, but told herself she didn't care. These were not people she envied or admired. Janis, the leader, was popular but not very bright. She had barely managed to pass grade eight. The other two were her lackeys, incapable of independent thought or action. While they had ruled the small kingdom of junior high, they were now little fish in a much bigger pond. Dana saw through their lively show of bravado. They were as nervous and anxious as she.

Moving to the back of the room, Dana chose a desk in the last row. In her old school she had been known as a quiet girl, a loner without the protection of a circle or best friend. She had grown used to standing by herself at recess, leaning against the fence, usually lost in daydreams. She didn't want to mix with others and rebuffed the few who tried to make friends. Unless specifically asked, she didn't participate in class nor did she join in school activities, sports or clubs. She resisted all efforts by her father and teachers to encourage her out of her shell. She did not want to be part of this world, she did not want to make friends.

"Some children are solitary," the principal had finally conceded to Gabriel. "You can either accept that or consider a psychologist."

Gabriel had decided to accept it, for the time being.

That she did well at school was Dana's saving grace. She liked to study and her projects were always well researched and presented. With tutors and hard work she had caught up on Canadian subjects to earn high grades. The French language was still a weak point. Her father wanted her to learn it to be fully Canadian, but she had yet to catch up with those who had begun the stream in earlier grades. Since she was already bilingual, being fluent in Irish, she was confident she would.

It was only when she had settled into her seat that Dana noticed the other student in the back, a few rows over. Now she understood why Janis and her coterie were making such a fuss. Here was surely the one whom they hoped to attract. Even Dana, who had no interest in boys, was not unaffected. The raven-black hair fell loosely around his face. The narrow cheekbones and firm jaw told of strong character. His clothes jarred slightly in the urban classroom but suited him perfectly: an outdoors look, rugged denim, dark-green shirt, brown leather boots. He seemed older than the class average or perhaps more mature, possibly because of his self-assured air. He did not look around but sat relaxed at his desk, reading a book. Dana tried to catch a glimpse of the title, but no luck. She was surprised at herself. There had been cute boys in her class before, she had never paid them any attention. But he was different. There was something about him.

Dana caught her breath. He had looked up suddenly to meet her gaze. The eyes were startling, a cool wintergreen. He seemed surprised to see her, as if he knew her somehow. He searched her features curiously.

The blood rushed to Dana's face. She turned away. It was not just from shyness. She was unsettled by his look, so keen and intense. When she found the courage to glance back again, he had returned to his book. She was relieved, but also a little disappointed.

Once the school bell rang and the day officially began, Dana settled into her usual state of "betwixt and between." With half a mind, she listened to what she had to learn and made notes when necessary. With the other half, she looked out the window, lost in thoughts of Faerie.

Beyond the asphalt grounds of the school yard, a line of old oak bordered the road. Where their leaves were beginning to turn, faint stitches of bronze trimmed the green. Grey squirrels scrabbled in the branches. They were so quick and busy, Dana smiled as she watched them. But what was that above the tree tops? A white blur in the sky. At first she thought it was a bank of clouds herded by the wind, then she realized it was a great flock of birds. A mild shock ran through her. *What were they?* There were so many of them, all different shapes and sizes, but every one was snow-white. She felt her heart lifting like a bird that wanted to fly too and she followed their flight with longing.

A harsh voice broke Dana's reverie, followed by an outburst of laughter from the class. Words filtered through Dana's confusion.

Woolgathering . . . daydreaming . . . featherbrain.

To her horror, she found herself in the glare of exposure. The whole class was staring at her with open amusement while the teacher scowled from the front.

It wasn't just the unwanted attention, the unkind words or even the embarrassment. Something else alarmed Dana. She knew instantly in a way she couldn't explain that she was under attack. That she had been singled out with deliberate malice. She fought through her bewilderment to face her tormentor.

Mr Grimstone. Aptly named, was Dana's thought when he first entered the room and announced who he was. Their home room teacher, he would also take them for English, first period, three classes a week. The universal reaction had been instant dismay. He was not the jolly pink-faced man who had made them laugh at orientation. "An unfortunate accident" was briefly mentioned, then Grimstone took command.

He was a tall grey man, lean and bony, with weak eyes behind his glasses and a thin sneer. When he spoke, spittle gathered in the corners of his mouth and his tongue darted out like a lizard's. He wore a grey suit, the same colour as his hair which fell in sparse locks to his shoulders. When she first heard his whispery voice Dana had dismissed him as harmless if decidedly creepy. Now she could hear the force behind the hiss, the surge of malevolence.

Her skin crawled as she met the dead look in his eyes. There was something terrible here, something far worse than his appearance. Something so cheerless that it would smother any spark of liveliness it encountered. She sensed his hatred. But what had she done?! His will seemed to press against her. She felt as if she were falling . . . falling backwards . . . into an abyss.

It is dangerous to approach evil. The best thing you can do is run away.

Dana had no idea who or what was speaking to her, but the soft voice fluttered in her mind like wings. It was all the encouragement she needed. Gathering what little strength she had, she hurried to make her escape, journeying in her mind towards Faerie.

Despite her panic, it wasn't hard. She had done it so often it was second nature. In a matter of moments she was running up the hill towards the great portal. Music and laughter beckoned from within. The light of the Summer Country warmed her face. There she would recoup, seek help and advice, before she returned to face her adversary.

It happened the moment she reached the dolmen. There was a blinding flash and a monstrous roar. Then her world blew apart. She saw the great stones leap into the air as if they were dancing. Then they crashed to the ground and shattered like glass. Pieces flew everywhere, strewn like broken bones in the grasses. Nothing was left standing.

Reeling with shock, Dana grew aware of a second horror. A greenish-grey mist hovered over the stone shards. She sensed a malevolent presence that didn't belong there. An acrid odour singed the air, dank and rotten like the breath of a graveyard. The thing was watching her. In one heart-stopping second of clarity, she knew it had come for her.

Too late, she tried to back away. Smoky tendrils snaked out to seize her throat. She began to choke. Overcome with terror she flailed wildly, but the more she struggled the tighter the thing gripped. As in a nightmare, she tried to scream but no sound came out. A deathly pall had fallen over that place, smothering all sound. Dana was losing consciousness. Darkness fell over her eyes.

Then words rang out like church bells in the distance.

"*Tabernac,* so she looks out the window. What's the big deal?"

It was like a splash of frosty water from a clear mountain stream.

Falling into her body with a sickening lurch, Dana was back in the classroom. She clutched her desk as she gasped for breath. Quickly she looked around. *What was going on?*

Grimstone's eyes blazed, but his attention was no longer directed at her. It was trained on the young man a few rows over.

"Ah. Jean Ducharme. Or should I say, *Monsieur* Ducharme? Our transfer delinquent from Quebec. Have you been introduced to your peers who are hardly that since they are so much younger than yourself?"

The words oozed like an oil slick over clean waters, but their target was not in the least perturbed. Jean Ducharme returned his teacher's glare with a mild look of disdain. The cool green eyes were steady as he responded to the taunt.

"I have fifteen years, *un peu* older than the others, *oui*. But my English is not good, so I am agreed to be here. In one year, I will meet my class. *Mais peut-être,* you cannot see this. You cannot see intelligence."

For a moment Grimstone looked as if he might explode. Then he shuddered visibly as he regained control. His face cooled to a mask. His tone was icy.

"I wouldn't advise you to keep up that tone and track, mister. I've seen your record. I could have you expelled in an instant."

Wide-eyed, the rest of the class struggled to hide their delight as they exchanged furtive glances. The year had barely begun and it was already showing great promise. They had all been immediately intimidated by Grimstone, but here was a new player challenging him. The girls cast approving glances at the hero in their midst. Dark-haired and handsome, older than the other boys, with a French accent and a shady past, what more could they ask for?

A light smile played around Jean's lips, but he didn't bother to reply. He simply shrugged.

Closing the matter with a scowl, the teacher turned his back on the class and began to write on the board.

Dazed and bewildered, Dana fought to stay calm. Her thoughts raced wildly. She had only begun to absorb the horror of the portal's destruction and the murderous assault, when she found herself facing a new dilemma. *There was another being in the classroom that was not of this world.* Like the electric aftermath of a flash of lightning, it tingled in the air around her. The smell of magic.

Had something followed her from the portal? Was it her attacker? She looked first at Grimstone and then at Jean. Her mind was on fire. It was one of these, she was certain. But which? And more important—*what?*

As the first shock wore off, Dana went on the defensive. There might be another attack. Through the rest of the class, she kept an eye on both her teacher and Jean. The two did not clash swords again but settled into an uneasy truce, ignoring each other. Grimstone also appeared indifferent to Dana, sometimes looking right through her as if she weren't there. She was beginning to think she was mistaken about him when the bell went off. As she grabbed her books to leave, she caught him staring at her. A cat watching a mouse. She saw the threat in his eyes before he could hide it. *I'll get you.* With a shudder she hurried out of the room. She no longer doubted that he was an enemy.

But what about Jean? She was not the only one interested in him. As the morning progressed, he was showered with glances like handfuls of confetti. Notes were passed his way. In the halls, spurts of French could be heard wherever he walked as his admirers hoped to woo him with his own language. In the cafeteria at lunch hour, clusters of girls hovered near his table. Some stood around awkwardly where he might see them, while others approached him directly to converse in French. The latter included young women from the higher grades. Word had spread like wildfire about the handsome new student who stood up to teachers.

Jean, for his part, was courteous to everyone who came near him. Those who spoke French, however badly, were rewarded with a half-smile and a fluent response that left them dazzled. He was *so* French. He was *so* hot. Despite all the fuss he remained aloof, like a visitor who knew he would be leaving soon. As the circles of girls eventually drifted away, he went back to reading his book.

Dana had no desire to join the crowd around Jean, but she did want to thank him for defending her in class. She also wanted to get closer, to investigate her suspicions. There was definitely something different about him, but could he really be linked to the attack at the portal? He seemed too . . . nice. A wolf in sheep's clothing?

She was eating her lunch alone in the far corner of the room. Like Jean, she had brought a book to read, but she couldn't concentrate. She was too upset. What had happened to the portal? What was after her? How could she fight it? What should she do? She had been warned long ago, before she left Ireland, that trouble lay ahead in her future, in Canada. The High King of Faerie himself had told her. But as the months and then the years passed by without sign or incident, she had relaxed her guard, eventually forgetting the threat entirely. Now here it was, out of the blue, and she wasn't prepared, wasn't ready at all. How could this have happened? Why had no one warned her? Compounding her fear was a sense of betrayal. Where was Faerie when she was attacked? Why had no one come to her aid? The more she thought about it, the more her heart beat wildly. The room closed in on her, the scrape of chairs, the din of voices. Like a cold hand around her throat, the truth finally seized her.

Her portal had been destroyed. Her bridge to Faerie was broken. She was alone and defenceless against an unknown enemy.

Dana sat up with a jolt as if struck by a blow. Instinctively she glanced across the room at Jean. Once again she met his eyes. He was looking straight at her, a question in that calm green gaze. Before she knew what she was doing, she was on her feet and walking towards him. Barely able to breathe, she willed herself across the unending stretch of floor. His quizzical smile seemed to encourage her forward. She had almost reached him when her way was blocked.

Janis did not see Dana coming. She was too busy fixing her hair as she struggled with an awkward phrase in French.

Gently, Jean waved her aside.

"*Excus'-moi* but we wish to speak," he said, indicating that someone was behind her.

Surprised and annoyed, Janis turned to find Dana. In one scathing glance she took in the rumpled clothing, the lank hair, the face without make-up. Her lip curled with scorn, then she flounced away without saying a word.

Withered by the look, Dana regretted she had come this far but Jean's voice was kind.

"*S'il te plaît,* sit down."

She remained standing but managed to stutter, "I . . . I . . . just wanted to say thank you . . . *merci beaucoup* . . . for speaking up this morning. It was really . . . good of you."

"*Ce n'est rien,*" he said with a slight shrug. "*Monsieur* Grimstone is not so nice, eh?"

As the pale-green eyes appraised her, Dana grew painfully aware of her appearance in a way that even Janis could not have brought home. For the first time, she cared how she looked in the Earthworld. She wished she had made some effort with her dress and hair. If only he could see her in a fairy gown with jewels! Though his own clothes were casual, he had a certain flair. She noticed that the wristband of his watch had beaded work of Native design. It featured the shape of a black bird, perhaps a raven. The boots also had a Native look, expensive and handmade.

Dana couldn't know what Jean was thinking but she was certain he found her unattractive, even repulsive. She began to edge away.

"*Dis-moi,*" he said. "What is this your accent?"

"I'm Irish."

His smile was so swift and embracing that Dana blushed.

"*Irlandaise! Magnifique!* The French and the Irish, we are always good friends. *C'est un très beau pays, l'Irlande.*"

"Yes, it's a beautiful country," she said.

He heard the catch in her voice.

"You are not happy here?"

"Yes. No. It's . . . complicated." She didn't want to explain. She had yet to decide if she trusted him, this mysterious and charming stranger. "What about you? This isn't your home either?"

"I am *Québécois*. Born in Rivière-du-Loup but we move around a lot. My parents, they are *artistes*. They get good jobs in *le théâtre* here. I choose this school to learn English better." A wry look crossed his face. "Maybe not a good idea."

"I'm so glad you did!" she burst out.

Dana thought she would die. Her face burned furiously. She had been lulled by their conversation as he was so easy to talk to. Her stuttering had stopped and, in a natural progression, she had sat down at his table. Now she couldn't believe she had blurted out her feelings like that! Worse still, she was suddenly aware of all the eyes that were watching them. She jumped up, almost upsetting her chair. She had to get away.

Jean looked surprised by her panic, and a little sad. He caught her arm before she could leave. His voice was grave.

"I want to say to you, about Grimstone. Beware this teacher. For you, he is *dangereux*."

Dana was startled. Before she could ask what he meant, he nodded towards the entrance of the cafeteria. There in the corridor, staring through the glass doors, was Grimstone. He looked from Jean to Dana and back again, eyes black with rage.

"*Prends garde,*" Jean said softly as he released her arm.

Confused and disturbed, Dana hurried away.

CHAPTER SIX

On THE SAME DAY, AT
the same moment in which Dana was attacked, Laurel Blackburn
pitched forward with a cry. She had been sitting in her supervisor's
office, discussing the subject of her thesis when the blow struck. It
was as if a balled fist had punched her gut. In that fleeting moment
of pain, a series of images flashed through her mind.

*A little girl with blond curls, three years of age, reaches out to touch
a hot stove. She lets out a cry as it burns her hand. Now the same little
girl, older at five, falls off a swing. She lands on the ground and gashes
her head. At nine years of age, she is cornered by a bully in the school yard
who pushes her against the wall.*

Laurel recognized the child immediately, her sister Honor,
even as she recognized the images. They were memories from
a time when she was small and her twin was in trouble. Being
the stronger of the two, she had run to rescue Honor on each
occasion.

The last vision was a new one.

*A dark wood overhung with shadows. Honor runs wildly through the
trees. Her hair is tangled, her gown torn. Tears stream down her face as she
cries out tragically. Our doom has fallen! The Summer Land is lost!*

"Are you all right?" Laurel's professor asked her.

Laurel straightened up. The pain was gone, but not the horror.

"Yes. I'm fine. Sorry. I have to go."

She ran out of his office.

Gwen, too, felt the blow that day. Late for a job interview, she was hurrying through a downtown shopping mall when it struck. Her knees buckled under her. She leaned against a store window.

"Oh God," she gasped.

The mannequins stared back at her blindly.

With the pain came an image that hurt her all the more. It was only a brief flash, but the details were seared on her mind.

A high hill cloaked with hawthorn. A pale grey sky above a damp green slope. A cold wind blows over the desolate scene. Two figures sprawl face down in the grasses. Neither is moving. One is an old woman, the other a young man.

As soon as the pain left her, Gwen ran for the subway. Her interview was abandoned. She had to get home. She had to call Ireland. The place in her vision was well known to her. Dunfinn, the fairy fort on Inch Island in Donegal. Worse still, she knew the two people she had seen lying on the ground. The old woman was Granny Harte, fairy doctress and friend. The other was Dara, the young man Gwen loved.

She heard the telephone ringing as she opened her apartment door. She ran to answer it.

"Gwen, something terrible has happened!" Laurel's voice shook.

"I know. Will I come over?"

"Please!"

Laurel's rooms were spacious for student accommodation. A narrow bedroom was partitioned from the wider living area where a built-in desk faced the window. Shelves ranged around the room full of books and papers. There was enough space to fit Laurel's sofa, arm chair and low wooden table. A colourful rug and paintings made the place cosy. Classical music soothed the air with the plangent sounds of cello and violin.

Gwen sat on the couch, sipping a mug of herbal tea. As she inhaled the grassy scent, she felt herself grow calm.

"St John's Wort?"

Laurel nodded, pouring herself a cup.

"It dispels dark forces. We need it."

"Tell me what happened," said Gwen.

Laurel was evidently distraught, no longer the cool and contained person Gwen had met the week before. Her face was pale, her eyes frantic. The blond hair straggled on her shoulders as she ran her hands through it.

"Honor and I always had this twin thing. We would know if the other was hurt or in trouble. The day she died, I collapsed on the floor. I knew she was gone."

Laurel choked. Gwen waited with sympathy till she was ready to continue.

"This was the same thing but stronger, as if she were consciously trying to contact me, to get a message through. Normally she arrives whenever she wants to, but there's been no sign of her since the vision. I have an awful feeling she can't get here. I tried to fall asleep to dream my way into Faerie, but I'm too upset."

"I felt something too." Gwen described her own dark vision. "I called Ireland right after you rang. All I got was Granny's answering machine. She and Dara were to meet the High King today at Dunfinn on Inch Island." She fought back the tears. "That's where I saw them . . . dead."

They were both overwhelmed by emotion. It was Laurel who rallied first.

"You don't know that," she said to Gwen. "You can't assume the worst when you don't have all the facts. For all we know these could be premonitions. They may not have happened yet and we could still prevent them. We've got to keep our heads."

Gwen heard the "we" and it steadied her.

"You're right. I'm being a dope. We don't know anything for certain yet."

"There's something else." Laurel hesitated. Her natural reticence struggled against her need to tell Gwen. "I rang Ireland too."

With sudden insight, Gwen understood. She knew the story: how Laurel had quested in the west of Ireland to find the Summer King. During the course of her mission, Laurel discovered that the king was the one who had killed her sister. But by then, she was already in love with his human side born separately in the Earthworld.

"You called Ian?"

Laurel turned away. Her voice was strained.

"We broke up a year ago. After that, I stayed away from Faerie since he spends half his time there as the Summer King. I decided to leave it all behind me, to get on with my life. But when I couldn't reach Honor . . . well, I thought he might know something as he lives in both worlds. I rang his flat but then I realized he'd be at work so I rang his father, the Reverend Gray, to get the number." A quaver crept into Laurel's voice. "Ian's missing. He didn't show up for work today and he didn't call in. That's not like him. He's a vet. He loves animals, especially birds. His parents are really worried. So am I."

She paced the room.

"I thought it was over, but I've obviously been fooling myself. As soon as I heard he was missing, it was like an arrow pierced my heart. I thought I would die."

"So whatever has happened involves him too," Gwen said, thinking. "But Granny said the battle would be in Canada, not Ireland."

"Ireland isn't the common denominator here," Laurel pointed out. "It's Faerie."

That was when the penny dropped for Gwen; the bigger picture that loomed over the image of Dara and Granny in trouble.

"It's here. Faerie's darkest hour."

Laurel nodded. "The Enemy has struck. Our mission has begun. The rescue of Fairyland."

Again Gwen heard the "our" and was heartened.

"So you're in this with me?"

"That's the way it goes, eh? Just like you said. You're in over your head before you know it. Honor and Ian are the two people I love most. I couldn't bear to lose them."

They stared at each other with silent resolve, two heroines who had quested once before for Faerie.

"We need a plan," said Laurel.

Gwen agreed. "I'll keep trying to get Dara or Granny. Hopefully Honor will contact you again, or maybe Ian. We've got to find out what's happening. Meanwhile, our original mission was to look after Dana. I have some protective charms and herbs. I was going to put them around her, secretly of course."

"Excellent idea," said Laurel. "I have a few spells of my own I learned on Achill Island. 'Red thread tied round branch of rowan.' Stuff like that. We should do ourselves as well."

"Of course. We could be targets too," Gwen said without flinching. "I've got the addresses of Dana's home and school. I've been keeping an eye on her. I even applied for a job at her high school. That would have been perfect, but no luck. We should do it right away. Either twilight or midnight. Threshold hours are the most potent. I say midnight, less chance of being seen. Is that okay with you?"

Despite the gravity of the situation, Laurel smiled at Gwen's air of command. It was such a contrast to her gentle features and femininity. Here indeed was the Captain of the Company of Seven. A warrior in pink.

"The sooner we do it the better," Laurel agreed. "The Enemy is on the move. Have you read the papers? A crime wave is hitting the streets. Something bad is working its way through the city."

"I should've got going before this," Gwen said guiltily. "With the job hunt and everything I've been really disorganized."

The same guilt struck Laurel.

"*Mea culpa*. It's my fault. If I had joined you when you asked . . ."

Gwen shook her head. "I gave up too quickly. I could've made more of an effort to win you over. To be honest? I wasn't that happy about another Canadian involved. I preferred to be the sole ambassador for Canada in Faerie."

That was the one that got Laurel. She let out a quick laugh. It was the first time Gwen had heard her laugh and it was a pleasant sound.

"You should laugh more," Gwen told her.

"With you around I have a feeling I will." Laurel's features softened. "After things ended with Ian I couldn't go back, not to Ireland or Faerie, even though I wanted to. It was my fault, you see. We were always arguing and I found it too difficult to reconcile our differences. He wanted to keep trying. He believed in us. But I said no." She shrugged sadly. "I think I'm just one of those people who ends up alone."

Gwen reached out to comfort her.

"You're not alone. We're in this together."

Later that night, shortly before twelve, Gwen and Laurel met at the corner of Brunswick and Bloor. Both wore dark clothing to blend with the night. Each had a bulging knapsack. Gwen had brought branches of ash and whitethorn as well as bunches of primroses gathered on May Eve. Laurel had sea salt, twigs of rowan and broom tied with red thread, dried daisy chains and old knives and scissors. Gwen had been taught her charms by Granny, the

Wise Woman of Inch. Laurel had learned hers from the sea fairies of Achill Island.

"Any news?"

Laurel shook her head. "Still no word or sign of either of them."

Gwen's shoulders slumped. "Same for me. When I couldn't get Dara or Granny, I tried the other members of the Company of Seven, Katie on her farm and Matt at home. All I get is answering machines or busy signals. I've sent emails too but no replies so far. I tried to reach my cousin Findabhair but she's still on the road. I left an urgent message with her manager. Hopefully she'll call me as soon as she gets it."

Laurel could hear the huge effort Gwen was making to stay optimistic. They were both clinging to the hope that despite all appearances their loved ones were safe.

"Come on," Laurel said, "we've got work to do."

They hurried up Brunswick Avenue to Dana's address. When they reached the big brownstone, they stared in dismay at its size. The charms had to be placed where they couldn't be removed or blown away by the wind. Lights shone in some of the rooms. Would they be able to strew the doors and windowsills without being noticed? Fortunately the house was surrounded by trees and bushes. Plenty of places to hide if someone came out.

"I'll take the back," Laurel whispered. "I can climb over the fence. You do the front."

It wasn't long before they joined up again.

"Finished?" they asked each other.

Both nodded uncertainly. As soon as they were a safe distance from the house, they broke their silence.

"I put some stuff on the sills," Gwen said, mystified, "but then I stopped when I got the strangest feeling."

"Me too! That it wasn't necessary?"

"Yes! Because—"

"The house is already protected," Laurel concluded.

They stared at each other, overcome by a huge and nameless excitement.

Gwen looked back up the street. "A beautiful presence," she said softly. She could hug herself she felt so good.

"And jolly as well." Laurel wanted to laugh, but she also felt shy. "Full of fun and laughter, but also sacred and powerful. The way you imagine Santa Claus when you're little."

They had stopped under a street lamp. Bathed in yellow light, they were both radiant with joy.

"We're not alone," Gwen breathed.

"Other forces are gathering around the girl," Laurel nodded. "This is good. This is very good."

"Okay, so let's get a taxi to her school," said Gwen. "It'll be a big job but I've got plenty of charms left."

"Me too. Her home and school should do it. Where else would you find a thirteen-year-old?"

When they reached Bloor, they eyed the road for a cab. Despite the late hour, the street was busy. Restaurants, pubs and coffee shops were bustling with late-summer trade. There was a mild chill in the air but the night was still amenable to strollers.

"How about celebrating with lattes and Nanaimo bars in the little café?" Gwen suggested.

"Work first, then treats."

"You are so like my cousin," sighed Gwen.

When they arrived at Dana's high school, their hearts sank. Not only was the large building locked and shuttered, it was ablaze with security lights and video cameras. Gingerly they approached the first window. Laurel flung a handful of salt through the metal grate while Gwen pressed a primrose petal onto the sill. Neither was prepared for the repercussion.

The flower and salt burst into flames even as a blast of hot air flung the two of them backwards.

They hit the ground with a smack.

"What!" demanded Gwen.

Stunned, they helped each other up.

Laurel regarded the school grimly.

"We're too late. It's been claimed by the other side. We're not safe here."

They hurried away.

Back at Laurel's they shared a pot of tea, any thought of treats forgotten.

"Oh God," said Gwen. "I was afraid of this. We're moving too slowly."

"We're dancing as fast as we can," Laurel countered.

Gwen's tone hardened. "We need help. We're in the dark and we're fighting shadows. Canadian battle or not, I'm calling up the Company of Seven. I'm their leader. They're my friends. They've got to come."

"If you can reach them," the other pointed out.

"I will," she said fiercely, "if I have to go to Ireland to do it. With her school compromised, the girl's in danger. We've got to act."

"You're right," Laurel nodded. "But we should also join up with Dana. It would be easier to protect her."

Gwen frowned. "Granny's instructions were clear. We were to be like guardian angels. Watch over her from afar."

"That doesn't make sense," Laurel argued. "Things are getting serious and she's only a kid."

"She's not just a kid." But Gwen sounded uncertain. After all, the situation had changed since she had last talked with Granny. "All right. We'll contact her."

Laurel was now having second thoughts herself. Talking about Faerie was never easy, how would it would go with a kid who didn't know them? She didn't particularly like children and Honor's description of Dana was hardly encouraging. A moody teenager. That's all they needed.

Gwen saw the look on Laurel's face.

"I'll do the talking," she assured her. "I'm good with young people, it's my job. You just have to be there. At least she'll recognize you since you look like the High Queen."

"Okay," Laurel agreed. "First thing tomorrow we tackle her."

Had that meeting taken place, all of them might have suffered less. But it was not to be. Gwen's premonition at the fountain would soon be proved true. Things were about to get worse.

CHAPTER SEVEN

THE VILLAGE OF CREEMORE, just an hour and a half drive north of Toronto, was given its name in the 1840s by Judge James R. Gowan. He called it after an Irish townland in his native county of Wexford. The family of the founding father of the village, Edward Webster, also came from that townland but they had emigrated to Canada long before the judge. While there is no recorded history of the moment, Edward and Judge Gowan may well have christened the village together over a malt whiskey in Kelly's Tavern. The judge himself never lived in the village and most of the Gowans who settled there were no relation to him. They hailed from Queen's County in Ireland, now called Laois. Nevertheless Dana's grandmother, Maisy Gowan, claimed some distant connection to the judge, thereby maintaining that her family tree was rooted in the two Gowan families and both Creemores.

The modern Creemore was a picturesque village of tree-lined avenues, old churches and stately brick homes. Nestled in the valley of the Mad and Noisy rivers and surrounded by farmland, it was a quiet sleepy place during the week. On the weekend the town would fill with tourists as well as city dwellers escaping to their cottages in the Purple Hills. The main thoroughfare of Mill Street was a browser's delight with quaint storefronts, hanging baskets and hand-crafted street signs. Antique shops, art galleries and tea rooms bloomed like roses. The village also boasted North America's smallest jail, little more than a shed.

Dana's grandmother was "bred and buttered" in the village, as she often said. Regardless of her marriage, she was always called by her maiden name since she belonged to one of the oldest and most respected families. Her husband, on the other hand, was a "blow in." Indeed Maisy had caused something of a scandal in her day when she married Gabe Faolan, an outsider and a Roman Catholic to boot. The fact that he was Irish helped to ease the shock. As time passed, his talents as a painter and teacher, as well as his charm, secured his acceptance in the small community. Though Maisy never regretted her marriage, and loved Gabe heartily till his early death at fifty, she always blamed "the Faolan streak" when her children misbehaved.

She was a small sturdy woman of endless energy with salt-and-pepper hair in closely cropped curls. On Sundays she dressed in a skirt and blouse with pearls or brooches and sometimes a hat, while the rest of the week saw her in track suits and running shoes. In her late sixties, she lived a busy life, working in her garden and keeping up the family home. She also served on various committees for the betterment of the village, including the Creemore Tree Association, the Creemore Horticultural Society, the Purple Hills Arts and Heritage Society, and the Royal Canadian Legion.

The Gowan home was just off the main street. Built by Maisy's grandfather in 1901, it was a fine big house of red and cream brick with stone quoins on the corners and gabled windows. Geraniums blossomed on the sills. A wooden verandah encircled the house and was furnished with a swing seat, two rocking chairs and wickerwork antiques. A wide front lawn ambled down to the road, shaded by maple and cherry trees. In the past, the rooms were heated with wood stoves whose pipes went up to warm the second floor before connecting to the chimneys. According to Gran Gowan, the house wasn't as cosy once the "newfangled" central heating was installed. But old-fashioned comfort was still to be found in polished pine floors, iron beds with goose-down quilts and open fireplaces. In the back yard was a drive shed where the horse and carriage were once kept. Now it housed Gran's pride and joy, a dark-green Triumph Herald that once belonged to her husband.

When Dana heard she was going to Creemore on Friday, she was overjoyed. The light at the end of a long dark week. It was her stepmother who had noticed how ill she looked on her return home that first day at school. Dana was so pale she was almost translucent and her eyes had a haunted look. She was immediately sent to bed.

"Is the moon in your womb?" Aradhana asked gently, as she brought her a cup of chamomile tea.

Dana smiled wanly at her stepmother's way of describing menstruation and shook her head.

"Your temperature is very high," Radhi said worriedly.

Her hand was cool on Dana's forehead and fragrant with the scent of jasmine.

In the days that followed, Dana had grown much sicker. Unable to eat, she complained of mysterious aches and pains. When she slept, it was fitful and she often cried out in her sleep. The nightmares were the same. She was back at the broken portal and under attack. In the distance, a shining figure tried vainly to help her. She could hear her mother's cries. As she called back to Edane, Dana would wake to the terrifying truth. She was alone, cut off from Faerie.

"It's most likely a virus," the doctor told Gabriel. "No use treating it with antibiotics. We'll give it a few days to work its way out and if nothing changes, I'll order some tests. Between you and me, it could be psychosomatic. Some kids are traumatized by starting high school. They adjust with time."

Gabriel sighed. He had thought as much himself though his wife wasn't convinced.

When the doctor left and Gabe went to cook dinner, Aradhana sat down beside Dana's bed. Taking the girl's hand, she spoke quietly.

"Is everything all right between you and your mother?"

Dana stared into the dark thoughtful eyes. Her stepmother's question showed how special Radhi was. Both Gabriel and Aradhana had discovered the truth about Dana's mother before they left Ireland. Gabriel had soon forgotten what he learned about his first wife, remembering only that she left him. It was the nature of Faerie. The spell of forgetting was woven like a wall around it. Adults in particular could not hold the reality of fairy existence for long. If they did remember, they inevitably dismissed the experience as a dream or their imagination. At one time Dana wished she could have shared that side of her life with her father, but his forgetting made things easier. She could move between the worlds without permission or explanation.

Up to that moment, she had assumed that Aradhana too had forgotten what she learned.

"I respect your privacy," her stepmother said, still holding Dana's hand. She chose her words carefully. "Your life with your mother is not any of my business. But I want you to know, my Irish Barbie, that if you need to speak of such matters you may do so with me. In India we live with many gods and spirits. They are not strangers to us."

Tears pricked Dana's eyes. She tried to speak. She felt as if she were at the bottom of a dark pit looking up at her stepmother who peered over the edge. She wanted to call out to Radhi but she couldn't. She hadn't the strength to divulge her nightmare.

By the end of the week, Dana began to feel better. It was as if a poison that had got into her system had finally worn off. When her father announced they were going to Creemore for the last family gathering of the summer, she couldn't have been happier. She loved her grandmother who doted on her and also her two aunts, Yvonne and Deirdre.

Though they were older, Dana's aunts tended to look and act like teenagers. At thirty-two, a painter and sculptor, Yvonne was a brash blonde who dressed in dramatic colours, usually scorched orange or red. She liked tight skirts and slinky dresses, stockings with seams, stiletto high heels and ruby-red lipstick. Younger at twenty-nine, Deirdre, also called Dee, was a filmmaker specializing in radical documentaries and political animation. Having shaved her head for years, she now sported a blue brush-cut. Slashed jeans and leather jackets were her preference along with hobnailed boots, but sometimes she wore pearls to "soften" the look. Given their own idiosyncratic tastes, neither would interfere with Dana's appearance despite their older brother's pleas.

"There's no such thing as a good influence," Yvonne told him. "As Oscar Wilde said, 'All influence is immoral.'"

"Is she saying 'grunge' do you think?" Dee wondered. "It's a valid statement."

"What," snorted Gabriel, "'I will not wash?'"

"'I will not be a slave to conventional forms of beauty,'" his sister corrected him. "Didn't you see my doc on youth and fashion? Does *no one* in my family look at my work? I'm a prophet in my own home, unrecognized and undervalued."

"I know all your work," Yvonne pointed out, "and Gabe was out of the country for that one."

In the end, of course, Gabriel knew it was hopeless. His sisters would never side with him against Dana. He was a parent, "One of them." She was a daughter, "One of us."

The barbecue cum corn roast was held in Gran Gowan's back garden with its broad lawn bordered by a fence and privet hedge. The smell of charcoal mingled in the air with that of hamburgers and hot dogs spitting on the grill. A pot of boiling water bobbed with yellow cobs of corn. On a cloth-covered table were bowls of potato salad, cole slaw and green salad, pickles and beet-root, baskets of crusty bread and pots of mustard and relish. Ice clinked in wet jugs of homemade lemonade sprinkled with white sugar. Since Gran Gowan did not approve of alcohol and barred it from the premises, the aunts had been forced to stash a cooler of beer in Dee's bedroom. Getting it up the stairs without their mother noticing had involved stealth and timing, but they were practised hands. Gran also didn't approve of the vegetarianism of her son and granddaughter who had brought lentil patties to accompany the corn and salads.

"I have no objections to Aradhana not eating meat," she stated in her no-nonsense way. "It's her religion and I would never stand between someone and their God. You two, on the other hand, are just being contrary."

As the afternoon meandered on and everyone had eaten their fill, the croquet set was arranged on the lawn.

"We'll divide into teams," Yvonne declared. "Radhi and Gabe, Maisy and Dana, Dee and me."

"Place your bets, ladies and gentlemen. We're going to take you to the cleaners," said Dee, swinging her mallet like a golf pro.

"There'll be no gambling here," Gran Gowan said mildly.

"Don't mind those two," Gabe said to his wife. "They're all bluff and bluster. It's the dark horses you have to watch out for, Dana and Mom."

Dana listened to the banter as she lined up for her shot. She felt safe with her family. *Clack* went her bat as it hit the hollow ball that rolled over the grass. When it sailed through the wire hoop, everyone cheered. She smiled shyly back at them. She could feel her worries falling away like leaves from an autumn tree.

By late afternoon the barbecue had cooled and the table was cleared. Aradhana went to her room to rest, while Gabe and his mother watched the news in the parlour. The two aunts stayed outdoors, sneaking gin into their lemonade from a furtive flask. They sent Dana into the kitchen to fetch some ice. That was when she overheard her father and grandmother talking in the next room. Both their voices were raised.

"... dreadful," Gran Gowan was saying, "even paler than usual. And she still has no friends! I've said it before, Gabriel, and I'll say it again, Toronto is no place for the girl. You've taken her from a small town in Ireland and dropped her into a big Canadian city. It's two years now and she has not 'adjusted.' By all appearances, she's getting worse. She should be here with me in Creemore. I know you love her, but you're too busy with your new job to look after her properly and you have a wife now as well. Dana was used to having you all to herself."

"Dana loves Radhi!" Gabriel protested.

"Don't interrupt your mother. That's not the point. I'm not going to stand by any longer and watch that bright lively child grow more miserable by the day. She's withering away with the loneliness. It's not natural. She would flourish here. Creemore is a close friendly community. She'd go to the high school in Stayner—a good size but not too big—and there are plenty of young people to be her friends, like that sweet Holly Durnford down the road."

"Dana's eccentric, like her aunts," Gabriel argued defensively. "They had no friends either and they grew up here in Creemore."

Gran Gowan was stumped by that truth for a moment, but she recovered quickly.

"Well, they had each other. Dana has no siblings. Which is another point. You've been married for two years now, more than enough time to get going on a family."

"Aradhana and I will have kids when we're ready!" Gabriel's voice thundered. This was forbidden territory.

"Hmph," said his mother, retreating quickly.

Dana could hear her father spluttering. Here was undoubtedly one of the reasons why he had lived in Ireland for so long. Gran Gowan had no qualms about interfering in her children's lives.

Dana backed away from the voices. Why was everyone always talking about her? As if she were nothing but a problem! She was overcome by the shame, the unfairness, the sheer awfulness of her life. It only compounded the nightmare of the week gone by. Her eyes flooded with tears. She barged through the screen door and out into the garden.

"Where's the ice, oh slow but faithful one?" Dee called out.

Her aunts were lounging on deck chairs on the far side of the lawn where Gran Gowan was unlikely to detect the scent of liquor.

Dana didn't answer, but ran blindly around the side of the house and onto the street. She wasn't paying attention to where she was going, she only wanted to get away. She didn't see the car parked across the road, a black sedan with tinted windows. Nor did she notice it move off to follow her as she ran down the street.

Like a panther stalking its prey, it pulled up to the kerb beside her. The passenger window slid noiselessly down.

Shocked by the sight of the driver, Dana stopped.

"Hello, my dear," came the whispery voice. "Fancy meeting you here. Small world, isn't it? I missed you at school all week. Are you feeling better now?"

Grimstone looked greyer than she remembered him. His pallor was sickly, his frame skeletal. The only part of him that seemed alive were the eyes that burned into hers.

"Would you like to come for a ride with me? Yes. Open the door. Yes. Get in."

Alarm bells rang in Dana's head yet she found herself inexorably drawn to Grimstone. Her hand reached out to open the car door. She knew it was all wrong—*what am I doing!*—but she couldn't resist. His voice was mesmeric. His eyes transfixed her.

"Yes. Get in," he insisted. "Come with me now."

She was almost in the car when she heard a shout. Slowly, with huge effort, she turned to see her aunts. They were running towards her.

"*Get in!*" Grimstone urged.

She felt pushed and pulled between two forces. His will was relentless, but the shouts of her aunts jarred against it. As they drew nearer, Dana could see the panic on their faces. Dee was ahead, boots pounding the pavement, with Yvonne close behind despite her high heels.

Grimstone cursed and reached out to grab Dana.

She stepped back just in time.

The car door slammed shut as the aunts arrived and the sedan screeched away.

Yvonne clasped her niece.

"Get the licence number!" she ordered Dee.

Deirdre squinted at the speeding vehicle as it disappeared down the road.

"I don't have my lenses in," she said, jittery with adrenaline.

Yvonne was the same.

"For chrissakes, how can you go around half-blind like that!"

"New perspectives. Fuzzy edges."

"Great. A myopic filmmaker."

"We're babbling," Dee warned. "Shock."

"You're right," her sister agreed. "We should call the police."

"Did you get a good look at him?" they asked Dana. "What did he say?"

Dana was bewildered. She was glad that Yvonne was holding onto her. She didn't feel right. Her head hurt and she felt loose and scattered as if she were coming apart. She had a vague sense that something terrible had just happened but she couldn't remember what. At the same time she was confused by the memory of a harmless conversation.

"I . . . it was . . . someone asking for directions."

"Oh yeah?" Dee demanded. "Then how come he took off like a bat out of hell?"

"And what were you doing getting into the car?" Yvonne asked, more gently. "You know better than that, kiddo."

Dana shook her head as she looked from one to the other. Tears trickled down her face. She had no idea what was going on. Could her life get any worse?

The aunts had calmed down. Their terror at seeing their niece being abducted was ebbing away. They began to question what they had seen. The more they thought about it, the vaguer their impressions grew. The only thing they were really sure of was Dana's distress.

"Tea room," Yvonne announced, throwing her sister a look. "Hot chocolate and chocolate buns with heaps of chocolate sauce and chocolate doughnuts."

"Chocolate and more chocolate," Deirdre agreed.

The Mad Hatter Tea House was a favourite haunt of the aunts. Everything about it was "darling." The wood-framed building was prettily painted in egg-shell blue with yellow trim. A line of pink flamingos marched past the front window. Inside, the big room was chock-a-block from floor to ceiling with shelves of teapots. Big ones, small ones, plain and patterned, delicate china or glazed ceramics, they came in every shape and colour; a black-and-white cow, a hen on her nest, ladies in long skirts, a honey-hive with bees, a piano, a chair. Each was a work of art and no two were the same.

The three settled into an alcove by the lace-curtained window. Though the menu offered sandwiches and other savouries, they went immediately to the desserts. By the time they had tucked into the chocolate mousse cheese cake and chocolate chip cookies, they had totally forgotten why they were there.

"Gran will kill us," Dana said, her mouth full. "She made a rhubarb tart."

"Hah! We'll eat that too," said Dee.

Yvonne dialled her cellphone.

"Maisy, we've gone for a walk," she said, winking at the others. "Put the pie in the oven. We'll be back soon."

The aunts had huge appetites and ate like horses without any visible effect on their weight. "Good breeding" their mother maintained. "Hyperactive madwomen" was their own prognosis.

"So why did we get so upset when that guy asked you for directions?" Yvonne wondered.

Dana shrugged.

"Toronto paranoia," Dee concluded. "Do you ever get the reverse kind? When you think you're following someone?"

"Oh yeah," Yvonne nodded, dropping brown sugar cubes into her coffee. "Everywhere you go, you keep seeing the same person and you think 'My god, am I trailing them?'"

Sitting between the two, Dana laughed at their antics. She was always happy in the company of her aunts. They expected nothing from her and accepted her as she was, no matter her mood. She wished she could tell them what was really troubling her, but it wasn't possible. Her fairy life had become a dark secret she couldn't bring herself to reveal.

"I still miss Ireland," she confided instead. "It's like an empty feeling in my stomach that won't go away."

"Try the cheese cake," Dee said. "It's almost as good as—"

Her sister frowned her into silence. Sometimes Deirdre was incapable of being serious.

"You're just like your dad," Yvonne said with sympathy. "We weren't surprised Gabe stayed so long in Ireland. Aside from escaping Mom, of course, he was always crazy about everything Irish— music, books, history, language, Irish this and Irish that."

"Irish Guinness," Dee added.

"The trouble is," Yvonne continued, "you haven't seen enough of Canada. All you've seen is Toronto and Creemore."

"Toronto's good," Dee interjected. "Creemore's good."

"Yeah but," said Yvonne. "There's so much more. Like Hugh MacLennan said, 'This land is far more important than we are. To know it is to be young and ancient all at once.'"

"How do you remember these things?" her sister said admiringly.

"There's been no time to travel," Dana pointed out. "We've had so much to do from the time we got here. Find a place to live, Gabe and Radhi's marriage, their new jobs, my new school."

"I rest my case," said Yvonne. "No time to smell the roses, to appreciate where you are and what you've got."

"I appreciate you two," Dana said fervently.

Her aunts beamed back at her.

"We're really glad you're here," Yvonne said. "We just hope someday you will be too."

They returned to Gran Gowan's in high spirits ready for the rhubarb pie and a family game of Scrabble. As the night grew darker, Dana was eventually sent to bed. Climbing under the thick quilt, she was nagged by a stray thought. Something important she had forgotten. *What was it?* But no matter how hard she tried, she couldn't remember. Giving up at last, she fell into a troubled sleep.

Later that night, when everyone else had gone to bed and all the lights were out, Grimstone returned.

CHAPTER EIGHT

Dana was standing on the sidewalk in front of her grandmother's house. Confused and groggy, she had no idea how she had got there or what she was doing. A black sedan drew up to the kerb. The door swung open. A whispery voice issued from the dark interior of the car.

"This time you *will* get in. Yes. You cannot resist."

Grimstone wasn't lying. Though it was the last thing she wanted to do, Dana felt compelled to obey him. As soon as she sat in the passenger seat, the door shut and locked of its own accord. Like a snake, the seat belt slid over her shoulder to bind her fast.

"You're mine!" Grimstone hissed in triumph.

"Where—?"

Her voice was small and strangled. She found it difficult to think or speak.

"Where are we?" she tried again.

Creemore was gone. Outside her window was a bleak landscape, sered and blackened by some ancient fire. As far as the eye could see, everything was dead or dying. The earth was torn up and thrown aside in clots of dank mud. Swamp willows crawled from the roscid hollows. A polluted snye trickled like ink past a tangled wood of withered larch and spruce. The sky was dull with ashen light.

"This is a dream," Dana told herself. "There's no reason to be afraid."

"You have every reason to be afraid."

Even as Dana sat spellbound in the car, her real self was sleep-walking through her grandmother's house. Unbeknownst to herself, she had slipped out of bed and was padding downstairs in her bare feet and pyjamas. When she reached the kitchen, she searched through the bundle of keys that hung on a hook near the stove. Then she left the house.

Still lost in her nightmare, Dana stepped across the damp grass to where the old Triumph Herald was parked. Not yet stored in the shed for winter, the antique car stood in the drive-way. Dana unlocked the door and slipped behind the wheel. From the time she was nine, Gabriel had taught her to drive their own Triumph out in the country, but it wasn't Dana who drove the car now. It was Grimstone who put the key in the ignition and reversed the car onto the road. It was Grimstone who drove through the silent streets of Creemore, past the stately homes of Gran Gowan's neighbours, past Creemore Public School and Recreational Centre, out beyond the town's border and into the countryside.

The old car was being pushed to its limit, heading northwest. The night was cool and clear, lit up by moonlight. The land rolled gently, fields of hay bordered by stands of forest. Careering around the steep curve of the mill town of Glen Huron, the Triumph sped onto an isolated stretch of road. The land grew marshy as it trailed the Mad River. Now the car bumped onto a gravel track. A warning sign said "Summer Road Only." August storms had already caused damage, leaving deep ruts and depressions. As the car struggled over them, going ever uphill, it bumped and slid. Dense tracts of ash and maple crowded the verges. Lit up by the headlights, the red candles of the sumac glowed like blood. Skirting the edge of the Bruce Trail, the Triumph was travelling along the gorge carved by the river as it flowed off the escarpment. The line of hills in the distance marked the boundary of the provincial park called the Devil's Glen.

Dana's foot pressed the accelerator to the floor. The engine screamed in protest. The car shuddered like an animal in pain. Its windows rattled like teeth. A new sign on the road—"Unopened Concession"—indicated worsening conditions ahead. The tires spat gravel as the car lurched in and out of the corduroy ridges.

"Nearly there," Grimstone whispered to Dana in his car, in her dream.

"Nearly there," Dana's lips whispered, as her hands gripped the Triumph's steering wheel.

She was coming to a bend in the road. Beyond it fell a sheer drop of cliff. She did not turn the wheel.

Outside, the forest seemed to lean towards the car. Branches of white pine scraped and tapped at the windows as if to waken Dana. But her mind had been taken too far away. She didn't see the forest. Nor did she see the swift creature that was running through the trees alongside the car.

The wolf had journeyed far that night, leaving the city miles behind him. In short steady bursts, he had reached his peak speed of forty kilometres an hour. Forsaking the pockets of nature trapped in urbanity, he had headed ever northwards to the promise of mountains. *Caledon. Albion.* Once across the Nottawasaga River, he had wandered in the Hockley Valley, through fields of baled hay, wild daisies and goldenrod. Avoiding villages, hamlets and farmsteads, he had travelled uphill along the rim of the Niagara Escarpment. From there he could see the glimmer of Georgian Bay in the north. Would he go that far? He felt something pulling at him, though he didn't know what.

The star on his chest blazed white against the black hair that blended with the night. The great head tapered to a glossy nose and wide mouth. His nostrils quivered as he caught the scent of other wolves in the area. Preferring to run alone, he didn't answer their howls but he was pleased to know they still roamed the region. Too many of his kin had been driven out by man or coyote. There were other animals abroad in the night and he detected them easily; red fox and porcupine, racoon and deer, weasels and muskrats, hare and grouse. The sour scent of a black bear surprised and delighted him. How good it was to meet wildness again!

In wildness is the preservation of the world.

Joyously, effortlessly, he loped on with smooth strides.

Only when he had crossed the Boyne River into the Mulmur Hills did the wolf sense the other preternatural creature abroad in the night. His hackles rose. The guard hairs on his body stood on end. He growled deep in his throat. The foul odour was unmistakable. His enemy was near, the monster that had tried to kill him in the city. Evidently it, too, had travelled that night. Was it pursuing him? He hunkered down in the tall grasses at the side of the road, all senses trained on the darkness.

The longer the wolf waited in the grass, on guard, the more confused he grew. Was he the hunter or the hunted? He did not feel like prey, yet all his instincts warned him to flee.

He didn't leave. Deep inside he heard it. The blood call. The cry from kin. From where it came, or how, he couldn't be certain but this he knew, one of his own was about to die. Had he stopped to ponder, the wolf might have guessed that this very call was the cause of his wanderlust that night. But he wasn't thinking, he was acting on instinct as he raced over hill and valley, through the Mulmur forests, towards the Devil's Glen.

On a height near a waterfall above the Mad River, the wolf's silhouette stood out against the moon. Below, along the edge of the gorge, lurched the only traffic on that lonely strip of road. Though he normally steered clear of humans, the wolf felt drawn to the Triumph Herald. His sense of danger was acute. He could see that the car was nearing a bend, but the wheels weren't turning. It was bound to drive over the cliff. A suicide perhaps? The amber eyes glowed with keen sight. He jerked back with surprise when he spotted the driver. A young girl sat rigid at the wheel, staring blindly ahead of her.

There was no time to wonder or question. The wolf threw back his head and howled the alarm. Then—in a magnificent arc of poised muscle and bone—he leaped from the height down onto the road.

In Grimstone's car, in her nightmare, Dana jolted upright. The call of the wolf had echoed through the gloom of the landscape. A wild cry of freedom that was life itself.

"NO!" screeched Grimstone at the wheel of his car. He grabbed at Dana.

Too late, she was gone.

In the Triumph Herald, Dana woke with a start. Horrified, she immediately saw her peril. The car was speeding towards the edge of a cliff. On the road in front of her, lit up by the headlights, stood a great black wolf with a white star on its chest.

She didn't stop to think. She pulled at the steering wheel with all her might. Had the car been modern, lighter and faster, it would certainly have turned over. She would have been killed. Instead, the old Triumph, slowed by its weight, obligingly crashed into the nearest tree by the road. It didn't buckle, the solid chassis held, but Dana was catapulted forward with a painful wrench. The windshield shattered. She was showered with broken glass. Blood trickled down her face and she could taste it in her mouth. Overcome with shock and terror, she looked wildly around her.

What was she doing in her grandmother's car? On a dark road at night? In bare feet and pyjamas!

Slowly she moved her arms and legs, instinctively checking for injuries. No bones broken. There were cuts and bruises but she didn't feel any pain. She was numb with shock. The car was crushed against a tree, but it too had survived. The key still turned the ignition. If she could just stop shaking, she would be able to drive. She needed to get help. She needed to get home.

A dark shape appeared at the window.

Dana was about to scream, when she heard a familiar voice.

"*Ouvre la porte! Vite!* Open the door!"

Dana's mind reeled. *What was this?* How could that be Jean, the boy from her class? He was peering through the window. Pulling at the door. It was locked. *What was he doing here?* He kept looking around. His fear was contagious. She sensed the danger too. Whatever had brought her to that place was near.

A wave of hysteria overwhelmed her. *It was Jean!* It had to be. Then a stab of doubt. An image of Grimstone flashed through her mind. A black car. A burnt landscape. Were they working together? Why else would Jean be there?

"*Câlisse,* girl! Open the door!" Jean shouted. "*Qu'est-ce que tu fais?* It's coming!"

"It's here!" she screamed back.

It arrived with a screech like a missile plummeting downwards. A horrible thud hit the roof of the car as if a body had landed. Then she smelled it in the air, a fetid odour. The stink of death.

Dana scrambled for the keys. She reversed full throttle. With a great crunching noise, the car pulled back from the tree. Jean was thrown sideways. She prayed that the thing on the roof was thrown off too. Turning the wheel back the way she had come, she put her foot to the gas.

Despite the squeal of protest, the car took off like a bullet. Dana was shaking uncontrollably. Tears poured down her face. A quick glance in the mirror brought new horror.

Two figures struggled on the road behind her. One was the great black wolf that had blocked her path. It reared up on its hind legs as it fought with ferocity, tearing and biting, snapping and snarling. The other was a ragged and shapeless thing that glowed with the florescence of decaying matter.

In that moment as she sped away, Dana quailed at the truth. The creature on the road was the same as the one that had attacked her at the portal. It had followed her to the Earthworld and was still trying to kill her! She almost cried out. But she was safe for now. She had escaped it again. Yet something felt wrong. What about the wolf? Should she have abandoned it? And what about Jean! Where did he come from? What was he doing there? Nothing made sense.

Despite the prickles of her conscience, Dana kept driving. Her instinct for self-preservation urged her onward. All she could think of, all she wanted, was to get home. She was grateful that the Triumph was like her dad's, a standard with the steering wheel on the right-hand side. Despite her state of shock, she was able to drive it. The car had taken a bashing. Cold air blew through the shattered windshield, chilling her to the bone. There was only one headlight to show the way. The shadows of the trees loomed over the dark road. The road itself was torn and broken. She had to slow down to manoeuvre the ruts. There was no other traffic at that early hour before dawn, but even if there were she wouldn't have stopped. Her enemy was out there. She couldn't trust anyone.

At first Dana wasn't sure where she was going, but eventually she came to a familiar signpost. Once she passed Glen Huron, she knew she was on the last stretch home.

Driving into Creemore, she was overcome with relief. She was also frozen with cold and shock. She could hardly think. What should she do? What could she say? Was her family still sleeping or had they discovered she was missing? Her last question was answered as she approached her grandmother's house.

There, on the front lawn, stood a ragged little group lit up by the red flashing light of a police car. Her aunts were huddled together, blankets wrapped around skimpy nightwear. Their faces looked pale and bleary without make-up. Gabriel stood beside them, eyes dazed. Aradhana held his hand. At the centre of the group was Gran Gowan looking, for the first time since Dana had known her, very old and frail.

A policewoman was ushering them back into the house when the Triumph drove up. Relief and joy mingled with stupefaction as they took in the crushed car and broken windshield, and the young girl behind the wheel, face caked with blood.

Dana caught the look on her aunts' faces. Their concern was eclipsed by awe at the scale of her wildness. Not even the antics of their own youth matched this.

She stopped the car in front of the police cruiser and stepped out shakily. Gabriel ran towards her. She opened her mouth to speak, but no words came out. As her father's arms reached out to catch her, Dana fainted away.

The rest of the night was a blur. Kind hands bathed her and changed her pyjamas. The scent of jasmine. Radhi's soothing touch. Then the downy dream of a soft quilt settling over her. Hot water bottles at her head and feet. People coming in and out of her room, speaking in low tones. One was a doctor. *No questions now. Shock and mild concussion. Cuts and bruises, a few stitches, but nothing serious. Keep an eye on her. Keep her warm.*

Once the worst was over and they knew she was safe, the repercussions began. Hovering between sleep and waking, she heard them in the hall.

". . . the whole neighbourhood," Gran Gowan was saying querulously. "We are thoroughly disgraced!"

"Oh come on, Mom," Deirdre pooh-poohed her. "It's nothing new. We used to terrorize the town and it's not as if they've forgotten. Old Nalty still glares at me every time I pass him."

"That's not what you're worried about, Maisy, you can't fool us," Yvonne said gently. "She'll be okay. You'll see."

Then came the most painful sound Dana heard that night. The mute defeated weeping of a little old lady.

Gradually the voices trailed away as everyone retired. Dana heard her door open again. A chair was placed beside her bed as someone sat down.

Gabriel's voice shook in the darkness.

"I know I've let you down, Dana. I haven't been a good father. But you've got to know that I'm trying to do what's best for you, for all of us. I love you, princess, no matter what has happened. That's all that's important, that you know I love you. Will you tell me what's going on? Will you let me try to help you?"

She didn't open her eyes. She didn't respond to his plea. How could she? He needed an explanation and she didn't have one. Even if she tried to tell him, he wouldn't be able to hear. He had forgotten the Faerie side of her life and she didn't think he would want to remember. It was the other world that had taken his first wife away, now it was trying to kill his daughter. Her throat burned with the things she couldn't say. She longed for someone who understood, who could help her through this nightmare. Why had Faerie forsaken her?

Never in her life had Dana felt so alone.

CHAPTER NINE

"I CAN SEE WHY YOU LIKE this spot," Laurel said when she saw the statue.

Gwen had suggested they meet at the Mackenzie monument on the west side of the Ontario Legislative Building. The sculpture by Walter Allward was different from the other statues of rulers and politicians that adorned Queen's Park. Perhaps this was the reason it was hidden away, along with the rock that remembered those who fought against Franco in the Spanish Civil War.

"He reminds me of a fairy king," Gwen nodded.

Laurel gazed wistfully at the figure cast in bronze. He strode across a lone stone wall with a book in his hand. His features were noble and majestic. There was something about him that made her think of Ian. As the Summer King, her former boyfriend was darkly handsome in his royal robes. In Faerie he wore his black hair long, bound with a golden circlet at his brow. In the Earthworld he preferred jeans and a leather jacket, with his hair cut short and a gold ring in his ear. While dealing with his two sides could be exciting at times, it didn't help that both were temperamental. Add Laurel's own volatile nature to the mix and their relationship had seldom been peaceful.

"We got along best when we were dancing," she murmured, smiling to herself. "We used to waltz all night on the summer lawns of his palace in Hy Brasil."

She let out a sigh, then forced herself to return to the present.

Gwen had collapsed on a bench nearby. Having run all the way from the subway to avoid being late, she was still catching her breath.

"Another interview?" Laurel asked her, noting the suit and high heels.

"Eat first, then talk," she pleaded. "I'm starving!"

They sat together and opened their lunches. Laurel raised her eyebrow at the sight of Gwen's sandwich, a large crusty roll stuffed with pepper salami and mozzarella. She herself had rye bread with shavings of cucumber on a spread of cream cheese.

Gwen noticed the difference too and grinned.

"Some people are slim, some are rounder. I like my food."

Laurel felt a twinge of envy. Gwen obviously liked herself as well.

The last of the summer sun glimmered through the trees and lit up the pink rose bushes around them. Though the road beyond was busy, the sounds of traffic were muted by the trees.

"Thanks for bringing me here," she said to Gwen. "It's magical. I never noticed this spot, though it's so close to Massey. I don't know the city that well. I grew up in Niagara Falls."

"There are little bits of magic all over Toronto," Gwen told her. "I started to find them after my first visit to Faerie. It's all a question of perception, isn't it? Not just where you look, but how. There's an old bank near Front Street. I spotted it one day when I was working part-time for the *Star*. There in the corner-stone of the building, half-hidden behind weeds and overlooking a parking lot, was this beautiful centaur! I could hardly believe what I was looking at. He was made of white marble. I admired him for ages. Then just as I turned to leave, I swear, he winked at me!"

They both laughed.

"I'm not surprised you see these things," Laurel said. "You have a very different attitude to Faerie than me. It's like being brought up in the same family but not having the same experience. Faerie has only been good for you. I can't say the same. First it took my sister away, then came the disaster that was Ian and me." She shook her head. "To be honest, most times I wish that world never entered my life."

"And you're studying folklore?" Gwen pointed out. "Why?"

Laurel laughed again.

"Touché. That's one thing I *can* thank Faerie for. I was always into sports, you name it, I tried it, but I never settled into one or trained enough to be a professional athlete. If it wasn't for Faerie, I would have drifted through university without knowing what to study or where I was going. I'm fascinated by the subject. My granddad was also a professor of Folklore, so I'm keeping up the family tradition."

"Faerie hasn't been all bad for you then," Gwen said. She had finished her sandwich and was starting on a chocolate bar. Laurel's dessert was a green apple. "But you want to know something? It hasn't been a total garden of roses for me either. Do you think being in love with a mortal king is any easier than loving a fairy one? Dara is the hereditary King of Inch. While that doesn't mean much in modern Ireland, it does mean a lot to the islanders as well as to Faerie and to Dara himself. Though he doesn't live on Inch all the time, he won't go too far away. We've talked about marriage, but then comes the hitch. No matter how much he loves me, he won't emigrate. As for me," she looked around at the shining blue sky, the sun-warmed greenery, "I'm Canadian. I don't want to move either."

The resignation in her voice touched Laurel. With sudden insight, she saw that Gwen's consistent good spirits were a hard-won battle. There was no solution to the dilemma of a long-distance relationship. Their love was not a fairy tale. They would not live happily ever after in one place together.

"Down to business," Gwen said, shaking the crumbs off her lap. "Any luck with Dana?"

Laurel shook her head.

"She didn't go in or out of her house all morning."

Gwen snorted with annoyance.

"And there was no sign of her at school again today. Something has happened to her!"

"I don't think so," Laurel countered. "Her parents have been going to work as usual and they look happy enough. They wouldn't be acting normal if something was wrong. We must be missing her somehow."

"We're being blocked," Gwen swore. "That's it!"

Laurel frowned. "Do you feel a spell around you? I don't."

"Me neither," she admitted. "But I swear I'll go crazy if we don't make some headway soon. I feel like a rat on a wheel. We're running in circles and getting nowhere."

"How's the job hunt going?" Laurel asked with sympathy.

"It's not," she groaned. "My feet are killing me, bloody high heels, and I hate interviews. Sucking up to people just to get hired, it's degrading."

It was so unlike her to be negative that Laurel knew things were bad.

"And I'm worried sick," Gwen went on. "*No one* has got back to me. Not one phone call or email. It's not like Dara. It's not like any of them."

The image that constantly tormented her flashed through her mind: Dara lying on the ground, limbs splayed and motionless. She was close to tears.

Laurel, too, was living in dread as each day passed with no sign of Honor or Ian. She felt cornered by a nameless threat, all the more sinister for being insubstantial. How did one fight shadows?

"What can we do that we haven't done already?" she said, exasperated.

"I've been thinking about that." Gwen pulled out a brown envelope from her shoulder bag. "I'm going to Ireland."

Not for the first time Laurel marvelled at Gwen's assertion, at the iron will behind her mild manner. She was even more surprised when Gwen handed her the envelope. Inside were hundreds of large bills.

"There's a small fortune here!"

Gwen nodded. "It came by courier the day Granny called me about our mission. It's from my friend, Matt, the businessman in the Company of Seven. He's a millionaire. Years ago, he was the sales rep of this company that was going bust and he got the workers together to buy shares so they could keep their jobs. Then the Celtic Tiger hit, the economic boom in Ireland, and they all got rich."

"I love stories like that," Laurel grinned. "But I can't take this. Your friend meant you to have it."

"I've split what Matt sent. That's your half. It's his way of helping the mission. If we need to buy anything or rent a car or whatever." Gwen looked suddenly uncertain. "I doubt he meant me to take a free trip."

"It's the right decision," Laurel assured her. "We're in the dark. We don't know anything and communications are down. I'd go too if I thought it would help."

"Only one needs to go," Gwen said. "I'm unemployed with nothing to lose. No point you falling behind in your studies. And you can keep trying to reach Dana."

"That's the plan then," Laurel agreed. "Good luck. Call me as soon as you get there."

★   ★   ★

Gwen was packing when Dara rang. She dropped the receiver at the first sound of his voice.

"I'm here!" she cried, scrambling to retrieve it.

Her heart was bursting with joy. Some part of her had been convinced that he was dead. She could see him clearly in her mind: the nut-brown hair falling around strong features, the mischievous look in his eyes, the slightly crooked grin. The first time they had met was on an island road when he knocked her down on his bicycle. She was only sixteen, under a fairy spell, and unable to move. He had hoisted her over his shoulders and carried her to Granny Harte's cottage. On holidays in Ireland, Gwen had become entangled with Faerie when her cousin Findabhair was abducted by Finvarra, the High King. Once Dara heard the story, he was quick to join her. Though she was shy and self-conscious, Gwen had liked him from the start. It was soon obvious that he liked her too. She would never forget the time they wrestled in the cold waters of Lough Swilly, and the heart he drew in the sand around his name and hers.

He loved to tease her and make her laugh.

"You have a brilliant laugh," he would say.

When she told him that she had never had a boyfriend, his reaction was instant.

"I can't believe no one has fancied you!"

And of course when she asked him if he thought she was fat, his response was better still.

"You're not skin and bones if that's what you mean. You're lovely. I couldn't help but notice when your clothes were wet."

Though they lived in separate countries, their love had survived across distance and time. They spoke often on the phone, sent emails and letters, and took holidays together whenever they could. Each tended to ignore the cloud hanging over them, the fact that neither wanted to leave their own country. They were young. They still had hope.

"Are you well, love?" Dara asked her now.

"Yes, I'm fine! Are you?"

He didn't answer the question, she noticed that immediately, and he didn't give her the chance to ask again.

"How is the girl? Is Dana all right?"

His words were abrupt. She heard the urgency and answered at once.

"I think so. I mean most likely, yes, or we'd know otherwise. We haven't been able to reach her in person but we've been to her home and—"

"Thank God."

His relief was audible.

"Dara, what is it?"

Ever direct, he gave her the full brunt of the news.

"It's worse than we could have imagined, even with the warnings. The gateways have been destroyed. *All* of them. The bond between Faerie and the Earthworld has been severed."

Gwen caught the cry in her throat. She forced herself to stay calm. She was the Captain of the Company of Seven. She needed a cool head.

"What are the consequences?" she asked. "How long can the worlds exist without each other?"

From her last mission for Faerie, she knew that the destinies of both worlds were inextricably linked. She had faced Crom Cruac, the Great Worm, the guardian of the balance between the worlds.

I lie curled on the branch of the Tree of Life that bears both Faerie and your world like two golden apples. Two orbs, two moons that eclipse each other, one fantasy, one reality, balanced side by side. Humanity cannot exist without its dreams, but for any dream to exist there must be a sacrifice.

Dara's reply confirmed her fears.

"You know yourself, mortals are the first line of Faerie's defence. Only humanity can fight the Enemy. Without us, Faerie is vulnerable to attack. And even if the Enemy doesn't destroy it outright, without human belief to sustain them, the fairies will wither away. As things stand, the Summer Land is doomed."

"Then so are we," she said gravely. "Faerie is the Land of Dreams. Humanity needs to believe in something greater than itself. We need our dreams to keep us going."

"The strike is against both worlds," Dara agreed. "The Enemy hates all life wherever it is found."

Against the horror that was threatening to overwhelm her, Gwen drew on all her strength and courage. This wasn't the first time Faerie had faced extinction. "The Rescue of Fairyland" was a mortal myth. It was also mankind's eternal duty.

"What must we do?"

"The girl is the key," Dara said, "even as Granny foretold. The Light-Bearer's daughter can restore the gateways. But she must act soon. The worlds have begun to drift apart. By the power of the next convergence—*Samhain*—they will align once more. But unless a bridge is there to bind them, they'll drift again. And if they do, it will be forever."

Gwen knew that the worlds collided at certain times in the year. These occasions were celebrated in Faerie as feast days even as they were once held sacred by the Celtic peoples: *Imbolc*, the spring festival at the beginning of February; *Lá Bealtaine*, May Day; *Oíche Lár an Tsamhraidh*, Midsummer's Eve in June; *Lá Lughnasa* or Lammas Day in August; and *Samhain*, the autumnal feast, which began on *Oíche Shamhna*, Hallowe'en.

"It's almost two months till Hallowe'en," she said. "At least that gives us some time. What must Dana do and how can we help her?"

The silence on the other end of the line was worse than a scream. Gwen's stomach clenched like a fist. *Here it comes.* Because she knew him so well, she had sensed it the moment she had heard his voice. He was hiding something.

"We don't know," he said at last. "We had hoped to learn more about Dana's destiny from the Faerie Council, but that's when . . ."

Gwen's vision flashed through her mind. Dara and Granny sprawled on the ground.

"What happened?" she whispered.

Again, he didn't mince his words, nor did he try to cushion the blow. He was the King of Inch. Like many such kings in modern Ireland, on Tory, Aran and other islands, he had no official authority; but the title was held proudly through the generations. In the realm of Faerie, however, it meant much more. The hereditary kings were the only Irish rulers acknowledged in that land. Dara had already proven his kingship in defence of the Summer Country. He was a hero there.

Now he spoke quietly without emotion.

"On the day the Enemy destroyed the gateways every member of our Company was attacked. Matt and Katie are both in the hospital. Some kind of coma. Matt collapsed over his desk at work. They thought at first it was a heart attack. Katie was found lying unconscious in a field, her cattle around her. As for Granny and me . . ."

For a moment his resolve wavered. He couldn't bear to hurt her and he knew this would.

"What?" she pressed, reminding herself that he was alive and talking to her.

"We were struck blind, Gwen. We're both blind."

"Oh my love," she sobbed.

Now that the worst had been said he moved to support her, speaking calmly and steadily to ease the shock.

"We were entering the portal at Dunfinn when the Enemy attacked. The High King and High Queen were on the other side, about to greet us. Suddenly the huge stones exploded and we were blasted backwards. When I woke up on the hillside everything was dark. I thought it was night, but we had gone to the fort just after lunch. I crawled around till I found Granny. She was barely conscious. That's when we discovered the truth."

He waited through the muffled weeping as Gwen struggled for control. It was dreadful these things had to be said over the phone. He wished he could have told her in person so he could be there to comfort her.

"We've been in the hospital since then," he continued. "We were released today. Judging by the state of Katie and Matt, we didn't fare too badly. We're disabled but not defeated. We'll manage, I can promise you that. Granny has ordered a computer that responds to word commands. She'll be in touch with you as soon as it's up and running. I've moved in with her for now. We can help each other. You know the two of us. The indomitable Irishry. We just need time to adapt. The worst of it is we can't come to join you. We'd be more of a hindrance than a help right now."

Gwen was still trying to absorb the enormity of what had happened.

"I felt the blow," she said, dazed. "I saw you struck down. Laurel felt it too. She saw her sister. But how come we weren't hurt?"

"Granny says the protective spirits of North America can block the Enemy. But you're not clear of danger. When the Enemy can't act directly, there are always those who will do its work."

A chill ran up Gwen's spine as she remembered Dana's school. She told Dara what happened.

"You must protect the girl!" he urged. "She's our only hope. This is her destiny. How she's to fulfil it we don't know yet, but

Granny will find out. You can count on that. There are methods of divination that don't require sight. As soon as we know something, we'll let you know. Until then, you must guard Dana. You must keep her safe."

"We can do it," she assured him. "Laurel and I are on it."

She managed to sound more confident than she felt. She was determined to match his resolve with her own. He had enough to deal with. She could hear the weariness in his voice. He was obviously still recovering.

As their conversation drew to a close and the first shock wore off, Gwen began to feel the first waves of real pain.

"Dara," she murmured.

"You must be strong, my love. There is always hope."

After they hung up, she stared blindly at the telephone. It took a great deal of willpower not to ring him back and tell him she was flying out that night. It took even more to ring and cancel her flight. She would stay and do her duty. He wouldn't be happy if she did anything else and nor would she. They were warriors, the two of them, soldiers in an ancient and eternal war. They had their parts to play. Their love would have to wait.

Gwen was about to ring Laurel to tell her the news when the phone rang again.

"Gwen?"

"*Findabhair!* Thank God you've called! Are you okay?"

It was over a year since Gwen had last seen her Irish cousin and that had been a flying visit. Findabhair was so immersed in her musical career along with her husband, Finvarra, that she had little time for anything else.

"Aside from being knackered, I'm grand," she said. "Too many days on the road. Too much *craic agus ceol*. I got your message. Sorry, but I haven't had a free minute till now. What's up?"

"We've got a serious problem," Gwen began. "Faerie—"

"Trouble in Paradise?" Findabhair's tone was wry. "Are we surprised?"

As Gwen outlined the situation, she thought she detected a coolness on the other end of the line, or was she imagining it? Long-distance calls were rarely satisfactory. California was even farther away than Ireland.

"How soon can you and Finvarra get here?"

"Sorry," Findabhair said brusquely, "but it's not on. We're in the middle of a major tour, Gwen. It took over a year to put this together. A lot of planning and money. We can't leave our backers high and dry. There are concerts booked solid along the west coast and then across Canada. We'll be in Toronto mid-November. We can meet up with you then."

Gwen could hardly believe what she was hearing. Perhaps she hadn't explained properly? Hadn't conveyed just how bad things were?

"That will be too late!" she cried. "We've got to open the portals on Hallowe'en. It's our only chance!"

"You're not listening to me, cuz. You'll have to count us out. I'm sorry about Dara and Granny and the others. I really am. But we're not in any position to help them. We can't sacrifice our lives for Faerie again. It's someone else's turn."

Gwen could hardly speak. "But you were High Queen and Finvarra was High King! How can you abandon the Summer Land like this? You know how important it is!"

"And you know I haven't been there since Finvarra lost his kingship." Findabhair's voice was cold. "He can't go back and I'd never go there without him. We did our bit for Faerie, Gwen, and we paid the price. We owe nothing to the Realm."

Gwen was speechless as the truth hit home. Neither Findabhair nor Finvarra would come to Faerie's aid. She had caught the bitterness in her cousin's tone. How long had it been there? A quick survey of the past showed Gwen what she had failed to see. It was actually several years since she had last seen Finvarra. Only Findabhair had made the effort to stay in touch. Even then, the meetings were always brief, and they rarely if ever talked about the other world. There it was before her, as plain as day to see, her cousin's disaffection from Faerie. How could Gwen have been so blind?

She knew the answer to that question. Laurel had more than hinted at it. When it came to Faerie, Gwen wore rose-coloured glasses. She couldn't see anything wrong with that magical land. Nor could she bear to think that others might not love it as deeply as she did.

"Finn, I'm sorry. I've been so stupid. I didn't pay attention."

"Don't," said Findabhair. There was an echo of sadness in her voice, then the usual dry humour. "It's not your fault. You were always a dope."

"That's me," Gwen sighed. "I miss you, cuz."

"I'll see you in November. We'll have a long chat then. And Gwen?"

"Yeah?"

"It'll work out. You'll see. As long as he has you, Dara will be fine. I really believe that. And you'll get the job done. Look, you quested all over Ireland without me, remember? You were the real hero of the Hunter's Moon."

"Thanks," Gwen said and she meant it. "Good luck with your tour."

Gwen knew she should ring Laurel with the latest news, but she didn't. Instead, she turned out the lights and lit candles around the room. She sat on the sofa and gazed out the window. Her apartment was on the thirteenth floor, high above the city, with a bird's-eye view of rooftops, streets and patches of greenery. In the lambent quiet, she watched the night fall.

She was mourning the loss of the Company of Seven. Her friends and comrades-in-arms would not be with her in Faerie's hour of need. Even as the Earthworld was severed from the Land of Dreams, so was she cut off from those who sustained her.

"The darkest hour is before the dawn," she told herself. "I must call Laurel. We've got work to do."

But she didn't move. Cloaked in loneliness, she stared out at the dark.

CHAPTER TEN

For the week after Dana's nightmare with Grimstone, Gran Gowan got her wish and kept her granddaughter in Creemore. The Triumph Herald was repaired at a body shop for vintage cars, while the family doctor gave Dana a clean bill of health. The police dismissed the matter as teenage antics in an otherwise respectable and law-abiding family. Remembering Dee and Yvonne, the sergeant had rolled his eyes. He was glad to hear the girl normally resided in Toronto.

As soon as the others had gone back to the city, Maisy Gowan turned her full attention to her wayward charge. The first thing to go was the nose-ring. Then the black clothes. Several shops in Creemore specialized in youth fashions and Dana was allowed to choose her new wardrobe as long as the colours were bright. The visit to the beauty salon was, for Dana, the oddest experience, especially since the clientele were her grandmother's age. However, she liked the hair style she got, long and tapered, and she listened politely to the advice on make-up and skin care. Indeed, she was prepared to do anything that Gran Gowan wanted in order to gain her forgiveness and regain her trust. Dana considered it a bonus when, in the end, she liked what she saw in the mirror. She also enjoyed spending time with her Gran, strolling through the town, sipping hot chocolate in the Tea Room, chatting on the verandah as the evenings grew short. All of it helped her to push the horror of that night away.

For Gran Gowan, the time was well-spent in more ways than one. She was pleased with the improvement in Dana's appearance, but more importantly, she had reassured herself that her grand-daughter was not "going bad." Though Dana offered no explanation for what she had done, she showed more remorse than her aunts had ever feigned when they were young and in trouble. Gran Gowan was satisfied that her grandchild was still a sweet and caring girl. By the time Dana was ready to return to Toronto, the two were fully reconciled.

Back at home, there was a tearful reunion between father and daughter. Gabriel was delighted with the change in Dana, not only the brighter appearance but her more open manner. She was obviously trying hard to make up for what had happened. Aradhana also welcomed her with open arms.

In her own bed that night, Dana stared at the ceiling. She couldn't sleep. Tomorrow she had to go back to school. The time with her grandmother had been a respite, the calm before the storm. Though much of what had happened on the Mulmur Road was a hideous daze, she knew one thing for certain. Somehow both her teacher and Jean were involved. How could she face them? More importantly, how could she protect herself? She was helpless, powerless.

Sick with dread, she turned fitfully under her duvet to face the window. She always opened her curtains at night. Outside, the street lamp shed light into the tree tops and the dappled shadows danced in her room. She blinked for a moment. What was that in the branches? A white blur. Her eyelids felt heavy as she struggled to see. Falling into sleep at last, a thought fluttered through her mind.

You must change your life.

*   *   *

The next morning, Dana steeled herself as she walked into the classroom. Her first surprise was that Grimstone was gone. In his place was a plump and pretty young woman with a pleasant manner. She handed Dana a note for her parents. The school regretted the unforeseen departure of Mr Grimstone but hoped everyone would be satisfied with his replacement.

The second surprise was that Jean was also missing. His seat was empty. Dana was baffled. What did it mean? It certainly confirmed her suspicions that the two were connected. Why else would they have disappeared at the same time? Yet Dana couldn't shake the uneasiness that plagued her. Something wasn't right. Every time she remembered Jean sprawling on the road as she reversed the car, she felt a wave of shame.

It was in the cafeteria at lunch hour that she heard the news. Two grade twelve girls in the queue ahead of her were talking about Jean.

". . . mugged. Found in High Park in a really bad way, early in the morning."

"What was he doing out so late?"

"Clubbing probably. He could pass for nineteen."

"Couldn't he just. I mean, isn't he hot?"

"I heard he was pretty beat up."

"Yeah, I read in the paper he was still unconscious. They say a gang got him."

"You don't think he's—?"

"Nah. Well, I hope not!"

A wave of nausea swept over Dana. She leaned against the counter. It was all her fault! How could she have left him there? Her act of cowardice filled her with self-loathing.

You must change your life.

As the whisper shivered through her, Dana knew it was true. Lost in her unhappiness the past two years, she had forgotten how to be strong, how to stand up for herself. Once upon a time she had quested alone in the mountains. She had faced the world boldly. But she had let herself grow weak and powerless. That had to change. Jean had been harmed because of her. It was up to her to do something about it.

She interrupted the older girls.

"Where is he? Do you know? What hospital is he in?"

They looked at her coolly—how dare a grade niner butt in like that?—but one glance at Dana's face convinced them to co-operate.

"St Michael's. In the ICU."

As Dana rushed out of the cafeteria, she bumped into her new teacher.

"Whoa, what's the hurry?" Ms Woods said with a smile. "I'm glad I've caught up with you. I was looking for you."

"Yes?"

Dana shuffled impatiently. She didn't have time for this. She had to get to the hospital. How could she leave the school without anyone noticing?

"I want to have a talk with you," her teacher was saying. "Since I'm new here, I'm interviewing everyone in the class, one by one. Nothing formal. Just a little chat so we can get to know each other."

Dana's impatience quickly turned to suspicion. Despite the smiles, pink dress and blond curls, she sensed that Ms Woods was not as soft as she appeared. Was there a hidden agenda behind her request? Dana wasn't about to trust another teacher, not after her experience with Grimstone. Was Ms Woods his replacement in more ways than one? She had to think fast.

"You want to interview me alone without my parents' consent? Sorry, it's not on."

Though her voice quavered as she challenged her teacher, Dana was determined to stand her ground. She couldn't risk being caught alone with a stranger. It might be a trap.

Ms Woods was surprised by the girl's refusal and before she could recover, Dana fled down the hall.

Her teacher's attention put an end to Dana's plan to skip classes. Everywhere Dana turned, Ms Woods seemed to be there, hovering in the background, watching her covertly. On guard at all times, Dana spent the day avoiding further contact.

As soon as school ended, she hurried home and went straight to her stepmother.

"I need to visit a friend in the hospital."

Aradhana's expression was pained.

"Your father has grounded you, Dana. You know that. I cannot go against his wishes. It is not an unjust punishment given what happened in Creemore. You will have to ask him yourself when he comes home."

"I can't wait that long!" Dana cried. "And he might say no. It's too important! *Please,* Radhi. I'm begging you!"

Dana's intensity jolted her stepmother. Dana had never raised her voice to her before. Aradhana grasped the girl's shoulders.

"Will you tell me what is going on?"

Dana's eyes filled with tears, but she shook her head.

"I . . . I can't."

Aradhana's voice was firm. "If you cannot trust me, I cannot trust you. That is the matter in a nutshell." She could see the girl was wavering and she was inspired to ask, "Has this to do with the Other world? Is that why you won't speak of it? You know I understand such things. Tell me and I will listen."

Dana almost gave in. She yearned to confide in someone. She felt so alone. Yet still, she wasn't ready to open up. She was afraid to. Her stepmother vowed to understand, but how could she?

Dana herself hardly knew what was happening. Her shame over Jean also kept her quiet. What would Radhi say when she heard about *that*? It was too painful to contemplate.

"I can't tell you, Radhi. I want to, but I can't." Dana cried as she pleaded. "You've got to believe me. I need to see this friend. I need to help him if I can and even if I can't, I need to try."

Aradhana heard the truth in the girl's voice. She also saw it in the tears that filmed her eyes, those startling blue eyes of another world. That her stepdaughter was different she had known from early days, but she didn't trespass on that other life. It belonged to Dana's mother. Yet Radhi often worried about Dana's unhappiness and wished there was more she could do to help her.

Gently she put her arm around the girl's shoulders. The scent of jasmine sweetened the air.

"Someday I hope you will learn that to ask for help is a strength not a weakness. I will let you go without further questions, but first you must let me do something for you."

Aradhana led Dana to her study, a little solarium at the side of the house. Vases of fresh flowers stood on the windowsills. Indian rugs and tasselled cushions covered the floor. A small altar was set up in a corner, draped with red-and-gold silk. Statues of Hindu gods and goddesses were surrounded by incense burners, candles and brass bowls of offerings. Amidst the statues were photographs of Aradhana's parents and relations, her brother Suresh and his restaurant staff, herself and Gabriel on their wedding day, and Dana in her school uniform back in Ireland. Of all the figures and images, one stood out above the rest. Bedecked with pearls and a golden crown was the plump merry god with the head of an elephant, the Lord Ganesh.

Aradhana placed her hands together and bowed before the altar.

"I was six years old when my mother died," she began in a low voice.

Slowly, gracefully she lit candles and incense.

"On that day I lay across my bed, weeping with grief. My child's heart was broken and inconsolable. I would let no one near me, not my *āyā*—my beloved nurse—nor my father nor Suresh. I screamed like a wild cat if anyone touched me. Finally they left me alone."

Gently she bathed the statues with drops of perfume.

"That is when he came to me. First I caught the fragrance of jasmine, then I heard the golden rattles. The ones he likes to carry. My head was buried in my arms but I could not resist looking up. There he was, resplendent in white silk and adorned with pearls. He lifted me in his arms and he kissed my face and when I looked into his beautiful dark eyes I saw that he was weeping too. Weeping for a motherless child. I wiped away his tears and he wiped away mine. And when I had stopped crying he danced with me, the way my mother used to dance with me. He didn't have to say the words, I understood his promise. He would always be with me, my dear guardian Ganesh."

Dana felt her heart lifting. Radhi *did* understand.

"One day I hope you'll come to Faerie with me," she said to her stepmother.

Aradhana shook her head mildly.

"It has been many years since I walked among the gods. It is much harder for adults, Dana. The *sādhu*s and the *gurū*s go that road but the rest of us are bound to this world, to the business of living, and that is how it should be. It is here we belong for the time that we live."

She placed her hands together in prayer. Touching her forehead, lips and heart, she bowed to her guardian.

"O Joyous One, beloved God most dear to my heart, Remover of Obstacles, hear my prayer. I love this girl as I would my own daughter. I appeal to you now to come to her aid. Bring to her your strength and guidance. Remove the obstacles that block her path. Beloved, will You come to her?"

Aradhana closed her eyes as her lips continued to move in silent prayer. Suddenly she stopped. Her face lit up like a sunburst. When she turned to Dana, her voice rang with happiness.

"He will help you."

Dana hugged her stepmother.

"I'm so glad you married Gabe."

"So am I," she smiled. "Now I must get dressed for work. Your father will not be home till tea time. You may go to the hospital, I will write Gabe a note, but I expect you to return as soon as possible."

"I'll do my best," Dana promised.

Aradhana sighed as her stepdaughter hurried from the room. She was more concerned than she had let Dana see. Still, she had done her best and that consoled her. What better help could she give than that of her God?

★   ★   ★

The Toronto transit system was a modern marvel that Dana had taken to from the day she arrived in Canada. There was no subway in Ireland and though she had gone on the Tube in London and the *métro* in Paris, she would definitely give the TTC first prize.

The silver train glided like a sea snake through the dark tunnels beneath the city. It emitted metallic shrieks as it scraped the tracks. Dana usually enjoyed the swift ride and the rocking motion as the train turned the bends. She liked to pass the time observing other passengers and noting the colours of each station. But today she sat hunched in her seat, sick with worry.

Museum. Lemon-yellow and bright like the sun.

She could see him in her mind, Jean Ducharme, wintergreen eyes studying her curiously. That disarming smile. The way his face lit up when she said she was Irish. *Irlandaise! Magnifique! The French and the Irish, we are always good friends.* He had stood up for her that first day in class. Then later he had warned her against their teacher. *For you, he is dangereux.* How could she have thought that he was her enemy? Whatever the reason he was on the road that night, she should have opened the door. She should have let him in the car.

Queen's Park. Royal blue for the Queen of Canada.

They said that he had been attacked by a gang, that his injuries were severe. It wasn't a gang, she knew, but a malevolent monster. The monster who had come to kill *her*. When she fled, leaving Jean behind, it had gone for him instead.

The train drove into the next station on a blast of wind. Chimes rang out as the doors swished open, then shut.

St Patrick. Pale green with a dark-green trim. Green for an Irish saint from the Emerald Isle.

He was unconscious. What if he never woke up? What if he died! Oh, how could she live with herself!

"Poor little girl with lots of worries, eh?"

The voice came from in front of Dana. The words were obviously directed at her. They seemed to fall on top of her head. No wonder, she realized, as she looked up. The speaker was quite short. Dana frowned. She had been warned not to talk to strangers, especially on the subway. Too many weirdos, as her aunts would say. But this little man did not look sinister.

His skin was the brown of oak leaves in autumn. His clothes were a quirky design of black and white with a black floppy hat, white T-shirt and checkered shorts with suspenders. His feet were shod in white leather sandals showing hairy toes. Along with dark sunglasses, he was wearing a Walkman that spilled out music, jazz or maybe reggae, Dana wasn't sure. Instead of turning the Walkman down, he raised his voice.

"A problem shared is a problem halved."

His accent was broad, very nasal and Canadian, almost singsong in tone, quite pleasant on the ears. His look was pleasant too, and so kind and friendly that Dana couldn't help smiling back. The train was crowded with office workers on their way home. Safe enough, she decided, if he tried anything strange.

"I . . . a friend . . . is in the hospital," she told him. "St Michael's."

The little man bobbed his head vigorously, displacing his earphones.

"St Michael's a good one. Patron saint of fairies, eh?"

Dana started. She looked at him closely. He peered back at her over the edge of his sunglasses. The eyes were big, an earth-brown colour darker than his skin. There was something innocent and childlike in his gaze, but there was no recognition. And she felt none herself. Still, she liked him and that encouraged her to talk.

"Do you know the old folktale about St Mike?" she said. "How he defended the fairies after the Great War against Lucifer? The fairies were in disgrace for refusing to take sides."

"There's no neutral ground in this war," the little man murmured.

"What?" said Dana.

He shrugged and clammed up.

"Anyway," she continued, "apparently St Michael argued that while the fairies weren't good enough for heaven, at the same time they weren't bad enough for hell. He suggested they should live on Earth. Some say that's how Faerie and our world got connected in the first place."

"He'd make a good lawyer," the little man commented.

Dana laughed. She leaned towards him confidentially.

"I don't really believe that story. You know what I think? I think Michael is their patron saint because he's their dream, their ideal. What could be better or more beautiful than a fairy? An *archangel*."

The little man cackled with glee.

"Oh that's a good one. I like that. Well worth some advice."

He glanced out the window.

"The Lady's station. Isn't this your stop?"

Queen Street. Light-blue, the favourite colour of the Queen of Heaven.

Dana had lost track of the time and her journey. She jumped up and made a dash for the door. Behind her came a shout.

"Put your hands over his head! That should do the trick!"

What? How! She spun around. Too late. The door slid closed. He was lost in the crowd. Dana stood dumbfounded as she watched the train rumble down the track. Then she shook herself out of her daze. Impossible. They didn't exist, not here, not in Canada.

Still, she hurried towards the exit with a lighter heart. First Radhi and now him. They had taught her a lesson. People could be magic too.

CHAPTER ELEVEN

Queen Street was bustling with office workers and shoppers. Dana hurried past a construction site that reverberated with the noise of drilling, men shouting and trucks unloading. On the road, traffic moved slowly. A double-carriage streetcar rumbled by, packed with rush-hour passengers. In the press of the crowd a grey figure looked out at Dana, but she didn't see him. She was threading her way up the street. Behind her glinted the department store windows of the Hudson's Bay Company. Ahead rose the red brick walls of St Michael's Hospital.

She didn't need directions. From a billboard high on the wall, a benign visage gazed gigantically down. A cloud-white angel against a blue sky, he wore his wings like a feathered mantle. His head was bowed, his arm raised. *Help Us Watch Over You. Give to Toronto's Urban Angel.* Cheered by the image, Dana headed for the entrance of the Victoria Street wing of the Intensive Care Unit.

The moment she set foot on the ramp that led to the glass doors, she knew she was in trouble. The lightest of sensations triggered the knowledge, a prickling at the back of her neck. *Danger.* She looked around quickly. The side street was empty. Then something stepped from the shadows.

Grimstone! His face was disfigured with livid scars. His eyes were black with rage. She recoiled at the sight of him, but worse was to come. Out of his body writhed hideous tentacles, green and viscid like decaying matter. Though the ragged shape had grown more solid, she recognized her attacker at the portal and the monster on the road. Now she knew without a doubt that Grimstone and her enemy were one and the same.

She made a bolt for the doors. A tentacle snaked out to lasso her. It coiled around her waist. She was stopped in her tracks. More tendrils slithered around her body to bind her fast. One curled itself around her throat and began to choke her.

She sensed the glee he took in killing her. *You're such an easy prey.* The whispery voice was cold and mocking. *Poor little girl. All alone and afraid. It's so easy to defeat you. You lack the will to defend yourself. You'd be dead already if it weren't for the wolf.*

The scars on his face, the wolf had done that! Dana rallied at the thought and began to struggle. His grip only tightened. The awful voice continued to taunt her.

Your hero is not here to save you. I've dealt with him.

She was overcome with shame. Her worst fears were confirmed. Jean *was* attacked when she left him on the road.

I wonder why I was even sent to kill you. Grimstone was gloating. *You're no threat to anyone. A weak and foolish child with no defences, no allies, no power.*

The darkness was gathering around Dana. Her head fell back in a swoon. The high walls of the hospital loomed like a fortress above her. The urban angel stared down. Was that a reproach she saw in his eyes?

Help us watch over you.

She heard her stepmother's words. *To ask for help is a strength, not a weakness.* Even her enemy had said it. Her isolation was something that made her weak. She had no allies.

"St Michael," she whispered, "patron saint of my mother's people. Grant me sanctuary."

As if in a dream, she saw the image move. The arm that was out of sight in the billboard came into view, wielding a weapon. The sword of light descended through the air and slashed at the monstrous limbs that held her. Screeching with agony, Grimstone recoiled. Dana was free. She raced up the ramp. More shrieks came behind her but she didn't stop to look. Catapulted forward, she charged through the doors.

Immediately she felt the hospital take her under its wing. She knew she was safe. Deep in her heart she heard a still voice. *He shall cover thee with his feathers and under his wings shalt thou trust.* This was not a place where Grimstone could follow.

Dana stopped to catch her breath and looked around the lobby. To her right was the reception desk, ahead were the elevators. On her left was an alcove built into the wall, illumined by lamps. It housed a marble statue of St Michael, the original of the image that graced the poster outside. With awe and gratitude, Dana approached the white effigy of the great archangel.

At the foot of the statue were flowers and cards from hospital patients. *Thank you, St Michael, for your intercession.* She repeated the words softly.

His head was bowed, his features serene. Calmly he regarded the vanquished demon at his feet. One arm was raised in triumph, the other held a sword against the serpent's neck. From his shoulders unfurled a swan's span of feathered strength. His composure bespoke a different world, a different way of being, not human but immortal.

A plaque on the wall told Dana about the statue, but nothing about the celestial being himself.

For almost a century, the statue of St Michael the Archangel has graced St Michael's Hospital as a symbol of hope for employees, patients and their families.

The artist and date of creation are unknown, but the name of "Pietrasanta" chiselled on the back of the statue indicates that the stone is from the same quarry in Italy where Michelangelo procured marble for his famous Pieta.

How the statue of St Michael made its way to Canada is unclear. What we do know is that during the latter part of the 19th century, the Sisters of St Joseph found the statue, dirty and blackened, in a second-hand store on Queen Street and bought it for $49—a sum they had accumulated from the sale of old newspapers.

Plaque unveiling
St Michael's Feast Day Celebrations
September 30, 1996

She stared at the demon under the archangel's foot, the writhing body, the cold ophidian eyes. St Michael had the power to conquer his enemy, but how could she possibly defeat hers? The statue gazed downward as if leaving her to solve her own dilemma.

Dana asked herself hard questions. She recalled Grimstone's taunts. Were they true? Was she really powerless? For the second time that day, she remembered how strong she had been when she was younger, how daring and full of spirit. And what of her birthright? Was she not of the immortals herself? The silver blood of Faerie ran through her veins. Light lived inside her. She had many gifts and strengths, but she had buried them deep, like treasures in a bog. Over the past two years she had lost her way and sunk into that bog. Her loneliness had only pushed her deeper, a great stone on her back. Could she rise up now?

With quiet resolve, Dana walked to the elevator. She had a job to do. She was here to right a wrong. Though she had no idea if or how she could do it, she was here to save Jean.

Admission to the Neurosurgery and Trauma Intensive Care Unit was strictly controlled. There was a waiting area with chairs and magazines and a locked door with an intercom system. The door was already opening as Dana grasped the handle. She smiled to herself. She knew who was helping her. This was *his* hospital, his domain. His angelic presence permeated the brick and glass, indeed the very air itself. As he guided her through the corridors, she seemed to be invisible. Doctors and nurses passed her without a glance. When she reached Jean's room, there were two attendants outside the door, one in a green uniform, the other in dark-blue. They spoke in low tones.

"Definitely a gang beating. The extensive injuries are typical, head trauma, deep shock."

The second attendant was visibly upset.

"Mindless violence! I hate it when the city goes this way. Wait and see, there'll be more. It always comes in a wave. As if something evil sets up shop and starts to feed."

The first shuddered.

"God, I hope you're wrong!"

As soon as they left, Dana went inside. Her first sight of Jean was a shock. She hardly recognized him. Hooked to monitors and intravenous drips, he was covered in bandages and plaster casts. The only distinguishable feature was his tousled dark hair.

Fighting back waves of guilt and sorrow, she approached his bed.

Put your hands over his head. That should do the trick.

Dana looked down at her hands. They were trembling. Once upon a time she could cup her hands together and a pool of light would well up in her palms. It was her inheritance, a gift from her mother. But a long time had passed since she had last called up her light. At first there was no need. When she wanted magic, she went to Faerie. Then there was no will. As a silent protest against her exile in Canada, she had refused to bring her light to the place she considered her prison. In the end, she lost the memory of how to do it, though she never admitted this to her mother or even to herself.

Dana knew she needed the light to help Jean. She had nothing else to offer him. But what if she couldn't do it? She was almost afraid to try. She looked at Jean. She had no choice. Taking a deep breath, she placed her hands together and willed the light to come.

Nothing.

Her heart sank like a stone. She tried again. And again. By the fourth time, she was crying. The loss was devastating. She had squandered her inheritance. She had lost her gift. Dana buried her face in her hands. That's when she saw it, through the film of her tears, a faint dusting of gold at the tips of her fingers. It was almost imperceptible. Tiny specks like dust. Hardly the pool she once possessed, but it was better than nothing. Would it be enough?

She held her hands above Jean's head. The light fell like soft rain upon him. Slowly, softly, it formed a halo. She closed her eyes. For a moment, she saw the green hill and the broken portal. She turned away. This was not her destination. Instead she thought of Jean, wherever he might be, and she reached out to find him.

"*Tabernac!* What you are doing here?"

He stood before her, tall and lean, the raven-black hair loose around his face, the wintergreen eyes bright with astonishment.

She shivered at the sound of his voice. It was like a cool mountain stream splashing over her. She was so happy to see him she almost laughed, but the laugh died in her throat when she looked around. She knew this place. She had seen it from Grimstone's car. It was even worse close up.

They were standing in a mire of dank peat and cesspools. Olid vapours issued from the ground. Nearby was a brake of barren trees, pleached and prickly like a field of barbed wire. In the distance lay a bleak prospect of crags that seemed to claw the dull sky. The air was acrid with the smell of charcoal. Jean's clothes and hands were smeared with soot.

"This place!"

"*Le Brûlé,*" said Jean. "You know it?"

"Do you?!"

He shrugged.

"It look like a place I get lost in one time, in eastern Québec. They are all over the country. This is spruce bog. Not so good. You step in the wrong way," he made a drowning motion, "you go down."

"Quicksand?" She looked around warily. "I know it from the night Grimstone tried to kill me. He took me here in his car, but at the same time I was somewhere else. On the Mulmur Road." She stopped, overcome with shame. Then she burst out, "I'm so sorry, Jean! For leaving you there! I was scared and confused, I didn't know who to trust, but still it was wrong. I acted like a coward."

"*Ce n'est rien,*" he shrugged again. "It was a strange night, eh? Who could know what happen?"

She was surprised by his indifference. Did he think it was all a dream, back then or now? But though he himself had no interest in what had happened, she wanted to know.

"Did Grimstone attack you? I saw a wolf fighting the monster. How—?"

"Yes, he attack me," Jean interrupted quickly. "The thing it was Grimstone, yes, but something else. It pick me up and throw me and then I am here. In this place."

"What about the wolf?" Dana asked. "Where did it come from? How did—?"

Again he cut her off. It was obvious he didn't want to talk about it. He changed the subject quickly.

"*Dis-moi,* are you really here or do I dream you?"

"I'm here," she said. "I've come to help you."

She saw the quizzical look but there was no sarcasm in his voice, only grave doubt.

"I think maybe not. For days I try. The bog is *dangereux* but worse are the *feux follets*."

"The what?"

"*Feux follets*. Crazy fire. They come from the ground."

"You mean will-o'-the-wisps?"

Jean frowned. "I don't know this word but it sound too nice."

He turned to show her his back. Dana gasped. There were scorch marks on his shirt and the back of his jeans. Worse still, where the fabric had been burned away, his skin was raw with livid burns.

"We've got to get you out of here," she swore.

Again Jean looked doubtful but Dana was thinking fast.

"Can we fight fire with fire?"

She cupped her hands together. Regardless of Jean's talk of Canadian spruce bogs, this was obviously a dream landscape, an otherworldly place. She hoped her gift might be stronger here. As the light welled up and spilled over her palms, she breathed with relief.

"Now if I could just do that back in the real world," she murmured.

Jean's eyes widened when he saw the light, but he didn't ask questions.

"*C'est bon,*" he said, excited. "We got a chance. I been here a while and know some things. See the mountain there? Every time I try to go that way, the *feux follets* they attack me. *Alors,* this tell me, that is how we go. Maybe with your fire we do it!"

The ridge was on the other side of the bog, beyond a tangled wood of withered trees. No discernible path led to it. Jean set off with Dana close behind. They skirted the trees and followed a sluggish stream where the ground cover was sparse.

"Don't look in the water," Jean warned over his shoulder.

Dana immediately glanced at the stream, though she hadn't given it a thought before he spoke. There in the sickly flow of the snye, she caught her reflection. Bloated and grotesque, it wavered in the turbid waters, half-strangled by oily tubular plants. Spellbound by the image, she watched herself thrash wildly even as she tasted the greasy stem that was invading her mouth.

"Câlisse!" cried Jean.

He had turned just in time to see her lean over the water, about to fall in. As he pulled her back he yelled, "I say not to look!"

"Everyone looks when you say 'Don't look'!"

But she was annoyed at herself. She would have to be more careful. She could hardly rescue him if she got trapped herself!

They were approaching the far side of the bog. The stream had widened to a dark river that couldn't be crossed and the only way forward was through the trees. Ragged branches of swamp willow and black spruce clutched at each other. The dank ground was gashed and pitted, and gnarled with old roots.

Dana was surprised when Jean took her by the hand. She was overcome with shyness, but she was also glad. He knew the way they should go. Together they pushed through the trees and brush, sometimes crawling beneath the briars. The bog made sucking sounds under their feet. When they waded through a pool that bubbled like oil, they were splashed by stinking mud. At last the trees began to thin and they could see the jagged outline of the ridge ahead. Then they broke from the bog. The ridge was only a short distance away but any hope of an easy escape quickly died.

Up from the ground in front of them rose a globe of green light. Small as an apple and seemingly harmless, it paused in mid-air as if looking around. Now another rose up, as big as a grapefruit, then another, larger still, the size of a football. As more and more joined the swarm, their appearance grew increasingly sinister.

"In Québec," Jean told Dana in an undertone, "we say the *feux follets* are sinners so bad they are not welcome in hell."

Dana stared at the fiery gauntlet that hissed and spat.

"How often have you faced this?" she asked, with horror.

"I stop counting," he said with a shrug.

She was inspired by his courage. Heart thumping, mouth dry, she steadied herself. This was why she had come. Despite Jean's strength, it was here that he failed. It was here that he needed her.

The swarm began to oscillate, flickering and flashing angrily. Before Dana had time to cup her hands, the crazy fires bore down.

"I think now we run, *non?*"

"Yes!" cried Dana.

Heads down, shoulders hunched, they charged for the ridge. It was like dodging gigantic bullets or burning hailstones. While Jean swerved with the skill of one who had done this many times, Dana held her hands high and called on the light.

"This is for you!" she cried to Jean, thinking of him in the hospital bed, covered in bandages.

The light streamed out like a golden banner.

The *feux follets* went mad.

They sped towards Dana, buzzing like giant kamikaze fireflies. One struck her left hand. She cried out at the searing pain, but didn't falter. Another struck her right hand.

"And this is for me," she thought, as the guilt and shame blew away like ashes.

A baptism by fire.

The golden banner had become a river of light that bathed the two of them. Whenever a *feu follet* came near, it drowned like a fly in the liquid gold.

"*Bravo!*" Jean yelled.

"Keep running!" Dana panted, not letting up her stride.

Yes, it was working. The crazy fires were in disarray. As more and more were destroyed by the light, they finally retreated.

Dana and Jean reached the foot of the ridge. As soon as they began to scale the height, the landscape dispelled like mist around them.

Dana was back in Jean's hospital room, beside his bed. His eyes fluttered open. Gently she moved her hands away, but not before he caught sight of the remnant of gold.

"Qu'est-ce qui se passe?" he whispered. "What are you?"

She was overwhelmed with relief and joy. She had done it! He was free from the nightmare in which Grimstone had imprisoned him.

But this was not the time for explanations. He needed to rest and recover.

She smiled. "I'm something different," she said. "Get better and I'll see you soon, *mon ami.*"

As his eyes closed in a deep and healing sleep, she left the room.

CHAPTER TWELVE

Dana's DREAM BEGAN BADLY.
She was sliding down a dark tube that undulated like a hollow serpent. When she finally emerged at the other end, she was floating in a black void, as if underwater. Her first instinct was to put her hands together and make light. The clash of metal rang out. Her hands were encased in heavy gauntlets made of iron, the bane of Faerie. For a moment she felt the touch of despair, but she thrust it aside. She would not go down into the dark without a fight. As soon as she struggled, she began to move upwards. She used the iron gloves like weapons, pummelling the void. Soon she was rising like a bubble to the surface.

As she burst out of the darkness in a surge of black spray, she found herself treading water in a cold mountain lake. Above her, the sky was rose-gold with sunset. All around were the great shadowy peaks of mountains. She swam to shore.

The dark tarn lay in a high hidden pasture. The tall grass glistened with evening dew. The earth was cool and damp beneath her bare feet. The iron gloves had disappeared and she was dressed in a long-sleeved gown that fell to the ground. She didn't wonder why she was dry despite her swim, nor did she question what was going on. She knew she was dreaming.

She walked through fields bordered with yellow whin till she came to a tall wooden gateway. It was guarded by stone statues of

Indian goddesses. An inscription was carved on the lintel above.

It's a funny old world.

Dana knew where she was. Gabriel had brought her here when they still lived in Ireland. It was a sculpture park outside of Roundwood in the Wicklow Mountains. Set up by an eccentric philosopher, the park featured statues made in Mahabalipuram in southern India. One figure in particular dominated the images.

"Ganesh!" Dana murmured.

Her stepmother's prayer had been answered. He had come!

She hurried into the park and there, as she remembered it, was the great statue of Ganesh in shining black granite. He looked round and jolly with plump limbs and toes, big belly and trunk, a generous spread of leafy ears, and eburnine tusks. Sitting cross-legged on a dais, he held a book in his lap. When Dana glanced at the pages they were blank at first, *tabula rasa*. Then letters began to take shape, darting like tiny fish in a pool. They spelled out words. *The Book of Dreams*. Dana noted the message though she didn't understand it. She looked expectantly at the statue, but it didn't move.

Not far from where she stood, a green garden hose lay in the grass like a snake. In India, priests would bathe the temple statues with water, oil and perfume. In the sculpture park, guests were invited to shower Ganesh. Remembering that, Dana retrieved the hose and stood on tiptoe to spray the statue. In the last rays of the evening sun, the water sparkled with light as it cascaded over the gleaming black figure.

The first sound Dana heard was a chuckle. It rose from deep inside the belly of the god. Then came the tinkle of anklets as his left foot twitched. The chest heaved slightly and the limbs stretched out. Colour was seeping like life through the stone. The white pearls of Hyderabad and the gems of Bangalore shone on the silver-grey elephantine skin. Now the eyes shot open, bright with wisdom and mischief and laughter.

Dana jumped back. Dream or no, he was overwhelming!

THE LORD GANESH.

Flap flap went the great ears like giant fronds in the wind. *Haarrooo* blew the trunk's trumpet call.

She intended to bow but wasn't given a chance. He leaped from the dais to catch her hands and danced her around the park with sweeping strides. Music filled the air as the other statues came to life. Ganesh playing the tabla. Ganesh playing the sitar. Ganesh playing the flute. Wild sweet music echoed through the air, singing of hot winds and red soil, bright silks and glass bangles, banyan trees and scented temples. *Indiahhhh.*

"You came!" Dana cried with delight. "Just like Radhi said you would!"

"My daughter calls, I answer."

His voice was rich and dark like chocolate. Hooting and laughing, he scooped her into his arms and swung her high as if she were a baby. Then gently he placed her back on the ground.

"I have many forms, many abilities, but I come to you this night as the Remover of Obstacles. For a short while only, I can lift the veil. For a short while only, I can remove what keeps you from your land and people. But you must act quickly. Your enemy is near and dreams are fragile. This one will soon be torn asunder."

Dana understood the warning. At the periphery of her vision, she could see the grey mist that crept towards the park. As it moved, it consumed the greenery and the other colours of her dream. Her heart beat wildly.

"Where should I go? What should I do?"

Ganesh took her by the hand and led her back to the lake through which she had arrived. On the shore near the water's edge was a coracle with oars.

"Go quickly, daughter. The answers you seek await you on the other side."

"Thank you, thank you so much!"

She lifted his hand and kissed it reverently.

The Lord Ganesh smiled.

"Fare thee well, little one. Give affectionate greetings to my beloved Radhi. Tell her to laugh more as it makes me happy. I have come to you at her request, but I will do so no more. Your gods are all around you, child of Faerie, you need but open your heart to them."

Dana climbed into the boat and took up the oars as Ganesh pushed her off with his trunk.

The mere was as smooth as glass. The oars sliced through the water as if it were quicksilver, propelling the skiff over the surface with ease. As the sun set, the sky above turned a dark-blue sprayed with stars. The night was still. The only sounds were the dip of the oars in the water and the lap of the low waves against the hull. The gentle rocking of the coracle was like a cradle, a womb. How long she rowed she couldn't be certain, but at last she saw a rim of land ahead. She rowed faster and harder.

As landfall drew near, Dana cried out with happiness. There on the shore was a shining figure with long fair hair.

Dana jumped from the boat and flung herself into her mother's arms.

"Child of my heart, blood of my blood," Edane murmured.

"Where have you been? What's going on? What has happened?"

Edane led her daughter into the dunes above the shore. A small campfire had been lit amidst the maram grass. The flames flickered in the dark.

"We are on the border of Faerie," Edane told her quietly. "The Lord Ganesh fashioned a dream to make a bridge that could bring you here. There was no other way, for there are no bridges left. We must be quick, dear heart. The stuff of dreams is delicate."

Her mother sat her down by the fire. A little feast was laid out on stones in the sand. Dishes of gold held fruits and wild berries and tiny seedcakes dipped in honey. A jewelled goblet brimmed with wine.

"Eat and drink while I speak," Edane said. "Your fairy soul is in need of sustenance."

While her daughter feasted, Edane roasted hazelnuts in a bronze pan over the fire. A sweet woody smell filled the air.

As she took the food and wine, Dana tasted the truth of her mother's words. How much she had hungered and thirsted for this, the fruits of the other world! In the long days of separation from the land of her spirit, she had been slowly starving to death. Yet even as she was refreshed and nourished, the dread rose inside her. She had never seen her mother so solemn.

"Hark to me, daughter," Edane said. "Our doom is upon us. The Enemy has risen to strike at our heart. The portals between Faerie and the Earthworld lie riven. Not only the gateways throughout Ireland but all the doors of perception that open to the fairy mind. All commerce between humanity and Faerie has been brought to an end."

Dana was stunned. This was beyond her worst imaginings.

"I thought it was just me," she whispered. "Is it war?"

Edane's eyes clouded.

"The same war. The old war. One that plays itself out again and again."

She sat down beside her daughter. With trembling hands, she fed Dana the roasted hazelnuts, one by one.

"The High King sends you this message, my child. The hour of your destiny has come. You are the light that will bridge the darkness. Only you can restore the gateways."

Dana's eyes widened. Shock kept the full import of her mother's words from hitting her, but she caught a glimpse of the huge task ahead. A short while ago, it would have broken her. But she had retrieved her light and rescued Jean, danced with a god and eaten otherworldly food. She no longer felt alone or powerless.

"You must find *The Book of Dreams,*" Edane said. "It holds a secret—"

She was about to place another nut in Dana's mouth when she dropped it. With a cry, she searched frantically in the sand at her feet.

"It's okay, Mum," Dana said but Edane looked stricken.

"The nuts of knowledge! The High Queen was to bring them to you. I pleaded that I might come in her stead for I feared that I would never see you again. Oh what have I done?"

Dana felt the same panic. She had been so happy to see her mother, so relieved to have contact with Faerie at last, but that relief had vanished once she heard the news. Worse still, she was being handed the greatest mission of her life and the wrong person was guiding her!

She tried to calm down. Her mother was already distraught. No use both of them losing their heads.

"Okay, so I'm to find a book," she said. "How? Where do I look? Should I return to Ireland? Or is it somewhere in Faerie?"

Edane frowned as she tried to remember.

"*The Book of Dreams* is in Canada. It is as the High King foresaw long ago. That was the reason you were sent to that land. Your destiny lies there."

Dana was appalled.

"*Canada?* But how? Why? That doesn't make sense. There's no magic there. I can't quest in that country. I don't know it at all!" A map of Canada flashed through her mind. "And it's *huge!*"

She might as well have been asked to search the ocean.

"The High Queen said you could do it," Edane insisted. "*The Book of Dreams* belongs to you. It is your inheritance."

"What did she mean?"

The question only heightened Edane's confusion and dismay. Again, Dana saw the mistake that had been made. Honor knew the answer, but her mother didn't.

Edane stiffened suddenly and looked out across the water. A grey mist was creeping over the lake towards them.

"Too little time! I have not said enough!" The blue eyes filled with tears as she began fade. "The Enemy will do anything to stop you. Be ever watchful and wary. Courage, my daughter. You are the Light that I bore. Remember always, I love you."

Dana reached out for her mother.

"I love you too!"

Behind her, the grey mist had reached the shore and was edging towards the dunes.

"Wake up!" Edane cried.

Dana woke in her bed, arms grasping the air.

"Mama," she whispered.

She got out of bed and walked to the window. Her face was wet with tears. The road below was deserted. It was the darkest hour, just before dawn. The street lamps shed light through the trees beyond her. The birds had yet to begin their morning song, but there was movement in their nests. In the distance came the silvery sound of wind chimes.

Dana was in no doubt about her dream. It was a message from Faerie, a cry for help. Not only had her portal been destroyed but all portals everywhere. Her mind reeled at the thought. The bond between the two worlds had been severed. The Enemy had truly struck at their heart.

The meaning of the dream was also clear. *The hour of your destiny has come.* A shiver ran through her. She had been given a mission, a task of overwhelming importance. For a moment she wavered. The fate of two worlds rested upon her! How could they expect so much of her, her mother, the High King and High Queen? Weren't they aware she could fail?!

Dana steadied herself. Fail or not, she would have to try. For better or worse, the job was hers. A sweet fragrance lingered in the air and she heard the faint sound of music. She was not alone. Great powers had already moved to help her. The words of Ganesh echoed through her mind. *Your gods are all around you, child of Faerie, you need but open your heart to them.*

Standing at the window, she watched the night transform. Slowly the darkness gave way to the ink-blue of pre-dawn, then the half-light that heralded the arrival of day. In the changing of the hours her resolve hardened. She would go out into Canada and quest for the book. *The Enemy will do anything to stop you,* her mother had warned. That explained Grimstone. If she had to fight him, she needed allies. It was time to end her isolation and ask for help. *Be ever watchful and wary,* Edane had also advised. Caution was important. But she already knew where she could place her trust.

Below in the street, across the road, he stood. She had been watching him as he skulked through the park, half-hidden by shadows. The amber eyes glowed like gold coins as he stared up at her window. The great black wolf with the white star on his chest.

CHAPTER THIRTEEN

Jean did not return to school till the end of September. During the time he was away, Dana prepared for her mission. At home in her room she practised calling up the light. At first it was weak and took all her energy and effort, then slowly but surely it grew brighter, stronger. When at last it welled like a pool in her hands she bathed her face in it, laughing and drinking and eating the pure light. Like fairy food it nourished her spirit. As the light grew stronger so too did Dana. She began to delve deep to find her powers, though she wasn't always sure what she might find. She had never asked her mother about her birthright. They had only played games and danced and partied. How she regretted rejecting the High Queen's offer to be her tutor! Since Honor herself had had to learn fairy arts, she would have been the best teacher.

No use crying over spilt milk, Dana told herself.

Alone, without guidance, she trained herself. There were certain fairy gifts she knew about though she had neglected to use them, including glamour, flight, enchantment and shape-shifting. Being part human, her skills were halved but she had power enough if she could wield it.

Since the attack at the hospital there had been no sign of Grimstone, but she kept constantly on guard. There were times when she felt oddly safe and secure, as if someone were watching over her like a guardian angel. Was it Ganesh? Or St Michael perhaps? Whoever it was, she was grateful for their protection.

At school, she had become adept at avoiding her new teacher. Though Ms Woods appeared to be kind and good-natured, Dana had already made up her mind. There was only one person she intended to trust and she was waiting for him.

The day Jean returned he walked slowly into class, avoiding the curious stares of the others. Though he bore no scars from his ordeal, there were shadows under his eyes and he was pale and thinner. He didn't look in Dana's direction nor did he respond whenever she tried to catch his attention. She finally had to accept that he was ignoring her.

Dana was crushed. Had he forgotten their time in the Brule together? Perhaps he only remembered the night on the road, when she left him to die? There was also the possibility that he had no memory of either event. Her heart sank. That would be the worst, for then she would mean nothing to him. She would just be another girl in his class. She couldn't bear the thought. She wanted, needed him to join her. She would have to convince him somehow. Her heart sank further. Having no experience with boys, she had no idea how to talk to them. Nor had she any girl-friends she could ask for advice.

After a long morning spent mustering her courage, Dana confronted him in the hall between classes.

"*Comment ça va?*" she said, unsure how to begin.

Jean frowned and shrugged, then tried to move away.

"Please," she pleaded with him. "I know it was my fault you were hurt. I'm really sorry, believe me. It's no excuse for my cowardice, but I honestly didn't know what was going on. I thought you were my enemy."

His frown deepened. She saw the wariness in his eyes. There was anger there too, but also confusion. Did he or did he not remember?

Dana could see he was wavering. It was now or never. She moved closer to him to block his path. Then, turning in such a way that he could see her hands while she shielded them from others, she called up the light.

Nothing happened. She was too nervous. She had never shown her gift before to another human being.

He made an impatient noise and was about to leave when at last the light shone.

Jean's eyes widened. But he didn't look as shocked as she had expected nor was he frightened. He grasped her hands and stared down at the light.

"What are you?" he demanded quietly.

"You asked me that before," she answered in the same low tone. "I'm more than I seem. I'm something . . . different."

"Le Brûlé!" he swore suddenly. *"Les feux follets!* It was no dream! *Maudit, c'est incroyable!"*

The green eyes flashed. All the anger and confusion vanished. Excitement lit up his face.

"Dis-moi. What is happening? What *aventure* is this?"

Dana was abashed by his intensity. She could feel the full strength of his personality trained on her and it threw her into a muddle.

"The w-w-olf," she stammered. "The . . . the one that follows you? He tried to save me that night. I want to thank him and maybe . . . could I meet him?"

It was as if a mask had clamped down on Jean's face. His eyes went cold. He backed away from her.

Dana understood instantly. She, too, was protective of her Otherworld friends. She, too, guarded her secrets. But sometimes you had to open up, to have faith in others. He was the person she was ready to trust and she needed him to feel the same way. Throwing aside her shyness, she rushed out her words.

"I've shown you my light. It's a gift from my mother who is a fairy queen. But I'm also half-mortal and I think it's my human side you'll accept more. My last name is Faolan. *Faol* is the old Irish word for 'wolf.' My father's people are the Clan of the Wolf. We belong to the wolf. She is our guardian."

It worked! He was caught, she could see it. A strange delight shone in his eyes. He grinned with a sudden flash of white teeth.

"*Alors,* the wolf in you wish to meet my wolf?"

She nodded vigorously.

"And you don't fear?"

"No!" Dana declared from her heart. "I love the wolf!"

"*C'est vrai?*"

His grin broadened. Mischief sparked in his eyes. He was so hugely amused that Dana was nonplussed. She sensed she was missing a joke somewhere.

Jean leaned towards her. His grin widened from ear to ear.

Disoriented, unsure what she was seeing, Dana found herself staring into a maw of bone-white canines. *Grandma, what big teeth you have.*

A laugh growled low in his throat.

"Like you, I too am more. I, too, am *différent.*"

A yellow-gold colour seeped into his eyes, drowning the green irises. The amber glare of the wolf stared out at her.

Instinctively she backed away.

"You!" she gasped. A cold fear gripped her. This was more than she had bargained for. This was not the wolf she knew. "You're a werewolf!"

His grin was wicked.

"So, not all wolves you love, eh?"

Dana recovered quickly, ashamed of herself.

"I'm sorry, really, I . . . I never met a werewolf. Not in Ireland or Faerie."

He shrugged good-naturedly. The wintergreen returned to his eyes.

"I am not werewolf," he said. "I am *loup-garou*. You know what is this?"

She shook her head.

"*C'est ça.* It's a French-Canadian thing. I tell you later. *Maintenant,* we go with chemistry. Do you do the work for this?"

"You mean the homework? Yes. We're doing an experiment with hydrogen."

"*Bon.* I sit with you."

Dana entered the science lab in a happy daze. New and peculiar feelings were bubbling away inside her. She felt as if she had taken a turn on the road and was now wandering through foreign territory. It was exciting and disturbing and promising and terrifying all at the same time. For better or worse, she was no longer alone. A new kind of magic had entered her life and with it, a boy. She wasn't sure which was more fascinating.

There was a lot of laughing as they struggled with a Bunsen burner that refused to light.

"We do the *feu follet,* we can do this," Jean assured her.

At lunch in the cafeteria, he came up behind her in the line.

"You eat with me, *non*?"

He was obviously not shy with girls. His manner was confident and easy-going.

Battling her own shyness, Dana followed him to a secluded corner. She was painfully aware of the looks cast in their direction. At one table, the older girls she had questioned about Jean raised their eyebrows at each other. At another table, Janis and her circle sat stupefied.

Indifferent to their audience, Jean drew up his chair next to Dana's. If he was aware of her discomfort, he didn't show it. Unwrapping a baguette of ham and cheese, he tore into it hungrily.

His manner towards her was both casual and intimate. To cover her embarrassment she spoke quickly, keeping her voice low so no one else could hear.

"How did you become a werewolf? Were you bitten by one?"

He waved his hand dismissively.

"*Mais non,* I tell you I am not this thing."

He bowed his head nearer to her.

"I am *loup-garou.*"

Then he took another voracious bite of his sandwich.

"It happen to *mon grand-père* . . . my grandfather . . . and he tell me of the others, my great-grandfather and his great-grandfather. The first one, he come from Poitou in France but it only happen here, *je pense.* To Roman Catholic men. He don't go to Mass for seven year, so he become a wolf at night. He can be *normal* again if he confess the sin to a *curé.* A priest. Then he go back to the church and he is *loup-garou* no more."

"The men in your family didn't go to a priest?" Dana grinned with sudden knowing. "They liked being a wolf."

"*Mais oui.*"

Jean's teeth flashed white as he threw back his head to laugh.

Dana couldn't help but laugh too. Their laughter was so loud and wild, they drew more looks. Dana no longer cared. She was caught up in the wonder of a Canadian fairy tale.

Enjoying her response, Jean was happy to go on.

"Unless the man confess, it stay in the blood of the *famille.* But not all the peoples. My father is not *loup-garou.* But my dear *grand-père* he see that I am. He wait for me outside the house the night I have seven years. When I turn, there is much fear. *Terreur.* Here I am a *petit* boy in my bed, then I am on the floor with four legs and so much hair and big teeth. I am all—how you say?— shivering. Then I hear the call to me. This howl in the night. This *cri de coeur.* A cry from the heart, yes, that is *liberté* . . .

freedom . . . the freedom of the wild. It's like a fire in my head, in my blood. I jump out the window to start my new life."

"Was it less scary being with your grandfather?"

"*Mais oui,* but also with the wolf comes *courage.*"

"Of course," Dana murmured, remembering.

"That first night we run together, I never forget. My parents, they live in Trois-Rivières at that time but *grand-père* he live in Labrador City. He invite us to visit at his house for my birthday. He know I am to turn that night and he want me to run free in the wild places with him. *Câlisse, c'était merveilleux!* I have not the words to describe. It is the winter. The land is all white with snow and the ice. The trees, they are tall and black like arrows that shoot into the sky. We run across the lakes that are frozen and across the white hills and over the rivers that are like roads . . . *c'était très beau.*"

Eyes shining, face aglow, he was lost in the memory of his first wild run. Dana could see that he was far away, running with the wolves through the cold white interior of Labrador and Quebec. Oh how she yearned to be there with him!

"Is it up to you when you turn?" she asked. "Do you have any choice about becoming a wolf or not?"

"*Toujours.* Always I choose. Except when the time is full moon. Then the moon calls to the wolf and the wolf come out whether the human like it or not."

Again, the wide grin.

"And during the day?"

Dana saw immediately that she had asked the wrong question. Where his face shone like the sun, it suddenly darkened as if crossed by a cloud. His features seemed to close in on themselves.

"It is not good to turn wolf by day. Then you stay wolf forever. You can never be human again. But I don't want to talk about this."

She didn't press him. She knew all too well from her own experience that magic was a two-sided coin. Enchantment could be beautiful and exciting, but it could also be perilous. Fairy tales did not always end happily. She sensed an old wound, some deep loss that he had suffered. Instinctively, she rested her hand on his.

"Back in Ireland, when I was lost in the mountains, a wolf came to guide me. She was my *anamchara*. That means 'soul-friend' in Irish. She . . . she died. I loved her so much, it was the worst thing imaginable. I've never spoken of her to anyone till now."

Her words took his breath away. This day was as astonishing for Jean as it was for Dana. He had never met anyone his own age who was like himself, who shared the same pain and joy. Until this moment, he hadn't known how truly alone he was.

He lifted her hand and kissed it lightly.

"The first time I see you, I wonder why you feel like *famille*. The wolf, he always know his people. Your wolf friend, she is gone. I will take her place. I will be—how you say this *beau* word in your language? *anamchara*—I will be your soul-friend. *Alors,* now tell me. Why do this monster want to kill you?"

For a moment Dana was overwhelmed, by his charm and by the generosity of his offer. This was what she had so dearly hoped for. That she could set out on her mission with a companion by her side.

"It has to do with a quest," she began, "like the search for the Holy Grail. Except it's not a chalice I'm looking for, but a book. *The Book of Dreams.*"

As Dana told her story, she grew afraid that Jean might not want to join her. After all, it was not his battle, the mission had nothing to do with him. He already knew from his experience with Grimstone that the dangers were real, could even be fatal. Why would he want to risk his life for someone he hardly knew?

She faltered at the end of her tale and waited anxiously. How would he respond?

The green eyes glittered with excitement. There was not a moment's doubt, not a second of hesitation.

"I do this with you! We go together! Already I meet the monster before the night I try to save you. He is my enemy too. He's the enemy of all that live."

Dana caught her breath. She could hardly speak she was so happy. How much her life had changed in so short a time! As if she had stepped out of the shadows and into the light.

"So where do we look?" said Jean.

She came down to earth with a thump.

"It's somewhere in Canada," she said lamely. "That's all I know. Talk about a needle in a haystack!"

"Needle?" He looked confused. "Haystack?"

"Sorry, it's an expression," and she began to explain.

His face cleared.

"*Ah oui,* it's the same in French. *Chercher une aiguille dans un botte de foin.*"

A shiver ran up her spine. She loved to hear him speak his own language.

"I have an idea," he said suddenly. "Can you run with the wolf?"

"I . . . I did once," she said. "It's been a long time."

He gave her a stern look.

"It is necessary you run with me. I can't help if you don't."

Dana's throat tightened. She had no idea if she could do what he asked. Her recent attempts to shape-shift hadn't gone well. It was one of the most difficult of fairy arts.

"Yes of course I can," she stated more confidently than she felt.

"*Bon!*" he said. "When can you do this? We go the whole night, eh?"

"How about on the weekend?" she suggested, thinking fast.

She needed time to prepare, not only for the magic but to cover her tracks. If she was going away overnight, she would have to do it in secret.

"*Bon,*" he said again. "Saturday. We meet *chez toi,* at your house. I know where you live. I go there as wolf."

"I saw you that night!" she said. "What—?"

He shrugged, but didn't bother to explain. He would make no apologies for the lupine side of his character.

They were still discussing their plans for Saturday when Ms Woods approached them.

Their teacher looked nervous. For the past two weeks she had been chasing Dana and had yet to catch her. It was obvious she was determined this time.

"Dana, it's really important that I talk with you. I understand if you're afraid or suspicious. Believe me, I know what's going on. Well, I don't know everything but I want to help you."

Jean looked surprised and interested, but Dana's eyes narrowed.

"I don't need your help."

Ms Woods frowned. Her presence in the cafeteria was already drawing attention. Teachers usually kept to the staff room. Some of the nosier students edged closer in an attempt to overhear. Who was in trouble? What had they done?

"If you would just come with me," she urged Dana, "where we could talk in private. If you'd like to bring your friend, I don't mind."

"Leave me alone," Dana said. Her voice was low and hard. "If you come near me again, I'll report you."

Ms Woods was taken aback, not only by the threat but by Dana's tone. Yet it seemed for a minute, as she regarded the two of them, that she also looked pleased.

"Very well," she said with a touch of sadness, as she reluctantly withdrew.

"You don't like?" said Jean, as he watched their teacher leave.

"I don't trust."

"She seem *gentille*. She don't feel bad like Grimstone. But who can know for sure, eh?"

"Exactly," Dana said. "And I'm not taking any chances."

"*D'accord*. So, we got a date for Saturday?"

Dana blushed furiously.

Chapter Fourteen

I T WAS LATE WHEN JEAN FINALLY
appeared outside Dana's house. She was watching for him at her
bedroom window, dressed and ready to go in jeans and parka. As
time passed, she had grown worried that he wasn't coming. But
there in the shadows beyond the street light stood the great
black wolf.

Dana glanced towards her bed at the lump under the duvet.
What should have been a simple enchantment had taken all week.
In theory she knew how to fashion a changeling: bind leaves,
twigs, branches and clumps of earth with a string of words, a spell,
to make a human shape. Getting the materials from the back yard
and up to her room was the easiest part. The magic itself had
eluded her and the first attempts left a rotting mess on the bed. It
took days of frustration to the point of tears before she managed
to weave the fabric of illusion. There, at last, lay the counterfeit
Dana with dark curls of hair, fair skin, similar height and weight,
wearing her pyjamas.

Gabriel and Aradhana had retired earlier that evening, but
there was always a chance they might look in on her. Aside from
the musty smell that lingered in the room, all seemed normal.

Dana leaned over the sleeping form for a final check.

The eyes shot open.

"Go 'way," it said grumpily.

Dana jumped back. The eyes closed again.

Perfect, she thought, if creepy.

She tiptoed into the hall and down the stairs. By the time she had shut the front door and crossed the road to the park, Jean had returned to his own shape to greet her. Hands plunged into the pockets of his jacket, he leaned towards her eagerly with a big smile on his face. Though the rest of him was human, the eyes glowed like gold coins.

She was happy to see him, but at the same time suffered an attack of shyness. She had grown used to meeting him at school, sharing lunch together and talking between classes. He was so natural and easy-going, she was able to relax in his company. But this was different. They were no longer surrounded by the security of school and other students. This was just the two of them, alone in the night. She could hardly believe what she was doing. She cast a glance back at the big house behind her. There was a light on in her father's bedroom, but the curtains were closed. What would he do if he looked out the window and saw her there with a boy! She caught Jean's arm and drew him into the park.

"I am late," he explained in a quick whisper. "I wait for *mes parents* to sleep. They know I go out sometime but then they worry. Especially since the night I get hurt. *Alors,* I try to go *en secret.*"

"Me too," said Dana. "So where are we going? Is it still a surprise?"

All week he had refused to reveal their destination.

"I bring you to my friends," he said now. "There is one who is special. A medicine man. We go to him for help."

"Medicine man? What's that?"

"You don't know? There are other words—*jongleur, sorcier*—I don't know in English. How you say a person who go between the worlds?"

"You mean like me? A fairy?"

"*Non,* he is human. He is born in this world but he travel to the other ones. He do this for power and to know things, but also to help the peoples when they are sick."

"Of course!" said Dana, annoyed with herself for being so slow. "In Ireland we call them a fairy doctor or doctress. I didn't know there were people like that over here."

His exasperation was quick.

"You think these things are only *irlandais?* This country has *beaucoup de magie!* Open your eyes, eh!"

Dana heard the echo of Ganesh's admonishment. *You need but open your heart.* She caught sight of a truth she had refused to see. Eyes opening, heart opening, a door opened in her mind.

"I was so sure there was nothing here," she said, shocked by her own blindness. "And that's all I saw. Nothing."

"*Alors, regarde chérie,*" he said with a wicked grin. "Canadian magic."

Even as he grinned he was already turning. Dana drew back involuntarily with a frisson of terror. Her instincts wanted her to flee. It was a natural reaction. As the old Irish adage warned, *Bí ar d'fhaichill ar an strainséir. Beware the stranger!* His features disappeared first. The face elongated to an elegant snout. As his back arched, he dropped to the ground, landing on all fours. *A stranger to humanity.* Hands and feet changed to great paws. Nails grew to claws. Black hair sprouted from every pore, piercing his skin and then his clothes, covering both like a coat. He expanded in size. *A stranger even to her fairy self.* There before her stood a great northern wolf, bulky enough to hunt the moose and the caribou. As the broad head reared back, she saw the point of the white star that emblazoned his chest. When he opened his mouth a great red tongue lolled out. The sharp fangs looked lethal. And yet, somehow, that wicked grin was Jean's.

Turning to leave, he trotted a short distance away and stopped to look back at her. The amber eyes were as cool as the moon. He snapped a quick bark. *Your turn,* it said clearly. *Turn.*

Dana's moment of truth had come. Metamorphosis, for fairies, was as natural as dancing, and the wolf itself was Dana's totem, but no matter how often she had tried that week she had yet to succeed. The changeling had been difficult enough, and that was only a simple enchantment. Shape-shifting was far more complex.

As Dana hesitated, afraid to tell him, she sensed the wolf's impatience, his lupine hunger to run wild, run free. With a final bark, he took off without her, running into the night.

She let out a cry. If she didn't move quickly, she would miss her chance. She wouldn't be able to run with him. The thought of facing him later with lame excuses was unbearable. She clenched her body in a furious effort to transform.

The first thing she felt was the cry of the wolf inside. It rose up like a pressure against her ribs, an excruciating pain, as if the creature were trying to claw its way out. She opened her mouth to scream. An impossible stretch of jaw let out a howl that tore through every cell in her body. It was a howl of longing to the full moon of her heart. A cry of grief for her soul-friend who had died in the mountains. A call-note of sobbing from her fairy self caged too long in human form and yearning to be free.

As the life force of the wolf struck her, Dana fell to the ground. She landed on her dewclaws and the immediate discomfort pushed her upright on all fours. There was no time to lose. She sniffed the air to catch Jean's scent and bounded after him, a hunter on the trail of her prey. The last changes were quick and graceful and occurred as she ran, till she was all fur and fang, sleek sinew and muscle.

Racing at a breathless pace, Dana had to wonder—how had she kept the wolf trapped for so long?!

To run with the wolf was to run in the shadows, the dark ray of life, survival and instinct. A fierceness that was proud and lonely, a tearing, a howling, a hunger and thirst. *Blessed are they who hunger and thirst.* A strength that would die fighting, kicking, screaming, that wouldn't stop till the last breath had been wrung from its body. The will to take one's place in the world. To say *I am here.* To say *I am.*

Travelling westward, she caught up with Jean and they kept a steady pace together. The cool night air flowed past like a river. They loped in smooth elastic strides, sometimes erupting into short bursts of speed. Dana knew they could run this way for hours, but she was already losing track of human time.

Like two large dogs they raced through Toronto's streets, moving swiftly and silently over the sidewalks, across the roads, through green patches of park. They stayed in the shadows and sheltered spaces, but it wasn't really necessary. No one paid them any heed, not the drivers whose cars sped through the dark night nor the pedestrians who had their own reasons for being out so late. Those who did notice dismissed them as strays. Both Jean and Dana were aware of the truth: the vast majority saw only what they wanted to see, what they believed to be real. Most people ignored the extraordinary and anything that might challenge their view of life. Anything that might frighten them.

An Irish fairy in the shape of a wolf, running beside a *loup-garou*, Dana was part of that silver thread of magic, that other world stitched into the fabric of reality. She could feel it all round her, humming like static on electric wires, fluttering like ribbons through the silent streets. The stuff of dreams. *There are more things in heaven and earth, Horatio, than are dreamt of in your philosophy.*

When they passed through a Chinese neighbourhood, Dana was startled to see huge creatures crouched ominously on the rooftops. At first she thought they were demons or gargoyles, then she saw they were dragons. Ruby-red, dark-blue, yellow and green, they perched atop shopping malls, restaurants and businesses. Many were fast asleep with no sign of life except for the puffs of smoke that occasionally rose from long snouts. Others dozed like giant iridescent lizards with one eye open, tails batting gently against scaly hides. Some, but not all, had wings tucked in at their sides. One of them winked at her and Dana suddenly knew. These dragons were the guardian angels of the community. They had emigrated with their people to bring them prosperity and luck.

The wolves continued westward as if tracking the sunset. When they reached the rolling green of High Park, Dana thought they might stop but Jean kept going. They skirted the cold waters of Grenadier Pond till they came to a halt at the edge of the South Kingsway. As it was Saturday night, traffic was still busy. They waited patiently for the way to clear. Once across the road, they slipped into the marshes that fringed the Humber River. Skulking along the river banks, past white oak and cottonwood, they surprised a blue heron asleep in the reeds. The river flowed southward into Lake Ontario, but they journeyed north to Étienne Brûlé Park.

The wolf that was Jean stopped at last and shivered violently. Rising up on his hind legs, he began to transform, slowly at first and then more quickly as the change gathered momentum. Finally snout, fur and claws receded as his human form emerged.

Following his lead, Dana unravelled too. Jean grinned a welcome. She couldn't speak at first, breathless with the speed and thrill of her journey, but she managed to grin back. She had never felt so alive and happy!

Jean waved his arm at the greenery that burgeoned around them.

"This is one place I go when I am *loup-garou*. There are others. Warden Woods, the Don Valley, High Park . . . all are good for the wolf. They are also good to hide *le canot* that run *la chasse-galerie*."

"The what?" said Dana.

She could see he was barely suppressing his excitement and she guessed this was the secret he had been keeping all week. He started to search the underbrush. Now he was pulling at something large. At last he dragged it out of the bushes.

"A boat?" exclaimed Dana.

It was a long graceful canoe, not a modern fibreglass construction, but a Native craft of birch bark artfully stitched over ribs of wood. The blood-red colour glowed in the dim light. The sides were painted with images and patterns. Dana could discern the shapes of raven and wolf, but there were other figures that made her uneasy. Grotesque faces grimaced at her with unmistakable malice. She backed away. There was something here that reminded her of Grimstone, something menacing.

Jean had already clambered into the canoe and was retrieving the oars.

"Allons-nous!" he said over his shoulder.

"What?" she spluttered.

Was this some kind of joke? But she didn't feel like laughing. She wanted to get away from that boat as soon as possible.

"Let's go!" he said again. "*Vitement*. Time flies. So do we."

Dana hung back. Her old doubts about Jean crept into her mind. She knew for certain that the canoe was bad. All her instincts screamed alarm.

"No," she said, taking another step back.

She was planning her escape. Having reclaimed her ability to shape-shift, she could easily change herself into a bird. No wolf could catch her if she flew away. Still, she hesitated. She wanted to trust him.

"What's going on, Jean? There's something wrong here. I know it. Please don't lie to me."

He had laid out the paddles fore and aft and was kneeling in the stern. Obviously he intended her to take up position in the bow. He regarded her gravely. There was bemusement in his look, but also a touch of sadness.

"You think I will hurt you, *chérie*?"

She was confused and torn by her emotions.

"No," she said, struggling to be clear. "It's the boat. I don't trust it."

His sigh was rueful.

"You are *sensible*. Sensitive? I don't tell you everything so you don't fear. *Je m'excuse*. This is not right. You are not *enfant*. *Alors,* I explain."

He rubbed his hand gingerly along the skin of the craft as if it were a wild horse.

"This is a spirit boat. A witch canoe. With it, I run *la chasse-galerie*. It flies through the air, like a boat goes over water. This is the good thing. Now I tell you the bad that you feel. The boat, he belong to a *diablotin*. A demon. A devil. This we fight—*comment dit-on?*—wrestle. Yes, that is the word. It is necessary we *wrestle* it. There is a battle of will between the one who own the canoe, the demon, and the one who row the boat, who is you and me. That is what makes *la chasse-galerie*. That is what makes the boat fly."

"You've done this before?!"

"*Mais oui*. All the time I want to go where is too far for the wolf. Like tonight. I want to go to my friends in the North. This is the *surprise* I have for you. We go to the north of Québec where live my friends."

Despite her misgivings, Dana was thrilled. A journey to Quebec, to northern Canada, with him!

He saw her indecision and argued his case.

"But think, *chérie,* this is not so strange a thing, eh? We do this all the times. We fight the demon inside us, *non?*"

She wished she could say she didn't know what he meant, but of course she did. With sudden unease, she reflected on the two years gone by. Had she fought her demons or had she succumbed to them?

Now he stood up and reached out to coax her in.

"You come with me, *non?*"

"Dark forces can be dodgy," she muttered, but she took his hand and stepped into the canoe.

"Without the dark," he shrugged, "it don't go. But you and me, we are strong together. One last thing it is necessary to remember. Don't call to God no matter what happen. If you do, the demon he let go of the boat and we fall from the sky. *Comprends-tu?*"

Dana understood perfectly. There was always a risk when you played with the dark.

Kneeling in the front, she took up her paddle. It felt light and easy to handle. She had never been in a canoe before. She wished she could sit behind Jean to copy his movements, but she gathered the more experienced person went in the back. Though she was anxious and unsettled, she was also excited. The night's adventure, it seemed, had only begun.

Despite her feelings about the spirit boat, Dana would have been disappointed if it didn't fly. A shiver ran through her when Jean called out the challenge that was also a spell.

"*Nous sommes ici!*" he cried. "Let's play the game of chance and fate! *Nous risquons de vendre nos âmes au diable!* We play for our souls! *Canot d'écorce, qui vole, qui vole! Canot d'écorce, qui va voler!*"

Like a dead thing slowly coming to life, the canoe began to shudder. Cold currents of air rushed towards them. Dana sensed the demon struggling to take form in the atmosphere around them. She could feel its ill will as it clutched at the vessel, eager to seize those who risked their souls for a night ride. She knew she was in mortal danger.

Now the boat shook so violently, her teeth were rattling.

"Fais-nous voyager!" Jean roared, *"par-dessus les montagnes!"*

As Jean uttered the last words of the spell, the canoe leaped upwards. It was as if an invisible hand had plucked it from the ground and flung it into the sky. For a moment they hovered over the park, several hundred feet in the air, hanging above the tree tops like a star.

"Regarde," Jean called to Dana. "When we run *la chasse-galerie,* the boat he sail through time and space. He give us eyes."

Below her, the air rippled like water. She had a bird's-eye view of the modern-day park; the site for campfires, the parking lot and washrooms. Then a wave seemed to wash over the scene. The trees were suddenly denser, much bigger and older. There was a clearing not far from the river. Smoke rose up from structures of hide and wood. It was still night-time and few were awake, but two men sat companionably by a campfire. One was Native, the other white, but both wore the same clothing of deerskin and furs. The white man looked up. Even from the distance Dana could see he was young, still in his teens. It seemed that he saw her too, floating in midair. His glance was swift and piercing, like an arrow.

"Who's that?" she asked Jean.

Jean laughed with pride.

"Étienne Brûlé. He come here long ago when the park is a village of the Wyandot peoples they call the Huron. Étienne is the first white man to see the Great Lakes. He have only eighteen years when he come to Canada with the French explorer Samuel de Champlain. Like you, Étienne was *sensible.* A special person."

He waved down at the young man who waved back with a smile.

"Now we go!" urged Jean.

A surge of power coursed through Dana as she paddled furiously. The canoe itself seemed to tell her what to do. She delved the air with her oar, first right, then left, as if paddling the craft over the surface of a lake.

The spirit boat flew swiftly over dark spears of pine and across the black flow of the Humber River.

The landscape unfurled like a map below them. To the south gleamed the waters of the great lake of Ontario. A jewel on the north shore, Toronto sparkled with a thousand lights. The magnificence of the city took Dana by surprise; the ivory-white spire of the CN Tower, the leafy parks and avenues, the elegant skyscrapers jutting upwards like crystal quartz. There were no cities like this in Ireland. Even Dublin, the capital, was only a big town compared to this glittering metropolis.

Up, up they flew into the atmosphere. The city lights blinked below like the gold and silver specks of the stars overhead. *As above, so below*. The canoe rocked on the cool currents of air.

Worse than turbulence in a plane, thought Dana, her heart in her mouth.

She was glad of her parka. The wind was harsh. When they passed through clouds, they were left chilled and damp. Above the clouds was the dark of night where the moon hung like a sliver of nail, a pale lunula.

Toronto fell away behind them. The countryside spread out in broad flat fields and low rolling hills ribboned with roads.

They paddled with energy, but it was hard work. The air, like water, resisted their flight. And so too did the spirit boat itself. In fits and shudders it would buck like a wild horse, trying to toss them out. Sometimes it veered crazily in another direction. As the canoe struggled against their will, they fought to keep it on course.

"It wants to go somewhere else!" Dana shouted to Jean.

"Mais oui," he called back. "It want to go to hell!"

She heard the truth behind the joke and paddled all the harder. This was the perilous game, the risk they took. Whoever mastered the boat chose its destination. Dana took heart from the knowledge that Jean had done this before, and by himself. She was determined not to let him down. Gritting her teeth, she worked so hard she started to sweat despite the cold. In the end, she had to admit she was enjoying herself. There was something to be said for taking up the challenge and pitting one's will against the dark. Wrestling with demons. You can't really know what you are made of until you are tested.

Guided by the Polar Star, they headed northeast, crossing the sky like a ship at sea. To the south glimmered the speckled band of the 49th parallel, the most populated region of southern Ontario. To the north lay a great soft cloth of darkness, the shadow of the vast terrain that was the Canadian Shield. To the east wound the St Lawrence River on its way to the gulf and the ocean beyond.

Another bright city sparkled ahead of them, a tiara crowning the brow of a hill. Ottawa, the capital. Dana gazed down curiously at the silver-green spires of the Government of Canada and the white vein of the Rideau Canal that shone frostily in the starlight. Jean called out the names of the many bridges that clasped the slender arm of the Ottawa River: *Pont Champlain, Pont des Chaudières, Pont du Portage, Pont Alexandra* . . .

For Jean, Ottawa was the marker buoy that pointed the way home. Steering the witch canoe due north, he urged them on to greater speeds as if they were shooting the rapids of wind. He was going home on night's dark wing, flying into the wild heart of Quebec.

"À gauche! À gauche!" he cried to Dana. "Left side only!"

The land below became an ink–black shadow of vast tracts of rock and bog and forest. The ground bristled with the pointed spears of trees, black spruce, jack pine, barren tamarack and balsam. Chains of lakes and winding rivers gleamed a faint silver. Except where sporadic points of light shone like lone ships on the sea at night, there was an overwhelming sense of the absence of man and the triumph of nature. *In wildness is the preservation of the world.* They were crossing the taiga, coniferous bogland on the fringe of the northern boreal forest that draped like a green scarf over the shoulders of North America. Beyond lay the majestic finality of tundra, a cold lonely land oblivious to the humanity that crouched on its borders.

How far into Quebec they journeyed Dana wasn't sure, but the occasional signs of communities grew fewer and farther between. After a particularly long spell of darkness, Jean pointed to a flickering light ahead.

"We are here! I bring us down. Don't paddle!"

She could hear him chanting in French as they began to descend. It was a steep drop to the ground. Her stomach lurched as they hurtled downwards. She let out a yelp.

"*C'est* okay!" he called out.

She put her paddle aside and held onto the canoe. The descent was rapid, cold and rough. The ground rushed towards them with frightening speed. It was all happening so quickly that Dana caught only flashes of where they were going: a dense forest, a small lake, a winding road. She was just getting used to the free-falling motion when she spied it ahead of her.

A ragged trail of grey mist in the air.

It was almost imperceptible, a smear of cloud, but she instantly sensed it was bad. At first she thought it was the demon of the boat. Then the twisted features came into view, scarred and familiar. The eyes burned like red coals.

Grimstone!

The phantasm charged straight at her.

"Oh God!" cried Dana.

The words were out of her mouth before she could stop them.

"NON!" shouted Jean, but it was too late.

Like a bird whose wings had been clipped in mid-flight, the boat lost all buoyancy and plummeted downwards.

Jean and Dana clung to the gunwales. The canoe was pitching from side to side in a last-ditch effort to toss them overboard. They managed to hold on, but their luck was running out. Below, there was nothing to break their fall. Only hard ground. They were riding a juggernaut on a dash to their deaths.

Jean grabbed his oar and began to paddle with fierce strokes.

"Dans l'bois!" he cried.

Dana spotted the trees ahead and understood. If they could land in the branches of an evergreen, they had a chance. But the trees were far away.

The ground rushed nearer.

Dana saw in an instant they would never make it. They were bound to fall short.

Jean roared as he paddled furiously, every inch of his body bent on the task. Now Dana roared too as she hurled herself forward against the bow of the boat. Calling on the power of her fairy blood, she drove the canoe with the sheer force of her will.

It was enough.

The spirit boat leaped forward in a last gasp of flight and crashed into a tree.

In the tense stillness that followed, the only sound to be heard was the protest of branches beneath the weight of the canoe. The craft teetered precariously. The tree's weave held. At last the boat settled, perched askew in the boughs like a great misshapen bird.

"Maudit, câlisse, tabernac," swore Jean.

He moved quickly to see if Dana was all right. She had fallen back into the bottom of the boat. Bruised but not badly hurt, she sat up shakily.

Jean peered over the side of the canoe.

"Pas de problème. We climb down. *Le canot* go first."

She expected him to be furious. With one careless word, she had nearly killed them.

His eyes glittered, but not with anger. He flashed a wide grin.

"That was some ride, eh?"

Dark hair tousled in the wind, white throat bare, he threw back his head to let out a wild laugh. It turned into a howl.

For a moment, Dana was stunned. Then she threw back her head and howled along with him.

Chapter Fifteen

CLIMBING DOWN THE PRICKLY spine of the evergreen wasn't easy. Pushing the spirit canoe ahead of them through the tangle of branches was trickier still. The sturdy craft was undamaged by the fall, but like a boat snagged in the rushes at the edge of a lake, it resisted their efforts. As they struggled downwards, Dana kept a lookout for Grimstone. Was he lurking nearby? Would he attack them again? But there seemed to be no sign of him.

At last the boat was wrestled to the ground and they were out of the tree.

The northern night was cold and silent. High above the dark tree tops, a shower of stars sprayed the sky. The air tingled with the frosted scent of pine. A fall of snow had left a hush of white.

Jean dragged the canoe into the undergrowth. Noting where they were, he tied a piece of string on a branch nearby.

At Dana's questioning look he grinned. "One time I forget where he is."

Her eyes widened at the thought. They could be stranded in the middle of nowhere!

"Do you know where we are?" she asked.

"*Mais oui, c'est mon pays.* This is my country." His voice rang with pride. "This is where the wolf run and where my friends live. Many mile to the east is Labrador City. That is where my *grand-père*—"

A tremor of pain crossed his features. He didn't continue.

Dana was curious, but she didn't trespass. Their friendship was too new.

Not for the first time Jean was surprised by the girl's sensitivity. She seemed older than her age. Something else had caught his attention though he was trying hard to ignore it. After running with the wolf and the night ride in the canoe, she looked unnaturally wild and beautiful. Like a spirit of the forest, not human at all. He was impressed by her courage and her quick thinking which had saved them. And he really liked being with her. She was brave and fun, an ideal companion for a *loup-garou*.

"Before we go to my friends," he said, "I like for you to meet someone else."

The amber light seeped into his eyes. He threw back his head and let out a howl. An echoing bay came from deep in the woods. Jean howled again. Again came the response, but it was closer now as the other wolf drew near.

As Jean continued to call Dana kept watch, but she was still caught off guard when the beast charged from the trees.

Silver-grey in the starlight, the wolf was huge with a powerful head and gaping jaws. It had the northern coat of long hair as well as thick underfur and a large bushy tail.

It leaped at Jean.

Dana let out a cry as the wolf's great paws pushed against Jean's chest and knocked him down. The wolf landed on top of him, growling low in its throat. Jean was quick to recover. He grabbed the animal in a head lock and twisted sideways till they were both rolling over the ground. Now Jean leaped to his feet, arms ready to wrestle. The wolf crouched low, ears pricked forward, waiting to pounce. The two began to circle and feint, sometimes bounding forward, sometimes dashing back.

By this time Dana knew they were playing, despite the throttling and biting. When the greeting game was over, they both sat panting. Jean put his arms around the wolf's neck. They stared at each other, man and beast.

Dana saw clearly the pain in Jean's face.

"We don't run tonight," Jean told the wolf. "I go with my friend to Grandfather. You come too, eh?"

The wolf studied Dana a moment, then loped into the woods.

Jean stumbled to his feet. His eyes were wet. As his head dropped to his chest, he let out a sob, a tortured sound.

Without thinking Dana ran to put her arms around him.

"What is it? Tell me!"

The night seemed to hold its breath there in the forest of snow and pine, with the moon and stars watching above. She had caught him by surprise when she caught him in her arms. The knife in his heart, the pain he had carried for so long, eased ever so slightly. Perhaps it was time to let go. Time to tell. To take out the knife and let the pain flow like blood.

"The wolf . . ." His voice rasped with laboured breath, as if torn from his body. "One time when I am small . . . when I have ten years, I stay with my *grand-père* in Labrador City. I . . . I climb a high tree to the top and then I fall down. My legs, they are broken. Maybe my back too. I bleed inside. The *hôpital* is too far away. It's winter and the roads are all ice and snow. My *grand-père,* he put me in a blanket on the sled. A man, he can't go so fast, so far . . . but a wolf is strong."

Jean pulled away from Dana. He was torn with grief and guilt.

"It is day. It is not the night. My *grand-père,* he . . . he . . ."

Jean let out a cry like a wounded animal.

"He turned wolf," Dana finished for him, feeling the echo of his pain inside, the wound she carried herself. "He knew the taboo, but he turned into a wolf in the daylight so he could save you. And he can never turn back again."

Again she reached out to hold him. His body shook against her as he wept unrestrainedly, letting out the tears he had held back for so long.

Only when he went still did she dare to speak.

"You have to accept the gift," she said quietly. "His sacrifice. His love for you."

Surprised by her words, Jean held Dana's face in his hands and stared into her eyes.

"How do you know to say this?"

Tears flowed down her face in response.

"Remember I told you about my *anamchara*? My wolf guardian who died? She died . . . to save me."

They held each other for a long time, two lost children who had finally found their family. Slowly they grew aware of the darkness lifting as the first hint of dawn crept onto the horizon. There was a moment, before they broke apart, when Jean gazed into her eyes, understanding at last why he felt he had always known her. She was his *âme soeur*, his *anamchara*. He went to kiss her, but then stopped. She was only thirteen. Too young. He might upset her. He stepped back awkwardly.

"We go to my friends. We go to meet the medicine man."

Dana was confused. She was certain that Jean had been about to kiss her, but then he didn't. Was it her fault? Did she do something wrong? Was there something she was supposed to do? Perhaps it was only her imagination. Wishful thinking. She had so wanted him to. Now he was acting strangely, not meeting her eyes. There was an awkwardness between them that wasn't there before. Dana was mystified. She knew nothing about boys. She couldn't begin to guess what he was thinking or what had gone wrong. Following him through the forest, she told herself to stop being silly. This was no time for fantasies. She had work to do.

Their feet crunched over the snow.

"My friends, they are Iynu of the Cree peoples," Jean told her as they walked. "The Cree are the biggest nation in Canada, but here in the north of Québec they are small. They share the land with the Naskapi and the Montagnais."

"*Crí*," Dana repeated in Irish. "That means 'heart' in my language."

Jean smiled. "*C'est beau*. 'Cree' is the name the French give them. The East Cree say they are Iynu."

"I've been in Canada for two years, but I've never met a Red Indian."

Jean winced, then corrected her gently.

"This is not so good to say. In English they are 'Native peoples.'"

Dana was embarrassed.

"That's what the Irish call them. We know very little about . . . Native peoples." She let out a sigh. "I only know what I've read. Their history is very sad, like Ireland's."

Jean nodded. "But *l'histoire* is not over while the people live. The First Nations, they are strong again."

Dana knew by his tone that the matter was close to his heart.

"Your canoe looks Indian, I mean Native. Did the medicine man build it?"

"He help me to make it and he teach me how to call the demon. With the spirit boat I can visit many times and see *grand-père* who live here too. After he turn, he don't stay in Labrador City. They will hunt and kill him there. Here is better. The Native peoples, they don't hate the wolf. They say he is their brother, like the dog."

When they broke from the forest, they faced a stretch of open ground. Most of it lay cloaked in snow but there were patches of moss-covered rock and coarse grass. In the distance, a scatter of buildings stood haphazardly like tents, as if the inhabitants didn't intend to stay. Behind the buildings gleamed a strip of lake. Nothing indicated they were on reserve lands. This far north, signposts were meaningless. If you didn't know where you were, you were hopelessly lost.

There was no highway or other access to the wider world beyond, but a dirt road led from the forest to the community.

They passed a big shack, boarded and dilapidated.

"That's the Hudson Bay Trading Post from the old time," he told her. "It don't open now but the peoples still are hunter and *trappeur.*"

"You don't think that's wrong?" Dana asked, surprised.

"The wolf is hunter," Jean pointed out. "I don't like when the peoples hunt for fun and they make a big joke about killing the animals. It's not the same here. These peoples, they don't kill the animal for fun. They do it for their life, for how they live."

Farther ahead was a small wooden church with a cross on the roof and a graveyard behind it. Beside the church was a low flat hall that served as school, library and community centre with offices for the band and government. Most of the houses were wood-framed bungalows with aluminum siding, television aerials and satellite dishes. There were no gardens or driveways, nor did they have basements due to the permafrost. The cars parked randomly were all four-wheel drives accompanied by snowmobiles. Life was organized around the reality of nine months of snow.

There was no one about at that hour of the morning. A few houses shone with yellow light and the flickering reflections of television sets. All around, the landscape glistened white with snow outlined by dark forest and the hills beyond. Above, the sky was ablaze with stars.

Jean pointed to the lake that glinted icily on their left.

"There's no road so the airplane bring the store, the food, the priest, the teacher." He started to laugh.

151

"What?" said Dana, laughing with him. She was happy to see him cheerful again.

"The airplane land on the lake in the summer and the winter. In the winter, he land on the ice. When he go again the little kids they run behind to catch—how you say?—the air that comes?"

He made a whooshing sound.

"The draft?"

"Yes, I think so. They hold open their coats and it's like they have wings. The air pick them up and they fly maybe a *mètre* from the ground." He was laughing again. "You see the plane go across the lake and all these little birds, they run and jump and fly behind it."

"Did you try it? I bet you did."

"May be," he admitted.

They were still laughing when they arrived at the place where Jean's friends lived. The house was a wood-framed structure like the others, but there was no wiring for television. The lintel and door posts were beautifully carved with the shapes of animals. As Jean knocked, Dana studied the designs of wolf and raven, then the door opened.

A young man, not much older than Jean, stood in the doorway lit up by the glow of a bare bulb behind him. He was darkly handsome with glossy black hair that fell to his shoulders and lively eyes. His chest and feet were bare. He looked slightly annoyed but also concerned. It was obvious he had just jumped out of bed and thrown on his jeans. The minute he saw Jean he let out a yelp and grabbed him in a bear hug.

"Loup! Enfin! Ça va?"

There was a lot of horseplay interspersed with laughter, rapid-fire French and words of another language Dana guessed was Cree. As the two fell into the hallway, she followed behind and waited patiently till they broke apart.

The young man looked at Dana with frank curiosity as Jean introduced them.

"We speak English, okay? She come from *l'Irlande*. Dana, this is my friend, Roy Blackbird."

"*Salut*. Hi there," said Roy, offering his hand.

His grip was warm and friendly. They grinned at each other with instant liking.

"So you finally got a girl, eh?" he said to Jean. "A real cutie."

Jean was able to ignore the statement while Dana blushed.

Despite the kidding, there was a peculiar gravity to the moment that all of them felt. A sense that they had met before. In other times and other places, these three had stood side by side in the fray *As it was, so it would be, now and always.*

Roy ushered them through the dim quiet house. Doors opened into rooms of bare walls and plain furniture. Dana saw immediately that no woman lived here. While the place was comfortable, it lacked decoration and a feminine touch. Its purpose was evident, to provide shelter for men who spent most of their time outdoors.

"Should've known it was you," Roy said to Jean. "Guess who's been up all night drinking tea and smoking? Wouldn't go to bed, like he knew someone was coming."

He brought them into the kitchen where a big wood stove dominated the room. The floor was bare linoleum. A government calendar hung on the wall. The furnishings were simple and functional, white cupboards and shelves, a Formica-topped table with wooden chairs, a refrigerator and battered washing machine.

In a chair beside the stove, an old man hunched over his cup of tea, smoking a pipe. He wore faded denim and a thick plaid shirt. His silver-grey hair was twisted in long braids. A red-and-black blanket draped his shoulders like a mantle, emblazoned with the same designs that were carved on the door.

It was the blanket that Dana noticed first, then she met the Old Man's eyes.

The room fell away. She staggered slightly. It was as if she had suddenly come to the edge of a precipice. She felt weak and dizzy. Never had she encountered such a powerful force. But though his gaze showed something profoundly deep and ancient, at the same time there was plenty of humour there. Dana found herself wondering if life weren't some huge joke being played on humanity.

He looked away from her and greeted Jean.

"*Bienvenue, Loup.* I been waitin' for you. I had a dream. We got work to do, eh?"

His voice was like his gaze, deep and grave and full of laughter.

Before Jean could answer, the Old Man stood up and nodded solemnly to Dana. She was overwhelmed by a desire to bow or curtsey, to show him respect. She knew how he would be addressed in the formal courtesy of Faerie. *Lord. King. Majesty.* But how to approach him here, in this world?

She stooped to take the edge of his blanket and brought it to her lips.

"I am honoured to meet you, Sire."

The old eyes crinkled. His laugh rumbled like thunder.

"Don't be too humble. It lacks dignity. Call me *Ne-mo-som.* Grandfather."

He took hold of her hands. She felt the rough rasp of his skin like the bark of a tree, felt also his immense strength. He turned her palms upwards and stared at them intently. Though she made no effort to call it herself, the gold light shimmered. He let out a grunt, then gently dropped her hands and gestured her to sit.

"Welcome, Skywoman's daughter. You got news of the Summer Land?"

Though Dana knew he was special, she was still astounded. Tears pricked her eyes. This was the first time another human being had known exactly who and what she was, had recognized and greeted her as herself. The irony that it should happen in Canada and not Ireland was not lost on her. She sat down shakily in the chair beside him. Jean had already drawn up a stool while Roy pottered around, filling the kettle with water, getting mugs from the cupboard, setting out milk and sugar. When the tea was made, everyone sat comfortably sipping the hot brew.

Grandfather regarded Dana with calm dark eyes. He puffed on his pipe, waiting for her to speak. When she did, her voice shook with emotion.

"Yes, my mother is a *spéirbhean*. A skywoman. And she lives in the Summer Country that has many names. I am of fairy blood but I'm also human. The news I bring you isn't good and that's why I've come, to ask for your help if you'll give it."

The Old Man nodded. "My people tell stories about the *ma-ma-kwa-se-suk* who come as if from nowhere, who live underground and in the rivers and the hills. They are also called *u-pes-chi-yi-ne-suk*. 'The little people.' Some say they are the ones who make the flint arrowheads you find in the ground."

"Elf-darts!" Dana exclaimed. "We say the same thing in Ireland!"

Grandfather tapped his pipe against the stove.

"When I was a young man, I went off with my uncle across the country. We wanted to see the land, test our skills with strangers, and hear the stories of other nations. In the east we sat at the fires of the people called Mi'kmaq. There I heard the tale of how summer came to Canada. How their hero-spirit Glooskap—like the one we call We'sa-ka-cha'k—went to the Summer Land to ask their queen for help. He wanted her to chase away Old Man Winter who was killing the people with too much cold. He sang her a song and she liked it. He was handsome and she liked that too. So she came back with him. Everywhere she walked, sunshine spread out from her feet. She melted the frozen ground and the snow and the ice. And she melted the cold heart of Old Man Winter. They sat down together and had a talk. He promised he wouldn't stay all the time, he'd let the summer come every year."

Dana marvelled at the story. She recognized it as yet another tale of Faerie, a land whose history could never be fathomed.

"That explains something," she said with a sudden grin.

"What?" asked Roy.

"We get awful summers in Ireland. The fairy queen must have given you ours!"

Everyone laughed.

"It's amazing," she said, shaking her head. "I thought Faerie only belonged to Ireland."

"We are all part of the Great Tale," Grandfather said. "We are all family."

Dana felt her soul shiver at his words. She knew it was time to tell her story. Hesitating at first, because she was ashamed of parts, yet knowing she couldn't leave anything out, she told them everything. When she came to the worst, how she had left Jean on the road with the monster that was Grimstone, her voice faltered. Roy looked angry but Jean interrupted to tell how she had fought the *feux follets* to save him. His friend was satisfied with that and the Old Man looked pleased.

"In the long ago past," Grandfather said, "we would make many preparations before going on a long and difficult journey. There was little time for you to prepare, Skywoman's daughter, but you did well and you have grown in your travels."

Dana felt like crying. She had come for his help. His praise and approval was more than she could have hoped for.

Grandfather stood up slowly. It was obvious he had come to a decision.

"Since we have been fenced into reserves, our nation has shrunk. There are fewer of us and ours is a different life now. But the council fires have not gone out and we still have our medicine. *Pu-wa-mi-win*—the spirit power that comes through dreams—is with us still. You've come to me for counsel. Some would say it's not our battle, it's for your people only. But we all got duties and obligations to each other. When evil comes, it strikes where it will. Only last week, word came that strange footprints were seen near the Peawanuck Nation on the Hudson Bay. It's been a long time since rumours of the *We-ti-ko* travelled."

Grandfather paused a moment to give Jean time to absorb this news. Dana didn't know what he was talking about, but she could see it wasn't good.

"Evil walks the land. Your enemy is calling up bad spirits to join him."

Dana was guilt-stricken.

"It's my fault. I'm so sorry."

Grandfather waved her words away.

"There are many things that strike terror in the hearts and minds of men. Evil goes where it wants. When it comes to us, we all got to fight it. *Comprends-tu?*" Grandfather said to Jean. "*C'est le combat éternel entre les forces du Mal et les forces du Bien.*"

"*Je comprends,*" said Jean.

"*Moi aussi,*" said Roy.

They were all standing now. Dana knew without being told that a pact had been made. Whatever might come, these three were with her.

"We go to the Medicine Lodge," Grandfather said. "The girl will journey. You boys will stand guard."

"*Grand-père* is here too," Jean told him.

The Old Man was pleased.

"*C'est bon.* We need all the power we can get right now."

He glanced out the window at the darkness beyond.

"Something bad is coming."

CHAPTER SIXTEEN

ROY MOVED THE JEEP TO THE front of the house and let the engine run. Jean hesitated before he got in. A wintry light seeped into the sky from the east. The air was cold and his breath streamed like mist. He looked around him worriedly.

Roy saw the look and understood.

"A wolf smells his own kind over a mile away. You know that. He'll follow us."

"*C'est vrai,*" Jean sighed. "I worry anyways."

"*Je comprends,*" the other nodded.

Roy stayed behind the wheel as Dana and Jean climbed into the back. They left the front seat for Grandfather who had told them to wait while he made his preparations. Though the heaters were on full blast, the jeep was freezing. When Dana shivered, Jean put his arm around her. Caught by surprise she stiffened, to her immediate regret, for he quickly removed it. The earlier awkwardness between them returned. She tried to shake it off.

"Thanks for bringing me here," she said to him. "If anyone can help, Grandfather's the one."

"He has power," Jean nodded.

"He got it young," said Roy, leaning over the front seat. "There are many stories about my grandfather. Remember what he said about travelling across the country? That was back in the

1930s. He was sixteen years old and his uncle was twenty-four. First they went east and then they went west. Between freeze-up and spring break-up, they walked and snowshoed well over 3,000 kilometres. They sat at the fires of many nations before they came home."

Roy and Jean sighed together. Dana knew they were wishing they had been there with him.

"Even before that," Roy went on, "the Elders saw he was *stabo*, a man who stands alone, who has no need of others. Some dreamed it. Others felt weak when they came near him. These are the signs."

"Yes!" Dana broke in, "I felt that when I met him! I felt dizzy."

"It's his power," Roy explained. "He has it from the *mista'bou*, the spirit who guides him. Today, when he sings and drums in the Lodge, he will ask his guide to help you."

Dana was overcome by the honour. Awe mingled with silence in the jeep for a while, then Roy changed the subject.

"I sent in my application for the Aviation Program at FNTI," he told Jean.

"*Fantastique!* I'm glad you do!"

Jean punched his arm with delight. He knew that Roy had been thinking about going to the First Nations Technical Institute in Tyendinaga.

"They got a residence and everything. I don't like to leave the Old Man but like he says, it's only Ontario. I'll get back as much as I can."

"I visit him too," Jean promised.

"It'll be great," Roy said happily. "Just two years and I can go for my commercial pilot's licence. I'll fly like a bird for Air Creebec!"

There was more talk about the flight training program but everything came to a halt when Grandfather stepped from the house. He looked magnificent in his ceremonial garb. The coat and leggings of deerskin were embroidered with porcupine quills. His moccasins were bright with blue and red beads. Most resplendent of all was the great black mantle of ravens' feathers that hung from his shoulders. He carried a drum under one arm and a rolled bundle under the other.

When Roy and Jean hurried from the jeep to assist him, he waved them away.

"Je suis ancien," he said, *"pas invalide."*

The younger men laughed.

Soon the jeep was speeding down the road and out of the community. They drove north, around the lakeside, towards a range of hills shrouded with forest. Though the air had lightened to a milky fog, the stars still hung in the sky.

Grandfather turned to Jean in the back seat.

"Have you told Skywoman's daughter how you and Roy came to be brothers?"

Jean started to laugh. Roy let out a whoop and slapped the steering wheel.

"Will I tell her how you hunt me down?" Jean called to his friend.

Roy and Grandfather laughed out loud.

They were all so merry Dana had to laugh too. She couldn't have been happier, driving across the frozen north of Quebec in that jeep with those men.

"When *grand-père* disappear," Jean said, *"mes parents* move from Trois-Rivières to Labrador City. My father search for many years. It's sad but I can't tell him the truth about his father. *Grand-père* he tell me always it is necessary to keep the secret. It is necessary to keep safe the wolf. But for him and me, the move is good. I run with *grand-père* all the time and he's not so lonely. But sometime, because I am young, I want to go far. To the north where there are no trees and sometime to the west. That is how I come here."

They were approaching the dense forest that bristled with jack pine, black spruce and birch. Though the trees rose up like an impenetrable barrier, the jeep bumped onto a narrow trail that led inside.

"I come here," Jean continued, oblivious to the jolting of the vehicle, "where lives the best young hunter and *trappeur* in the land. *Son nom?* Roy Blackbird. He see me in the wood one night and the trouble begins."

"The black wolf with the white star on his chest!" Roy exclaimed. "He was *magnifique*. There he stood in the moonlight, a dream of power. I told the Old Man, 'I got to hunt him.'"

Grandfather shook his head. "I warned him. 'This is sacred. For such an animal to appear can mean your life or your death. We don't hunt our brother, the wolf, unless he takes our food.'" The Old Man shrugged. "He didn't listen."

"I couldn't," Roy said. "The black wolf was in my head, in my heart. I couldn't rest till I got him. I tracked him from dusk till dawn. He brought me deep into Nitassinan, the lands of the Innu."

"A good chase," Jean agreed.

"We were equals," Roy explained. "Before I set out, I would sing the song of the wolf. The song I made to help me catch him. It was cunning against cunning. Strength against strength. The hunt went on for weeks until we headed into winter. Now I knew the time was coming, the hour of his death. For the wolf, like all animals, grows weaker in the winter. I began to regret the day I would kill him. It came to me that I would be sad in the world without him."

Grandfather nodded. "This is a truth the good hunter knows. Animals can live without humans, but we can't live without animals. We'd die of lonesomeness."

"Why didn't you stay away?" Dana asked Jean. "Why didn't you stop being a wolf till he gave up the chase?"

Jean shrugged. "I don't think that. How to say this? Something go between the hunter and the one that is hunted. I feel it with him. It's in my blood. For me, it's not right to hide the wolf. It's the coward act."

The jeep had come to a stop in the dark heart of the forest. The silence pressed around them. No one moved as Jean finished his tale.

"That last night, he trap me in the mountains near to *un escarpement*. It's too high to jump. I am too *fatigué* to run. I see him hold up the gun. Death is coming. I don't think to turn human. I am wolf. I wait to die."

Dana held her breath. Jean paused.

"Rien," he said at last, echoing his amazement from that time. "No shot. No bullet."

Dana let out her breath again.

"Couldn't do it," said Roy. "Even before I cornered him, I had a feeling I wouldn't. Good thing, eh?"

The two grinned at each other.

"I see the gun point to the ground," Jean concluded. "Then this hunter, this great enemy, he lift his hand to say farewell. Also, to salute me. Then I know he's my friend. My brother. I turn in front of him. Except for *grand-père,* I don't do this before."

Roy let out a whoop as he recalled that indescribable moment when he saw a wolf change into a man.

"Lucky I seen some strange things with the Old Man or I would need clean pants, eh?"

When the laughter died down, Grandfather spoke quietly.

"It's good to tell stories of courage and friendship, and to laugh together. This gives us heart. Now let's do what we've come to do."

Just beyond the jeep was a clearing in the trees and within the clearing stood the Medicine Lodge.

The framework of the Lodge was made of young trees, strong and supple enough to bend without breaking. Embedded in the ground, one held the centre while the others made a circle around it. The outside poles were slanted to the middle and lashed together with lariats of *shagganappi,* tough twisted rawhide. A circular hoop on top of the structure positioned the canopy of moose hide that covered the frame. A corner flap was left open to act as a door. Beside the Lodge, a fire pit had been dug, with logs and kindling waiting to be lit.

Jean let out a low whistle.

"The Shaking Tent."

"We made it two weeks ago," Roy said. "I asked the Old Man who it was for and he said, 'We'll know when they come.'"

There was enough room inside for several people, but Grandfather told the young men to stay outside and light the fire.

"You must guard the circle," he told them gravely. "Allow no one or no thing to enter. We must not be disturbed."

Roy and Jean stood shoulder to shoulder, a determined look in their eyes. Dana knew they would die before anything entered that space. Once again, she sensed that she had always known them and they had always stood by her.

There was a sudden noise in the underbrush. Out of the trees bounded the grey wolf that was *grand-père.* In the early morning light his coat shone like polished silver. He rushed to Grandfather and bowed his head in greeting. The two gazed at each other with friendship. Then came a series of barks and whines from *grand-père.* Grandfather frowned.

"He has seen things in the woods. That is why he was delayed. He hid in the bushes and watched. I know some of what he describes, *esprits du mal* of the northern lands. The Bag o' Bones they are called, skeleton creatures who fly on the wind and perch in the tree tops. But there is something else he speaks of that is strange to me. It is like *Ka-pa-ya-koot*—'he who is alone in the wilds'—but it is not the same. *Grand-père* says that first it comes in the shape of a dark cloud."

"Grimstone!" Dana said. "My enemy!"

"He is near," Grandfather said. "We must hurry."

The Old Man led Dana inside the tent and closed the flap behind her. The air was rich with the smell of earth and musky moose hide. Though the space was pitch black, she wasn't afraid. She felt strangely at home.

A match was struck. The scent of sulphur grazed the air. Shadows danced across the walls as Grandfather lighted a lamp. He invited Dana to sit on the ground, then knelt to unravel his bundle. The deer hide opened like an animal leaping in flight. Feathers, pebbles, bones and small carvings were arranged on top of it.

"What is the sacred number of your people?" the Old Man asked her.

"Three."

He lit a bundle of sage and sweetgrass and smudged the air three times around her. The sweet-smelling smoke was soothing.

"Four is the sacred number of my people," he told her, as he smudged the air around himself four times.

Now he lit a small heap of tobacco in a bowl and placed it at the centre of the hide. Humming and singing, he moved with quiet purpose. His words seemed to curl with the smoke that filled the Lodge.

"This place was given to me to make the dance. I have never mocked it. I rely upon it."

Despite the calm of the Old Man's voice and movements, Dana felt anxious. She could feel the tension in the air. She sensed that what they were about to do was dangerous. But there was no question in her mind of turning back. This was her battle, on behalf of her people, and with great good fortune she had found allies in her cause.

Grandfather shook his rattle in the four directions, calling on the spirits of the East, South, West and North to join them in their circle. Then he shook the rattle above his head to call the spirits of the sky. Then he tapped the rattle on the ground to call the spirits of the earth.

Dana could feel the power gathering in the tent. Whispers and low voices shivered in the air. Invisible presences pressed against her. With every word the Old Man spoke, the feeling intensified.

"All creation flowed out of the mind of the Creator. Not only earth and fire, water and plants, animals and humans, but also the mysteries, those who inhabit the other worlds and those who can walk between the worlds, the spirit helpers, the demons, the dreamspeakers and the windwalkers."

He crouched in front of Dana. His eyes were like an eagle's, piercing her soul. He waved his hand over the deerskin and the sacred objects upon it.

"This is the Medicine Wheel. This is the circle that is life."

"*Roth Mór an tSaoil,*" Dana said softly, in Irish. "The Great Wheel of Life."

The Old Man looked pleased.

"You will journey well. Close your eyes, Skywoman's daughter, and I will drum. Let the beat of the drum be the beat of your heart and the beat of your wings. Let it carry you where you need to go."

For a moment Dana wavered. Shouldn't she ask about *The Book of Dreams* and how she might find it? Isn't that why she had come? But her trust in the Old Man was complete. She was prepared to do whatever he said. Closing her eyes, she surrendered herself to the spirit of the journey. She would go wherever she needed to go.

The beating of the drum began.

It was strong and steady, like a heartbeat, rapid like a wing beat. Great soft leathery blows reverberated against her ear drums. Softly pounding. Softly pummelling. Softly pulsing. The sounds beat against her skin as if she were the drum, thrumming and throbbing. She began to feel drowsy. Her head fell to her chest. There were more drums drumming now. And other sounds too. Wood crackling in a fire. Dogs barking. Wolves howling. Voices singing. Now she heard the high-pitched screech of a bird. Was it an eagle?

An eerie siren wailed overhead as a blast of wind struck the Lodge.

The tent shuddered wildly. The poles creaked and snapped as they twisted out of shape. The moose hides flapped as if coming apart.

Though her eyes were still closed, Dana felt an immensity of space open up. Behind her closed lids, motes of light burst into flame.

Another waft of sage and sweetgrass engulfed her.

Louder and louder came the voices and the singing chorus, driven relentlessly by the beat of the drum. The clamour was explosive. The centre couldn't hold.

Oh-oh-oh-whi!

Was that the Old Man calling?

Yei! Yei! Yei! Yei!

She was weak with terror. It felt as if everything were bursting its seams, as if she herself were coming apart. She wanted to open her eyes.

"Do not fear the shaking of the tent."

Grandfather's voice came from far far away. Dana's heart leaped as she realized the truth.

Something wonderful was happening.

Her journey had begun.

CHAPTER SEVENTEEN

SPLASH!

Dana gasped as the icy water struck her face. Those nearest to her laughed and continued to paddle. She was no longer in the dark smoky Lodge. She was in a canoe like the spirit boat, but much bigger and crowded with men and supplies. Her companions were burly, dark-haired and bearded, dressed in buckskin with fur caps on their heads. Some were Native, and all had the weathered skin of those who lived outdoors.

Coureurs de bois.

The words flew through Dana's mind like a flock of birds, carrying with them the knowledge of what they signified.

Runners of the woods.

Explorers and adventurers, hunters and fur-traders, these were the intrepid men destined to become folk heroes. Once upon a time they travelled the mighty waterways of North America, from Hudson Bay to the Gulf of Mexico, from the Atlantic Ocean to the Rocky Mountains, across plain and woodland, over mountain and prairie. They spoke the languages of the Native peoples and adopted their ways to survive. Often they married and lived amongst the tribes. Oh the fierceness of them! Full of life and vigour, voices raised in song, strong backs to their work, paddling in unison as they guided their canoes over the rush of the river.

Assis sur mon canot d'écorce
Assis à la fraîche du temps
Oui, je brave tous les rapides
Je ne crains pas les bouillons blancs!

Les canayens sont toujours là!
*Eh! Eh! les canayens sont toujours là!**

The canoe bounded over the foam, plunging and rising on the crests of white water. Only skilled oarsmen could guide this frenzied movement, avoiding the rocks that jutted up like knives. They held that bark craft steady with their paddles, reading the waves and the shapes of the currents, keeping in the best stream to ride the rapids. They were one with each other, one with the canoe, a live thing swifting downriver. Twisting and turning! Shooting round bends! Leaping like a salmon!

On both sides of the river crouched the jungle of black forest. The majesty of trees soared to the sky. The air was so fresh and clean, so free of human toxins, it was like champagne. The aromatic resins of pine and balm of Gilead oiled the breeze. The leafy shadows rang with the cries of birds and animals: the melancholy call of the loon, the screech of the hawk, the roar of a black bear. A moose crashed through the trees. On the river bank, the brown furry bodies of muskrat and beaver scurried busily. Like the air, the waters too were clear

---

Seated in my bark canoe
Seated in the coolness of the day
Yes, I brave the rapids
I do not fear the white foam!

The Canadians are here, hurrah!
The Canadians are here!

and clean, brimming with white fish, maskinonge, trout and bass.

It was all so real and vivid that Dana was thrilled beyond words. She too had the skills of the others, delving the water with mighty strokes. She too sang lustily in the raucous tongue of the *voyageur canadien*. That she found herself amongst these men didn't surprise her. She had set out on a Canadian journey. Who better to guide her than the *voyageurs*?

> *Je prends mon canot, je le lance*
> *À travers des rapid's, des bouillons blancs*
> *Et là, à grands sauts, il avance*
> *Je ne crains mêm'pas l'océan.*

> *Les canayens sont toujours là!*
> *Eh! Eh! les canayens sont toujours là!**

Distracted by the beauty of the setting and her work in the canoe, it was a while before Dana noticed the man who paddled beside her. She didn't recognize him at first with the thick black beard, but he looked very handsome in buckskin and with his hair tied back in a ponytail.

"Jean!" she cried out.

"*Qu'est-ce que c'est?*" he shouted back, over the noise of the river and the others singing.

---

*I take my canoe and I launch it
Across the rapids and the white foam
And then by great leaps it advances
I am not afraid even of the ocean.

The Canadians are here, hurrah!
The Canadians are here!

Apparently he didn't know her, at least not as Dana. Perhaps this wasn't Jean, but one of his ancestors? He was Québécois, of an old family from France. The blood of the *coureurs de bois* surely flowed in his veins. But was she in the past or traversing a dream landscape? Either way, with him beside her, Dana felt easier in this new world.

Vive la Canadienne!
Vole, mon coeur, vole!
Vive la Canadienne!

Et ses jolis yeux doux, doux, doux—
*Et ses jolis yeux doux!**

They were moving swiftly through a vast canvas of wilderness. The wooded shores were overhung with trees, their topmost branches festooned with green vines. Amidst the dense tangle bloomed delicate blue harebells and the wild Canadian rose. Where the river swirled around chunks of rock and cedar-crowned islands, the shores seemed to tremble. Where the river widened, the waters rushed into ink-black pools and a cold steam rose above the rapids.

Lost in that stern and rugged beauty, Dana felt the unchanging stillness of centuries. There were times when the *voyageurs* broke off their singing. Awed by the great solitude that held them in its palm, they gave mute witness to the purity of life without man.

Dana paddled blissfully. A fine mist hung like a veil upon the water. The quiet was so profound, she was shocked when an arrow landed with a *thwock* in the side of the canoe.

---

*Hurrah for the Canadian girl!
Fly, my heart, fly!
Hurrah for the Canadian girl!
And her soft pretty eyes.

"Attention!" shouted Jean.

She didn't duck fast enough. He pushed her down even as a hatchet spun past. It sank into a tree on the river bank.

The others in the canoe were now shouting and cursing as they paddled faster. They were under attack.

Dana looked around wildly. She heard the howl of a wolf. A grey streak ran through the trees on the shore.

In the canoe, Jean frowned, as if remembering something.

"Grand-père," Dana whispered.

Was he trying to warn her?

The other men were tense. They sensed something strange was happening. Many blessed themselves with the Sign of the Cross.

"Que'est-ce que c'est que ça?" they asked each other.

"What is it?" Dana called to the wolf.

The wolf ran along the river bank to meet someone. As the canoe caught up, Dana saw it was Grandfather. He looked younger, more vigorous. His hair was as black as the cloak of raven feathers that fell from his shoulders. He was gazing up at the sky. Now he raised his rattle and shook it like a fist. The jingling sounds rained over the forest. Behind it, like thunder, came the drums.

Following Grandfather's gaze, Dana looked up too. Dark clouds roiled in the upper atmosphere. An angry storm was brewing.

The Old Man's voice boomed through her mind.

"Your enemy. I see his face. It's indescribable. The hatred is great. Against you, against the Summer Land."

"Where is he?" Dana cried.

All she could see was the storm approaching. First they were pelted with rain, hard relentless drops like bullets. Then the air grew frosty and the rain turned to hailstones. The river rose in spate. The canoe careened. It took all the skill and strength of the men to keep them from capsizing.

Grandfather's voice was urgent.

"Name your enemy! It will lessen his power!"

"I can't see him!" Dana cried again.

It was like a nightmare. The name was on the tip of her tongue, something from her past. From Ireland? From Faerie? She couldn't remember.

There was more movement on shore. A young man stepped out of the trees, a bare-chested warrior with hide leggings and breech-cloth. His hair was tied back, his skin oiled and painted. As she recognized Roy, Dana saw how like his grandfather he was. He fitted an arrow to his bow and aimed at the sky. With a war cry, he released it. The arrow flew into the clouds and burst into flame.

The storm retreated.

"Name your enemy," Grandfather insisted again.

The river grew calm. The *voyageurs* relaxed. Dana understood that Roy had bought her some time. But no matter how hard she tried, she couldn't remember.

Now the drums beat faster. Or was that her heart pounding? She let out a cry.

No longer in the canoe with the *coureurs de bois*, she was airborne in the spirit boat. High above the ground, she was flying like an arrow into the heart of the storm. Below was the rushing torrent of river, above was the tempest.

Kneeling midships, Dana was the only human aboard and the only one paddling. Behind her, astern, was the grey wolf that was *grand-père*. Ahead, in the bow was the black. He turned around to look at her. His golden gaze was sombre.

"Jean," she whispered, her heart lifting.

He turned back to stare ahead into the storm.

Dana felt strengthened by the presence of the wolves as well as the two others, the great black ravens that perched on the gunwales on either side of her. She wasn't alone as she flew into the darkness to face her enemy.

The attack was sudden and horrific. On the winds of the storm came the most terrifying of creatures, screeching and chattering like nightmarish gulls. They appeared to be human skeletons with some organs still intact—the tongues, windpipes and lungs that allowed them to scream. Their voices were terrible to hear. Swooping down like vultures, they rushed at the canoe. Dana felt faint. Each time they dove near, it took all her willpower not to jump overboard.

One of the ravens cawed at Dana, then lighted on her shoulder. A familiar voice sounded in her ear as Grandfather spoke.

"They are hungry ghosts. Bag o' Bones we call them. They live in the clouds. In the fall, when the wild geese leave and the winds and the snows come, you can hear them in the tree tops as they chatter and cry. From the northwest they come, out of the lands of Hudson Bay. To the southeast they go, deep into Labrador. Your enemy has called them. Darkness goes to darkness."

The raven spread his wings and flew into the sky. The other raven followed. With sharp beaks they pecked at the skeletons, with talons they clawed them. With strong wings they beat them back. The screeches of the creatures were deafening. The ravens cawed. Black feathers fluttered, white bones rattled.

Dana swallowed her horror. She had work to do. She must name her enemy.

"I know his name in this land," she told herself. "His name is Grimstone."

A new name on an old evil to cloak the truth, to hide in the shadows.

The storm clouds darkened. A ragged shape emerged.

Frantically Dana cast her mind back, to the fairy tales of her childhood that her father used to tell her and the stories she had heard in Faerie. There was an ancient one, an elemental, who hated the pleasures of fairy life. He preferred misery and discord. He caused so much mischief he was finally banished to the shadowlands beyond the Summer Country. No longer able to pester the fairy folk, he chose to plague mankind. The weather was his vehicle. He could present himself in a sudden shower of rain or the flash of lightning before a thunder storm. His face often appeared in the cold mists of morning. Cowled in fog and dank cloud, he carried sickness in the folds of his cloak and released it where he walked.

Was this the one whom the Enemy had called into service? Was this the one who had been sent to kill her? The grey mist that surrounded him seemed to confirm her suspicions, but the murderous monster with the tentacles was something different. Had he devised a new shape to carry out his mission in a new land?

"I know who you are," Dana cried.

In truth she wasn't certain but she had to take the risk. Grimstone's face was now clear in the clammy grey mass charging towards her.

"*An Fear Liath!* Grey Man! You're only a shadow! The Enemy's servant!"

As the cloud burst in shock waves of air and water, the spirit canoe was thrown into a tailspin. Capsized in midair, Dana was flung out.

She was falling

falling

falling into a country far below her.

A great river wound across the land like a cold white serpent scaled with ice. *Dehcho*. All around the river, the land slept beneath a blanket of snow, frozen muskeg laced with small lakes. The ground bristled with dark fir. As far as the eye could see was a vast terrain of ice, snow, frost and cold.

Mon pays ce n'est pas un pays, c'est l'hiver.

My country is not a country, it's winter.

Her free fall was slow and oneiric. A dream of flying, not falling. She had time to muse on the frozen mosaic below. Slowly she grew aware of a pattern in the flow of the ice on the water. A purpose in its progress. Was it deliberate? The ice seemed to say something in the way it moved. Now she noticed the same message in the creep of moss over frost-shattered stone. What could it mean? Who was speaking to her? Something moved in the east. She strained to see it. Like a line of ink it came trailing through the snow. Now she saw what it was. *La Foule*. The Throng. The mass migration of the caribou, a flowing river of the wild reindeer's run. They too seemed to say something in the way they ran, their grand movement a cipher inscribed on the earth.

Here was a script far older than any mankind had invented. The secret language of the land. If only she could read it! What was it telling her?

Dana saw she was falling into northern Quebec, a dark rug of land pitted with lakes. She spotted the forest where she and Jean had landed in the spirit boat. The tree tops quivered with Bag o' Bones like ragged crows. They came flying at her, screeching and chattering, but she simply fell through them. She could see the clearing where the Medicine Lodge stood. It looked so tiny, like an ant hill in life's forest. She looked for Jean and Roy, but she was falling too fast and everything was blurred.

With a thump, she landed inside her own body, back in the tent, beside the Medicine Wheel where Grandfather was drumming. Was the journey over? Her heart sank. She hadn't found what she was looking for.

Not yet.

The drum was still beating. She took heart from its sound.

"I won't leave the wheel till I find the answer!"

As she sent her cry out into the universe, she opened her eyes to gaze on the Medicine Wheel. The deerskin, which she now recognized as caribou, bore markings she hadn't noticed before. She was surprised to see the chevrons and spirals. They were the same designs carved on the ancient stones of Ireland and the portals of Faerie.

Grandfather's drum sounded a new beat. Low and chthonic it came from deep in the earth, from the heart's core. Stronger magic was being made.

Dana's head was throbbing. She could hardly breathe. Acrid tobacco smoked the air. But she was getting closer, she could feel it.

The markings on the Medicine Wheel began to move. They looked like stars spiralling in a galaxy. No, like birds in flight high in the atmosphere. Or were they clouds swiftly crossing the sky? She kept her eyes on the designs as they played over the deerskin. She had seen these patterns only a short while ago, in the ice and the moss and the wild run of the caribou. She struggled to understand them, to decipher their code. If she could read the patterns, she would have the answer.

"*Roth Mór an tSaoil,*" she murmured. "This is the great wheel of life. *My* life."

Suddenly the pieces fitted together and made the shape of a book.

"*The Book of Dreams!*" Dana cried.

Before she could touch it, the book fell open and the pages of white paper fluttered like wings. They flew upwards in a flurry of white leaves and white feathers, white-winged birds flying into the air, around the tent, around Dana's head. They were singing to her in a beautiful tongue, a language she didn't know though it was strangely familiar, painfully so. Her ears ached to hear the words. Her heart longed to understand them.

She caught the gist of what they were singing, something about a Promise and a faraway Country.

Tears filled her eyes. The song was so grand, so beautiful, so true.

And now another marvel in that marvellous journey. She was so taken by surprise, she let out a cry. The caribou hide suddenly leaped to its feet, a great wild deer with antlers branching. Though alive, it still bore the designs of the Medicine Wheel on its flanks. For one quivering moment, it stood there paralyzed, nostrils flared, eyes wild with terror. Then it bounded out of the Lodge and into the night.

Dana didn't stop to think. She jumped to her feet and chased after it.

Outside the tent, she paused at the sight of Jean and Roy. They stood guard by the fire, watching the trees around them. They didn't appear to see her, but *grand-père* hunkered down and growled low in his throat.

"Qu'est-ce que c'est?" Jean asked him.

Dana was already rushing away, into the trees, after the caribou.

At first she thought she was a wild deer herself, running on four legs with speed and agility. *Hind's feet in high places.* But she didn't feel like a deer. She felt savage and ferocious, propelled by a hunger that raged through her blood. She was beginning to suspect what she was when she saw the others, running alongside her. Hair bristling grey and black, they streaked through the trees, two fierce wolves with fiery eyes. She was hunting in a pack with *grand-père* and Jean! Above the tree tops, cawing loudly, were the birds known to hunt with wolves, two black ravens.

Dana's blood was afire. She could smell her prey, smell its fear and its death. In the heel of the hunt, it all made sense. The deer was the answer, the secret she sought. She had to pursue it, to track it down, to eat and drink it.

Both were caught, the Hunter and the Hunted, on the Great Wheel of Life.

The trees began to thin out. Dana was gaining on her quarry. She could hear it panting. There were flecks of foam on its flanks. Her heart almost burst with the strain of the chase. It was just ahead of her now. Something huge and nameless, but she could almost name it. Something on the tip of her tongue, at the edges of her vision, in the back of her mind. She was approaching the answer.

The deer ran into a clearing. The mists of morning rose from the ground like the breath of the earth. A fire had been lit. An early breakfast was being cooked. There were figures seated around the fire, faint shapes barely visible like trails of sunlight. They turned at the sound of her arrival.

She couldn't see them clearly. They were already dispelling, all flickering and flashing and fluttering in the air, a spray of white feathers, white leaves, white pages.

"Please!" she cried, "Don't leave me! Tell me!"

Boom! Boom! Boom!

The drum was loud and rapid. Like someone hammering on the door, banging to be let in. She knew it was Grandfather calling her back from the journey, calling her home.

"No wait!" she cried, "I've almost got it! I'm almost there!"

Her wail quickly changed to a howl when the caribou suddenly crashed out of the trees. Antlers lowered, it charged at Dana. She didn't stop to fight. She turned and ran, back through the woods the way she had come.

The Great Wheel had turned. It was her time to be hunted, her turn to feel the terror of the stalker, Death.

Ears flattened against her head, eyes white with fear, she fled the thunder of the hooves behind her. At any moment the horns could impale her.

With a final gasp of desperation, Dana broke from the trees where the Medicine Lodge stood and flung herself through the door into the tent.

The drum was silent.

She opened her eyes.

Grandfather was rolling up his bundle. The air was grey with stale smoke.

"I was so close!" she sobbed.

There was no time for tears or regrets. No time for reflection. The tent was shaking violently. The ropes that bound it together were coming undone. The hides were flapping against the framework. The poles strained and snapped. Things were falling apart.

"What is it?" Dana said, though she had already guessed.

Grandfather had finished wrapping his bundle. He stood a moment to listen.

A storm was raging outside the Lodge. Gusts of wind battered the tent. The cry of the gale grew louder, moved closer.

The Old Man's eyes were dark.

"Your enemy is here."

Chapter Eighteen

OUTSIDE THE TENT, THE THREE guardians were still on duty despite the lashing rain. The fire had gone out. Both Jean and Roy were drenched, while *grand-père's* fur clung to his skin. Each time the wind gusted, they were whipped with streaks of water like cat-o'-nine-tails. Heedless of their misery, they stayed at their posts.

"Home!" Grandfather shouted, as thunder rumbled in the distance.

They ran to the jeep and piled inside. Though morning had broken, the storm darkened the air. The trees tossed and swayed in threatening motions around them. Trunks creaked, branches snapped. Nature seemed to conspire to hold them there. As soon as Roy attempted to move the vehicle, the wheels spun in the mud. The ground was sodden. The storm itself was pitched to a frenzy. Fork lightning split the sky. Peals of thunder crashed above them. *Grand-père* buried his head in his paws with a whine of pain. The wheels continued to spin.

"We push!" Jean swore, climbing back out of the vehicle.

Grandfather went to follow, but Roy caught his arm.

"I need you to take the wheel, Old Man."

As Roy got out behind Jean, Dana came after him.

"Stay inside!" they shouted.

"No!" she shouted back.

The three pushed with all their might as Grandfather put his foot to the gas. The jeep leaped out of the rut just as a bolt of lightning hit the Medicine Lodge. First came the strike like the report of a gun, then the explosion as the tent burst into flames.

"I'm so sorry, Grandfather!" Dana said, as everyone scrambled back into the jeep.

Roy was behind the wheel again. Grandfather had taken the rattle out of his bundle.

"*Ce n'est rien*. It's only a thing of hide and wood. The power is here and here."

He touched his head and his heart.

Now came the brunt of the assault.

A blast of wind hurled itself against them. It was as if a rhinoceros had charged the jeep. The vehicle juddered like a wounded animal. The headlights burst as if struck with a crowbar.

"*Go!*" Grandfather cried to Roy.

Roy drove as fast as possible though he could hardly see. The headlights were out and a grey fog had descended. Trees loomed in front of him as if to attack. He veered to avoid them, flinging his passengers from side to side.

"I can't see the trail!" he shouted.

The Old Man was chanting as he shook the rattle.

"We need light," he called over his shoulder.

Jean was already rummaging in the back of the jeep. Under the tools and tarpaulin, with the hunting and fishing gear, he found a flashlight.

The battery was dead.

"*Tabernac!*" he cried with frustration.

The jeep grazed a tree and bounced off sideways. Again they were struck by the force of the wind. Already off balance, the vehicle tipped dangerously and was about to turn over.

Grandfather's song rose higher, his rattle shook louder.

Roy pulled at the wheel and steadied them up. Onward he drove, cursing the darkness.

"We need light," Grandfather called again, looking directly at Dana.

Despite all the times she had called on her light, she couldn't imagine enough power to counter this darkness. But she had to try. She saw the surprise on Roy's face when her hands lit up, but there was only enough to brighten the jeep.

"Can you help me?" she asked Grandfather.

His reply was stern.

"Skywoman's daughter, your friends are in danger. Those who stood guard and who helped you on your journey. *O nobly born, remember who you are!*"

His words were the catalyst that pushed her further. She clapped her hands furiously. Like a shooting star, the light flew out from her palms in a fiery arc that pierced the windshield. An explosion of light lit up the woods and revealed the trail.

Roy let out a whoop as he steered the jeep onto the track. With the way shining before him, he sped through the trees. As they broke from the forest, leaving the storm behind them, howls of delight mingled with the real howls of the wolf.

It was wonderful to return to Grandfather's house, where wet clothes were changed and hot tea brewed, where there was toast and sardines and chunks of cheddar. Grandfather sat down by the stove with his pipe. *Grand-père* stretched out at his feet, flank to the heat. As the thick fur dried, the room smelled of steamed wolf. The others sat around them contentedly. All were satisfied with the work they had done.

Grandfather spoke first.

"Now, Skywoman's daughter, the best hunters dream the way to heaven and on their return they make a map. Tell us your journey."

"You were there, all of you," she said, looking around at them. "*Grand-père* as well. Don't you remember?"

Roy and Jean looked surprised.

"Our spirits were with you," the Old Man explained, "but the journey was yours. You must have got a good one, your enemy's real mad."

As soon as Dana tried to tell her tale, she found the details escaping her. It was all a jumble, a mazy collage of bright images and events. Jean grinned with pleasure when he heard he had travelled with the *coureurs de bois*. Roy sat proudly as she described him as a warrior. Whenever she faltered, Grandfather would gently nudge her.

"Did you see the thing you seek?"

She nodded vigorously.

"*The Book of Dreams*. It was there right in front of me, but it kept shape-shifting. It was part of the patterns and the white birds and the land. Oh it's all so mixed up," she floundered.

"Was there a song?" he asked.

"Oh yes! How could I forget? The white birds were singing it. It was so beautiful, but I couldn't understand the words."

She frowned as she struggled to remember.

"The words were in the land as well," she said. "The patterns, the secret language, it was everywhere, in everything. Does this make any sense at all?"

Grandfather's pipe was empty. Both Roy and Jean offered him tobacco from a pouch near the stove and they signalled to Dana to do the same. They knew the Old Man was about to give a teaching. As the sweet scent of the smoke filled the room, he spoke in a slow and measured tone.

"It has always been the way of the First Peoples to live in harmony with the land. The land, the plants, the animals and the people all have spirit. It is important to encounter and acknowledge the life of the land. From such encounters come power. The power of the spirits rises up from the land.

"You've lost two homelands, Skywoman's daughter, the land of your birth and the land of your spirit. And you lost power when that happened. Now you want power from this land 'cause what you're looking for is here and this is the land where you live. But you don't know the land and you don't know its spirits. When the land tries to speak to you, you can't hear. You're deaf to the words. You don't know the language.

"You're an outsider here, Skywoman's daughter, and you learned the truth in your journey. The land won't yield its secrets to a stranger."

Dana nodded dumbly. It was a hard lesson but she understood all too well. How could she hope to quest in this country the way she had in Ireland? She loved Ireland with all her heart and soul. Her new country she had made no effort to cherish. Only because of Jean had she even been able to see its beauty.

"I want to change that," she said now, with solemn resolve. "I'll do what you and your uncle did. I'll travel the land till I get to know it, till I'm no longer a stranger. Then hopefully it will tell me about *The Book of Dreams*."

Grandfather was pleased.

"This is a good decision. You are going on a vision quest, to acknowledge and encounter the land. Let the four directions be your map. If you go the road with heart, the spirits will guide you."

The long night was over. The storm had dissipated and day had come. They could hear doors opening outside, voices calling through the air, engines starting up. The community was waking, coming to life.

Grand-père sat up, alert.

"Don't worry, my friend," Grandfather told him, "we'll get you back to the forest. Is your spirit boat near?" he asked Jean.

"Oui."

"Take care when you fly. The one who follows Dana will always be near. The demon of the canoe is his ally now."

"I named him!" Dana suddenly remembered. *"An Fear Liath!* The Grey Man. He's an Irish elemental who acts through the weather. That's where the storm came from. But he has a new shape as well. A horrible one that kills."

"He's no longer alone," Grandfather warned her. "He has called up other bad spirits to join him. You saw the Bag o' Bones when you journeyed. There are others who will come. The We-ti-ko who cries in the cold heart of winter, whose own heart is ice. D'Sonoqua who kills in the west and eats her prey. There are many dark spirits known to the First Nations. Then there are those known to Jean's people, *les diablotins, les feux follets, les lutins, les fantômes* and more. When the white man came, he brought his devils too and he himself was *le Diable* to us. All these will join your enemy, for they are his brothers and sisters. In the spirit world, all are kin."

"So many against me!" Dana said, dismayed.

There was great kindness in Grandfather's look.

"You are not alone either. Others will come to your side. I dreamed this long ago. When darkness calls to darkness, light will go to light. For even as they are kin, so too *we* are family."

It was time for them to part. Roy offered to drive Dana, Jean and *grand-père* to the woods where the canoe was hidden.

"I don't know how to thank you," Dana said, her voice shaking with emotion.

She was reluctant to leave. She felt safe and at peace in the presence of the Old Man.

He clasped her hands in his.

"You got strong power, Skywoman's daughter, make sure you use it."

He turned to embrace Jean.

"A word to you, *Loup*. The place where a man lives shapes his character. The song of the bird in the air is the song of freedom. The one in the cage sings the song of captivity. Cities make men weak. Too many people, too much misery and bad spirit. The land of the forest with its lakes and rivers is the land of your heart. Keep its spirit with you till we meet again."

Then he laid his hand on *grand-père*'s head.

"It's good to have your kind under my roof. The raven and the wolf will hunt together again."

Outside, the day was clear and frosty. Their breaths streamed like smoke in the air. The community looked worn and exhausted after the storm. The ground was littered with broken branches, loose stones and clods of earth. The few people who were out were wrapped up warmly. A man called out a greeting to Roy who waved back.

In the jeep, they were all too tired to talk. Jean put his arm around Dana. She leaned against him for warmth and comfort. Roy grinned and winked at his friend.

"How's *your* girlfriend?" Jean asked him.

"Which one?"

Deep in the woods, Jean said his farewells.

"*À bientôt,*" he said quietly to *grand-père*, holding the wolf's great head in his hands, staring deep into his eyes. "Don't forget me. I return soon."

The wolf shook his mane of grey hair and licked his grandson's forehead. Then he loped away into the trees.

Jean watched him go. He turned to Roy.

"*J'ai peur* . . . he forget one day. Who he is. What he is. Maybe I come back and find he's all wolf. Maybe he forget me."

Roy mirrored his sorrow.

"Me and the Old Man, we do our best. We watch out for him."

"You're a good friend."

"I'm your brother."

They embraced.

Before Roy left, he chucked Dana's chin and gave her a big smile.

"Look after *mon frère*. 'Bout time he got himself a girl."

Dana smiled back shyly.

"Thanks for everything. I'm really glad we met."

"*Moi aussi*. We'll meet again, eh?"

As the jeep roared off with Roy beeping his last goodbye, Jean pulled the spirit boat out of the bushes.

"I'm banjaxed," Dana said, in despair.

The last thing she felt like doing was paddling home.

Jean clearly felt the same way, but he shrugged it off.

"There's no choice, *n'est-ce pas*? We rest here, we are late at home. I think *nos parents* can't take this?"

"Oh God no," Dana agreed.

"Don't say this word in the *canot*," he reminded her.

She clapped her hand over her mouth.

"Should I gag myself?"

She stifled a giggle. She was giddy with fatigue and over-excitement. Jean looked concerned for a minute, then had to laugh. Though she was visibly collapsing, her eyes sparkled with mischief. How different she was from the first time he had met her! When did that quiet plain girl turn into this adventuress? She was so much more than she appeared. So young, yet belonging to a race as old as the world. Grandfather and Roy, his dearest friends, had accepted her completely. They recognized the wolf and the warrior inside her, even as he did. And there was something else he recognized. The solitary nature of her life and the secret burden that rested upon her. Like him, she was alone and lonely.

"We need some fire to fly this boat," he decided.

Before she could ask what he meant, he pulled her against him and gave her a long kiss.

For a moment Dana struggled—because he had caught her by surprise—but it was only a moment and it quickly passed. She soon knew what he meant. The joy of the kiss fired her veins. Her heart almost burst with it. He kissed her longer than she thought was possible without taking a breath. When he let her go, she saw the same fire in his eyes that burned in her heart.

They clambered into the witch canoe and grabbed the oars. Their energy crackled in the air like blue sparks of electricity.

"Allons! Allez!" Jean cried.

Dana let out an echoing yell.

"Coureurs de bois abú!"

In a matter of seconds they were airborne and flying.

Far above the clouds, they met the rising sun as it blazed in red-gold splendour across the sky. Dana felt the bite of the upper atmosphere and turned her face to the light.

Jean began to sing as he paddled and she soon joined in. She would never forget the songs of the *voyageurs*.

A screech was carried on the wind towards them. The visage of the Grey Man appeared briefly in the clouds. But he hadn't a chance here, no luck at all. The canoe shone like burnt gold as it sailed through the morning, a flaming arrow. And the two singers in the boat sang with the unquenchable fire of new love.

> *Vive la Canadienne!*
> *Vole, mon coeur, vole!*
> *Vive la Canadienne!*

Chapter Nineteen

Flying faster than they had imagined possible, Jean and Dana reached Toronto in the late hours of morning. They landed in a secluded spot in the Humber Marshes. Though they had passed many towns and countless people, no one had looked up or taken any notice of them.

"Is the witch canoe invisible?" Dana wondered.

"Je n'sais pas," Jean shrugged. "They don't believe, they don't see, eh?"

Pale and tired, they hid the boat and made their way to the subway.

Both were too exhausted to talk as the train rumbled eastbound. Dana got off first, barely managing a goodbye. Jean had farther to travel and was already nodding back asleep, his head bumping against the window as the train pulled away.

Certain that the changeling couldn't have lasted that long, Dana dreaded going home. How would she explain another disappearance? By the time she had sneaked in the back door and hurried to her room, she discovered there was no need. The house was enjoying a lazy Sunday afternoon. Her room had been undisturbed. The bed was still made up as she had left it. Under the duvet, the changeling had disintegrated into a mess of dirt and wet leaves. Dana removed the soiled linen and stuffed it in her closet. She would clean up later. Crawling onto her mattress, she fell fast asleep.

Several hours later she woke with a start, overwhelmed by the sense that she had forgotten something. Memories of her adventure flooded her mind: the spirit boat, Jean and his friends, the journey with Grandfather, the quest that awaited her and the kiss, oh the kiss! She jumped out of bed. How wonderful life was! She felt ready for anything.

Washed and changed, Dana reached the kitchen door in time to overhear yet another argument about her.

"She is a teenager," Aradhana was saying. "They sleep late because of their hormones and the upset of their body clock. It is not laziness."

"You always take her side!" Gabriel complained. "Are you going to be like this with *our* children too?"

"All children in this family will be treated the same."

"That's not what I meant and you know it!"

Gabriel's exasperation ended in a fit of spluttering punctuated by a hiccup. They both burst out laughing. Smooching noises followed which Dana chose to ignore. But she was pleased. Evidently her absence hadn't been detected since no one tried to wake her, thanks to Radhi. Yet again Dana recognized how lucky she was that her father had married this wonderful woman.

A pang of guilt. They were only newlyweds. Had she helped them settle into their life together? She knew the answer to that question. The past two years hadn't been easy. For the first time Dana considered that the move to Canada might have been hard for the others. For Radhi, it meant leaving her beloved brother behind as well as the restaurant they ran together. For Gabe, the changes were also drastic. After ten years away, he was once again near his strong-willed mother. There was also the new job which was a full-time position. In Ireland he had worked as a gig musician along with giving lessons and even busking on the streets. There had been less money, but also less responsibility and far less pressure. Being newly married was, in fact, a bonus, not a problem. His wife made life easier for him.

"I sure don't," Dana thought to herself.

It was such a long time since she and her dad had had fun together. They were once so close they could read each other's minds, finish each other's sentences. She winced as she realized that she had blamed him for everything, because she didn't like Canada the way he and Radhi did.

Well, things could change.

Dana burst into the kitchen and greeted her father with a hug.

"Morning, Da. I'm making pancakes. Would you like some?"

"Good *afternoon,*" he responded, but there was no force in the reprimand. He was too surprised by the greeting as well as the offer. "Hm, yes, pancakes would be nice . . . for lunch."

"I'll make them Canadian-style, with bananas and maple syrup."

Now he looked worried. She always insisted on "Irish" pancakes, cooked thin and rolled up like crepes with lemon and sugar.

Aradhana smiled and poured herself some tea.

"So how's work these days, Gabe?"

"Well it's . . . there's . . . I mean . . ."

It took a while and a few more questions, but she eventually got him talking about his students and his new office and the usual power politics in the department. Even as he talked she saw his features relax, saw how pleased he was that she was interested, that she cared. It was like the old days when he told her about his gigs. He even mimicked the voices of some of his colleagues till the three of them were laughing hysterically.

As they ate their lunch, Aradhana remembered to tell Dana about the phone call.

"A boy called Jean rang you earlier. He asked that you call him when you get up. His number is by the phone."

"A *boy?*" Gabriel's good humour disappeared in an instant. "Who? How? When? Where?"

The look they both gave him was like a stone wall. He knew he had lost before he even began. He threw up his hands.

They were all laughing again.

When Dana rang Jean, the kiss they had shared hung in the air between them, teasing and embarrassing them. After the initial hellos, a silence fell on the line.

"You are fine today?" Jean managed at last.

"Yes," Dana replied.

Long pause.

"You?"

"*Oui. Bien. Très bien,* I sleep a long time."

"Me too."

"*Pas de problème* at home?"

"No. You?"

"*Non.*"

Another long pause.

Dana was racking her brain to think of something to say. They had just shared the most amazing adventure together, why couldn't she talk to him?!

Jean cleared his throat.

"So . . . I see you tomorrow at school?"

"Yes. Yes. See you then."

She was both relieved and disappointed to end the call. As soon as she hung up, she screeched for her stepmother.

"*Radhi! How do you talk to boys?*"

★ ★ ★

When they were back at school, it was easier for Dana. Face to face, she felt more comfortable with Jean. There was something about him, his open nature and the way he was so at ease with himself, that helped her to talk and act naturally as well. Besides his manner, she liked the way he looked. Now she understood why he dressed as he did. His clothes suited the North, the leather boots and tight jeans, the woollen shirts, the beaded armband. Her own appearance had become more dramatic, with tops and shirts of bright fabrics to liven up her jeans and Indian jewellery that Radhi had given her. She had started to wear her hair in different styles, sometimes loose on her shoulders, sometimes braided or tied up. It wasn't only her new appearance that made her attractive. Having emerged from her cocoon, she was bursting with life. Her happiness brimmed over in smiles and laughter.

Jean wasn't the only boy who noticed the difference in Dana. When he saw the others looking her way, he moved his desk next to hers.

Dana was pleased by the move, but it took all her willpower not to blush whenever he leaned close. She kept thinking about the kiss they had shared. To distract herself, she concentrated on what they needed to talk about. The task at hand. The next step in the quest.

"I've been thinking about Grandfather's advice," she said to him. "Where we start doesn't seem to be so important as long as we do the four directions. We should just pick one and go."

"*D'accord,* but if we go far we need time," he pointed out. "*La chasse-galerie* is fast but not like a rocket."

"This weekend would be perfect then. With the Thanksgiving holiday we'd have an extra day. But how will we do it? I can't just take off. My dad would have a fit."

"*Je comprends,*" Jean nodded. "It's the same for me with *mes parents.* I don't like them to worry."

Their heads were close together as they talked in low voices. The first class of the morning had yet to begin. They were so engrossed in their conversation they didn't hear the sniggers. One of the other boys had put his hand over his heart and was making exaggerated grimaces of true love. They also didn't notice their teacher enter the room and walk casually in their direction. She hovered nearby, taking her time to open a window.

As soon as Dana grew aware of Ms Woods, she signalled to Jean. They both stopped talking and opened their books. Dana was certain the teacher had been eavesdropping, but how much had she heard?

At the end of the day, when Dana returned to her home room to pack up her books, she found the note. It was tucked discreetly in the corner of her desk. Handwritten on cream-coloured paper with a border of gold spirals, it contained an urgent message.

Time is running out. The worlds are drifting apart. You must restore the gateways on Hallowe'en or they will be closed forever. You are not alone. The Companions of Faerie are with you. Please let us help you!

The letter wasn't signed but Dana was certain of its author. She sniffed at the paper. There was a faint smell of apples. She wished she could show it to Jean, but he had already left for hockey practice. A few students lingered in the classroom, preparing to leave. Ms Woods sat at her desk, blond head bent over test papers, apparently busy. But Dana could see the suspense in her posture, as if she were holding her breath.

Dana read the note again. Could she believe it? She had been told long ago there were friends of Faerie in Canada, including the High Queen's twin sister. Ms Woods didn't look anything like Honor. It could be a trick, another attempt by her enemy to get her alone. What about the deadline? That was disturbing. Hallowe'en was only four weeks away. While Dana hoped to find *The Book of Dreams* as soon as possible, she wasn't aware that time was an issue. Edane hadn't mentioned it. But then, Dana winced, her mother wasn't exactly the most reliable source.

Again she glanced at Ms Woods. She was torn with doubt. If her teacher had knowledge of the mission wasn't it best to find out? But what if this was a trap? And even if it wasn't, did Dana really want her help? The thought of someone else involved in the quest didn't appeal to her. She preferred it was just herself and Jean.

Ms Woods looked up hopefully as Dana approached her desk, but the smile died on her face as the girl hurried past.

Dana had made up her mind. She would talk to Jean first. Together they would decide what to do about the note.

Going home on the subway, she kept a lookout as always for the little man. Would he ever show up again? Had she imagined he was special? Now that she had met Jean and his friends, now that she was deep in a Canadian fairy tale, she viewed the world around her with different eyes. There *was* magic here. Knowing that, she looked for it everywhere, in the dark tunnels of the subway, on the crowded city streets, in the green patches of park. As usual it played hide-and-seek, a veiled presence lingering at the edges of reality.

Dana left the subway at Spadina station. From there it was only a short walk home to Brunswick Avenue. But as soon as she stepped outside the station doors, she was struck by a blast of wind and music. She stood stock-still, a wolf catching the scent. Silvery notes winged through the air. It was an Irish tune. No, not quite. There was something different about it. She hurried towards the sound.

At the major intersection of Bloor and Spadina, the early rush hour traffic had begun. Cars jammed the road, people crowded the sidewalks. On the other side of the road across from Dana was a small square. White flagstones were laid around a grassy knoll planted with young trees. Scattered over the flagstones was a sculpture of huge black dominoes. They were set out as if for giants to play, some end to end, others in a pile. Wooden benches bordered the square and there was a space marked out for street performers.

The musicians were out of sight behind a wall of people who had gathered to listen. Dana strained to see them as she waited impatiently for the lights to change. Their music echoed infectiously. A tumult of merry reels, jigs and hornpipes rang out over the noisy traffic. Suddenly Dana caught sight of a familiar figure in the crowd. Despite the blue jeans and leather jacket, she would have known her anywhere. Honor, the High Queen of Faerie! How did she get here?!

Dana waved wildly to catch her attention. Would the lights *never* change?

She was certain Honor had seen her, but when at last the light turned green and Dana raced across the road, there was no sign of the High Queen. Had she imagined her?

Dana's disappointment was quickly dispelled when she caught sight of the musicians.

Shabbily dressed in jeans and old sweaters, the three men were remarkably ugly in an interesting way. All were of stocky build and very short, no more than five feet, with bulbous noses and bulging eyes. The fiddler's hair was a crane's nest of red curls with a bushy beard to match. The tin whistler's ponytail was a piebald black-and-grey. The drummer, who played a hand-held *bodhran,* was as bald as an egg. All of them had tufts of hair growing from their ears and nostrils.

Their music was fast and frenetic. They played as if their lives depended upon it. In a dazzling display of virtuosity, tune chased after tune without stopping for breath. The tin whistle trilled like birds at dawn. The drum rumbled like thunder. The fiddler's bow skipped over taut strings, a dancer leaping.

Standing in a half-moon around the musicians, the audience jiggled and jittered like puppets on a string.

"Ize the bye!" someone shouted and everyone cheered.

"Newfies go home!" cried a lout from an apartment balcony up the street.

He quickly retreated when some of the crowd shook their fists at him.

Oblivious to the discord, the red-haired fiddler was bent almost double as he strained and sweated over his instrument. He finished the medley of airs with a frenzied flourish. There was an uproar of applause. Coins cascaded into his open case.

Dana edged to the front of the crowd. The little men were so comical she wanted to laugh. Then the fiddler caught her eye. The look he gave her drew her up short, as if they shared a secret. When he started the next tune, he gave her a quick nod and a wink to let her know it was for her.

First came a shivery quiver across the fiddle strings. Then a high-pitched whoop. Suddenly the three men burst into song. Their voices were rousing yet melodic. The words and the music rushed towards Dana like a wave to engulf her.

> *Cold wind on the harbour*
> *And rain on the road*
> *Wet promise of winter*
> *Brings recourse to coal*
> *There's fire in the blood*
> *And a fog on Bras d'Or*

THE GIANT WILL RISE WITH THE MOON.

She was no longer standing on a street in Toronto. She was somewhere else. A damp green place cupped by a range of low hills. Behind her, a grey sea crashed on the shore. She could smell salt and seaweed. The taste of salt was on her lips. In the first sweep of joy, she thought she had been transported back home to Ireland. Then she caught the sharp scent of pine in the air. The hills were cloaked with fir. The landscape was more bleak and rugged than any she knew.

> *The wind's in the North*
> *There'll be new moon tonight*
> *And we have no circle to dance in her sight*
> *So light a torch, bring the bottle*
> *And build the fire bright.*

THE GIANT WILL RISE WITH THE MOON.

It was early evening. The light was dusky but no stars were out. On her right, in the distance, was a scatter of houses. To her left, a rough road meandered into the hills. Her eyes followed the worn path that wove from the road to the highest peak in the hills. Her heart beat quickly. On top of the hill was an ancient stone circle. Jagged rocks stood out against the sky like the silhouette of a great crown. At their heart burned a bonfire. Illumined by the flames, the stones flickered fitfully. Dana blinked. The stones were men, short stocky men similar to the street musicians! They were singing and shouting and waving bottles in the air.

> *'Twas the same ancient fever*
> *In the Isles of the Blest*
> *That our fathers brought with them*
> *When they went West*
> *It's the blood of the Druids*
> *That never will rest.*

THE GIANT WILL RISE WITH THE MOON.

Dana was back on the sidewalk in Toronto. The musicians had finished their song and were packing up to leave. She ran over to the fiddler as he closed his case.

"Wait!" she cried. "Please."

The three stopped what they were doing to stare at her. All had grey eyes, cold and glittering, like the sea in her vision. Though she was looking down at them since they barely reached her chin, Dana had the sudden sensation that they were truly immense. As tall as the stones on the hill top. She was completely unnerved. How could she have thought them comical?!

"I . . . I'm going on a journey," she stuttered.

They continued to stare without speaking.

"But I don't know where I'm going," she said desperately.

Still they kept silent, their faces stony.

"The song you were singing, about the giant?"

"It be one of Stan Rogers," the fiddler spoke at last.

"Where does he live?" she asked.

"He don't bide here no more," came the answer.

Looks were exchanged between the musicians, a mingling of sorrow and gladness.

Dana could have cried with frustration. It was obvious they weren't going to divulge their secrets. She had already taken out some money to give them. She handed it to the fiddler. Regardless of their reticence, she was grateful for the music.

The red-haired man grinned with mischief.

"Ho byes. A generous hand, a generous heart. When I thinks about it, maybe we ought to tell her what she wants to know."

The drummer shook his head.

"You knows it ain't like that. We can't do no more."

The tin whistler agreed.

"You can't get blood from a stone, that's for darn sure."

Dana caught her breath. She was sure they knew something. Why did everything always have to be so tricky?

"Why are you here?" she demanded. "Do you know me? Are you Companions of Faerie?"

She was met with blank looks. The drummer let out a giggle.

"A little birdie told us all about ye."

She was about to ask more questions when the fiddler raised his hand.

"Now, lass. What can be said is said and was said in the song. You seen The Place of Stones in the music. You'll know it when you sees it in the world."

Their faces convinced her they could not be swayed. Still, she was beginning to understand that they had given her more than she thought. The song was the clue. What was the place mentioned? She had heard them say "Bradore." It sounded French. Somewhere in Quebec? She would have to ask Jean.

"Go raibh maith agaibh," said Dana, thanking them in her own language.

They nudged each other, pleased with the words, but it was evident they were impatient to leave. The tin whistler kept looking at his watch. The drummer was thirstily eyeing the Irish pub up the street. He tipped his cap in farewell and off he went, dashing across the road against a red light.

"Good luck to ye," mumbled the drummer before bounding after him.

The fiddler hesitated.

"Don't be afeard where ye go, lass," he told her kindly. "The morning star shines on my own countrye."

Then he too darted across the road, dodging the traffic and ignoring the blare of horns from irate drivers. Arms and legs akimbo, he held his fiddle above his head as if he were forging a river. When he reached the other side he turned back to her, beaming.

"Mind now," he shouted, "we are all family!"

Dana could hardly wait to get home to ring Jean with the news.

"Bras d'Or?" he repeated. "*Oui, je connais.* It's not Québec, *non.* It's a big lake on Île Royale. Cape Breton Island. I never see this place but I think you are going to like it. They say it look like Scotland and also your country."

"Where the morning star shines on my own countrye," Dana said softly. "Yes, we'll go there."

They were over the moon. They had a destination.

"So how we do this?" said Jean.

"There's someone who might help."

Dana told him about the note from their teacher.

"This is strange, eh?" he said. "But remember she try to talk with you? What do you think?"

"I'm not sure I trust her, but between the two of us we should be able to tell if she's an enemy or not. One could ask questions while the other watches her reactions."

"Good cop, bad cop?" Jean suggested.

"Something like that," Dana laughed.

"Bon," said Jean. "We do this tomorrow."

As it turned out, Ms Woods had already moved to help them as Dana discovered when Gabriel came home.

"Your teacher rang this afternoon. Radhi got the call before she went to work. Something about a field trip this weekend? Did you forget to tell us?"

Dana was too surprised to answer right away, but her father didn't notice.

"That rules out Thanksgiving in Creemore. Your Gran will be disappointed but it gets me off the hook, *buíochas le Dia.* Don't repeat that."

"So," said Dana, recovering, "can I go?"

"Sure. It sounds good and I can't believe there's no cost. She says she's looking after transportation and everything. Talk about last-minute arrangements. Do you have a list of things to bring?"

"No, but I know what I need. The usual stuff."

Dana's head was spinning. Between the musicians and Ms Woods, things were happening fast. It seemed forces were moving at last to help her. Or was it that she had finally let them? The words of Lord Ganesh echoed through her mind. *Your gods are all around you, child of Faerie, you need but open your heart.*

She rang Jean back immediately only to find he was about to call her. His parents had come home with the same news.

"*Bon.* We take the help she give us, but tomorrow we go to her. We see who she is, what she is."

Alas, however, they never got the chance. For earlier that day Gwen Woods had met Grimstone.

CHAPTER TWENTY

T HE DAY GWEN WAS OFFERED THE
teaching job at Dana's school, she went straight to Laurel to tell
her the news. The porter at Massey College recognized her and
waved her through the gates. As she hadn't called ahead, she caught
Laurel off guard. There was no time for the other to hide her
tears or her red and swollen eyes.

Laurel kept the door half-closed.

"I need to be alone," she mumbled.

"I don't think so," Gwen said firmly.

By the time they were both sitting down with cups of green
tea, Laurel was ready to talk.

"I just can't help thinking about it," she said. "If everyone in
Ireland was attacked, then Ian would have been too. He could be
lying somewhere in a coma, or worse."

Gwen nodded with sympathy. The thought had occurred to
her also, but she had kept it to herself so as not to upset Laurel.

"He could also be safely in Faerie," she pointed out. "You said
he lives in both worlds. If he was there when the portals went
down, he'd be stuck on the other side."

Laurel nodded and blew her nose.

"That's what I tell myself on good days."

Gwen glanced around the room. Given that Laurel was a
perfectionist, the state of disorder spoke volumes. Clothes were

strewn on the floor. Books and papers lay everywhere. Obviously this was not a good day. On the desk was a photograph in a jewelled frame which Gwen hadn't seen before. The young man was striking, with raven-black hair, pale features and the startling blue eyes of Faerie. He looked thoughtful and moody, like an Irish poet.

"Ireland's a small place," she said. "Do you want me to ask Dara about it? Maybe he and Granny can do some kind of search, with or without magic. I'm sorry, I should have thought about that before."

"You have enough to think about," Laurel said, "and so do they. The mission is the important thing."

"Ian's important too," Gwen argued. "Everyone is." She put her arm around her friend's shoulder. "We have to hold onto our hopes and dreams. It's the only way we'll get through this. Isn't that what the mission is all about?"

Laurel sighed and nodded. "My hope and my dream is to see him again."

"That a girl," said Gwen. "Are you ready for some good news?"

Laurel was delighted to hear about the job. Like Gwen, she felt the tide had turned in their favour at last.

"You'll be Dana's teacher!" she exclaimed. "That can't be a coincidence!"

"There's no such thing as coincidence," they said together and laughed.

"It'll be a piece of cake to approach her now," Gwen said. "She's far more likely to trust her teacher than some stranger off the street."

Dara was also overjoyed when she rang him with the news. All of them needed a boost to their spirits. Despite every effort to date, Granny had been unable to counter the spell that held the Irish Companions in its grip. Katie and Matt were still unconscious and she and Dara were still blind. Nor had she divined a way to restore the gateways. Though her auguries continued to point to Dana, they showed little else.

"The situation's hopeless but not dire," Dara said with typical humour. "We're working away. Granny's the brain and I'm the dogsbody. She has me out on the road at all hours, getting lashin's of this and lashin's of that. I can't drive, but I've got two feet and a cane. Don't I know the island like the back of my hand?"

Given the Enemy's attacks against them, both Granny and Dara agreed that the Canadian Companions should join up with Dana. But Gwen's plans to make immediate contact died her first morning on the job. The girl was not only absent that day, apparently she had been since school began. When Gwen made enquiries in the office, she was handed reports on an illness and a car accident with doctors' notes attached.

"No wonder we couldn't reach her!" Laurel said when Gwen told her. "Is she all right? Do you think she was attacked?"

"I don't know," Gwen said uncertainly. "The two medical reports didn't sound serious. Could it just be a coincidence? You know the party line on that. We'll have to wait till she returns to school. They said it should be soon."

The day Dana arrived back in the classroom, Gwen saw instantly that their fears were confirmed. The girl was pale and fragile-looking, like a porcelain doll, and her eyes had a haunted look. There was no doubt that she had suffered some trauma. Though she seemed both shocked and relieved to see a new teacher, she also kept looking around. Was she afraid, or searching for someone?

From the front of the class, an astute teacher can tell a lot about her students. The faces turned towards her reveal so much about their feelings and attitudes, the ease or hardship of their lives. Some are bright with laughter and mischief, others sullen or rebellious. There are those who look perpetually bored, in contrast to the ones who demand to be challenged and stimulated. Then there are those whose features are closed like a door. For whatever reason, usually painful, they just want to be left alone.

It was to this category that Dana belonged, Gwen saw that immediately. The girl was evidently a loner with no friends in the class. Despite her long absence, no one greeted her or asked how she was. She went quickly to the back of the room and slumped into her desk. At lunch time, she sat by herself in the cafeteria, reading a book.

From the day Gwen started her job, she had been conducting interviews with her students to get to know them. She decided to use that as an opportunity to be alone with Dana and casually introduce the subject of Faerie. Since the girl was shy and withdrawn, Gwen knew she needed to tread carefully, but she was not prepared for an outright refusal.

"You want to interview me alone without my parents' consent? Sorry, it's not on."

Before Gwen could recover, Dana had sped down the hall.

"Something to do with her last teacher?" Laurel suggested that evening when they met for supper to discuss the situation.

Laurel was picking her way through a Caesar salad. Gwen had a big plate of spaghetti *alla carbonara,* with a creamy sauce and strips of smoked pancetta.

"Definitely," said Gwen. "I did a little detective work in the staff room. His name was Grimstone and he sounded pretty grim all right. No one liked him. In fact, I got the distinct impression they were afraid of him. Seems his disappearance was a relief to everyone."

"He held the school for the Enemy!"

Gwen nodded. "It gets worse. He was a last-minute substitute. The teacher who should've been there was murdered."

Laurel was shocked.

"Gwen, you've got to be careful."

"I am, don't worry. I'm up to the yin yang in protective charms, plus I've put them around the school. The place is clear now, I guess with him gone. But do you see the good of this? Grimstone has disappeared and Dana is still here. Whatever happened to her, she survived, while he's gone. Looks to me like we're being helped."

"Could she have fought him off herself? She is the Light-Bearer."

Gwen was scooping up the rich sauce with her spoon.

"I'd like to think that, but from the looks of her I can't. She's no warrior. She's the weak and nervous type. There's no sense of power there at all. No wonder your sister was worried."

"Then she needs us. We've got to join her. We're running out of time."

"I don't want to rush things and scare her off," Gwen said worriedly. "She won't trust anyone after being attacked—especially her teacher!"

"Maybe I should talk to her?" was Laurel's proposal, though she didn't look happy about it. "Since I look like Honor . . ."

Gwen saw the grimace. It didn't bode well. The girl needed to be handled sensitively.

"Give me a few days," she suggested to Laurel's relief.

The waiter with the dessert cart was on the far side of the room. Gwen waved him over, quashing the other's efforts to decline.

"This is my treat. Don't be a kill-joy. We're celebrating my first real pay cheque as a full-time teacher. And none of your low-fat nonsense," she added.

Laurel laughed and gave in.

As they tucked into dishes of Italian ice cream with chocolate wafers, Gwen brought up the new topic as tactfully as she could.

"Granny says she might be able to help with Ian though she can't make any promises. She needs something personal of his. Do you—?"

"Yes," Laurel admitted, looking away with embarrassment. "I have one of his shirts. Oh God, this is so—"

"And it's a good thing you do too," Gwen said matter-of-factly, "or she wouldn't be able to work the spell. Now eat up all those calories so we can go back to your place and get it. I'll send it by courier. The sooner Granny has it, the sooner she can try to find him."

Gwen's tone helped Laurel to regain her composure.

"Thank you," she said quietly.

"What are friends for?"

The next day at school, Gwen was astonished to see the difference in Dana. The girl looked transformed! Though she still sat in the back and kept to herself, her aloofness was suddenly dignified, even queenly. She had lost the haunted look. There was an air about her of quiet triumph, as if she had accomplished something important. She also looked immensely pleased with herself, like the cat that got the cream. In the days that followed, Gwen saw the steady increase in strength and vitality. The girl's features seemed to glow. At the same time, Dana became more evasive and wily. No matter how often Gwen tried to cross her path or speak to her in private, Dana slipped away. She was adept at escaping, disappearing around corners, out of classrooms, down hallways.

"As elusive as a fairy," Gwen told Laurel.

They had been taking turns watching over the girl. Like guardian angels, they followed her from home to school and back again, to make certain she was safe.

Though they didn't admit it, they were also spying.

Gwen now believed that Dana had a mission, that somehow, someone, somewhere had set her on the quest to restore the gateways. All the changes in the girl pointed to it. There was a definite air of determination and purpose.

Laurel wasn't convinced.

"How could she know anything? The portals are down. There's no contact with Faerie. If there were, we'd have heard by now."

Gwen recognized the logic of Laurel's argument but nonetheless she trusted her instincts. Dana was questing and growing from it. If only the girl would let them in!

Gwen's opening came the day Jean returned to school. She knew one of her students had been mugged, but she didn't connect him to Dana right away. When he first entered the classroom, he didn't even look at the girl. It was at lunch time, when Gwen was passing the cafeteria, that she saw them together. Her attention had been caught by the sound of wild laughter. She was so surprised to see Dana with a friend that she stopped and stared. It was Jean, the boy who was attacked! Gwen's mind raced. Was he involved then? She studied Dana. The girl looked flushed and happy. In an instant Gwen saw the relationship and knew what it meant. She could have been looking at herself and Dara the first time they met, brought together by a Faerie mission. She felt an ache in her heart, but she was glad. Her instincts were right. Dana *was* on the quest and not only that, she had a companion.

It was time to act. With some trepidation she decided to approach them. She would have to talk fast. Teachers rarely entered the student cafeteria and she didn't want an audience. At the same time, she needed to convince the two that she was on their side and ready to help them.

Dana's rebuff was so forceful it took Gwen's breath away. This was not the weak and nervous girl who wasn't fit for a quest! The rejection notwithstanding, Gwen was delighted by the show of strength. She looked from Dana to Jean, liking what she saw in the young man's features. Here was strength of character and someone who could be trusted. Though she was disappointed they wouldn't speak to her, she was pleased. Together they inspired confidence. There was hope for the mission.

Laurel brushed aside Gwen's certainty that the two were on the quest.

"No offence to your instincts, Gwen, but we need something tangible. *Give me the facts, ma'am, just the facts.* She knows the portals are down since she, like us, would be cut off from Faerie. And she obviously knows the Enemy is after her, if she has been attacked. Maybe she knows something, maybe she's growing stronger, but it's still imperative that we find out if she has the power and knowledge to restore the gateways.

"Our job is to watch over her," Gwen argued, "and to assist her if we can. But the mission is hers, not ours. If she doesn't want our help, we can't force her. We have to trust she's up to the task. It's her destiny."

"You're wearing your rose-coloured glasses again. You're seeing what you want to see."

"That's unfair," Gwen protested.

She was hurt by the remark, but Laurel was relentless.

"Fair or not, time is against us. I say grab Dana by the scruff of the neck and find out what she knows. If you don't, I will. This can't go on any longer. We've been sensitive enough for her sake. The mission is more important than any of us."

It wasn't the first disagreement they had over strategy but it was the worst. Laurel's tone was belligerent. Gwen felt cornered.

"All right. I've got an idea. I'll write her a note. If that doesn't work, you can confront her yourself."

"Fine," said Laurel and she hung up the phone.

Gwen sighed as she stared at the receiver. She missed the Company of Seven. Laurel was not the easiest person to work with sometimes.

The handmade paper was a gift from Dara. The golden spirals were a Faerie design. Gwen took time to frame her note, then wrote it with quill and ink. It was important that her words were strong and true, that the message appealed to Dana. As a last flourish, she sprinkled the envelope with her favourite apple-scented perfume.

When Gwen arrived in class the next morning, she noticed immediately that Jean had changed desks to sit beside Dana. The two were deep in conversation, oblivious to everyone else around them. It wasn't Gwen's nature to eavesdrop, especially on young people whose privacy was sacrosanct, but she couldn't help herself. Sidling along the outside aisle, she took more time than was necessary to open the window near them.

She heard very little before Dana spotted her, but it was enough. She was elated. Confirmation at last! Dana *was* on the mission and so too was Jean. They had been discussing how to get away for the long weekend. Here was the opportunity Gwen had been hoping for, the chance to show her good faith and gain their confidence.

As soon as she was free, Gwen called Laurel. Together they devised a plan. Gwen would arrange "a school trip" for Dana and Jean. She had the money to finance their travels and she would accompany them. Between the note declaring her a Companion of Faerie and real assistance, they were bound to accept her.

"You'll miss Thanksgiving," Laurel said sheepishly. She was feeling guilty about their row the night before, especially since the other had been proven right. Gwen being Gwen, of course, didn't say 'I told you so.' "Maybe we should flip a coin? Or both go? It's fairer."

"No point two of us missing the turkey," Gwen said. "You told me yourself, your parents are really looking forward to your visit. I see mine regularly. It won't be that big a deal."

"Are you sure?"

"Hey, I'm the one who's off on an adventure. Food isn't everything." Gwen gasped. "Did I say that?"

"You've convinced me now," Laurel laughed. "Okay then, I'm going to head off today to beat the rush on the buses. I expect a full report when I get back."

"You've got it."

"And Gwen?"

"What?"

"Be careful, eh?"

The plan was a good one, but like all plans it wasn't foolproof. With only two days till the weekend, Gwen had to act fast. First things first, she needed parental permission. That was the easy part, a few phone calls. It was her efforts to make contact with the young people that failed disastrously. She had hoped to catch Jean before he went home, but she hadn't counted on his leaving early for hockey practice. The worst came when Dana read the note and hurried from the classroom without looking back.

For a moment Gwen sat stunned, too disappointed to react. Then she grabbed her coat and ran after the girl.

She was well used to tailing Dana from her turn on watch, but today everything conspired to confound her. First the principal stopped Gwen in the hall to have "a little talk" and praise her work. She almost screamed with frustration. That delayed her getting to the subway. Dana's train was already leaving the station as Gwen hurried down the stairs, cursing her high heels. Racing back up the escalator and onto the street, she hailed a cab to Brunswick Avenue. Early rush hour traffic meant slow progress, then the one-way system left her halfway to Dana's house. Throwing money at the driver, she jumped out of the taxi. One quick look around and she saw the emergency. She had arrived just in time.

On her left, a short way up the street, Dana was unconcernedly walking home. To her right, near a large abandoned convent, something was taking shape in a gurge of grey matter.

Something wicked this way comes.

She wasn't sure what she was looking at, but she could see it was all wrong. The smear of grey coalesced into a human shape, tall and pale with hideously scarred features. But it wasn't human. Out of its body writhed great tentacles like tumid worms. Gwen caught the smell. A sickening odour that clawed at her throat. She didn't stop to think. The ghastly face was turned towards Dana. The hatred in its eyes was shocking to see. She didn't have to be told that it was about to attack the girl. Before it could move, Gwen ran to fight it.

Grimstone was caught off guard. He knew he had to reach Dana before she got to her house. Her home was under the protection of One far more powerful than he. Intent on catching her on the street, he didn't see Gwen till she barrelled into him.

He didn't know who or what Gwen was and he didn't care. All he sensed was an adversary whom he had to kill. Though she was kicking and flailing, he soon caught her in his grip. His glee turned quickly to contempt. She was only human, hardly worth the effort. She had no strength, no weapons, no fairy blood.

He moved with horrible speed, dragging her to the yard behind the convent. He didn't want to be disturbed while he enjoyed himself killing her. He took a cold delight in the fact that he would do the deed on once hallowed ground.

"You dare to challenge me?"

Gwen shuddered at the sound of his voice, so dead and remorseless.

"I'll dispatch you with enough time left for the fairy girl. Then I'll murder her too."

The tentacles coiled around Gwen's body like that of an octopus. A quick grip and a snap was what he intended. There was no time for the slow play of torture. It would be over in seconds.

"Not on my watch," Gwen hissed through clenched teeth.

She wasn't weak nor was she powerless. She was well-equipped with protective charms. To combat a creature like this, it was better than packing a pistol. She had already taken the first charm from her pocket. It was clutched in her hand, a little sprig of holly with dark-red thread. Before the monster could tighten his grip, she released the charm and uttered the spell.

Let the briar that spreads, let the thorn that grows, pierce and perish your flesh.

Though she had barely managed to croak out the words, the effect was instant.

Grimstone released her with a screech and fell to the ground, squirming in agony. Every part of him was pierced with fairy thorns. The tentacles flayed the air. He was maddened by the pain.

Staggering to her feet, Gwen grasped the next charm. She knew the battle had only begun. Though it was a long time since she had fought for her life, she was ready to do it. She could feel her adrenaline rushing, her courage rising. Once a warrior in Faerie, always a warrior.

The second charm comprised dried leaves and flowers in a pouch of woven hemp. Gathered on May Eve, these were seven herbs which nothing natural or supernatural could injure: vervain, St John's Wort, speedwell, eyebright, mallow, yarrow and valerian. Quickly, she shook them into her palm. They had to be taken separately—one by one—to obtain their power. Would she have time? As soon as she swallowed the blade of yarrow, she felt it course through her veins. She was instantly stronger. Now for the speedwell. Yes! Her limbs tingled. She could move more swiftly. The eyebright would improve her sight and reflexes if only—

Grimstone had recovered. He charged at her. His rage was palpable. He was burning with it. Smoke rose from the pavement where he passed. He had underestimated his opponent. He was about to correct that mistake. The moment he saw what she was doing, he lashed out furiously. The tentacles whipped through the air, each one a sharp and deadly weapon.

The speedwell helped Gwen to dodge the full impact, but she couldn't avoid them all. One tentacle sliced across her face to gash her forehead. Blood ran into her eyes. The world went red. Another whistled through the air and tore at her hand.

She let out a cry.

The pouch of magical herbs was ripped from her fingers.

She reached for her last weapon to fight in earnest. A thin switch of hazel, peeled bare and white, she wore it tucked into her belt like a dagger. Now she brandished it like a sword. Springing forward with a cry, she attacked the monster, laying into him with her own deadly fury.

Back and forth they moved in a dance of death.

Gwen darted with the swiftness the speedwell gave her while the yarrow strengthened her arm as she smote and jabbed. Whenever she landed a blow with the wand, Grimstone shrieked in agony. Sacred and powerful, the hazel had secret properties that defied all demons. Though Gwen herself knew little of its mysteries, she was a trueheart and a braveheart and she used it well.

But the monster was a mystery too, if a dark and loathsome one, and it had power of its own. The Enemy had not sent a fledgling to do its evil work. The thing that had taken the name of Grimstone was much older and more terrible than Gwen could have known. Despite the grave injuries she inflicted upon him, slowly but surely he gained the upper hand.

Gwen continued to fight valiantly. Long before she had begun to lose, she knew she had won. Dana was safe at home and out of harm's reach. Gwen had done her duty, she had served the cause well. Her king would be proud of her.

She knew her time was coming. Despite the strength of the yarrow, her arm grew tired. Despite the swiftness of the speedwell, her steps began to falter. The hazel would work its magic as long as she could wield it, but the time was near when it would drop from her hand.

Grimstone's blows rained relentlessly down. Gwen could no longer fend them off. She staggered beneath their force. The pain was unbearable. The tears fell without shame for a life lost too young.

Now her arms fell to her side. Now the monster coiled around her once more.

She felt his rage, his ravening hunger. There would be no mercy.

But even as he choked the breath from her body, she let out a last cry.

Come merciful word, singing word and the good word also. May the power of these three holy things set me free from evil.

Her words shimmered in the air like silver. For a moment the monster drew back. The cry rang out like the song of larks in the clear air. A clarion call to all that was bright and beautiful.

But it was only a moment. With implacable malice, Grimstone bore down. The stink was overwhelming. The foul smell of the murderer. Gwen felt herself falling backwards into darkness. Her heart fluttered wildly like a bird in its death throes. As her eyes closed on the world, she whispered the name of the one she loved most, her greatest grief in parting.

Dara.

CHAPTER TWENTY-ONE

THE NEXT MORNING AT SCHOOL, DANA AND Jean were surprised to find their teacher absent. They exchanged glances when the vice-principal hurried into the room, flustered and annoyed. No explanation was given as he took the class, but it was obvious that something had happened.

"What's this?" said Jean at lunch. "You think she run away from us?"

Dana was mystified.

"It doesn't make sense. She sent the note and called our parents. That seems to prove she's on our side. But then she didn't mention *The Book of Dreams*. So she doesn't know about the quest, yet she knows about the gateways. That could put her in the Enemy's camp. And what about the Hallowe'en deadline? My mother didn't say anything about it."

Jean looked equally confused and uncertain.

"She can be bad, she can be good. Maybe she try to help us? Maybe she try to trap us? How do we know?"

"We don't," Dana said, thinking about it, "until she turns up again. But I think we should go this weekend. We'd be following Grandfather's advice and the three musicians. I trust *them*."

"*D'accord*. We take the time she give us and when she come back we see what happen."

Though Dana was happy with their decision, still she was

unsettled. She couldn't shake the feeling that something was wrong. What could their teacher's disappearance mean? Was she in trouble? Should they do something about it? But what could they do? Who could they tell?

"If we go tomorrow," Jean was saying, "that give us *biens le temps,* many time to go to Cape Breton."

"We should take sleeping bags," she suggested, "and maybe some food. Bring everything to school. Our parents will take for granted we're leaving from here."

Once they began making plans for the trip, Dana forgot about Ms Woods. The thrill of adventure was in her blood. That Jean was going with her made it all the sweeter.

The following day, at the end of school, they collected their things from their lockers. As they planned to retrieve the spirit boat at dusk, they went out for supper.

In the restaurant, Dana suffered an attack of shyness. This was too like a date. Sitting across from Jean, she did her best to look calm. They decided to share a pizza with pepperoni and ham on his half, olives and green peppers on hers.

"In Ireland you get sweet corn on your pizza," she told him.

"Câlisse," he shuddered.

Then he ordered garlic bread for two.

"If one eat garlic, it is necessary *all* eat garlic," he told her with a wink.

She blushed to the roots of her hair and changed the subject quickly.

"Do you feel bad lying to your parents?"

He considered her question seriously.

"Non. For them, the truth is not good. I can't tell my life as *loup-garou* or what happen to *grand-père.* It's more pain for them. *Et toi?"*

Dana sighed. "Sometimes I wish I could share the magic with my dad and especially my stepmother. But the dangerous stuff rules that out. They would only worry and try to stop me. In the end, it's better that I keep it to myself."

She looked a little sad. Jean understood. He knew the loneliness of living with secrets. Her hand was resting on the table. He reached out to clasp it and they stayed that way till their food arrived.

As the sun began to set behind the city towers, they made their way to the Humber Marshes. Once they had taken the witch canoe from the bushes and clambered aboard, they soon left Toronto far behind them.

It was different this time, Dana realized that immediately. It was much easier to run *la chasse-galerie*. Their last journey had bonded them like true *voyageurs*. They paddled like a team, as if with one mind. Though the dark stream of the boat's demonic force struggled against them, they kept it firmly in check. With almost effortless ease, they steered due east.

Dana knelt in the bow, gazing ahead. It would be up to her, once they reached Cape Breton, to recognize the place she had seen in the music. But before then, they had a long journey ahead of them.

High in the atmosphere, the wind was biting. She had bundled up warmly in her parka with scarf and mittens. When they were preparing to leave, Jean had pulled a knitted cap over her head and ears. It was similar to the one he wore himself, with a long tapering end.

"*Tuque québécoise*," he declared. "The best thing for the head!"

"I brought a thermos of hot chocolate."

"Like we go on a bus?"

They laughed.

They were flying away from the setting sun into the dark night of the east. Ahead of them lay the great province of Quebec and the St Lawrence Seaway, the mighty waterway that would be their route.

"Tell me stories about your country," Dana called back to Jean. "In Ireland we say that a song or a story shortens the road."

"I have *beaucoup*," he warned her. "*Mon grand-père* and before she die, *ma grand-mère*, they tell me many story."

"I want to hear them," she assured him.

He told her tales of John the Bear, *Teur-Merisier, Talon-Rouge* and Ti-Jean the Giant-Killer, after whom he suspected he was named. There were also tales of the devil—*le Diable, beau danseur*—who seemed to have a penchant for French-Canadian parties and dances. He would always appear as a dark handsome stranger, richly dressed with a fine beaver cloak and an ebony cane. In the heart of winter, he drove a magnificent sleigh pulled by a glossy black horse with silver bells and harness. The prettiest maid at the dance or party would inevitably be fatally attracted to him But just as he was about to carry her off and steal her soul, some innocent would unmask him, usually a child. They would prove that he was limping because of his cloven hoof, or they would show where the floor had been burnt where he was dancing. Then the Devil's game was up and he would be chased away as everyone made the Sign of the Cross and the *curé* came running.

Jean made her laugh as he described the games his *grand-mère* taught him as a child: *arracher la souche,* pulling up the stump, *sauter le rapide,* shooting the rapids, *plonger le loup marin,* diving like a seal.

"She come from Notre Dame d'Île Verte," he said. "I show you when we pass."

"Our Lady of the Green Isle," Dana translated. "That's beautiful."

"Now you tell the story," he insisted, "or sing *une chanson irlandaise.*"

"This is like a road trip with my Da."

She was about to take her turn with a song when she noticed something strange below. The land seemed to have patches of darkness and light, as if it were day in one place and night in another. The more she gazed down, the more confused she grew. She wasn't sure what she was looking at. There were moments when she saw things she couldn't possibly see from that far up, as if she were only metres away. Then she realized the truth. Like gazing into a crystal ball, she was viewing the land with magical sight. As well as the bright vistas of modern cities and townlands, she could see layers of time on top of each other, as if time itself were a heap of events, a great collection of moments.

"Jean, I can see all kinds of things down there! Is it me or the boat?!"

"*Le canot,*" he said, laughing. "How to explain in English? Remember when you see Étienne Brûlé? This happen sometimes with *la chasse-galerie*. The flying, she make *une ouverture sur le Grands Temps*. A big hole in time? No, I don't mean this."

"An opening in the Great Time." She understood what he meant. "It's the same with Faerie! Time and space go all weird around it. More like a circle than a line or, better still, a spiral."

"*Oui, c'est ça! Exactement!*"

He waved grandly at the panorama below.

"*Regarde, chérie. Regarde mon pays.*"

Running north from the great seaway were strips of land like parallelograms, the old estates of *seigneurs* and *habitants*. This was farmland carved from the ancient forests of New France. Whitewashed houses perched neatly amongst apple orchards and cereal crops. Cows grazed in the pasture, pigs snuffled in their pens. In the fields, women toiled alongside the men. In the air wafted the rich smells of tourtières and stews, along with the sweet sticky scent of maple sugar rising from *les cabanes à sucre*.

As the spirit boat passed over Montreal, another name came whispering through the cobbled streets and around the corners of tall buildings and sidewalk cafés. *Hochelaga.* At the confluence of the Ottawa and St Lawrence rivers, at the foot of a hill not yet called Mont Royal, stood a thriving Iroquois community. Palisaded like a town, with fifty longhouses, it overlooked tilled fields of corn and maize.

On sped the canoe past *Trois-Rivières* and *Cap-de-la-Madeleine* to *la Ville de Québec*. Again the layers peeled away like an onion. Beneath the majestic walls of the city and the great star-shaped fortress called *le Citadel,* Dana could see another settlement. *La Habitation* was a simple quadrangle of wooden buildings with a stockade and moat. It stood on a point where the St Lawrence narrowed, a *kebek* as the Algonkian people called it.

She saw how the Natives kept the first settlers alive, teaching them to grow squash, maize, beans and pumpkins. They also showed the white men where the blueberries grew and how to make maple syrup. Most important of all, in the long cruel winter, they taught them to boil the bark and leaves of *annedda,* the white cedar, to make a brew that fought the deadly scurvy.

"I have a bad feeling about what comes next," Dana said to Jean.

They had both stopped paddling, transfixed by what they saw below, history unfolding like a never-ending story.

"It don't get better," Jean agreed.

A new sound reached the flying canoe. Musket fire and the screams of men. A horrific scene emerged.

On the Plains of Abraham, in the shadow of Quebec City, two armies gathered. Two old countries waging war for new land. Thousands of British troops were mustered on the grassy field below the western walls of the fortress. They had already bombarded and destroyed much of the city. Had the French waited for reinforcements, the outcome might have been different. But they didn't wait. The battle was short and bloody, less than half an hour, and both leaders were killed. General Wolfe lay dead amongst his troops on the battlefield. The Marquis de Montcalm would die from his wounds the next day.

The spirit canoe quivered violently.

"We go!" Jean cried out. *"Vite! Rapidement!"*

Soon they began to notice a pattern. It happened each time the tapestry below wove a tale of death and destruction. Wherever the shadow of the Enemy worked its way through human history, the canoe shuddered with delight. *He was a murderer from the beginning.* Feeding off the darkness below, the demon would gain in strength and ferocity. Then Dana and Jean had to struggle with all their might to keep control of the craft.

The demon was at its worst whenever they encountered the devastation wrought by the settlers on the First Peoples of the land. Without pity or remorse, the Europeans burned villages and crops, enslaved men, women and children, and slaughtered all who opposed them. Sometimes in the crowd of slaves or the bodies of the slain, Dana thought she recognized Grandfather and Roy. She would turn away with shame. She couldn't bear to see.

She felt weighed down by the grief of centuries. Why was human history a trail of tears?

When they passed a small island upstream of Quebec, she felt a sharp pain in her heart. The wooded isle was sculpted with coves and capes. On a rocky promontory overlooking the river stood a high Celtic cross, carved in stone. A tombstone to mark the site of mass graves.

"My people are buried here!" Dana said with sudden knowledge.

The sorrowful sound of keening was carried on the wind, a wake of fiddles and the clatter of bones. *Oileán na nGael.* The Island of the Irish. She heard the whispers of the thousands who perished in this place. Some had crossed the Atlantic in "coffin ships" to escape the Great Famine. Others had come seeking new lives and freedoms. Here they died of disease and malnutrition, meeting death in their dreams.

"I know this *complainte*," Jean told her, for he too heard the music and the whisperings. "This is Grosse Île. There are more graves in Pointe Sainte-Charles. With them lie the French also, the ones who try to help. Like I tell you, *chérie*," he smiled sadly, "the French and the Irish are always good friends."

They continued to follow the St Lawrence as if it were a highway. The great river had yet to freeze and was busy with sea traffic. Amidst the modern vessels, Dana caught sight of ancient canoes and ghost ships.

Now they passed over high cliffs sheering into choppy waters. *Cap au Diable*. And on the south shore, *Rivière-du-Loup*.

". . . *où je suis né!*" called Jean. "Where I am born!"

"What's it like?" Dana asked as she peered down, but they had already passed it.

"I don't know. We move soon after. We move all the time."

"You're a true *voyageur!*"

"*C'est vrai!*"

How long they travelled along that shining seaway, Dana had no idea. Hours seemed to pass like minutes and sometimes a minute contained eternity. Again and again, the land told its tales with all the colour and verve of a local storyteller. Then a silence fell over the country, like a book closed at bedtime, and they paddled on through the darkness beneath the sky of stars.

They heard the gulf before they saw it, a mournful sound in the distance, the plangent murmur of the sea. When they reached the estuary of the Gulf of St Lawrence it looked as wide as an ocean.

Jean steered the canoe south. To their left, in the distance, was the dark silhouette of Île d'Anticosti standing guard at the gateway of the great river's mouth. To their right, ahead of them, was Prince Edward Island. *Abegweit* the Mi'kmaq called it. *Cradle in the waves*.

They had journeyed through a long night towards the rising sun. The waters of the gulf gleamed in fiery splendour. The sky blazed gold. Soon they came in sight of Cape Breton Island.

Dana scanned the rocky landscape and the sea-washed shores. Nothing looked familiar.

"Let's go inland," she suggested, trying not to sound anxious.

What if they had come all this way for nothing? What if they couldn't find The Place of Stones? She suffered a pang of doubt. What if it didn't exist except in a song that she could hardly remember!

They had begun to descend. Jean was looking for a place to land.

"We don't fly near the lake," he warned. "There's fog on Bras d'Or."

His words triggered her memory. Dana recalled the song clearly as if he had just sung it.

There's fire in the blood and a fog on Bras d'Or.

"That's it!" she cried. "A fog over Lake Bras d'Or! We've got to fly through it!"

There was a moment after they sailed into the fog when they both regretted the decision. It was a moment of intense cold and damp and milky blindness. Both were all too aware that a huge deep lake lay somewhere beneath them. If they were going to land on a body of water, they would rather see it first. They held their breaths as they continued to paddle and only released them again when they flew out of the haze.

There in the clear light of day was the place Dana sought.

Where the lake opened its arms to embrace the Atlantic was a little cove with a scattering of houses. The village was sheltered by a ridge of low hills. The highest peak had a crown, a jagged circle of stones.

"That's it!" Dana called out, delighted. "The Place of Stones!"

They landed the canoe on the stony shore of the cove. The air was salty with sea spray. Other boats lay upturned on the stones, small wooden craft painted in bright colours.

"It's like the west of Ireland," said Dana.

"There is nowhere to hide *le canot,*" Jean observed, looking around.

The hills nearby were all grass and grey stone. There were few trees in sight.

"It'll be safe here," she said, thinking of home. "This is fishermen's country."

Though he understood what she meant, Jean wasn't happy. He didn't like leaving the canoe out in the open.

"How about a picnic?" she suggested, to distract him. "It's time for breakfast."

They spread a sleeping bag over the stones and opened their knapsacks. Each had brought supplies for the weekend.

"You never eat meat?" he asked her curiously.

He had rolls of ham and beef, while she had cheese and egg salad sandwiches.

"I won't eat anything that had a face."

"This I can't do," he said with a shrug and he wolfed down his food.

When they had finished their meal, they debated on whether they would rest or explore. After travelling all night, both were pale and bleary-eyed.

"The Place of Stones is on the highest hill," Dana said, surveying the range.

"Maybe we go to the village first, eh?" Jean stifled a yawn. "We see who live there."

"Sounds good to me."

Dana stuffed a few chocolate bars into her pocket, then rolled up the rest of her things in her sleeping bag and stowed them under the canoe. She could keep going for a good while yet. When she was only eleven, she had quested for days through the mountains in Ireland.

Jean was impressed. Here was a girl as keen and able for adventure as he was.

"What?" said Dana, when she caught his look.

"I like we do this together," he said simply.

His words made her smile. Remembering how alone she had been for most of her quest in the mountains, she felt the same way.

Hand in hand, they walked towards the village. Tired they might be, but they were ready for anything.

CHAPTER TWENTY-TWO

İT WAS BARELY A VİLLAGE, A HANDFUL OF SMALL houses perched on the rocks like a scatter of gulls. There were no paths or gardens. The cottages were made of stone wedged together without mortar or cement. Their roofs were thatched, some as tightly as cloth, others less tidily with weeds and wild-flowers sprouting from the eaves. There were lace curtains in the windows and pots of red geranium on the sills. The place had an Irish or Scottish air but where Dana expected to see sods of peat, woodpiles were stacked against the walls. There was no sight or sound of the inhabitants but they were evidently at home. Smoke curled from the chimneys, sweetening the air with the scent of burning wood.

Dana and Jean stopped at the first house and waited uncertainly. The stillness was eerie. When they knocked on the door, no one answered. A big ginger cat sat on the windowsill eyeing them coolly. The door was of the kind Dana had seen in rural Ireland. Built in two pieces, the top could open separately like a window to let in fresh air. The old people would lean on the bottom half and call out to their neighbours who passed on the road.

"Maybe we enter?" Jean suggested. "This look like the kind of place my *grand-mère* say '*la porte est sur la clanche.*'"

"The door is on the latch?" guessed Dana. "That's what the Irish say!"

She hesitated. If the villagers were friendly wouldn't someone have come to meet them by now?

Jean was about to open the door when a voice inside began to sing. The high quavering notes belonged to an old woman, but she had the power to move her listeners. She sang in French, in a strong country accent incomprehensible to Dana. Jean closed his eyes to listen.

Pourquoi me fuir, passagère hirondelle
Ah viens fixer ton vol auprès de moi
Pourquoi me fuir lorsque ma voix t'appelle
Ne suis-je pas en exile comme toi? *

Though she didn't understand the words, Dana felt the sorrow. It was like the pain she had suffered when they flew over Grosse Île.

"Jean, what is it? I feel like crying."

"Naturellement," he said quietly. "It's a story like your peoples. She sing about the Dispersion of the Acadians. Some go to Cape Breton. They don't forget what happen."

The cottage door swung open in front of them though neither had touched it. Inside, a family huddled in the corner. The father was shielding his wife and children. The two little girls were no older than ten. The baby was clutched in his mother's arms. All stared in terror at the door.

Everything happened so quickly, so shockingly, that Jean and Dana could only watch. First came a wave of sound from

---

Why do you fly away from me, little swallow?
Come, take a rest from your flight and settle beside me,
Why fly away when my voice calls to you?
Am I not an exile like you?

behind—screams and cries, gunshot, wood cracking, glass shattering. Then soldiers rushed in, passing through the two as if they were ghosts. With bayonets pointed, the soldiers forced the family out of their home, oblivious to the mother's pleas and the screeches of the children. Then they ravaged the house, smashing furniture and crockery, tearing cloth and curtains. When they were finished, they set it all alight.

> Dans le désert le destin nous rassemble
> Ah ne crains pas de rester près de moi
> Si tu gémis nous gémirons ensemble
> Ne suis-je pas plus à plaindre que toi?*

Stunned by the wanton destruction, Jean and Dana followed the family out onto the road. Everywhere were scenes of mayhem. The air was choked with the acrid smell of a world on fire. Whitewashed farmhouses were burning furiously. Fields of crops were ablaze, crazed animals ran amok. A line of refugees trudged down the road, hundreds of men, women and children, empty-handed and bereft. Many were wounded and bleeding. Some had seen their loved ones murdered in front of them.

No house was spared as more and more families were driven from their homes. The soldiers shouted and cursed in English. The victims cried and pleaded in French.

"They live in Acadie for more than one hundred year," Jean told Dana. "They are farmers, *catholique*. They don't fight against the English but they don't take the oath to the English king. *Alors,*

*Fate brings us together in the wasteland of our misery
Do not be afraid to rest beside me
If you cry, we will cry together.
Am I not more wretched than you?

they must go, in ships without food, without water. They lose their home, their family. Many lose their life. For *eight year* it happen to many thousand of the peoples and no one stop it."

> *Tu revoirras ton ancienne patrie*
> *Le premier nid de ton amour hélas*
> *Un sort cruel qu'on fit ici ma vie*
> *Ne suis-je pas plus a plaindre que toi?*★

Dana's heart ached as she watched the stream of human tragedy, ordinary people in the wrong place at the wrong time.

Would this war never end?

She grasped Jean's arm.

"Are they all gone?"

"Non," he said, looking a little less devastated. "Some come back to Canada. They suffer much, but they survive. Many go to *Amérique.* You know this word 'Cajun'?"

"You mean the music? My dad loves it."

"Music, food, stories," Jean nodded. "Cajun is *Cadien. Acadien.* The Cajuns are . . . *comment dit-on?* . . . the children of the children of—?"

"Descendants?"

"Oui. C'est ça. They are the descendants of the Acadian who survive in *Amérique."*

"Not all that is gone is gone forever," Dana murmured.

As the scene dispelled like mist around them, they found themselves standing once more at the door of the cottage. The

---

★*You will see your homeland again*
  Your first beloved nest. Alas
  It's my sorry lot to make my life here
  Am I not more wretched than you?

voice within had stopped singing. The half-door opened. An old woman peered out at them. She was grey-haired and regal, with gaunt features and dark lively eyes. Her nose was hooked like a beak, her clothes were black. She wore a feathery shawl around her shoulders.

"I am the *Cailleach Beinne Bric,*" she said brusquely. "You are welcome to Ailsa Craig. Come in, sit you down."

The cottage was a single-room dwelling with whitewashed walls and a loft overhead reached by a ladder. A cavernous hearth dominated one end of the room. A black cauldron hung on a hook over the fire. Half the space was domestic with an old settee, table and chairs, and a wooden dresser filled with dishes. The other half, near to the door, was a makeshift shop and pub. A high counter fronted shelves of tinned goods, dried herbs, rolls of twine and various tools. Bunches of onions and garlic hung from the ceiling. There were stools at the counter and chairs nearby. The floor was checkered with black and red flagstones, worn and swept.

Dana and Jean sat down near the fire while the old woman made tea in a black kettle. She moved with an ungainly grace, kicking her long skirt in front of her. When she poured the tea, it trickled out like treacle, a dark-brown mixture with leaves floating on top. Once dollops of cream and sugar were added, it was surprisingly good.

"Did ye ever hear the tale of tea?" she asked them, eyes bright with mischief. "When 'twas first brought from China, the people of Europe hadn't a notion what to do with it. They boiled up the leaves, threw away the liquid and ate it like cabbage."

She made a face and pretended to spit. As they laughed together, the strangeness was eased amongst them.

"May we offer you something to go with the tea?" Dana asked politely. "There's an Irish saying that you shouldn't arrive at a house with one arm as long as the other."

She slipped the chocolate bars out of her pocket and onto the table.

The old woman looked pleased. She took one for herself and put the others on a plate.

"You've good manners," she said. "In turn I will help you. Why have you come here?"

"We're looking for something," Dana said. *The Book of Dreams.*

The old lady nodded. "Well, you'd best ask the giant about that. Blessed with serendipity, Fingal is. Not too bright in the head, but he's good at finding things."

"The giant!" Dana was excited. "The song that brought us here was about him. Can we meet him?"

The old woman didn't answer. Glancing out the window, she was suddenly distracted and spoke quickly to them.

"Hear me now and do as I say. You be the first of my visitors this day, but not the last. Mind, the Enemy has friends in every tale. If you are found here, all will be lost. Do you understand me now?"

Even as she was speaking, she hurried them over to the ladder and up into the loft.

"You have journeyed far," she said. "Rest here awhile."

Dana frowned at the single bed with straw mattress and quilt.

The *Cailleach* snorted impatiently.

"If you enter our world, you must bide by our rules. There is nowhere else you can go. I mean you to hide here where you will be safe."

With a shrug to Dana, Jean crawled under the bed. She followed after him, though she didn't look happy.

The old woman trailed the quilt over the side of the bed till they were hidden completely. Then she went downstairs to tidy her house.

They were snug enough in their hidey-hole. The floor of the loft was made of slender branches plaited like a mat. It was rough but pliant, and comfortable to lie on. Best of all, they could see through the weave into the room below.

"I think I'm in a *conte merveilleux*," Jean whispered to Dana.

"A wonder tale? It does feel familiar," Dana agreed. An unpleasant thought struck her. "What if she's a witch and intends to eat us?!"

Jean squinted down at the black cauldron over the fire.

"The pot fits only one, Gretel."

He snickered.

She gave him a dig with her elbow.

"I'm serious," she hissed. "Remember what she called herself? The *Cailleach Beinne Bric*. She sounds Scottish to me, but Scots and Irish Gaelic are quite alike. At first I understood her name to be the 'Wise Woman of the Speckled Company.'"

"*C'est beau.*"

"Yes, but *cailleach* can also mean 'hag' or 'witch.'"

"Now you say! Okay, we don't sleep. It is necessary we regard her."

The first hour was easy. Despite their fatigue, they were too anxious to close their eyes. They kept a sharp watch on the old woman as she swept the floor and stocked the shelves. When she was finished her housework, she busied herself preparing food. Dana grimaced at the cod heads lined up on the table, with their empty eye sockets. One by one, the old woman stuffed each head with a wet doughy mixture and put them in the cauldron. The more items that went into the pot, the better Dana felt. There couldn't be room for much else.

And the more time passed without incident or excitement, the harder the two found it to stay awake. Their eyelids grew heavy. They had to fight off the sleep their bodies craved. Whenever one fell into a doze, the other gave a quick nudge. But inevitably it happened—both nodded off at the same time.

They slept without dreaming, perhaps because they were in a dream already. Minutes turned to hours. The sun rose in the sky to burn away the mist on Bras d'Or. The surface of the lake gleamed like glass.

A loud knock on the door woke them!

Before they could figure out how long they had slept, the shock of the visitor drove all thought from their minds.

In through the door he strode, a fierce and black-robed rider clad in high leather boots and with a goad in his hand. From outside came the sounds of his horse snorting restlessly and pawing the ground. Dana nearly choked when the visitor passed beneath her. His shoulders were empty. *He was headless*. In fact, he was carrying his head under his arm like a hat! It had the colour and texture of mouldy cheese and glowed with the phosphorescence of decaying matter. Worse were the gruesome wet lips that grinned from ear to ear and the dark wicked eyes that surveyed the room.

Dana covered her mouth to keep from crying out.

The *Cailleach* was unruffled.

"Good day to you, Dullahan, will you have a drink?"

A hoarse voice issued from the bloated lips of the head.

"Gie us a beer."

A glass of black porter was put on the counter.

Upstairs, the spectators watched with fascinated horror. Though they didn't want to look, their curiosity compelled them. How would he drink it?

As the glass was held to the head's mouth, it guzzled thirstily.

"*Maudit, câlisse, tabernac,*" Jean muttered.

Dana bit her lip. She wasn't sure if she wanted to scream or laugh.

Slam went the glass on the counter. Pop went the head onto the horseman's shoulders. He stretched his neck to work out a cramp, then threw a gold coin to the old woman who caught it adroitly. With a salute of farewell, he marched out the door.

The *Cailleach* had no sooner bitten the coin and put it away than another knock came on the door. Several creatures entered, each more beautiful than the last, two men and a woman holding a child by the hand. They had scales instead of skin, iridescent aquamarine, and their hair was like long green strands of seaweed. Their fingers and toes were webbed. Around their shoulders they wore capes of sealskin.

Were they mermaids or merrows or selkies? Dana wondered.

She hoped to discover the answer from their talk, but they didn't stay long. In a smattering of French and Scots Gaelic, they bought a few bags of salt and left shortly after.

The third party of visitors created an uproar. Their arrival was heralded by a whirlwind of noise that battered the thatch of the roof and the walls of the cottage. Jumbled all together were many sounds: the flapping of wings of a flock of large birds, the rolling wheels of many carriages, loud laughter and singing, bells ringing, dogs barking. Then came a banging on the door like the hammers of hell. Voices were raised and raucous. They were like a drunken crowd shouting to be let in.

"'S FOSGAIL AN DORUS 'S LEIG A 'STIGH SINN!"

Not in the least bothered, the old woman remained at the counter. She stood on one leg, head cocked as she listened.

The noise receded from the door and moved around the cottage towards the back wall. Circling the house, it came back to the front and the door opened with a blast of wind.

In trooped the oddest sight yet. They weren't quite giants but they were bigger than men. They had to stoop as they entered. They were broad with great bellies hanging over their belts. Their hair and beards sprouted like birds' nests. Half their number were black-skinned with raven locks. The other half were ruddy red with manes of ginger. All wore denim dungarees and buckskin jackets. Some had caps or tuques pulled over their ears. Their feet were shod with homemade larrigans, laced stovepipe leggings with moccasined soles. They were a handsome lot in a rough wild way. But though they didn't appear to be mean or bad-tempered, they couldn't be thought harmless.

Their leader wore a headdress over his face and shoulders. It was the great hollowed head and hide of a bull with its horns intact. Commanding the centre of the room, he chanted loudly.

> *Tháinig mis' anseo air tús*
> *A dh'úrachadh dhuibh na Calluinn*
> *Chá ruiginn a leas siud innseadh*
> *Bha í ann bhó linn mo sheanar.*
> *Théid mí deiseil air an fhardaich*
> *'S tearnaidh mí aig an dorus*
> *Craicionn Calluinn 'na mo phócaid*
> *'S maith an ceo a thig bho'n fhear ud:*
> *Chan eil duine chuireas r'a shróin é*
> *Nach bí é rí bheo dheth falláin.*★

★I came here first of all
To speak to you of the Calluinn
It's for the best that this continues to be told
Even as it was from the time of my grandfather
I'll go sunwise around the house
And I'll arrive at the door
The Calluinn skin as my pouch
And good will be the smoke coming from it:
There's no one who will hold it to his nose
That won't have health all his life.

When he finished speaking, he lifted the bull hide from his head to reveal a face half-red, half-black. He marched over to the old woman and offered her the skin. In a formal manner, she inhaled its odour. Then he brought it to the others so they could sniff it one by one.

In the rafters, Jean and Dana caught a whiff of the raw brutish smell.

"*SLÁINTE!*" the leader roared at the finish. "HEALTH AND LONG LIFE TO YE!"

"*SLÁINTE!*" they all roared back.

The ritual completed, the wild men sat down. Some took seats near the window to gaze out at the twilight. Others bellied up to the bar.

"Spruce beer!" the leader demanded. "And it's the black spruce we want!"

The *Cailleach* put bottle after bottle onto the counter, all steaming with heat. A sweet putrid scent filled the room.

"Good woman, ye kept them in horse shite!" cried one of the men.

For the next few minutes the only sounds were those of corks popping, throats gurgling, loud sighs and grunts.

"Any grub?" someone asked.

The murmuring amongst them was friendlier now.

"Salt herring, *ceann groppi,* blue potatoes, oatcakes and bannock," the old woman announced.

There were cheers and shouts of "good on ye!"

From the cauldron on the fire, the *Cailleach* dished out a big mess of food for the men. It looked awful, especially the cod heads stuffed with liver, but the smell was hearty and, for the two upstairs, a welcome respite from the pongs of bull hide and manure. As the men fell on the food with drunken hunger, Jean and Dana conversed in low tones.

"They look like goblins," Dana said. "*Fir Dhearga* and *Fir Dhubha*. The Red and the Black Men. But they're very big. I didn't think their kind were found in this part of the world!"

"*Les lutins* we call them," said Jean. "This is not so good. They are *très dangereux*."

While the men were busy eating, the old woman clomped up the ladder and into the loft. She carried two large yellow bags which she set down near the bed.

"Climb inside," she whispered urgently. "Be quick, be nimble. The night is falling. The moon is rising."

Neither of them moved.

"Why do you want us to do this?" Dana hissed. "What's going on?"

"Do not seek to know too much about us," came the stern reply. "This is the only way you will get what you want. You, especially, must take care," she said to Dana. "Raising the giant is man-magic. It's not safe for girls. Stay hidden till he rises but remember this—you must call out to Fingal before the goblins do. Now be of good courage and do what I say."

Still they hesitated, fearing a trap and wondering if they might yet wind up in the pot. The *Cailleach* was growing impatient.

"Get in or get lost!" she hissed.

Fighting down feelings of panic and claustrophobia, Dana crawled into one of the bags. Reluctantly, Jean followed into the other. The material was soft like suede or pigskin and there were air holes to help them breathe. Once the old woman tied the ends shut they were smothered in darkness. With astonishing strength, she heaved the bags over her shoulders and carried them downstairs.

"Ho byes, the Hag has bags for us!" the goblin chief shouted.

"Haggis and baggis!" cried another.

"They're not for the likes of ye," she said shortly. She put the bags on the floor. "They're a meal for the giant. Little pigs for his breakfast."

Dana and Jean gasped at her words. One of the men came near. They could hear him snuffling around them.

"Fee fie foe fum, I smell the blood of a tasty hu-mawn."

A cacophony of howls and laughter followed.

Dana was seized with the urge to get out of the bag and started to kick wildly. She felt the *Cailleach's* hand on her head. The touch was kind and firm and strangely soothing.

"It's no business of yours what's in the bag," the old woman told the goblins curtly. "Just mind you take it up the hill when you go."

"And who says we're going up the hill?" the chief demanded.

A tense silence fell over the room. They were seconds away from a hullabaloo. Suddenly the top half of the door burst open. The big ginger cat jumped up on the sill. In a high-pitched cater-waul it screeched into the room.

"Awake the Sleeper!"

Then the cat ran off.

The old woman looked triumphant.

"The *cat sith* has spoken."

The men exchanged glances. A low grumbling rose amongst them. One spoke up gruffly.

"The wind's in the north."

Another nodded.

"There be new moon tonight."

This elicited mutters of "aye" and "that's true."

The goblin chief slammed the counter.

"We have no circle to dance in Her sight!"

The *Cailleach* was distributing bottles of scotch and whiskey. Her tone was persuasive.

"So light a torch, bring the bottle and build the fire bright."

The chief glared at her, then looked out the window at the darkening night. The first stars had appeared. He gave a hard nod to the others.

"The giant will rise with the moon."

It was the signal they were waiting for. They jumped up as one man. Coins were showered on the counter as they prepared to leave.

"Don't forget the bags," said the *Cailleach* mildly.

Dana and Jean were hauled over burly shoulders and carted out the door.

It was a rough passage down the road and up the hill. The two were jarred and jolted with every step the goblins took. When the men broke into a jog, it was all the more bruising. There was a lot of loud talk and grunting, wild laughter and yelling. After what seemed an eternity of discomfort, they were unceremoniously dumped on the ground. The loud voices around them moved a short distance away.

"Are you there?" Dana whispered, trying to see through an air hole with no luck.

"Oui," came Jean's low reply. "You okay?"

"More or less."

They struggled to loosen the ties on their bags. Cautiously they peeked out. They were in the hills that overlooked Lake Bras d'Or. The landscape rolled in dark shadows around them. Below glinted the cold waters of the lake. Above shone a clear night sky sprayed with stars and a sliver of new moon. But where was the circle of stones they had seen from the air? They were on the highest hill top. The ground was tamped earth with coarse patches of grass. Just beyond them, the goblins were busily building a bonfire. Some piled up sticks of driftwood and dried branches. Others lit torches soaked with petrol. One of them emptied a canister of gasoline over the kindling and threw in a match. The great WHOMPFF of flames made them all jump back. When they recovered from the shock, they screeched with laughter.

"Ye singed Black Murphy's ears, ye omadhaun!"

Red sparks showered the night air as the wood crackled and burned. The men stood around the fire, torches held aloft, gulping their whiskey. A fiddle appeared amongst them, then a *bodhran* drum and a tin whistle. Dana squinted through the dimness at the three musicians. Could it be? As she looked over the circle, she understood the *Cailleach's* warning. The men looked bigger and wilder in the firelight. Their faces were flushed from heat and exertion, their eyes crazed with drink. They were hard men engaged in a hard man's ritual.

Up rose the shivery sounds of the fiddle, then the shrill of the whistle and the thunder of the drum. The men sang in harsh melody.

> *Cold wind on the harbour*
> *And rain on the road*
> *Wet promise of winter*
> *Brings recourse to coal*
> *There's fire in the blood*
> *And a fog on Bras d'Or—*
> *The giant will rise with the moon.*

They began to dance as they sang, weaving in and out of each other with surprising grace. They held their torches and their bottles high, footing it lightly over the rough ground, then stamping their feet down with great crashes that shook the earth. Whether it was the firelight or the night shadows or the nature of man-magic, both Dana and Jean found their sight wavering. In place of the goblins, a great circle of stones took shape to form a rampart around the bonfire. Then out of the stones stepped a new group of dancers, dark-robed men with gold torcs at their necks and blue spirals painted on their faces.

> 'Twas the same ancient fever
> In the Isles of the Blest
> That our fathers brought with them
> When they went west
> It's the blood of the Druids
> That never will rest—
> The giant will rise with the moon.

The music grew more frenzied, the singing more frantic, and the dancing increased in speed and complexity. The bonfire flared like solar explosions. The stars in the sky spun deliriously. A vortex of energy was mounting in the circle.

The stones and the Druids melted into the darkness. The goblins returned. They were as drunk as lords. They stomped and bellowed and shook their fists at the moon.

> And crash the glass down!
> Move with the tide!
> Young friends and old whiskey
> Are burning inside
> Crash the glass down!
> Fingal will rise—
> With the moon!

Now the dancing reached such a pitch of ferocity and aggression that Dana and Jean hung back, appalled. Where could this end but in murder? They were about to make a run for their lives when the circle turned again.

No longer stones or goblins or dark-robed Druids, they were ordinary men, familiar men. Yes, there they were, the three musicians she had met in Toronto! They played their instruments and they sang and they danced in the company of other men like themselves. Maritimers from the coasts and islands, from Newfoundland, Nova Scotia, New Brunswick, Prince Edward Island and Cape Breton. They sang with passion to a fever of music. They drank their bottles dry and crashed them to the ground till the glass splintered and sparkled like the stars above. In young and old voices, men's wild voices, they sang with ardent fervour to warm the cold heart of the moon. Throats hoarse with whiskey and cigarettes and age, they were men of the sea and men of the mines, hard men who lived hard lives, ekeing out a living, battling bad governments and poverty and hardship, their lineage not forgotten, the blood of the Druids in their veins, the memory of the ancient stones, the blood sacrifice and the Otherworld so close to their own. The fire was in their blood, in their voices, in their music, in their indomitable will to survive, to live on. Whooping it up around the bonfire, they waved their torches and their bottles of whiskey, roaring full-throated a song lusty with life.

The wind's in the north
There'll be new moon tonight
And we have no circle to dance in her sight.
So light a torch, bring the bottle, and build the fire bright—

THE GIANT WILL RISE WITH THE MOON.

O see how he rises! Rising up from the waves! Rising up from the deep! Up out of the deep of the great lake of Bras d'Or! Wet and shining like the stars, dripping water and kelp and sea-wrack, *wet out of the sea and luminously wet,* knobbled with barnacles,

gigantic and beautiful against the night. *FINGAL THE GIANT!*
He it was who once strode between the northern shores of Ireland
and Scotland, who had crossed the broad Atlantic, wading through
the swell with massive legs like tree trunks, over the heaving waves
of the cold vast ocean to follow the ships that bore his people,
those who told his stories and sang his songs. He couldn't let them
go without him. Like a faithful dog he followed, nearly drowning
at times as he sank beneath the water then rising again to plough
the main till at last he arrived in the new land, exhausted beyond
belief. He collapsed on Cape Breton Island where he could hear
them singing in the Gaelic. It was early in the morning and the
sun was rising over the great lake of Bras d'Or. He saw the gold
light reach out like arms to greet him and he fell into its warm
embrace for the merciful sleep of the deep. And there in his wet
sea bed he still lies at peace. But he will rise, oh yes he will rise, on
the night of the new moon if you sing his song with enough fire
in your blood and your voice to wake him.

With slow heavy tread, the giant waded out of the lake. As
each gargantuan footstep landed on the ground, it sent tremors
through the earth. He was huge beyond imagining. Bigger than
the hills he crossed to reach the bonfire where they had called his
name.

Now he towered over the goblin hill and lowered his head for
a closer look. Dana and Jean were expecting a terrifying visage.
They were surprised, then, by the big round friendly face with its
bald head and cauliflower ears and a bushy beard like a bird's nest.
The grin was broad and toothless.

"I do *love* that song, byes. We're havin' a party, eh?"

Chapter Twenty-Three

Dana was so surprised by Fingal's affability, it took her a moment to act on the *Cailleach's* instructions. Then, with heart beating wildly, she struggled out of the bag and ran towards the giant.

"Yoo hoo! Hello there! Help!" she shouted as loudly as she could.

The reaction was instant. A clamour broke out amongst the goblins. Screeching with rage, torches held like cudgels, they charged at Dana. Jean had crawled from his bag and was running to join her. He turned as he ran, eyes golden, face elongating to a snout, black hair sprouting from every pore in his body. As he moved between Dana and the goblins he dropped on all fours, baring his fangs and snarling and snapping. In the flaming shadows of the bonfire, he looked all the bigger and more savage.

At the sight of the fierce beast, the wild men fell back. But it didn't take them long to recover. Brandishing their torches, they circled the wolf warily, waiting for their leader's signal to attack.

Fingal's big hands reached down to scoop up Dana and Jean.

"Now, lads, be pleasant," he boomed. "The lass got the first word in, ye know the rules. Away ye go now and thanks for the song. See ye next new moon if ye're up for it."

With a lot of grumbling and blue cursing, the goblins did as they were told and headed back down the hill.

The giant lowered his big face to peer at the two in his palm. Dana flinched. The eyes were as big as moons and the nostrils were like caves.

"Pay no heed to the lads," he said to Dana. "They work too hard, them fellas. Won't take no holidays. Makes wee Jock all cross and cranky."

He patted the wolf lightly with his baby finger.

"Nice doggie, don't bite."

Jean unravelled to his own form.

The giant's eyebrows shot up, almost leaving his head.

"That's a good trick, bye. I never seen that before. A Frenchie, I betcha. *Loup-garou,* eh?"

Normally Jean would have been offended by the remark, but the giant was so mild-mannered and obviously a bit dim, he let it pass.

"Now what is it ye want, lass?" Fingal asked Dana. "I'll do your bidding this night."

Dana shouted to be heard.

"The *Cailleach* said you could help me."

"*An Cailleach Dhubh?* Aren't ye the lucky one to be gettin' advice from the likes of her. She be the sister of Aoife, her that was the wife of Mannanan, the Irish Lord of the Sea. I shouldn't be tellin' ye this now, but I can't help meself. I've always been partial to a wee bit of gossip. I've heard tell that Aoife stole secrets from her husband. The language of nature, it was, and all the wisdom it can give. Well he killed her for that, didn't he. She was of the crane family so he made a bag of her skin and put the secret language inside it. Now her sister got a hold of the bag. She's not a crane, mind, she's—"

"A cormorant!" Dana burst in with sudden insight. Images of the old woman flashed through her mind, the feathery shawl, the hooked nose, the high-stepping gait. She wasn't human at all but a bird-woman. "Of course! *An cailleach dhubh*. 'The black witch.' It's the Irish name for the cormorant and they *do* look like witches with their raggedy black wings."

"Anyhows," the giant continued with his story, "once the *Cailleach* got the bag, she had to scarper from the wrath of Mannanan. She flew all the way across the ocean till she dropped down here in Cape Breton, almost dead. And here she stayed. A bit like me own tale," he finished.

"She said you have the gift of serendipity," Dana told him, "and that you could help me find what I'm looking for. *The Book of Dreams*."

Fingal scratched the top of his bald head. The rasping noise was like a saw cutting through a tree.

"Can't say as I've heard of it. But there's another one wandrin' about the place lookin' for a book. Brendan's his name. A saint from the Old Country travellin' about like a sailor in a wee boat. I could find him for ye. Ye could be lookin' for the same thing, eh?"

Before Dana could respond, the giant strode from the hills and headed straight for the ocean. When he reached the seashore, he waded into the deep water without a second thought. Soon Cape Breton was a shadowy land behind them.

Cupped in the shelter of Fingal's hands, Jean and Dana kept watch through the lattice of his fingers. They were crossing the waves as if crossing a plain. On their left rose the jagged coastline of Newfoundland. In every other direction swelled the far-flung sea.

"I know some saints," Jean said to Dana, "but who is Brendan?"

"He's Irish, " she told him. "Very old. He sailed to Canada in a leather boat, long before the Vikings or the French and English."

She caught his grin of disbelief.

"It's not as daft as it sounds," she said. "An Irishman proved it was possible in the 1970s."

Jean didn't look convinced and Dana was about to give him more details when the giant made his announcement.

"We're goin' to drop by the girlfriend." His face reddened; they could see it glowing in the dark. "She'll point us in the right direction."

He popped his two companions inside his breast pocket to protect them from the gale-force winds. The fabric of his shirt was coarse but warm and they were able to peer over the edge. The Canadian coastline had disappeared entirely. The stars in the sky drowned on the rim of the horizon. They were treading the cold lonely miles of the Atlantic.

When they finally spotted her, a distant figure on the waves, she was like a mirage in the dunes of a watery desert. Huge and stolid, like the colossus of Rhodes, she stood alone on an outcrop of rock. At first they thought she was a statue. She was coppery bronze, with a greenish sheen wherever the water had tainted her metal. Her dress was that of a warrior, chain mail and helmet, but she bore no weapons. Her features were strong, stern and aquiline, with metallic eyes that stared blindly out to sea. Her head swivelled on her shoulders as they approached.

"We'll be gettin' a few riddles to answer," Fingal warned his companions. "Ye know the drill. Ours is not to question why, just to do or die."

Dana was alarmed. A surprise test!

"What kind of riddles?"

Jean wasn't too happy either.

"Do or die? In my *grand-mère*'s tales, if you say the wrong answer, it's always bad."

"Don't let it bother a hair on your chinny chin chin," Fingal assured him, though the giant was gulping nervously. "A few questions about life, the universe and everything. Three will do the trick. That's the magic number. Don't suppose either of ye knows the *Saltair na Rann?*" They shook their heads. His sigh was glum. "Sure nobody reads the oul books nowadays."

He trudged up to the Bronze Lady till they stood face to face. "Greetin's, hen, how's it goin' there?"

The metal jaws clanked as she opened her mouth to speak. Her voice had the timbre of organ pipes in a church.

"What is the number of the hosts which the noble wave of the clear sea reveals?"

Fingal scratched his head as he mused upon the question. Dredging deep in his memory, he fished out the answer and produced it proudly.

"The hosts of the air cannot be numbered."

Dana thought the Lady's impassive features warmed ever so slightly. Was that the hint of a smile on those great bronze lips as she gave him the nod?

Fingal looked pleased as punch, but his face went blank at the next question.

"What is the name of the multitudes which dwell there on the other side of the solid earth?"

"Your turn," he hissed to the two in his pocket.

Dana and Jean conferred in a panic.

"Australians?" Jean suggested.

Dana shook her head. Close, but not the right word. Something she had read somewhere? A song or a tale she had heard in Faerie? At last the answer dropped onto her tongue.

"The Antipodeans!" she cried.

A second metallic nod grated. They were almost there. Jean waited nervously. In all fairness, it was up to him to answer the last question.

"And the bright sun, whither does it go?"

He grinned with relief. He wasn't the weakest link.

"À l'ouest. It goes into the west."

The bronze head nodded for the third time.

Jean and Dana let out a cheer along with the giant. They had passed the test!

"Here's the question, m'dear," Fingal said to his girlfriend. "Has ye seen that little Irish monk fella, the one in the skin boat? He came this way once upon a time if I'm not mistaken."

"Indeed I saw him," she said. "A holy man, a saint and a mage of power. And he saw me."

They heard the faint echo of surprise in her voice.

"Can ye tell us where he went?"

"I can."

The Bronze Lady remained still for a while. Fingal waited with placid patience. He was evidently accustomed to long delays in their discourse.

At last she swivelled on her feet and pointed due north.

"He went thataway."

"Much obliged. Thank ye kindly," her boyfriend said cheerfully.

He leaned forward to plant a few slobbery kisses on the metal lady's lips.

Dana and Jean were caught by surprise and nearly fell out of his pocket. They clambered to safety, smothering their laughter as they did their best to ignore the loud noises of the giant's affection.

At last he had said his farewells and proceeded north.

Dana looked back. In the clear starry night, the Bronze Lady stood stark and glittering above the cold waters. Arms akimbo she moved with heavy grace, pointing in different directions like a giant weather vane.

"Who or what is she directing?" Dana called up to Fingal. "The wind? The waves?"

"Can ye no' see?" The giant was surprised. "That's a great shame now, for ye canny see the beauty of her work. What she does for the soul-birds who wander the world."

"Soul-birds?" Jean frowned. He translated the words in his mind, trying to make sense of them. "The souls of the dead?"

"Och no, they go elsewhere. The souls of the living. There always be parts of them flyin' to and fro."

"What?" they said together.

"It's a shame ye canny see them. Can ye not open your eyes a bit wider?"

His words triggered an echo in Dana's mind. *You need but open your heart.* She made an effort to try harder. Calling up her fairy sight, she gazed back over the starlit waters. Now she saw that the Lady was not alone.

All around the bronze figure they flew, like white spray from the sea, like white flurries of snow. Hundreds and thousands of birds—white birds!—they flocked in circles and lines and spirals. From the four corners of the earth they arrived in droves and flew straight to the Lady. Over and around her and to her they flew, from the tiniest hummingbird the size of an insect to the great whooper swan. There were many that Dana could name—gulls and guillemots, razorbills and fulmars, gannets, puffins, skuas and terns—and there were many she couldn't. Exhausted from their journey, some rested on the Lady's head and shoulders. Others hovered on the wing, waiting for her instructions. What inspired her directions?

Dana was seized by a desire to understand, to know. Were these the birds she had seen in the Medicine Lodge? Were they singing her song? She couldn't hear them. She was too far away. The loss and longing was an ache in her heart. As the yearning to join them grew inside her, she suffered the strangest sensation. The yearning itself emerged from her body in the shape of a white bird. On a rush of wings and wind, it flew over the waves, compelled to meet the others.

Dana was in two places at the same time. She was still with Jean in the giant's pocket even as she flew with the white bird towards the Lady. The first impression that struck her when she reached the other birds was the overpowering sense of loss. She could hear it in their cries, the dark call-notes of sobbing. Despite the beauty of their flight and the airborne ballet, all were grieving for something.

Now as she gazed on the Lady with the white bird's eyes, Dana saw a different figure. No longer a warrior made of metal, she was a shining angel—*Cara Mia,* Mother Carey—all kindness and loving and comfort itself. Her outstretched arms welcomed the weary travellers, calling and encouraging and showing them the way. She knew each bird and called them by name, knew whence they came and where they would go. Indeed she knew the number of feathers they had on each wing.

Awed by the Lady's true nature, Dana watched her at work.

A new flock of birds arrived, exhausted and despairing. Ready to drop to a cold grave below, they sang a dirge. It told of how they had suffered and how much they had lost. It seemed that they had been given more than they could bear. The Lady listened to their song and pointed South. A surge of images struck Dana, of blue skies, warm breezes, sunlight and laughter. The birds flew away with new hope. Now another group arrived. They too were bereft, but their song was robust, a heroic opera of challenge and survival. The Lady pointed North. Dana caught a glimpse of rugged terrain, high waterfalls and glaciers. With glad cries, the flock moved on.

It was a beautiful dance between the soul-birds and the Lady. She guided them to what they needed, to the place where they would heal. Dana wanted to join the dance, to find her place. Could the Lady send her where *she* needed to go?

Like a lost lamb to the shepherdess, she rushed towards the outstretched arms. Did the angel smile? Recognition shone in those eyes. There was no doubt that she knew who Dana was. The arm pointed northward, directly at Fingal's back as he trod through the waves. Before Dana knew what had happened, she was fully back in her body.

A wave of disappointment washed over her. She almost had it! It was something that the Lady knew. And the soul-birds too. And the *Cailleach* and her sister, Aoife. Yes! The knowledge that the crane stole from the Lord of the Sea and the cormorant kept in the black witch's bag. What was it? She had glimpsed it before, in the language of the land. The truth was all around her, but it was encrypted in code, in the secrets of fairy tales.

"What are the soul-birds?" she demanded of Fingal.

"I canny explain, pet. It's too deep for me. Sure ye can ask Brendan when ye meet him. He's a saint and a scholar. He'll tell ye."

"But where do they come from?" she insisted. "What do they mean? You must know something!"

Jean saw the glint in Dana's eye, the set of her mouth. She could be stubborn when she wanted her way. He didn't mind that in a girl, but this wasn't the right place. There was no point badgering Fingal. The giant was doing the best he could and without complaint. He was soaked to the waist with the cold dark waves breaking against him.

"Och, sure I know nothin'. Giants aren't the brightest pennies in the purse, doncha know?"

"Are there many in Canada?" Jean spoke up to change the subject.

"Oh aye, there be giants everywhere! We were upon the earth from the very beginning. And there's lots of room here, eh? I've heard tell the Old Countries are all landfills and motorways. Here there still be wild places. That's what a giant likes. Plenty of room."

Jean saw Dana's impatient look, but before she could bring up the soul-birds again, he pressed on.

"You know the others?"

"Oh aye, plenty of them. There be a whole clan of French ones live up in the big tunnels in Churchill Falls. Came from Normandy they did, a long time ago. They used to live in the swamps of Labrador. Hard life, that, ye get eaten alive by the black flies in the summer and freeze your butt in the winter. They were some happy byes, let me tell ye, when the hydro-electric plant was built and all them tunnels carved. Great place for a giant to live, all snug and out of the weather.

"Then there's Joe Mufferaw out in Renfrew County. Lives in them there hills in the Ottawa Valley. He's only half-giant, mind you, not as big as some, but a good lad. Him and me and a lot of the others are new to the country, in a manner of speakin'. We came with the settlers from across the sea. The native giants now they're the big ones. Bigger than the great red cedar. There's the Sasquatch out west, furry nation. What with all the clear fellin', they've been leavin' the forests and headin' up into the mountains. Can't say as I blame them. Some of us has to lie low, ye know. Humans don't take too kindly to giants. Could be 'cause some are carnivores, makes a fella unpopular. I'm not," he added quickly. "I'm vegan meself. But there's some likes the taste of human flesh, if ye know what I mean."

"I'm hearing more than I want to," Dana whispered to Jean.

She had given up hope of learning more about the soul-birds.

The giant's monologue came to an abrupt end when he let out a yell.

There ahead in the darkness, a small boat bobbed on the waves. Absurdly small, it looked like a walnut shell afloat on the ocean. Though the white sail hung limp in the calm air, they could still make out the design it bore. A Celtic Cross emblazoned in crimson.

"Ahoy, Brendan!" Fingal called.

"Ahoy!" came a hoarse reply.

The man on watch was the first to see them. Another crawled out from the narrow shelter where he had been sleeping. Both gawped and rubbed their eyes. There was no mistaking what they saw before them: a gigantic grinning man with two small figures perched on his shoulder like parrots.

"Visitors for Brendan," Fingal shouted amiably.

Before anyone could react, he had deposited Jean and Dana on the deck of the boat. Then, with a friendly wave, he strode away across the water.

Chapter Twenty-Four

![decorative celtic knot border]

THE STRANGE BOAT WAS NOT UNLIKE A FLOATING bird's nest. Banana-shaped, with square sails on two masts, it was an untidy muddle of ropes and supplies. It had obviously been at sea for many weeks and had survived rough times. Everything was wet or damp. The smells were overwhelming: wet leather, musty wool, pungent sheepskin and grease. The two astonished crewmen were as bedraggled as their boat. Both were hairy and bearded, and their eyes shone wildly from outstaring the Atlantic too long.

"*Cá bhfuill Naomh Bhreandán?*" Dana asked them, assuming they spoke Irish.

The men looked back at her blankly. She and Jean were already suspecting the worst. They began to notice the anachronisms around the boat. There were bright yellow tarpaulins over the bow and stern. Sheets of plastic protected electronic equipment. There was a radio telephone and a life-raft dinghy. Hardly the gear of a saint who lived before the Vikings!

"I think," Dana said slowly, "there's been a mistake."

"Is Brendan here?" Jean asked the men.

Once again the sailors looked confounded. Two more crewmen joined them. One was a tall young man with an easy air of command.

"I'm the skipper," he said, in an Anglo-Irish accent. "Tim's my name. That's George with the flashlight, our sailing master.

Trondur, there, with the head of curls is an artist and hunter from the Faroe Islands. And last but not least, the gangly one with the big feet is Arthur. We call him 'Boots.' As for Brendan," Tim made a sweeping gesture with his arm. "*Brendan* is the boat."

Their fears were confirmed. Fingal had left them in the wrong place. Jean looked dismayed, but Dana didn't.

"This is the *Brendan* voyage!" she cried, delighted. "What's the date? What year is it?" she asked the captain.

"It's June 13," he said, puzzled, "1977."

"*Câlisse,*" Jean swore.

"The last trip! How exciting!"

She knew the story well, it was one of her favourites, the life-saver that had helped her survive a dose of chicken pox at the age of nine. Gabriel had taken a week to read the book to her, as they pored over pictures and maps. The author was the captain himself, Tim Severin. A true tale of heroic adventure, it described how he built a boat of leather and wood following instructions from a mediaeval manuscript. Then he set sail with a crew of three men to prove that Brendan the Navigator, an Irish saint, could have reached Canada in the sixth century A.D., long before the Vikings or any other explorers.

Regardless of the mistake Fingal had made, Dana was thrilled.

"You're Irish," Tim said to Dana, having recognized her accent. He turned to the other Irishman in his crew. "Well, Boots, it's either my dream or yours."

Boots was well over six feet with a shock of yellow hair and a genial air of disorder. The youngest member of the crew, he was also the untidiest and managed to look even more dishevelled than the rest.

"Can I not even get away from you lot when I'm havin' a kip?" he responded.

"You're both barmy," said George, mildly. "It's not my form to fall asleep on watch. I must be dreaming wide awake."

They believed him. Tall and thin, a former English army man with a piercing glance, he was meticulous about his work and duties.

"Mass hallucination?" Boots suggested.

"Salt water in the rations?" Tim worried.

Trondur continued to stare at the visitors without speaking. Big and burly, he had the hands of an artisan. He looked like a Norse god with his curls of chestnut hair and bushy beard. From an ancient Faroese family who had lived on the same site for eighteen generations, he was a quiet man, shy to speak English.

"Strange things happen at sea," he said at last, "but I think they are not so much problem."

"Right then," Tim decided, nodding to the newcomers. "We'll play this out and treat you as guests. Do please join us for supper. You can tell us your story and we'll tell you ours. The past week has been pretty dull. Dream or hallucination or no, we could do with the diversion."

Everyone was pleased with the captain's decision. After braving gales, storms and rogue waves in their perilous voyage from Iceland to Greenland, the journey on to Labrador had been cruelly monotonous. Winds from the south plus calms and pea-soup fogs had slowed them to a crawl. With nothing to do and nothing to see, they were badly in need of some entertainment.

While the meal was being prepared, Jean and Dana conferred.

"Do you think the giant will come back?" Jean said.

"He's got to," Dana pointed out. "Right boat or not, wouldn't he have to bring us home?"

"We don't ask him this. Only to help us find the book." Jean touched his head. "He's not too smart, eh?"

They found it hard to stay worried as they were soon immersed in the *Brendan* voyage. The crew gave them sweaters of oiled wool to pull over their jackets as well as mitts and scarves. It helped to ease the cold wet chill of the Atlantic. All around them heaved the dark swell of the ocean. Sitting on damp sheepskins, they shared a night picnic illumined by the ship's lantern high on the mast. Overhead spread a vast panoply of stars. Though much of the larder had long been consumed, they were offered smoked sausage and smoked beef with the green mould scraped off, hazelnuts, oat cereal, the last of a truckle of cheese, as well as dried whale meat and blubber brought on board by Trondur. He had also hunted at sea, providing them with fish and fulmar which tasted like pigeon.

Being vegetarian, Dana kept to the nuts and cheese, but Jean was ready to try everything, including a slice of strong-smelling blubber.

"Is good," Trondur assured him. "Very good."

Jean almost gagged. It was like rubber soaked in machine oil.

Hot drinks finished off the meal, a choice of beef extract, black tea or coffee, along with dessert. The Skippers Special was a tasty sweet mush of stewed apricots, biscuits and jam.

Jean and Dana leaned against the gunwales, sipping their drinks. They were getting used to the strange feel of the boat. Despite the creaks and the groaning of wood, the overall quiet was profound. The leather muffled the slap of wave against hull. Like a living creature, the boat flexed with the water and its sides pumped in and out as if it were breathing. Cupped inside, they felt curiously disembodied, like Jonah swallowed by a whale.

"*Moi*, I have a strange *canot* also," Jean said, looking around with admiration. "How do you make her?"

"Heart of oak, bark of ash," Tim said proudly.

"And forty-nine oxhides to cover the frame," George added, "soaked in oak-bark liquor and coated with wool grease, then hand-stitched together. Our fingers ached for weeks."

"We're depending on two things to stay alive," Tim explained, "our sailing skills and the *Brendan's* ability to survive at sea. In many ways it was easier for the original Brendan. For one thing, the weather was milder then. But more importantly, the saint and his monks had generations of knowledge and experience behind them in the building and sailing of skin boats."

While they were talking, they heard the low roar of an airplane overhead. It was disorienting to be on an ancient boat out in the ocean with jet planes flying by.

"We are proving that Brendan and his sailor-monks could have done this," Tim insisted. "It's no longer a fairy tale recorded in an old book. Once we cast off in our *Brendan,* we became like St Brendan himself. At the mercy of wind and weather, we have delivered ourselves into the hands of Fate, like the *perigrinni* of old."

"Perigrinni?" said Jean, "What is this word?"

"Pilgrims. People who set out on a journey for sacred reasons. Usually they're looking for something special or holy, like the Grail or the Isles of the Blessed."

"Ah oui, je comprends. This is you, also, *non?"* he said to Dana. "You are *La Pèlerine."*

Dana liked the title.

Now the crew wanted to hear their story. As the tale of the quest for *The Book of Dreams* unfolded, they were enthralled to hear of fairy queens and portals, the *loup-garou* and *la chasse-galerie,* the Cree Old Man and the Medicine Lodge, the *Cailleach* and Fingal, the Giant.

"If this is a dream, someone here's got one hell of an imagination," said Boots. "Who's been boning up on Canadian folklore?"

Both George and Trondur shrugged, it wasn't them.

Tim regarded his visitors thoughtfully. He was not a superstitious man but he was a visionary, someone who was willing to go further than most in thought and action.

"If this is a dream," he said quietly, "it's what Jung calls a Big Dream. We appear to have crossed paths in time and space, in a netherworld between realities. I can see why we've met. Both of us are questing between Ireland and Canada. You know, each of us is born to do something special in our lives and it's our mission to find out what that thing might be. I was meant to go on this voyage. I've thought about it and planned it since the first time I read the *Navigatio Sancti Brendani Abbatis*. I guess in a way that old manuscript was the book of *my* dream."

Dana's mind was racing. So much of what he said made sense to her. She was about to ask his advice about her own mission when George suddenly sat up and looked around.

"We're moving faster!"

"Look lively," said the skipper.

They were all up and moving quickly. The sailing master was right. They were no longer travelling a steady course through quiet waters. The boat was speeding along at a clip. The wind had risen and the sea was choppy.

Crack-crack-crack.

"Damn, what's that?" said Boots.

George scurried up the mast with a flashlight and trained it on the water.

"Hey, I do believe it's ice!" he cried. "We're running into ice!"

The boat was hitting lumps of ice at speed. They rattled and crackled against the hull like ice cubes in a glass.

"Drop the sails!" Tim ordered. "We could be knocked to pieces! Our only chance is to stop!"

The crew worked frantically to lower the sails but the boat was still speeding. George climbed higher up the mast and shone the flashlight over the water. They were surrounded! Caught in a floe of icebergs! Grotesque sculptures of every size and shape muttered and grumbled as they rubbed against each other on the waves.

Dana shuddered. It was like a herd of sea monsters growling at the boat, out there in the cold night.

"This ice shouldn't be here," Tim swore. "I know the ice chart by heart." Then a slow horror dawned. "If a freak gale swept over the main ice sheet along Labrador, it could burst the whole thing open!"

Jean and Dana, who were doing their best to keep out of the crew's way, exchanged glances.

"Grimstone?" Jean muttered.

"Could be," Dana nodded. "The Grey Man is an elemental. He has power over the weather."

"Big one dead ahead!" George cried.

Tim pulled the tiller as far as it would go to steer around the huge chunk, but no luck. *Crash.* It was like hitting concrete. Everyone staggered with the shock. Now a series in succession. *Thump! Thump! Thump!* A quick battering and the boat spun away. Worse loomed directly in front of them. A berg twice the size of the boat rolled in the water like a hippopotamus.

"Hang on tight!" Tim roared.

As they struck head-on, the boat tremored with the impact. George was flung off the mast. Hanging onto the halliard and dangling in midair, he was in danger of being crushed between the ice and the boat.

Trondur rushed to help him down.

Crash!

Another collision. The loud protest of wood.

Could the *Brendan* survive this punishment?

There was no escape. They were hemmed in by pack ice, mile after mile, floe after floe, driven towards them by gale and current.

There was nothing they could do but fend off the attack as best they could, using wooden poles and their own hands and feet.

On the shelter roof, arm around the mainmast for support, George acted as lookout.

"Two on the port bow, another to the starboard side! Mind the gap!"

Above all, the *Brendan* had to avoid where the ice bumped together. If caught in the middle, the boat would burst like a ripe fruit.

For an interminable time, it seemed, they wove in and out of the floes, clattering over table tops of ice or scraping along the sides. As Tim said himself, it was "a cross between bumper cars and a country square dance."

At one point Dana thought she saw Grimstone's features leering in the ice. Then the squall hit.

Down came freezing rain and hailstones, cracking like bullets off the tarpaulins. The water rose ominously. Waves began to thrash and pound the boat. Deep troughs threatened to swallow them up, then tossed them over the crests in a welter of foam. The full strength of the Atlantic was hurled against them.

Well-used to storms at sea, the crew reacted instantly. They pulled on foul weather gear and threw spare oilskins to Dana and Jean. With the hoods drawn over their faces like cowls, they all looked like monks.

"Trondur, handle the headsail sheets!" the skipper shouted. "Boots, take the mainsail and look after the leeboards. George, you're the best helmsman, take over steering. I'll handle the pilotage. This is going to be tricky."

The wind was rising rapidly and so too were the waves. With a thunderous roar, a solid sheet of water crashed into the boat. *Water water everywhere.* The bilges were filled to the brim. The cabins were awash. They were too low in the sea. Water lapped over the gunwales, sloshed back and forth in the boat. While the bilge pump squirted it back into the ocean, Jean and Dana bailed with pots and saucepans. No one had to tell them that survival time in freezing water was five minutes or less. They felt the threat of death lurking in the night.

Tim stood near Dana, eyes red with exhaustion and the sting of salt spray. His voice echoed a moment of despair.

"What on earth are we doing out here in this lonely half-frozen part of the Atlantic?"

"We're following a dream," she said.

Nodding as he remembered, he managed a smile.

"Times like this you really have but one choice. Whatever will happen will happen, so you either face it as a coward or you face it as a hero. It's up to you."

The sinister dance with the ice and the storm went on for hours. Yet despite the battering and the drenching rain, the deadly cold and numbing fatigue, the little boat held. Three things kept them alive. Along with the *Brendan*'s ability to survive at sea and the skill of its sailors, there was a third factor. Courage.

Then their luck ran out.

The worst that could happen did happen.

The *Brendan* was trapped between two icebergs as if caught in a vice. The boat shuddered like a wounded animal. Everyone rushed to push it free. Too late, the damage was done. Sea water swirled in the bottom of the boat.

"We've sprung a leak!" George cried.

Trondur agreed. His voice echoed doom.

"I think stitching is broken by ice. Water in stern of *Brendan* is not so much problem. Water in bow is big problem."

"It could be anywhere," Tim said, looking around frantically. "We won't find it in the dark."

Climbing under the protective plastic that sheltered the radio, he put in a call to the Canadian coast guard. In calm terse tones, he warned them to stand by for a Mayday call. Yet even as he spoke, he knew the truth. If they went down, no one could reach them in time.

"We'll have to work the pump and wait for first light," he announced. "Then we'll find the tear and fix it."

No one groaned at the thought of more work. No one questioned how they could make repairs while the boat was still in the water. Whatever would happen, would happen. They were ready to face it.

Through the last hours of the night, while the storm raged around them, they worked the bilge pumps. Two thousand strokes per hour were needed to keep afloat. Worn out from fighting the storm and the ice, they all took turns including the visitors.

Dana insisted on doing her share of the work. Holding her breath, she squirmed through the dark wet tunnel of tarpaulin to reach the handle of the pump. They had told her to keep turning till her arm got sore, then switch hands. Aching with tiredness before she began, she still managed to follow instructions. She rocked back and forth with the mechanical motion of arm and torso. Though drenched and frozen with cold, she soon worked up a sweat. She discarded her oilskins. The monotony of the action was almost as painful as the wear on her muscles. She counted her portion of strokes to help her keep going. No matter how bad it got, she wouldn't give up. She knew in a way that the others couldn't that she was to blame. She was the cause of the ice and the storm.

At last her turn was done. When she crawled out of the space, the men gave her a cheer. Eyes bleary, exhausted, she staggered to her feet.

"What's that?" Boots called from the bow. "Do you hear it?"

Something large was moving through the water towards them.

Dana's heart sank. What would Grimstone send now? They couldn't take much more.

Then he emerged, through the hail and the waves, the big familiar shape of Fingal the Giant.

"Ahoy *Brendan!*" he called.

"Ahoy!" Tim called back.

"Got the wrong boat," Fingal shouted. His round face hung over them like a friendly moon. "The girlfriend set me right. Got to go further back in time. So if ye don't mind, I'll just take my little friends, thank ye kindly."

Dana turned to Tim and the rest of his crew. They were long past questioning what was happening around them. Red-eyed and spent, they were barely managing to keep on their feet.

"It's almost dawn," she told them. "When the light comes and the weather lets up, you'll find the leak."

"We can't go!" Jean protested. "Not like rats from a ship who sink!"

"We must," Dana insisted. "The ice and the storm were sent by Grimstone. He's after me, not them. He'll leave them alone once we go. They won't be safe till we do."

Jean wasn't happy. It seemed wrong to escape with the giant and abandon the crew to their fate. The *Brendan* needed the extra hands to work the pump.

"It'll be okay," Dana urged him. "I remember this part of the story. They find where it's torn and they mend it in the water. They survive and the boat survives, but if we stay they won't!"

Reluctantly, Jean accepted her logic. He shook hands with the men and wished them safe home.

Dana's farewell was quick but pointed.

"The storm will stop as soon as we go. I'm sorry we brought you bad luck. Things will go better from now on. I can tell you this, I know all of you as heroes."

Their haggard faces lit up. Hope was all they needed to keep going.

Fingal scooped up Jean and Dana and popped them into his pocket. With a final wave, he strode away, leaving the *Brendan* behind to disappear in the mists.

Jean was still feeling guilty.

"They'll make it," Dana assured him. "I remember how the book ends. The Newfoundlanders threw them a *céilí*, a big party that went on all night."

They snuggled inside Fingal's pocket. It was gloriously dry and warm. Outside, the gale howled.

"Will Grimstone fight the giant?" Jean wondered.

It wasn't long before his question was answered.

"Hould onto yer britches," Fingal warned them suddenly, "here comes trouble!"

A violent lurch followed his words. The giant was under attack. They scrambled to get a look out. As Dana had predicted, the storm had left the *Brendan* to pursue her instead. Now it raged against Fingal. The waves rose in a towering frenzy to match his size, then collapsed against him with vicious intent. Spume erupted like geysers. Water blinded his eyes. He was thrown off balance.

There was no doubt about who or what was driving the storm. Grimstone's visage screeched in the squall. His watery maw opened to swallow the giant.

"No!" cried Dana.

Fingal floundered. Arms flailing in the foam, he tried to tread water, but the waves pushed him under with malicious glee. It was a fight to the death. Though he struggled manfully, even the giant knew that the storm was killing him.

He sank beneath the surface. Water rushed into his pocket. Dana and Jean were thrown into the sea. They spluttered and kicked, attempting to swim but the water was too cold, too wild. A big hand grasped them suddenly and held them up high.

He would not let them drown. Not while there was breath in his body.

Now a mountain of water crashed against Fingal. It was the seventh wave. The one all sailors dread. The one that takes you down to Davy Jones Locker. Despair in his eyes, he began to sink for the last time.

But just when all seemed lost and the twist in the tale was a tragic ending, hope sailed over the horizon in a leather boat. From its mast flew a great sail emblazoned with the sign of the Celtic Cross. In its bow stood a man garbed in the robes of a monk. His arms were outstretched to the heavens as he prayed to his God to banish the storm.

CHAPTER TWENTY-FIVE

FINGAL'S HEAD WAS DISAPPEARING UNDER the waves when the leather boat reached him. In the bow the mediaeval monk stood fast, holding a wooden cross aloft. His brown cloak swirled around him in the wind, his face was lost in a deep cowl, but his prayers rang out with power and clarity. The squall gathered in force like a furious tornado and charged towards him. A burst of light struck the tempest.

The sudden calm was profound. The seas lay still. A warm breeze played gently over the lapping water. Dawn brought the morning with a rose-coloured sky.

The giant righted himself in the water and leaned over the little boat. Once again the monk lifted his cross.

"Death is above you!" cried the saint. "What is your ransom?"

"I hain't with the storm demon," Fingal hurried to explain. "I've a couple of pilgrims to join ye. Will they do for a ransom? Ye're Saint Brendan the Navigator, right?"

The giant and the monk were both speaking Gaelic. Dana translated for Jean and the two waited anxiously for Brendan's reply.

Still cowled, the saint's eyes flashed as he stared at Fingal.

"I have the Two Sights," Brendan declared. "The ability to see in the world of the body and the world of the soul. The Second Sight tells me that you are good. Your spirit shines."

The giant blushed with pleasure.

"Thank ye kindly. That's a great compliment comin' from a saint."

Gently he lowered Dana and Jean onto the boat.

"If he canny help ye, no one can," Fingal told them, switching to English. "He's a magus and a Druid. Ye saw his power over the winds and the water."

"I also have the Gift of Tongues," Brendan interjected in English. "That was not my power you saw, but the power of my God. He is *Dia duilech,* God of the Elements, even as he is *Coimdiu na nduile,* Lord of Creation."

"Well, ye've got power on your side, then. Would ye be on for givin' them a hand?"

"I will if I can," Brendan replied.

"I'm off then," said Fingal.

"Thank you so much!" Dana called out to him. "I hope we'll meet again!"

"When the Kingdom is restored," boomed the giant.

"Merci beaucoup!" called Jean.

"À bientôt," came the reply, sailing over the water as the giant disappeared.

How strange to find themselves on the original of the boat that would one day be called *Brendan*! Made of oxhide stretched over a wood frame, it was surprisingly like the one they had left behind in the future. But this boat was a lot bigger, could almost be called a ship, and it had a larger crew. It was also much more at home on the ocean. Dry and even cosy, it was not as open to the elements as the modern version. Two huts of woven wattle stood on deck, reminiscent of an ark. The large one midships housed the crew, while the smaller one in the stern was the private quarters of the saint. The huts were round in shape like the beehive cells hermits used in Ireland.

Overhead, sheets of tanned leather hung between the masts to catch rainwater for drinking. Dried fish and plucked birds dangled from poles. Bags of cereals and other provisions were stowed under the gunwales.

Like Brendan, the crew were also monks. Eight were awake and manning the vessel while another four slept off watch. They wore clerical garb adapted for sailing, woollen tunics like sweaters over baggy trousers, all oiled to be waterproof. Most of the crew were big country men with raw red faces weathered by the elements. They moved about the boat with the ease of practised sailors.

"You are welcome here," Brendan said to Jean and Dana.

Only now did he uncover his head. As the cowl fell behind him, the two gasped with recognition. Dana almost laughed out loud. No wonder Tim was haunted by Brendan's voyage! For here he stood again, an older version of himself, still tall and slim, but with lines in his face and streaks of silver in his hair. The eyes were the same, shining with an unquenchable thirst for adventure. He was dressed like his crew with the addition of the broad mantle that marked his status as an abbot. Like the other monks, he wore the Celtic tonsure, head shaven from forehead to mid-pate, with long hair falling onto his shoulders.

He took in the plight of his visitors, wet and shivering before him, and called out to his men.

"Dry clothes for our guests, then bring them to my cabin. Bring also food and drink."

After their dousing in the frozen Atlantic, it was heaven to pull on the rough dry fabric of the monkish clothes. The weave was tight and thick, providing instant warmth.

"So Brendan is Tim!" Dana said to Jean. "I wonder if the others are here?"

"We look for them," Jean nodded.

Once changed, the two were taken to Brendan's cabin. The wattle-and-daub hut was built to keep out wind and rain. It was warm and snug, with rush mats on the floor, woven hassocks for seats, and a brazier burning clumps of sod. A low table held the monk's writing materials, feathered quills, sheaves of parchment and pots of pigment and ink.

Brendan directed them to sit as their food arrived, hot mint tea sweetened with honey and a platter of fruit and unleavened bread. They were both exhausted but the refreshment revived them, as did the mischievous grin of the cook. By far the tallest of the crew, he was well over six feet and had to stoop inside the hut. He also had enormous feet encased in hide boots.

"Boots!" cried Dana.

"What name is this?" he laughed. "I am called Artán. 'Little Art' it means."

That made everyone laugh.

The food he brought was delicious. The grapes were as big as apples and though the bread was unleavened, which meant a lot of chewing, it was seasoned with herbs. There was an odd purple-and-white fruit the size of a football and dripping with juice. It was like nothing they had seen or tasted before, a mixture of strawberries, blueberries, plums and oranges.

"A gift from the heavens," Brendan told them. "The fruit was brought to us by a flock of white birds singing celestial hymns."

"I think I know these birds," said Dana, surprised.

The saint studied her closely. A silver rim formed around the iris of his eye, like a corona around the moon. The Second Sight. In a melodic voice, he chanted.

> *Are your horns the horns of cattle?*
> *Are your ales the ale of Cualu?*
> *Is your land the Curragh of the plain of Liffey?*

Are you the descendant of a hundred kings and queens?
Is your church Kildare?
Do you keep house with Brigid and Patrick?

Jean looked dismayed. More riddles! But Dana understood the nature of the questions.

"It's a greeting. He's asking if I'm Irish and what province I come from."

She answered the saint in the same formal manner.

"I am of Ireland and the holy land of Ireland. I am of the province of Leinster that is the plain of Liffey. But my companion is not. He is of—" she paused. What did the early Irish call the land to the west? *"An tOileán Ór."* The Golden Island.

The saint was satisfied with her response.

"The giant declared you pilgrims and the Second Sight tells me this is true. Are you practising *ban martre?*"

It was Dana's turn to be dismayed. She could translate the words literally but had no idea what they meant. *White martyrdom?* They obviously referred to something mediaeval that she knew nothing about.

He saw her confusion and explained, "There are three kinds of martyrdom that pilgrims practise. In *glas martre,* green martyrdom, you become a hermit or ascetic. You give up the comforts and delights of life such as family, friends, food, drink. In *derc martre,* red martyrdom, you shed your blood in God's name. A noble death. *Ban martre,* white martyrdom, is exile. You leave your home, perhaps forever, and journey for a divine cause."

"You could say I'm in exile," Dana said, thinking about both Ireland and Faerie, "and the quest I'm on isn't for something ordinary. I'm searching for *The Book of Dreams.*"

"A book! You are looking for a book?"

275

With great excitement, Brendan produced a jewelled box from his desk. Inside was a manuscript of fine parchment. The vellum sheaves were inscribed with gold orpiment and illustrated with ornate borders and drawings painted in coloured inks.

"The manuscript is composed of quinions," Brendan said proudly, "quires of five sheets laid on top of each other and folded. Hence a gathering of ten leaves makes twenty pages."

Dana's heart was beating wildly.

"*The Book of Dreams!*" she cried.

She could hardly believe it. Her quest fulfilled!

But her joy was quickly dampened.

"No, my child," he said gently. "It is *The Book of Wonders*. The reason I am on this *imram,* this voyage upon the sea which is also a pilgrimage. I will tell you my tale."

As he spoke, they followed his words through the manuscript where pictures depicted what he described. There he was, a younger Brendan, renowned abbot and founder of many monasteries. He was also an accomplished sailor who had already travelled to Wales, Scotland and the Orkney Islands. One day he was doing his rounds in the great monastery at Clonfert where three thousand monks lived under his rule. Psalms rose from the nave of the church. Pots clattered in the steamy kitchens. Men delved with hoe and spade in the vegetable gardens.

When he came to the scriptorium, Brendan lingered a little longer. This was his favourite place. He liked to watch the monks at their work, dipping their goose-feathered quills into ink-horns and trimming nibs with their pen knives. The pages of vellum were carefully cut, then ruled with lines. Coloured powders were mixed with water to make ink. Most of the young scribes copied psalters or gospels to be used in the monastic schools. Only a chosen few, the artists, illuminated the manuscripts prized by Christendom. The monks wrote in Latin and Old Irish and a hybrid Hiberno-Latin. It was a labour of love, but once in a while they noted their complaints, jotting personal glosses along the margins.

Is scith mo chrob on scribainn.

My hand is weary with writing.

Tria digita scribunt, totus corpora laborat.

Three fingers write, but the whole body labours.

Brendan stopped at the desk of a young scribe new to the monastery. As he leaned down to peruse the monk's work, the shock on the abbot's face told a tale in itself. The scribe was recording the story of a fabulous journey across the sea to a magical land behind a rampart of fire.

Brendan was incensed.

"I do not credit the details of this fantasy!" he cried. "Some things in it are devilish lies and some poetical figments. Some may be possible but others are certainly not. Some are for the enjoyment of idiots!"

At the end of his tirade he seized the pages of the manuscript and flung them into the burning hearth. The young monk hung his head in shame. The others continued to scribble silently, without looking up. Brendan was the abbot. His word was law.

That night the saint had a dream. He was standing in the chapel. Suddenly he heard the sound of wings and a great bird settled on the altar. It shone like the sun.

"A blessing upon you, priest," said the bird.

Brendan fell to his knees.

"Are you the Paraclete?" he asked, bowing his head.

"I am the archangel Michael sent to chastise you for burning a book. Who are you to question the infinite wonders of life? Between heaven and earth, more things exist than you can know of. Who are you to doubt the power of the Creator?"

It was the saint's turn to hang his head in shame.

Then the angel charged him with a mission. He was to set off on a sea voyage to seek out the marvels described in the manuscript he had destroyed. In recording all that he saw and experienced, he would restore *The Book of Wonders* to the glory of God. Not until he found the Land of Promise could he return home to Ireland. Only then would the book be completed.

Jean and Dana turned page after page of the manuscript. Each adventure on the voyage was more wonderous and exciting than the last. There was an island where it was always dark but the soil was lit up by glittering carbuncles. The Liver Sea was a nightmare of still waters that held the boat fast, but after prayers from Brendan a wind blew them free. When they came to a smoky land where volcanoes spewed ashes, the inhabitants threw lumps of coal to chase them away. Many times a herd of friendly sea monsters surrounded the boat, and once a great leviathan rose up from the water to carry the leather craft on its back.

"Whales!" said Jean, when he saw the illustration.

"This is the seventh year of my pilgrimage," Brendan told them. "Many wonders have I seen and recorded, but *Tír Tairngire,* the Land of Promise, eludes me still. So my voyage continues without end, for a journey is not completed until one goes home."

He returned the manuscript to its jewelled box.

"Thus you see," he concluded with wry humility, "the penitent became a pilgrim and the pilgrim a writer. Today I shall transcribe the tale of the giant who brought me two young visitors. You will be part of *The Book of Wonders.*"

Dana was taken aback. An idea struck her that made her head spin.

"Could I be like you?" she wondered. "Am I creating *The Book of Dreams* while I'm searching for it?"

"The dreamer is the dream?" Jean nodded.

Brendan folded his hands in front of him.

"To what end do you travel?" he asked. "I know my destination. *Tír Tairngire*, the Land of Promise, the Land of Wonders. It is a place where there is no grief or sorrow, no sickness or death."

His words sent a shiver through Dana. The description fitted Faerie! Could she and the saint be trying to reach the same place? The manuscript he had burned certainly sounded like a book of fairy tales. She felt dizzy. Her own story seemed to twist and turn like the knotted borders of Brendan's manuscript. He was in her tale even as she was in his.

If I'm writing my own book, she thought to herself, I could be a third or even halfway through by now!

"I think we're going the same way," she said to him. "I think we're on the same quest."

He smiled at her serenely.

"Indeed, my daughter, we are all going the same way. We are all on the same quest. For life itself is a peregrination through a foreign land and we are all travelling Home."

"I understand what you say," Jean spoke up. "It makes my heart want to fly like a bird."

The saint rested his hands on their heads. Though they couldn't describe what they felt, each suddenly wanted to be quiet and alone.

"Go now and rest, my children. Leave all your worries aside. I will pray and meditate upon this matter. The next step we take, we take together."

Out on deck, Dana and Jean were surprised at how mild the weather was and how tranquil the ocean. Warm breezes bathed their faces. The water lapped against the leather hull, rocking the boat gently like a cradle.

"It's just like Tim said," Dana pointed out. "The climate was nicer at this time."

A voice called from the lookout near the top of the mainmast.

"Na péistí! Ansin!"

"Sea monsters!" said Dana.

The rest of the crew stopped what they were doing and hurried to look. No one looked afraid.

"There!" Jean cried.

The ocean was alive with leaping bodies. Their appearance was sudden and miraculous, a natural wonder of the far-flung seas. The first to arrive were dolphins, gambolling in the waves like calves in a field. Then came the white-bellied whales who surfaced in bursts of spray before diving again with a huge flick of their tails. To watch them was sheer delight!

One of the monks began to chant quietly. Words and phrases drifted through the air as he quoted from the Bible where it described the leviathan. *His eyes are like the eyelids of the morning. Sorrow is turned into joy before him. He maketh the deep to boil like a pot. He maketh a path to shine after him. Upon earth there is not his like.*

Jean's eyes, shining like the sky, didn't leave the sea till the school had passed them.

"It's like magic, *n'est-ce pas?*"

Dana knew what he meant. Wasn't this what the saint was sent to discover? The beauty of the world. The wonder of creation.

Nearby, two of the crew began to quarrel. One was a big burly man with curls of brown hair. He clutched a manuscript bound with wooden boards. The other was tall and thin with piercing eyes. He had taken a book out of a white satchel. Both were excited and agitated as they pointed at the whales who swam in the distance.

"Never mind those two, they are always at it," Artán said, coming up behind.

He leaned on the gunwales with a genial grin.

"What are they arguing over?" Dana asked.

"Brother Sigisbert has a book he copied in Wales. The *Liber*

Monstrorum, a catalogue of curious and unusual animals. He's an unusual animal himself, being a Christian Saxon. All his people are pagans. Brother Fnör, from the land of Thule, has a book from his own country. The *Physiologus* is a bestiary of fabulous creatures. They like to argue, you see, over the names of the animals we meet in our travels."

Dana and Jean laughed as they recognized the two men. Sigisbert was a dead ringer for the sailing master, George, while Fnör was the spitting image of Trondur.

Some people are destined to be together, Dana reflected. She glanced sideways at Jean. Didn't she feel the same way about him and Roy?

"Do you get homesick?" she asked Artán, who was so like Boots.

"There are times when I long for the green hills of Ireland," he admitted. "It has been seven years since I last saw them. But I am a monk of Brendan. I would follow him to the ends of the earth. And I suppose," the eyes sparkled with mischief, "I am to blame for this voyage."

"How—?" Dana stopped when the truth struck her. "You're the young monk who was writing the fairy tales!"

"Mea culpa," said Artán.

"Where do you get the stories?" Jean asked him. "Do you make them yourself?"

Artán's features softened as he gazed out to sea. It was obvious he was remembering something. Or someone.

"I was not always a monk," he said with a little smile.

Jean grinned as he understood.

"Ah oui, je comprends."

"What?" said Dana. "What?"

They kept laughing and teasing her but finally Artán confessed.

"It was before I took orders," he explained. "I met a beautiful girl one day in the woods. She stole my heart and almost my soul. I had to choose if I would stay in this world or join her in another." He let out a sigh. "I made my decision, yet I never forgot the wondrous tales she told me or the beautiful songs she sang. It was these I recorded in the scriptorium when I should have been copying the Epistles of St Paul."

Dana smiled at his chagrin.

"It's just as well you did," she pointed out. "Think of what you would have missed!"

"Did the abbot not order the two of you to rest?" Artán said suddenly. "On this boat, as in the monastery, we must obey him."

After all their adventures, a rest was welcome. They slept for hours in the crew's hut on mattresses of down as soft as any duvet. At noon, Artán brought them bowls of steaming chowder and hot griddle-cakes.

"Do I dream this?" Jean said.

"When the seas are calm we enjoy our comforts," Artán grinned. "I can light a fire in the big cauldron and cook over it with smaller pots. When you are finished Brendan will see you."

He handed them their clothes which had been hung out to dry. Reluctantly, they traded the loaned woollens for their synthetic fabrics.

Refreshed from their rest, they returned to Brendan's cabin. The saint was looking lively himself. His eyes flashed with excitement.

"A new adventure awaits us! After deep prayer I remembered a tale in *The Book of Wonders* about an Island of Glass. It is the sacred abode of a mighty female spirit who is served by a Druidess. In that cold white country, there comes a day when the sun does not rise and yet another day when it does not set."

Brendan closed his eyes for a moment as he chanted.

There is an ancient tree in blossom there
On which the birds call the hours of life.

"The birds again!" said Dana, "The white birds? They've been following me from the beginning, but I don't know what they mean."

"What is this word 'Druidess'?" Jean asked.

"That is the Irish name for her," Brendan replied. "She is called *Angakuk* by her own people. She has certain powers and can walk between the worlds."

"Ah oui, jongleuse," said Jean, "like the Old Man."

"A shaman," Dana nodded. "Isn't that what you are?" she asked Brendan. "Didn't the giant call you a mage?"

The abbot shook his head vigorously.

"Before this journey, I did not even credit such things! I was a monk, a scholar, the founder of monasteries, but nothing out of the ordinary." His grimace was both rueful and amused. "Look at me now after one touch of an angel! I have the Second Sight and the Gift of Tongues, I am a sailor tossed upon the ocean in search of marvels, an explorer, a writer of fabulous tales." He let out a chuckle. "But no, I am not a mage, though many think me so. I am simply a man who follows God's will."

Out on deck, Brendan barked his instructions like any skipper. Where the boat had been sailing in a leisurely fashion towards the south, they now tacked in the wind and pointed north. The change in course had an instant effect. No longer sluggish in the water, the craft took flight like a bird on the wing, clipping along at speed.

Brendan looked pleased.

"As always when one goes in the right direction, things become easier."

They smelled the ice before they saw it, a cold breath that frosted the air. It wasn't long before small chunks were rattling against the hull like cubes in a tumbler. In the distance, a jagged floe moved slowly like a herd of white beasts across the plain of the ocean.

"The Sea of Glass," Brendan said with quiet awe, "even as the book described it!"

The cold began to seep into their bones. Artán handed out blankets to be worn as cloaks.

Now directly ahead of them a mountainous land came into view. As they drew nearer, they saw it was covered with snow. Between the land and the boat, the river of icebergs ranged like a barrier.

The crew needed all their skill to manoeuvre the boat through the floe. The deadly lure and majesty of the ice was breathtaking. Some pieces were sculptures of clear crystal, others were opaque white. The underwater ledges glowed a deep green while the crags above the surface were a glacial blue.

"Look for a crystal pillar," Brendan ordered, "with a wide-meshed net. That will point the way to go."

Everyone kept watch till at last it was sighted, a shining column of ice surrounded by churning water. Flakes of frazil fanned out around it, looking indeed like a net. Landfall was in sight. In a straight line from the pillar, as if it were a transit buoy, they could see a sheltering fjord on the coast.

Not a word was spoken as the boat sailed into the natural harbour. The stillness and beauty of the landscape was profound. They were approaching the edge of a glacier where bergs calved into the sea. The water was a silvery blue. A cliff of white ice towered above them. Behind it sheered a stark line of mountains draped in cold mist.

Sigisbert rammed a wooden plank into the glacier to form a bridge from the boat. Dana and Jean stared at the icy wall before them. How could they possibly climb over it?

Fnör gave them fur jackets as well as crude snowshoes. He hung the latter from their backs until they needed them.

"Gifts from the land of Thule," he said.

Despite the protests of his monks, Brendan insisted that only he and his guests would go.

As it turned out, the glacier was not as difficult to climb as it appeared. The ice was solid and layered in places to allow their feet purchase. Where it was too smooth for climbing, the saint went first with a sharp knife to carve out footholds. Like Good King Wenceslaus's page, Dana and Jean followed in his steps. At last they reached the plain above.

An arctic panorama spread out before them. A vast land with a backbone of mountain. Frozen peaks and glacial valleys, ice fields and nunataks, all ranged silent beneath the cloak of snow. There was no sign of life, either human or animal, in that great white landscape.

"Where on earth are we?" Dana said. Her breath streamed in front of her. "Are we on earth?"

Jean glanced up as he strapped on his snowshoes. He knew where he was. The recognition had sounded in his heart and soul.

"It's Canada," he said. *"Le Nord."*

CHAPTER TWENTY-SIX

J EAN FINISHED LACING HIS SNOWSHOES AND
stood up.

"I think this is Île Baffin, part of Nunavut. We go north of Labrador, *n'est-ce pas?*"

"That makes sense," Dana said, thinking about it. "Like Tim, Brendan was supposed to have sailed past Greenland. Who's to say he didn't go to Baffin Island before he went south to Newfoundland? The glass sea and the pillars of ice are in his legend."

She had finally managed to strap on her snowshoes and was ready to take her first steps. Moments later she was face down on the ground.

Jean hurried over, trying not to laugh as he helped her up.

Her face was caked with snow. She spluttered and spat. When she started to laugh, he joined in.

"It's all very well for you," she pointed out, "you're used to this. We hardly ever get snow in Ireland. I feel like I'm wearing tennis racquets on my feet."

"It will get easy," he assured her, "but if you walk too much you get *mal de raquette*. I tell you when to rest. *Mais vite,* we must hurry."

Brendan was already some distance ahead, gliding over the snow in his long monk's cloak like a ragged brown swan. He wore a floppy brimmed pilgrim hat and leaned on a staff. On his back he carried a satchel packed with provisions.

They set out after him, tramping across the snowy plain towards the craggy chine of mountains.

"Does anyone else live here?" Dana asked Jean. "I mean besides the shaman? Are there Eskimos here?"

"This is the land of the Inuit. Their name mean 'the People.' They live here for many thousands of year. 'Eskimo' is a name the Montagnais give them that mean 'Fish-Eater.' "

Dana groaned.

"There are so many races here. I'll never get them right."

Jean laughed.

"This is good about Canada, *non*? All the peoples."

They chatted companionably as they hiked through the snow. It was their first chance in a while to really talk together as they had been so busy with the quest. Jean asked about her background. Dana told him about her childhood in a small town in Ireland, how she was raised alone by her father till she was eleven.

"That was a big year," she told him. "Imagine discovering you're the daughter of a fairy queen!"

"Like I find I'm *loup-garou*," he nodded. "At the same time wonderful and *terrible*."

"Exactly!" Dana said. "Then we came to Canada. I think I liked it at first, I can't really remember. It was kind of a shock to leave everything I knew behind, our house, our street, my school, my best friend. Things just got worse as time passed. I desperately wanted to go home. To be honest, I hated it here."

He heard the past tense and smiled to himself.

"Do you know why?" he asked her.

Dana looked around at the glittering scene of snow and mountain, the clarity of blue sky and brilliant light.

"I don't know how, but I thought there was no magic here."

Jean stopped and gazed into her eyes that shone with the same blue brilliance as the sky above.

"Who whisper this lie to you?"

She caught her breath.

"You think the Enemy?"

"Perhaps," he shrugged. "Or maybe it was you, eh? You tell yourself the lie because you want to believe it?"

She heard the pain behind his words, something to do with himself and not her.

"What lie have you told yourself?" she asked quietly.

His smile was sad. She was getting to know him too well, this girl.

"That *grand-père* will one day be human again."

They had reached the end of the ice field. Before them rose another wall of sheer ice and snow, the end of a glacier that streamed down the mountain. It was much higher than the one they had scaled in the fjord.

"We can't climb that," Dana said, dismayed.

Brendan agreed and made no effort to ascend. Instead, he walked alongside the icy cirque.

They followed behind him.

"*It is enough to write the rough white cradles in the snow,*" he murmured to himself.

"That's lovely," said Dana. "What does it mean?"

The saint's features were ruddy in the cold. His eyes shone, silver-rimmed.

"She is somewhere here. Cradled in the snow. We need only find her."

Hours passed in that day of endless light and still they tramped beside the glacier. Their eyes were blind with the whiteness and the brightness. Dana and Jean were beginning to doubt Brendan's wisdom when at last they saw it. There ahead of them stood a miracle in that barren land. A branching tree rimed with frost.

"That is the sign," Brendan said happily, rubbing his hands together. *"There is an ancient tree in blossom there, on which the birds call the hours of life."*

That there was neither blossom nor bird didn't deter them, for they had spotted the opening in the ice behind the tree. The jagged crack in the glacier was large enough to enter.

One by one, they squeezed through the crevice to a chamber within. The scalloped walls emitted a cold blue light that dappled the air. Melodious sounds echoed frostily. The crinkling of ice. The chime of falling water. Fissures laced the walls, branching out into tunnels.

Brendan chose a passageway and entered boldly.

"Sometimes it doesn't matter the way you go," he told his companions, "only that you do. I believe, in this place, all paths lead to the centre."

He was soon proved right. They had not gone long through the snowy passage when they came to the mouth of the *Angakuk's* cave. They knew they had arrived when they saw her handiwork, the first sign of humanity on the island. The archway was decorated with pieces of stone and bone in intricate designs that complemented the ice.

They stooped to go inside the cave, moving slowly so as not to alarm her, but their care was unnecessary. She was obviously expecting them. Seated on the skin of a polar bear, she waved them to sit down as soon as they entered.

It was like being inside a frozen cloud. The cave glimmered with ice draperies and embroidered snow. The natural ledges and shelves in the walls held a profusion of objects: the whorled horn of a narwhal, the tusks of a walrus, stone implements and carved statues, harpoons and long knives. The floor was covered with furs, white seal and arctic fox.

The strange beauty of the cave was captivating, but it was the woman who caught and held their attention.

She seemed incalculably old, brown and wizened like an autumn leaf. Her eyes were black stones set in Asiatic features. Her grin was toothless. She wore the skins of the caribou and a beaded headdress that dangled over her face. Across her shoulders was a mantle of grey-and-white feathers.

Dana felt a wave of terror. Here was one of the ancients of the world. How dare they intrude? They had not been invited. They had no right to be there!

Sensing her fear, the *Angakuk* reached out for Dana. The old hands were strong and gripped Dana's like claws. The girl couldn't have pulled away if she tried. Now the shaman spoke to her. The words were like the sound of birds, clicks and whistles like a stonechat and the high trills of a lark. Dana was about to explain that she couldn't understand when Brendan spoke up in the *Angakuk*'s tongue. The old woman nodded. Cackling to herself, she let go of Dana and rummaged in her cloak. She took out two pebbles and handed one each to Jean and Dana. The stones were small and bluish-grey. She spoke quickly to Brendan.

"Put them under your tongue," he translated. "Then you'll understand her."

The pebbles were smooth from the sea with a slight salty taste. Sure enough, as soon as they put them in their mouths, they understood the shaman.

"Stones are the children of the earth," she told them. "They have been here since time began. They know all the languages of the world."

"Wise and noble woman," Brendan addressed her politely, "I would like to present you with gifts from my people."

Her eyes lit up. She grinned with delight.

"Are they things you found as you travelled in your *umiak*?"

"They are," he smiled.

"Then they will have power, for your journey is sacred. I have dreamed it."

Brendan took the gifts from his satchel and placed them before her, naming each and their origin.

"Four rods of yew with prophecies cut in *ogham*. They come from the branches of the lone tree that grows on *Inis Subai,* the Island of Joy. In a land where the mountains glow like fire, these gold-and-silver leaves were forged by giant smiths. And the fruits of summer, *toirthe samruid,* were gathered on the island that is the Paradise of the Birds."

As the old woman accepted each gift, she held it to her forehead and bowed towards Brendan. Each time she did this, he bowed in return.

Having completed the greeting ritual to both their satisfactions, the shaman was ready to get down to business.

"Why have you come to me?" she asked directly. "I am the *Angakuk* of the People. When the Inummariit have a question they want answered—Where is the seal? Where is the polar bear? Where is the caribou?—they come to me. I journey to Adlivun to see the Goddess. She knows where all the animals are. They are her children and her gift to us. She tells me where they are and I, in turn, tell the hunter. What animal do you seek?"

"Must it be an animal?" Dana asked.

It was the first time she had found her tongue. Though she was overawed by the shaman, she was beginning to doubt that the *Angakuk* could help her. The old woman's magic belonged to the Inuit. Dana was a stranger and not of the People.

"The spirit of an animal is in everything you seek," the shaman said sternly. "If you cannot see this, you are blind. You will never find what you are looking for."

Dana blanched at her reprimand, but the old woman was right. Thinking back over the quest, Dana realized that many animals were indeed involved: the wolf that both she and Jean were kin to, the ravens who were Grandfather and Roy, the deer she had chased in the Medicine Lodge, the throng of caribou that showed her the secret language, the *cailleach* who was a cormorant and her sister, the crane, the whales in the sea . . . Were there others? She was still reflecting when she found herself staring at the shaman's cloak, the grey-and-white feathers. That's when she knew. It was like a burst of light in her head. Of course! There *was* a single creature who had followed her throughout the quest, whose role eluded her, who seemed to convey some hidden significance she couldn't fathom.

"The white birds!" she cried. "The singing soul-birds! They keep showing up, but I don't know what they mean."

The *Angakuk* cackled with glee and rubbed her hands.

"You are not so blind after all. I will go to Adlivun. I will ask Taluliyuk about your birds. She knows a lot about birds."

"You'll do this for me?" Tears pricked Dana's eyes. The kindness of strangers. "But I'm not one of your people."

The old woman's response was quick and irrefutable.

"We are all family."

The shaman had no sooner spoken when a fiery arrow flew into the cave and lit the stone lamp beside her.

"It begins. I go."

Closing her eyes, she began to shake her head till the long beads of her headdress swayed back and forth. A low humming came from under her breath. With mesmeric slowness, she rose to her feet. Now she twirled with ever increasing speed. As she twirled, she chanted. The high-pitched notes sounded like bird-song and the sigh of the sea.

Once the *Angakuk* sang, everything went strange. The air in the cave dimmed as if the sun had set till only the lamp shed light like a candle. The cave flickered with shadows, the greatest being that of the dancing shaman cast upon the back wall. She seemed to tower over them. At first her song was unintelligible, arcane speech known only to her, but eventually words took shape to form a story and the story itself took shape in their minds.

Once upon a time there was a beautiful woman named Taluliyuk who spurned all the suitors who sought her love. Then one day a handsome young man came over the waters from a land far away. He wore grey-and-white clothing, his eyes were dark. His voice was as sweet as a bird's as he wooed her with promises.

O lady, come with me
To the land of my people
There you will dwell
In comfort and light.

It is a land without sorrow
Without sickness or death
A land without hunger
Without darkness or night.

Of course she went with him. He had promised so much. But when she arrived in his land in the North, she discovered his deception. He was not a king of the Otherworld, but a king of the birds. For he was a fulmar who had taken human form in order to court her. He brought her to his tent of fish skins, all torn and tattered. The wind blew through it constantly and she was always cold. There was no oil in her lamps. He fed her raw fish.

After a year of discomfort and misery, Taluliyuk sent for her father to take her home.

Aja, her father, came in the season when the ice broke in the water. He grew angry when he saw the plight of his daughter and he attacked his son-in-law. They fought long with each other till Aja killed the King of the Fulmars.

"You can come home with me now," he told his daughter.

Taluliyuk and her father were on the sea when the birds discovered the death of their king. They cried and lamented till they raised a storm to kill Aja.

Afraid for his life, Aja relented. He told the fulmars they could have Taluliyuk back and he threw his daughter into the sea. She clung to the side of the boat with all her might. Aja cut off the tips of her fingers, but still she held on. The bits of her fingers turned into whales. Now he cut the middle joints of her fingers and they turned into seals. When the fulmars saw the animals in the water, they were appeased. The death of their king had been ransomed with new life. They departed with the storm.

Then the sea opened to swallow Taluliyuk and she sank down into the Underworld. There she dwells to this very day, in Adlivun that lies under the waves.

The story ended but the shaman's song didn't, for the tale was only the prologue, the antechamber to the throne room. Now they entered the dark heart of the matter. The *Angakuk's* voice rose higher still and she screeched out shrilly.

> *That woman down there beneath the sea*
> *She wants to hide the animals from us*
> *These hunters in the ice house*
> *They cannot mend matters*
> *Into the spirit world*
> *I will go*

Where no humans dwell
Set matters right will I.

They were submerged in a heavy darkness at the bottom of
the ocean. Around them moved two-dimensional creatures, flat
eels and pseudopods and sleeping leviathans. Slowly they grew
aware of something else in the depths, magnificent and misshapen,
something so old and immense they could hardly comprehend it.
At first they thought it was an idol from a giantish city long lost
underwater. Then came the beginning of terror when they saw it
stir. The thing in the deep was alive.

Taluliyuk.

The *Angakuk* was there too, singing and dancing in the water.
With arms outstretched, she spun in the depths like a starfish.
Slowly, reverently, she approached the sleeping Goddess. Taluliyuk's
green hair swayed like seaweed. The shaman took out a whalebone
comb and gently raked the tangles of long hair, all the time singing
like a mother to her child.

Close your eyes, here I am
I'm right beside you
I'll close mine and together we'll dream.

The lips of the Goddess murmured with pleasure. Having lost
her fingers, she couldn't comb her own hair. In turn, she would
reward any shaman who requested her help in this way. And now, in
the strangest moment of that strange chthonic journey, the three
visitors found themselves with the *Angakuk* inside Taluliyuk's mind.

Inside her dreaming.

They were here and there and everywhere all at the same
time. They were with every living thing that was upon the earth.
They breathed, slept, hunted and fed with countless numbers of

animals. Every fish in the sea, every bird in the air, every creature great and small that walked, crawled or flew. Wherever an animal was, there was Taluliyuk, living in them and with them and through them all their lives.

Subtly and courteously, the song of the *Angakuk* changed inflection. A question was asked. *Where are the soul-birds?*

In a dizzying ascension, like a plummet upwards, they were hurled into the sky. There! A great flock over Canada, like a spread of clouds. A shining vista of white birds brooding over the country *with ah! bright wings*.

They felt the ripple of Taluliyuk's surprise. These were not her children, not of her body. She called out to the strangers.

In a rush of wings and wind, a mellifluous sibilance, they answered her call. Dropping out of the skies towards the shaman's cave, they alighted on the branches of the tree outside.

Even as the birds fell from the sky, so too did the shaman's three supplicants. Gently they settled back into the cave. They opened their eyes. The *Angakuk* lay on the floor, deep in a trance. Her mouth opened briefly to whistle a word.

"Go."

It was only when they were in the tunnel and Dana looked back to wave farewell did they discover that the dream wasn't over.

"Look!" she cried to the others. "Our bodies!"

There they were, the three of them, eyes closed in sleep, still seated near the *Angakuk*.

"*Tabernac!*" said Jean.

Brendan crossed himself hurriedly. "We are souls alone without their vessels. Another wonder to record!"

The *Angakuk* called out once more. Her tone was urgent.

"Go!"

They hurried through the tunnel and out onto the ice. There, another marvel awaited them. The branching tree had grown immense, almost touching the sky. Its boughs were laden with birds, hundreds and thousands it seemed, all white and shining, of every kind: gulls, ducks, eiders, owls, linnets, ravens, snow buntings, gyrfalcons and eagles, all fast asleep, heads tucked under wing.

As she gazed upwards into the haze of feathered white, Dana felt a deep thrill inside her. The thrill of recognition. The Faerie blood that enlightened her veins knew the truth. These birds were kin.

"What are they doing here?" she said breathlessly. "They belong to Faerie!"

A single white feather floated down from the tree and drifted towards her. She caught it gently and held it to her cheek. Her face was wet with tears. The longing for home surged through her.

Brendan was also enthralled by the birds. The silver rim of the Second Sight seeped into his eyes.

"The souls of the just in the Mystical Tree," he murmured. He turned to Dana. "This flock of angel-birds hail from the Land of Promise. They came here for you. Hark now to their message."

It was as if a wind had shaken the great branches of the tree. All the birds began to move, ruffling and rustling as they stretched and preened. As soon as they opened their mouths to sing, Dana remembered. The song she had heard in the Medicine Lodge. The message that tantalized in stray thoughts and dreams. *Sleepers awake! O nobly born, remember who you are!* They were singing her truth out into the world, the knowledge that was hers from the dawn of time but forgotten at birth. Her heart's truth. Her soul's knowledge.

And, again, as before, she couldn't grasp it. For they sang in a secret language that was lost to her.

"Do you understand what they're saying?" Dana cried to the saint.

Brendan had closed his eyes as he listened to the choir of the birds.

He was about to answer when Grimstone struck.

It was easy for a being who controlled the weather to attack in a land where climate ruled all. They heard him first, an eerie howling in the wind, then they saw the white tornado that sped towards them. Over the glacier it flew, hoovering up snow, firn, ice and debris, gaining in bulk as it approached. Before Dana could even attempt to flee, the whirlwind struck her.

Everything went white. The song of the soul-birds ceased abruptly. Dana was blinded by a blizzard of snow and ice. She sensed him at the cold heart of the flurry, her enemy, Grimstone. She sensed also his hatred. It was mindless and implacable. It wouldn't cease until she was dead. There was a moment when the malice almost wore her down and she felt the touch of the deadly frost of despair. She, herself, was turning white and cold.

Then she heard it, high up in the air, the chant of the *Angakuk*. The snow that was smothering her suddenly melted into water. The crystal flakes became bubbles as Dana sank down,

down,

down into the sea,

where she faced the gargantuan shape of Taluliyuk.

The shaman was still combing the green hair of the Goddess. One of Taluliyuk's great eyelids opened. She stared at Dana.

Mirrored in the dark pupil, Dana saw herself trapped in the whirlwind. She saw Brendan lifting his arms to pray, saw Jean running across the ice to save her. His eyes were golden. He was about to turn, though the wintry sun shone pale and clear.

"NO!" she cried, "You mustn't!"

It was a dream but a dream of power, she knew. Whatever happened to their souls would affect their bodies. If he became a wolf now, he would be so forever.

"Please!" she begged Taluliyuk. "Please don't let him do this! I'd rather die!"

The eye of the Goddess didn't blink, but Dana could see that her look was kind.

All will be well.

Something huge moved across the glacier with fantastic speed. A stone giant tromping over the ice. Its head, limbs and torso were formed of massive rocks. Its feet crashed to the ground. With each step, the earth shuddered, the ice cracked.

With stony ferocity, the *innunguaq* attacked the whirlwind. Tearing at the innards of the swirling snow, it seized Dana from the heart. Then it reached down to snatch Jean, and it hurled the two of them away from the glacier, away from Baffin Island, far out of the North.

With a blur of light and a violent jolt, they landed body and soul on the shore of Ailsa Craig. Nearby, where they had left it, was the flying canoe.

After the white frost of the Arctic, they were assaulted by a riot of smell and colour. The landscape was a shock of blues and greens. The air was vivid with the scents of seaweed and pine.

"Taluliyuk, she save us," said Jean, looking around him dazed.

Only a short while ago, he had made the same decision that *grand-père* had made. He had chosen to turn wolf in the daylight to save someone he loved. Though he was surprised, on reflection, at how easy it had been, he was glad it hadn't been necessary.

Dana stared down at her hands. She was clutching a white feather.

"We didn't get to thank her and the *Angakuk*," she said with a pang. "Or to say goodbye to Brendan."

She was still stunned by Grimstone's attack. He seemed to be able to follow her anywhere, like a relentless hunter tracking his prey. So far she had been lucky. There was always someone there to help her. She shuddered to think that a time would come when no one would intervene. When she would have to face him alone.

Her fingers closed around the feather. She could only hope she would be ready.

Jean was studying his watch the way one does after crossing many time zones. It took awhile to make sense.

"Monday morning!" he said at last. "If we go home now, I don't miss the turkey!"

Dana managed to laugh though she was feeling light-headed. Too much had happened. She could hardly think. There was something she needed to say to Jean, about his almost turning wolf in the daylight to save her. But it was too big a thing to broach right now. She was too shy and awed by its significance. She suspected that he wasn't ready to speak of it either.

"Let's go home to Thanksgiving," she agreed.

CHAPTER TWENTY-SEVEN

WHEN DANA GOT HOME LATER THAT DAY, SHE let herself in with her own key. She was thinking of what she would say if there were any questions and how she could avoid lying. The quest had changed her that way. The person she had been over the past two years was not someone she wanted to be any longer.

Her father and stepmother were in the kitchen. She could hear their voices.

"Who'll tell her?" Gabe said.

Dana's heart skipped a beat. He sounded anxious. Had her deception been discovered? She hesitated at the door and considered eavesdropping further, but changed her mind. That was something else she would no longer do.

She hurried into the kitchen before they could say more.

They were having Thanksgiving dinner. Candles and lace adorned the table. There was no turkey, of course, but there was a feast nonetheless. They were delighted to see her.

"You are here in time!" said Aradhana. "Will you eat?"

"I'd love to! I'm starving!"

Gabriel gave her a big hug, then dished her out a bowl of hot chestnut soup.

The main course had already been served, but she soon caught up. After a pineapple boat of curried lentil and tomato salad, she started on the almond croquettes with cranberry sauce and potatoes au gratin.

"I'm glad I didn't miss this!" she said, her mouth full.

As they questioned her about the weekend, she did her best not to lie. Apparently Ms Woods had promised to bring her home without stating a time. Neither her father nor her stepmother had any suspicions about the "field trip."

"I learned a lot about Canada," she said. "Amazing things. But I'm really glad to be home. Really glad."

The warmth in her tone was obvious. Gabriel and Aradhana exchanged happy glances.

"How about a game of Monopoly after dessert?" Radhi suggested. "We have not played for so long."

Gabe groaned. "You always wipe me out."

"Of course," said Radhi. "I am a businesswoman. You are an artist."

"What's for dessert?" Dana wanted to know.

"Spiced apples in chilled cider."

"Yum."

★   ★   ★

The next day at school there was no sign of Jean. Alarmed, Dana tried to ring him between classes but with no success.

At lunch she tried again but still got voice mail. Upset and worried, she sat alone in the cafeteria, wishing he were there. The last time they had talked together was the flight home in the spirit canoe. They had both been pleased and happy with their adventure, certain they had fulfilled the Old Man's instructions.

"We went east and north," Dana said. "That only leaves two directions."

THE BOOK OF DREAMS

"We live in the south already," Jean pointed out. "Maybe we go west next time?"

"Sounds good to me. If Ms Woods is right and there *is* a deadline, we've got a good chance of making it."

The reminder of their teacher set them wondering again about her disappearance.

"*Peut-être* she come back tomorrow," Jean said. "We talk with her then."

"If she's a Companion of Faerie, it would help," Dana agreed. "There's so much to figure out."

But though they had discussed all the amazing things that had happened and the people they had met, neither had mentioned one particular incident.

Sitting in the cafeteria, Dana's heart beat quickly at the thought of it. Jean had almost turned wolf in the daylight to save her! He had almost given up his human life for her sake! She was awed and humbled that he would do such a thing. And though she tried hard not to be, deep inside she was thrilled. Did that mean he loved her?

She gazed dreamily into space. A shiver of joy ran through her.

Followed by a jolt of horror.

Her hands were shining with light!

She clamped down on the flow and glanced around her in panic. No one was looking. She almost cried with relief. What would she have done if someone had seen her? She would have to be more careful!

Unnerved by what had happened, she hurried to finish her lunch. She wanted to call Jean again.

"Is it okay to sit here?"

Dana was about to point out there were empty tables nearby but she didn't get the chance. The girl sat down opposite her without waiting for permission. Dana frowned. She knew her vaguely. Georgia Cheung was a top student as well as the class beauty with her long black hair and almond eyes. Though generally admired and popular with her peers, she didn't belong to any one circle or group.

"Sure. Work away," Dana said uncertainly.

Georgia had her food on a tray, a noodle dish she had heated in the microwave. The smell of prawns and spices wafted towards Dana, making her mouth water. She was glad that Aradhana had made her lunch that day or she would have been jealous.

Georgia took out chopsticks and began to eat, eyeing Dana's samosas.

"They look good," she said.

"My stepmother's specialty," Dana nodded. "When my dad makes lunch, it's peanut butter and jam. Sometimes I make lunch myself but it's nicer when someone else does."

Georgia agreed heartily.

"My great-granny always makes mine. She's better than a restaurant."

They munched together companionably for a while.

Then Georgia dropped her bombshell.

"I saw what you did. The thing with your hands."

Dana choked on her food.

Georgia leaned over to clap her on the back.

"I don't know what you're talking about," Dana spluttered.

"Sure you do. You can't put me off, I know about magic."

Georgia continued to eat, giving Dana some time to recover.

"Don't worry," she assured her. "Your secret's safe with me." Then she giggled. "Don't you love when you get to say clichés in the right place like that?"

Dana didn't mean to laugh, but she couldn't help it. Georgia's tone was full of humour.

"You're Irish, right?" Georgia asked her.

Dana nodded, happy with the change of subject.

"And you're Japanese?"

Georgia made a noise like a buzzer.

"Wrong. Chinese ancestry."

Dana got flustered and began to apologize.

Georgia waved her hand breezily.

"Don't sweat it. I can't tell the difference myself. I'm Canadian. My background's a real mix. Mom's Hungarian-Irish. I told her about you. 'The quiet girl.' Dad's Chinese-Jamaican. I know more about the Chinese side of things, because my great-granny lives with us. So, where's your boyfriend today?"

"My—?" Dana blushed furiously. "He's not . . . I mean . . ."

It was Georgia's turn to be apologetic.

"Open mouth, insert foot! I'm always saying the wrong thing."

"Me too!" Dana burst out.

They laughed together.

"I don't know if he's my boyfriend," Dana confided. "I don't know anything about boys or going out with them."

"I could tell you a few things," Georgia offered. "He's really cute," she added. "Definitely boyfriend material."

"He is, isn't he," sighed Dana and they laughed some more.

For the rest of lunch they talked about boys, school, the other kids, their classes, their teachers, everything that was important in the day-to-day life of a girl. Dana felt the happiness well up inside her. This was what she had missed for so long, a friend she could talk to and share things with. She appreciated that Georgia didn't mention the light again. And what could she have meant by that comment about magic? Dana was curious to know, but at the same time she was cautious. Their friendship was promising, but too new to test.

When the bell rang, Dana made a decision.

"Would you like to swap phone numbers?" she asked shyly. "You don't have to if—"

"Great idea. I was going to suggest it myself, but I thought you might think I'm pushy." Georgia grinned. "I am, in case you hadn't noticed."

They met on and off for the rest of the day as they shared several classes. Dana still hadn't reached Jean, but Georgia's steady stream of chatter kept her distracted.

"What about that Grimstone guy, eh? Definite child-molester material. He picked on you, didn't he? I bet you're not sorry he's gone. Did you notice how we seem to lose teachers a lot? Do you think they're all buried in the basement?"

At the end of the day, Dana was disappointed to discover they lived in opposite directions.

"Call me!" Georgia shouted as she ran for her bus.

Dana was still waving after her, when she noticed the young woman on the far side of the street. Her heart leaped in her throat. She *had* seen her that time, in the crowd near the musicians. *Honor!* She was here! The High Queen of Faerie!

Overcome with joy, Dana raced across the road.

"Your majesty! How did you—?"

"Oh no Dana," she said, "that name does not belong to me."

Dana was already realizing her mistake. The difference was subtle but evident all the same. This young woman was not as happy or as light-hearted as Honor. She was, of course, her twin sister whom Dana had been told about.

"I'm Laurel," she confirmed. "Honor's sister. A mortal who lives in this world. Do you know where Gwen is? I've been trying to reach her. When I rang the school today, they were all strange about it and told me to contact the police. I know she was going out east with you and—"

Laurel stopped when she saw the blank look on Dana's face.

"Ms Woods didn't come with us," Dana said. "We were going to talk to her about the trip, but she wasn't at school."

Laurel looked as if she might faint.

"Oh God," her voice shook. "When did you last see her?"

Dana thought back. She, too, was beginning to feel shaky. Something was very wrong.

"We left Friday. She was already gone the day before. Yes, because that was the day the vice-principal took over. We thought she might be back today, but she didn't show up."

"She's been gone almost a week!"

Laurel struggled for control. Something was screaming inside her.

"It's my fault," Dana said slowly as the horror dawned. "She wanted to be friends, but I didn't trust her."

"Don't be ridiculous," Laurel said sharply. "How could it be your fault? You're only a child. You're not responsible for what's going on." She put her hands to her head. She had to think. She couldn't collapse now. "I'll have to contact the others and let them know what's happened. It's not your problem. We'll deal with it, don't worry. But right now, you and I need to talk. Are you on your way home?"

"Yes, I—"

"Fine, I'll go with you. I live near Brunswick."

"You know where I live?!"

"We've been watching you. Watching over you. Sorry, it was necessary. We've been trying to guard you, Gwen and I. That must have been . . ."

Laurel bit her lip. She couldn't think about that right now.

Dana was suffering the same thought. Had Gwen been hurt— or worse—trying to protect her?

"It must have been Grimstone!" Dana said, sickened.

She described the servant of the Enemy who had come from Ireland to kill her and how he had first appeared as her teacher.

Laurel looked grim.

"We figured it was him, but far too late to help you. I'm sorry. We did our best to guard you, but we didn't move fast enough. Thank goodness you were able to fight him yourself."

A trace of admiration had crept into Laurel's voice.

"Now tell me everything," she said. "Gwen was convinced you know about the mission? The closing of the portals and the need to restore them by Hallowe'en?"

Dana nodded dumbly, but she was slow to respond. Though she knew she could trust Laurel, she was reluctant to share her story. For one thing, she hadn't warmed to the High Queen's sister. Laurel's manner was adult and bossy. She obviously considered Dana a child. Ms Woods had been friendlier and more likeable. Dana regretted rejecting her. Worse still, that rejection may have doomed her teacher.

"I need to know where you are in the quest," Laurel insisted. "I can't help you, or Gwen, unless I know what's going on."

It was the need to help Gwen that spurred Dana to speak. She told about Edane's visit and the quest to find *The Book of Dreams*. Then she related how Jean had brought her to Grandfather who advised her to travel the four directions. She described her adventures on Cape Breton Island with the giant and Brendan and the *Angakuk*. Throughout her story she made it clear that Jean was her chief support, but she managed to exclude both the *loup-garou* and *la chasse-galerie*. Dana knew how fiercely Jean kept his secrets. She glossed over the question of how they journeyed with vague references to her fairy abilities.

When she was finished, Laurel shook her head with amazement.

"You've done so well. Beyond anything we could have expected. I must apologize. I've underestimated you, I guess because you're young. To be frank, for the first time since all this began, I believe there's a real chance we might succeed."

Dana heard the approval as well as the apology and couldn't help but be pleased. The High Queen's sister was obviously not someone who was easily impressed.

It was Laurel's turn to tell what she knew. She, too, chose to edit what she said. She didn't mention the fate of the Companions in Ireland. There was no point in burdening the girl with more bad news. Instead, she sought to encourage Dana with what support there was.

"There are others in the background working to help you. Even though we can't all come to you in person, you are not alone. Whenever the Enemy strikes against you, it means we have failed to hold the line. But I want you to know that we will fight to the last for you and your quest."

"Thank you," Dana said quietly and she meant it.

They had travelled by subway, talking in low tones. When they reached Dana's stop, Laurel continued to accompany her along Bloor Street and up Brunswick Avenue. As they passed the old convent, Dana stopped abruptly.

"What is it?" said Laurel.

Dana stared at the empty building. The dark bulk seemed vaguely sinister. Most of the windows were nailed and boarded. Part of the wall was charred as if from a fire.

"I felt something," she said. She looked around warily. "Something cold."

Laurel shivered. She reached inside her pocket for the protective charms she always carried. Her heart skipped a beat. Her pocket was empty! She had been so distracted and disturbed when she couldn't reach Gwen that she had forgotten to bring them.

Laurel caught Dana's arm. As they hurried up the street, she spoke quickly and urgently.

"I've made up my mind. We must go west. There are two other Companions of Faerie in Canada, Findabhair who's Gwen's cousin and her husband, Finvarra. He was once the High King of Faerie, but he's mortal now. They're musicians, on tour, in Vancouver at the moment. I don't know why they haven't joined us yet, Gwen was a bit vague about that, and right now I don't care. It's time they got on board. It can't be a coincidence that your instructions include travelling west too. You know yourself there's no such thing as coincidence in these matters. Obviously we should travel together."

The more Laurel spoke, the more dismayed Dana grew. She was glad to think of a line of support at her back, but she wasn't happy with the idea of others joining her quest. She preferred to think of the mission as something she and Jean did together. They were fine on their own. They didn't need anyone else.

"You should stay here and find Gwen," she suggested. "I'll go out west with Jean."

Laurel's disagreement was instant and vehement.

"Listen to me, Dana. You mustn't involve Jean again. He's a mortal and not a Companion of Faerie. This has nothing to do with him. I understand how you feel, he's your boyfriend, and he has helped you through a lot. But if you care about him, you'll leave him out of this. It's too dangerous. He has no way of protecting himself. If he is harmed, it will be your fault as well as mine."

Dana felt a surge of resentment against Laurel. How dare she interfere like this! Then she faltered. An image of Jean flashed through her mind. How he looked as he lay unconscious in the hospital swathed in bandages. Another image quickly followed. Jean on Baffin Island, racing towards the whirlwind that was Grimstone. His eyes glowed amber as he made his decision to turn wolf in the daylight. Dana's resentment changed to anguish. Laurel was right. Her quest put Jean in constant danger. She couldn't bear to think of him getting hurt or worse, losing his humanity because of her. It was selfish of her to keep him involved, especially now that there were others to help her with the mission.

"All right," she said, with a heavy heart. "I'll go west with you."

"Good," said Laurel. "Now how can we convince your father to let you go?"

They had arrived at Dana's house. They were standing on the pathway in front of the big brownstone.

"I'll talk to my stepmother first. She understands these things a lot better than my dad. It will be easier for him when he hears you're going, but I'll have to decide how much I want to tell him."

"I'm sure you'll do fine," Laurel said. "If they want to meet me, I'm available. We have a slight connection, I believe, that might help matters. Your dad knows my grandfather, Professor Blackburn. You could mention his name. Here's my number. Call me tonight. I'm not far from you, at Massey College on Devonshire Place. If you need me, I can be here immediately. Oh, and I have the money for our trip, so tell your dad that. I'd like to book our flights tonight. The sooner we go the better."

Laurel was about to leave when she stopped and looked up at the house.

"By the way, that's one powerful protection spell you wove here."

Dana smiled.

"Not me, my stepmother's guardian. She's from India. He's the Lord Ganesh."

"Ah, that's it," Laurel said softly. "You will always be safe here."

Again she hesitated. It was obvious there was something else she wanted to say.

"What is it?" Dana asked her.

"I know your story, I heard it in Faerie, but I get the impression you don't know mine or Gwen's?"

Dana shrugged sheepishly.

"Actually, I didn't even know your names. I always went to my mother in Faerie, she's a *spéirbhean,* not one of the Gentry. She didn't hang around the Court much, where the harpers tell the tales, and neither did I. To be honest, I was never interested in human tales, especially ones about Canadians and Faerie. I blamed the bond between the two countries for the reason I had to leave Ireland." She let out a sigh. "I didn't want to be here."

Laurel listened with sympathy.

"I understand. I've had my problems with Faerie too. It's not always a picnic. Too bad, though, if you had known our stories we might have met sooner."

Dana winced. And things would have been different. Gwen would still be there.

"I'm not accusing you of anything," Laurel said quickly. "Things happen. There's no point looking back with anger or regrets. Believe me, I know."

The echo of pain in Laurel's words touched Dana. For the first time, she thought she could like this young woman.

"Perhaps you could tell me your story when we travel?" Dana said. "It's a long flight out west, isn't it?"

Laurel smiled. The girl was less difficult than Gwen had described. She could even be charming.

"Good idea. Talk to you later then."

Dana hurried into the house, calling out for Aradhana, but a note on the table explained that her stepmother was working late. Gabriel was at home, practising in his studio. The sound of the silver flute trilled through the house. She would leave him be and wait for Radhi. She tried to ring Jean again, but there was still no answer. Then she tried Georgia, but her line was busy. Restless, she forced herself to do her homework. With all the excitement of the quest, she was falling behind in her school work. Lost in study, the time passed quickly. When the telephone rang, she raced into the hall.

"I've got it!" Dana shouted to her father.

It was Jean.

"At last!" she said. "Were you sick today?"

"I'm in Québec. With the Old Man and Roy. *Grand-père est disparu.* No one can find him. I come here as soon as they tell me."

"Oh no." Dana felt a cold panic. "Do you think it's Grimstone?"

"I don't know," he said honestly. "Each year *grand-père*, he is more and more wolf. It may be this. Tonight I go to the Shaking Tent. I find the truth."

"Can I help at all?" she asked desperately.

Two people near her had disappeared. Could it just be a coincidence? *There's no such thing as coincidence in these matters.* The more she thought about it, the more sinister it seemed. Having failed in his attacks against her, was Grimstone striking at her friends and the circle that helped her? She felt threatened, hemmed in on all sides. She wanted to tell Jean about Ms Woods and Laurel, but she decided against it. She had already chosen to exclude him from the quest to keep him out of danger. But was it too late? And what about *grand-père*?

"*C'est* okay," Jean assured her. "With Grandfather and Roy, I find him. And you? *Comment ça va?* Anything happen today?"

"I made a new friend at school," she said, avoiding an outright lie. "I'll introduce you when you get back. Don't worry about me. Find *grand-père*."

"*Bon.* I call you as soon as I know. But you, *fais attention.* Be careful, eh?"

"I will," she said. "And Jean? You'll take care too, won't you?"

"I'm fine. This is the best place to be. But I worry for you. I don't want to be—*comment dit-ons 'chauvin'?*—chauviniste? You are strong, but still I worry. You will wait for me, yes? I ask you?"

"I promise," she lied. So much for good intentions.

There was nothing left to say, yet neither hung up. Dana could hear him breathing on the other end of the line. Her heart ached.

"Dana?"

"Yes?"

"I am missing you."

"Me too. I miss you too."

"*À bientôt, chérie.*"

"Yes. Soon."

When the line went dead, she stared at it awhile. Then she ran to get Laurel's number. She needed to talk about *grand-père*'s disappearance. She was worried sick. The number Laurel gave her rang for some time and was then redirected.

"Porter's lodge, Massey College. Can I help you?"

"Oh. Yes. Hello. I'm trying to reach Laurel Blackburn?"

"I'm sorry, she's gone."

"*What?*"

"She left today. I don't know when she'll be back."

Chapter Twenty-Eight

Dana felt sick. This couldn't be happening. "What do you mean? I only met her a while ago. She told me to call her."

"It was some family thing, I think," said the porter. "I can't tell you more. Sorry. That's all I know."

In shock, she could hardly think. Family thing? The other Companions? That hardly made sense. Laurel wouldn't go away without telling her. Unless, oh God, like Ms Woods . . .

Dana started to shake. The fear was overwhelming. She was drowning in it. She buried her face in her hands. For a moment she was lost in darkness, then the light welled up. The golden warmth bathed her face like the sun. *O nobly born, remember who you are.* Dana straightened. She was stronger than this. She remembered what Tim had said on the boat. *Whatever will happen will happen. You either face it as a coward or you face it as a hero. It's up to you.* She wiped away her tears. Something terrible had happened and she had to face it.

She went to her father's studio.

"Sorry to bother you, Gabe, but I need you right now."

Gabriel looked up from his music to regard his daughter. Something in her tone had caught him. She didn't sound like a child. Nor did she look like one. Tall, calm, with serious features, a young adult stood before him.

"What's up, sweetheart?"

"Could you give me a lift to a friend's? She's staying at Massey. It won't take long. I could walk, but it's getting dark and the campus makes me nervous."

He didn't ask questions. He was pleased that she had asked for his help. Things had been slowly improving between them and he was following his wife's advice to let it happen naturally.

He was curious that she knew someone at Massey College. She explained that Laurel was a student who had come to her school to talk about folklore.

"You know her grandfather," Dana told him, "Professor Blackburn."

"Of course I do! He's the one who got me the job. What a coincidence!"

"Hmm," she said.

When they arrived outside the college gates, Dana asked him to wait in the car.

"I won't be long. Maybe you could meet her some other time."

Heart in her mouth, she hurried into the college residence. She was still hoping for a last-minute reprieve, a simple explanation, or even the return of Laurel herself.

The porter's lodge was directly inside the gate, a small cupboard of a room with notice boards and mail slots. The porter, a student, sat behind the wooden counter reading a book.

"I'm Dana Faolan, a friend of Laurel Blackburn. She didn't come back by any chance? Or maybe she rang? Or left a message?"

The porter looked contrite.

"You called earlier, didn't you? Sorry, I only remembered after you hung up. She left something for you." He took a thick envelope from Laurel's mail slot. "She left it earlier today. Said you might pick it up at any time."

A glimmer of hope. Perhaps Laurel *had* been called away by the other Companions? She could have tried to ring when Dana was talking to Jean.

"This guy came for her, tall, badly scarred face."

The porter shuddered though he tried not to.

The death of hope. Dana stood stock-still as she absorbed the news. Her worst fear confirmed. There was no mistaking the description. Again she fought off the terror and held onto her courage. She had to get help for Gwen and Laurel before it was too late.

Oh please, she thought, let it not be too late.

"Everything okay?" Gabriel asked her, as she got into the car.

"She's not there right now," Dana said quietly.

There was nothing else to say.

Back home, Dana hurried into her bedroom and tore open the envelope. The contents gave her a shock. A wad of money! There was also a note.

Dear Dana,

I'm so sorry. If you are reading this it means I have failed you despite my best efforts. I'm leaving this for you in case something happens. You mustn't look for me or try to help me. There isn't time. If there's hope for any of us, it lies in the quest and the restoration of Faerie. Go west as soon as you can. Find Finvarra and Findabhair. Tell them to help you. Time is running out. The portals must be restored on Hallowe'en when the two worlds cross. Use the money for your quest. Again, I'm so sorry if you are reading this. Be of good courage. I trust we'll meet again when the Kingdom is restored.

Yours,

Laurel Blackburn

Dana wanted to cry. Somehow Laurel had known that Grimstone was coming for her. Yet, despite the terror she must have been feeling, she still thought of the quest. A true Companion of Faerie. A true hero.

"I won't let you down," Dana said softly.

Attached to the note was a schedule with venues and dates. It took Dana a moment to understand what she was looking at: the itinerary of a musical group called "The Fair Folk." Findabhair and Finvarra! She studied the dates. They had arrived in Vancouver a week ago and would still be there over the weekend. Then they toured eastward with engagements in all the major cities. Dana frowned. They weren't due in Toronto till early November. If Hallowe'en was the deadline weren't they arriving too late? Perhaps they had other plans. Well, she would soon find out.

Dana knew what she had to do. She would go out west to meet Findabhair and Finvarra. Not to ask for their help with the mission, but to tell them what had happened to Gwen and Laurel. She was counting on the two of them to save their companions. She herself would continue the quest alone. She had done it in Ireland, she could do it in Canada. According to Grandfather, something awaited her in the West. She would go to meet it. This was *her* mission. It was time she took full responsibility for it.

Dana packed her bags with quiet purpose. Then she went into the kitchen where Gabriel was making supper. It was spaghetti *alla napoletana,* a favourite from the days when they were a family of two. Loreena McKennitt was singing melodiously on the tape player. *And now my charms are all o'erthrown. And what strength I have's mine own.* Seeing what needed to be done, Dana cut the crusty loaf on the table and buttered the slices before sprinkling them with garlic and basil. Gabriel had cooked the pasta and tomato sauce and was tossing a green salad. They smiled at each other as they worked together, humming along with the music. It was like the old days in Ireland when they made meals together.

In that cusp of time, Dana allowed herself to feel safe and happy. This was the calm before the storm. The night before the battle. She knew that evil was at the gate, crouched and waiting, but she also knew it couldn't get in. No dark thing could pass the Lord Ganesh's protection. She would enjoy this moment with her father. Gabe himself was full of cheer, looking younger and livelier than he had in ages.

When Aradhana came home from work, they all sat down to the meal together. Though there was plenty of laughing and joking, Dana felt sad. Soon she would end this bright moment. Her bags were packed. She was leaving that night. No matter what they said, they couldn't stop her. She planned to tell Radhi first, then she would break the news to Gabriel. The three of them had faced a similar crisis in the past. She hoped that fact might ease the pain. On her last quest, Dana had left home without telling her father. At least she would give him fair warning this time.

It was when they were eating dessert that Dana noticed something odd. Radhi and Gabe were exchanging furtive looks. Did they suspect something? But how could they? After supper, Gabe insisted on washing the dishes alone and shooed the two females into the living room.

"For a talk," he said nervously. "That's what women do. Talk to each other. Talk."

Aradhana was trying to smother her laughter. Gabriel shot her another look.

Intrigued and a little anxious, Dana sat down.

"What's up?"

Aradhana beamed at her stepdaughter and took hold of her hands.

"Dana, I will not beat about the bush. Your father is a typical man in such matters, that is to say, a coward. I am going to have a baby. You are going to have a sister or brother."

Dana fought to control her features. Her stepmother's face shone with joy. No wonder Gabe looked so happy! If only she could feel the same way. But the timing was disastrous. She couldn't possibly tell them anything now. It would be far too upsetting. They wouldn't be able to handle it. She would have to leave without letting them know and then call from Vancouver.

The loneliness descended on Dana like a pall. To hide her dismay, she hugged her stepmother.

"I'm really happy for you, Radhi. I really am."

Her stepmother's embrace was scented with jasmine. Holding back the tears, Dana rested her head on Radhi's shoulder. She could heard her father in the hallway, talking on the telephone.

"Thought you both should know. Yeah, aunties again! Well, someone has to pass on the genes. Neither of you will ever be mature enough to have kids."

Dana's eyes widened. She *wasn't* alone!

Racing into the hallway, she grabbed the phone from her father and sent him back to the living room.

"Can I come over?"

"Something wrong?" her aunt Yvonne asked immediately.

"We need to talk," Dana urged. "Invite me to stay the night. No, several nights. *Please.*"

Few adults respond correctly to the melodramatics of a teenager, but Dana knew she was talking to one who would.

"*Pas de* prob. Put Gabe back on."

Gabriel was sitting with Aradhana. He looked puzzled when Dana called him back to the phone.

"What? But?" he stuttered into the receiver.

Dana could see the day was won before Yvonne had even finished.

She hurried back to her stepmother.

"Listen, Radhi. I'm going away for a few days. To visit my aunties. Please don't feel bad. It has nothing to do with your news. I'm really happy for you both, believe me, but I've got something to do."

Aradhana took Dana's face in her hands and gazed into her eyes.

"Dana? Does this—?"

"Don't make me explain. I can't say more. Trust me, please?"

Aradhana didn't look happy, but she could see that Dana was adamant. At last she nodded.

Dana hugged her again.

"Your baby is going to be very lucky to have you. Just like I am."

*   *   *

Dana's aunts lived in the loft of a chic warehouse that accommodated an art gallery, a craft shop and several studios. The loft was spacious, all skylights, wooden beams and open planning. They had furnished it in a colourful style with futons, Afghan rugs, wall-to-wall artwork, shelves of books to the ceiling, and a music system that would serve a nightclub. The two sisters had been living together for over a decade, having discovered they couldn't tolerate anyone else on a permanent basis.

Yvonne greeted Dana with a hug, and casually waved her brother away.

"You've missed Mexican night, kiddo. You should have rung earlier."

Her aunt was wearing a red-and-yellow poncho over embroidered mariachi pants. Behind her, the glass dining table was littered with leftover tacos and dregs of salsa. A half-empty bottle of tequila partnered a salt shaker and slices of lime. The lights were dimmed, candles flickered around the room and The Gypsy Kings sang full-throated from the speakers.

"It doesn't matter," Dana said. "I don't eat meat."

"You could've had the refried beans," Dee called from the kitchen area.

She came out carrying a big bowl of nachos and a smaller bowl of guacamole. Dressed in black, she wore tight leggings with a tatty sweater torn at the elbows, and big clumpy boots. Her brush-cut had changed colour from blue to pink.

"Refried beans," she repeated. "Could they have thought up a less attractive description?"

"Could be a direct translation," Yvonne suggested.

"You can eat this," Deirdre told her niece, setting the bowls on the table. "Suitable for vegetarians and quite delicious. Also quite green."

She burst into song.

> *How are things in guacamole?*
> *Has the green gone brown and yucky yet?*

Dana looked puzzled. Between fits of laughter, the aunts attempted to tell her about an Irish-American stage play whose theme song was "How Are Things in Glocca Mora?"

"Finian's Rainbow," Dee said with awe. "Classic kitsch. First it was a cornball Broadway musical, then it really went bizarro-world when they made it a movie."

"Oh gawd, Fred Astaire's abominable brogue!" Yvonne screeched. "And Petula Clark was his daughter!"

They howled till tears came down.

"I bet Coppola gets nightmares remembering that one," Dee said.

"He was only twenty-nine," her sister pointed out.

"*I'm* twenty-nine and you wouldn't catch me making a clunker like that!"

Dana sank into a bean bag chair. Being with her aunts was always a leap into mayhem and madness.

"'Bout time you came to see us," Dee told her. "The last time you were here, it was almost a year ago. Your birthday, remember? We had to take a taxi to Gabe's and drag you out."

It was true. That was at the height of her rebellion against Canada. She had simply refused to go anywhere where she might enjoy herself. Most of the time she had stayed in her room, escaping to Faerie. How much things had changed!

"Don't mind her," Yvonne said, throwing her sister a look. "If you want to be moody, you go right ahead. It's a teenager's prerogative."

"I would like to visit more often," she assured them.

Dee grinned triumphantly at Yvonne.

"But I'm not really here for a visit," Dana announced. Time was running out. She had to state her case. "I'm here to ask for your help. I have to go out west, to Vancouver. I've got the money. I just need you to take me."

Producing the brown envelope, Dana emptied a pile of bills onto the table.

Her aunts' eyes went huge. Both were remembering the same thing. The night she stole their mother's car.

"Who did you rob?" Dee asked outright.

"It's the baby, isn't it," Yvonne said gently. "It's totally freaked you out. You're being replaced and—"

"No," said Dana, exasperated. "I'm really happy about the

baby. That's got nothing to do with it. And I didn't steal the money! How could you think that? This is something else, totally and utterly different."

Her aunts were exchanging looks. "Humour her," their glances said, "the poor thing has cracked under the strain."

Aware that she was fast losing her audience, Dana was ready to grasp at straws. She glanced at the bookshelves that lined the walls, cluttered with fantasy and mythic fiction. There was an entire shelf of Charles de Lint alone. She saw her chance. An opening into the truth. She pointed to the books.

"Did you ever think, either of you, that this kind of stuff— magic, I mean—could be real? Could exist in the world?"

They were caught off guard by the question. They had been concentrating on Dana and were suddenly thrown back on themselves. They started to giggle. Both looked younger and a little shy.

Deirdre rubbed the pink stubble on her head.

"Hey, you're looking at two people who spent a whole weekend in Ottawa searching for Tamson House."

Dana understood the reference to *Moonheart* which they had urged her to read.

"Didn't find it," Yvonne sighed.

"Yet," said Dee.

Dana took a quick breath. The moment was ripe. It was now or never. She put her hands together and offered her palms to her aunts. The light spilled over like liquid gold.

Deirdre's face drained of blood. There was always a moment of terror when the Otherworld knocked. *Every angel is terrifying.* A healthy fear of the unknown was ingrained in every animal, including humans.

"Okay, breathe through it," Dee ordered herself quietly. She got up to pace the room. "That's it, breathe. Life just got a lot more interesting. *Breathe.*"

Yvonne sat so still she seemed to be in shock, but in fact her mind was racing.

"It's to do with your mother, right?" she said finally. "Gabe's first wife? I always knew there was something weird happening there. The whole thing was too odd and Gabe could never really explain it. Where she came from, who she was, why she had no family and then—poof!—she disappeared. Am I right or am I right?"

"I found her just before we left Ireland," Dana nodded. "She's . . . she's a fairy queen."

Both aunts let out a long-drawn *ahhhhh*.

Then Dee let out a whoop.

"That makes you half-fairy!" She grinned at her sister. "We're the aunts of a half-fairy! If we were her godparents, we'd be a fairy's godmothers. She'd be our fairy god-niece."

"You're babbling," Yvonne warned. "Get a grip. I don't want to slap you."

"Cause you'd be sorry."

When they eventually managed to calm down, Dana told her story. Except for the truth about Jean, she left nothing out. Her aunts were so thrilled and excited about the wonder of it all, the aspect of danger didn't really sink in. Of course there was no question that they would help her. They would all go west and as soon as possible! With the decision made, they were galvanized into action, leaving their niece breathless.

The first call was to Gabriel. Dana would stay longer than a few days, maybe a week or more, nothing to worry about, they would get her to school, help with the homework. He and Radhi should enjoy the break. After all, they won't have any time for each other once the baby was born.

Dana listened with awe as her aunts played their brother like a song. Obviously it had always been this way. They had always run circles around him.

The next call was to a friend who was also a travel agent. Apologies for the late hour but this was an emergency, they needed return tickets to Vancouver ASAP.

Dee had begun to count the money at this point. She yelled gleefully to Yvonne who was still on the phone.

"First class!"

That made it easier. They could fly out in the morning.

"We'll call your school first thing tomorrow," Yvonne concluded. "You've got a dose of something. You'll be back in a few days."

"You guys are amazing," said Dana.

"She said 'you guys'! Did you hear that?" Dee crowed. "We got to her at last! A fairy Canuck!"

Dee was pulling out suitcases from a wardrobe and tossing in clothes as she sang.

My bags are packed, I'm ready to go
I'm standing here, on your big toe . . .

Chapter Twenty-Nine

"We are so dead if Gabe ever finds out," Dee said mildly.

She looked out the airplane window. The sun shone palely above a sea of cirrus. Below, the landscape played hide-and-seek with the clouds. They had been flying for hours, over green and brown countryside, through various time zones, across plains and prairie.

"Yeah," said Yvonne with the same lack of concern.

"Do you feel as if you're wandering through a dream?"

Dee was still absorbing the fact that she was heading for Vancouver on someone else's money. The luxury of first class was as good as she had hoped. The flight attendant kept giving her things, delicious food, hot towels, free perfumes, expensive magazines.

Yvonne shook her head vigorously.

"Not in the least. I feel exquisitely awake. As if I've been doused in the ocean. Every nerve is tingling. I'm totally alive."

Dee reflected on her words.

"I have that too," she finally agreed. "That's a better description. It's the way I feel when I'm making a film, when it's all coming together but still at the stage where anything could happen."

"Absolutely," Yvonne concurred. "It's as good as art and nearly as good as—"

They grinned at each other and cackled like witches.

Dozing in the seat across the aisle, Dana smiled to herself. Her aunts were worse than two kids. And in more ways than one. She couldn't believe that Deirdre had hogged the window seat. Gabriel always gave it to Dana on their travels. When Yvonne objected, Dana thought her older aunt was taking her side but no, she wanted the seat for herself. After a spirited exchange involving colourful words, they came to a time-sharing arrangement that didn't include Dana.

"You need to rest," Yvonne said, quite unfairly. They had all stayed up late talking. "You're younger than us."

Only in years, Dana thought to herself but she didn't argue, knowing it was futile. She promised herself to be first on the plane on the flight home. With her aunts, it was obviously every woman for herself.

Now the two were discussing the adventure in low tones. They had finally reached the realization that there might be danger and they were worried for their niece.

"Things could get scary," Dee was saying. "Remember those strange little men screeching up and down the hall at night?"

"That was the dark rum," Yvonne pointed out. "You didn't see them again when you cut it out."

The flight got bumpy over the province of Alberta as they crossed the brown foothills of the Rocky Mountains.

"I don't want to die," Deirdre moaned. "Not now. Not ever."

Yvonne didn't speak but she looked anxious and her knuckles were white as she gripped the arm rests.

Dana wasn't afraid. It was far less turbulent than the flying canoe. She saw her chance.

"Come on, let me near the window. You both have your eyes shut!"

Conceding defeat and welcoming the distraction, her aunts

changed seats to let her in. Dana pressed her face to the window. Below, the drifts of cloud parted to reveal a vast mountain range powdered with snow. The stark peaks undulated like an ocean of living rock. Dana shivered with awe. There was power and majesty in these mountains. She had flown into the west to meet them. What would they teach her?

When the plane landed, they took a taxi to their hotel. The driver was surprised by their encouragement to go the long way.

"Ah, Vancouver," Yvonne sighed, "Queen of Cities."

"Traitor," said Dee, though she was also looking around her with joy.

"What's that?" asked Dana.

Yvonne explained. "If you come from Toronto you can't even hint that Vancouver might be better. Though it so obviously is and everybody knows it."

"Traitor," said Dee again.

"Don't you have that in Ireland?" Yvonne asked her.

Dana thought a moment.

"No. Everyone in Dublin says the West is best. It begins when you cross the River Shannon."

"What is it about west coasts?" Yvonne mused. "Why do they have all the ambience? The *je ne sais quoi*? There's California too."

Beyond the cab window, the cityscape opened to embrace the Torontonians. On one side glimmered the blue Pacific Ocean, on the other sheered a grandeur of mountains. Cradled in between, like a sunburst of crystals, was Vancouver itself, all elegant architecture and spacious streets, arched bridges and sandy beaches, museums and quaint pubs. Overhead, the Skytrain glided like a silver serpent. The weather was crisp and sunny in contrast to the prairies where it was already snowing. Some of the trees still blazed with autumn colour while others stood naked, leaves heaped at their feet like discarded garments.

Their hotel was old and old-fashioned. It had been a stylish apartment building in its day, but now the lobby and elevators were somewhat shabby. Their room had an antique charm. The furniture was 1950s with its oversized lampshades in beige and brown, stuffed armchairs, wooden furniture and comfortable beds. The carpet was worn and the television huge, but the bathroom was spotless with an abundance of thick towels.

"We could have paid more for more," was Deirdre's comment.

"I just couldn't," said Yvonne. "I always stay here when I come to Vancouver. She's like an old lady friend. I would feel I was betraying her if we went to some tarty new place."

Dee rolled her eyes at Dana, but obviously didn't mind. Their room overlooked English Bay with a panoramic view of beach and promenade. Sea gulls periodically landed on the windowsills.

"Wait till you taste the food," Yvonne said. "Especially breakfast. Seriously yum. Bacon and eggs, fruit cup, pancakes with syrup, big pot of coffee."

"I want that right now," Dee decided, picking up the phone. "Why put off till tomorrow what you can eat today?"

"She knows nothing about deferment of gratification," Yvonne said to Dana, then she called to her sister, "The same for us!"

As they ate the food with plenty of appreciative noises, they discussed their plans. Dana had brought The Fair Folk's itinerary with her. The venue listed beside the Vancouver dates was "The Moon in the Bog, Whelan's Tavern, Gastown."

"I think it's safe to say The Moon in the Bog is a club on top of a bar," Dee said.

"New Irish bar," Yvonne nodded. "I've heard of it but haven't been there yet. That means you can't go," she said to Dana. "They serve alcohol."

"Yahoo!" said Dee, but when she saw Dana's face, "I mean, boo hoo!"

"We'll have to meet them for you," Yvonne continued, throwing Dee a look. "If we can't bring them back here, we'll arrange a meeting for tomorrow. We know the story, we can fill them in. Okay?"

Dana did not look happy.

"Can't we just put loads of make-up on her?" Dee said to Yvonne. "She's taller than us. She looks at least sixteen."

"Which is still not the legal age," her sister said archly. "Look, we're in pretty deep here already. Could you imagine if we got arrested with a minor and then they contacted Gabe?"

"Right," said Dee. To Dana she added, "Watch TV till your eyes bug out and run up the room service bill."

"Maybe we could reach them before their show?" Dana suggested.

Deirdre was looking at the itinerary. Beside "The Fair Folk" was a little blurb on the group describing their music—"a Celtic fusion of trad, folk and rock"—then the names of the musicians, "Findabhair and Finvarra."

"How do you pronounce this name?" she asked Dana. "Find-a-bear?"

Dana had to laugh. "It's an old Irish name, linked to Guinevere. You pronounce it 'Finn-ah-veer.'"

"Nice. And, yes, that's a good suggestion. I wasn't ignoring you. I just don't feel like making a bunch of phone calls."

"I'll do it," said Dana.

While her aunts unpacked, she rang the tavern, the club and The Fair Folk's hotel, to no avail. She left messages at each number giving her name and "The Companions of Faerie" for reference. Her lack of success left her crestfallen.

"They could still call back," Yvonne comforted her. "And if not, I promise you, we'll bring them to you as soon as we can."

It was too early for the club to open, so the three went for a walk along the promenade of English Bay. Crowds of people strolled along with them, enjoying the sunshine in the late afternoon.

"Very west coast," said Yvonne.

There were musicians busking with guitars and fiddles, youngsters skateboarding, lovers walking hand in hand. Two old men played chess at a stone table beneath a big tree, while a young woman contorted herself into yoga positions. The pale sand on the beach was strewn with grey driftwood. Ducks bobbed on the waves. Gulls screeched overhead. They bought popcorn and ice creams and sat on a bench to watch the world go by.

Back in their room, Dana's good humour dispelled as her aunts dressed to go out. Dee donned a black leather cat suit with a long zipper and metal jewellery, while Yvonne put on a slinky red dress with stiletto heels. Clouds of perfume wafted from the bathroom.

"You look divine, Mrs Peel," Yvonne said to Deirdre.

"You too, Madonna," came the reply.

"You're supposed to be on a mission," Dana accused them.

"You never know who you might meet on a mission," Dee pointed out.

"Heroes?" Yvonne said to her sister.

They grinned at each other.

"Now don't wait up," Dee said to Dana. "We're bound to get tanked."

"Just try and remember why you're going," their niece pleaded as they left.

The club was not what Dee and Yvonne had expected. The pub on the first floor was sleek and expensive. Upstairs, The Moon in the Bog was Celtic chic, a cavernous space with a big stage and dim lights. The walls were painted to look like stone with ancient spiral designs. Afro-Celt music shivered through the speakers. A well-dressed crowd slowly filled the room.

"Not your average grotty find-your-roots gig," Dee commented.

"Don't be cynical," said her sister.

"I am not 'dog-like,'" she retorted.

They headed straight for the bar and ordered pints of Guinness.

"Mmm good," said Dee, after a long swallow of the black porter.

"You've got a moustache," Yvonne warned her.

"I should hope so," said Dee, licking the creamy froth from her lip. "It's bad Guinness if I don't."

As the show started, they turned to face the stage.

Dressed in black like the night, both Finvarra and Findabhair were tall, lithe and beautiful. There the resemblance ended. Where her hair was blond and spiked like icicles, his jet-black mane fell in a blunt cut to his shoulders. Her skin was fair with diamonds piercing her ears, nose and eyebrow. His colouring was nut-brown, his eyes sloe-black. She wore a dark gown sprayed with stars, slit up the side to reveal a shapely leg. He wore black leather pants and a silken T-shirt that hugged his chest. Both had dark-blue spirals tattooed on their faces and kohl around their eyes. They were unashamedly flagrant and fey.

The aunts approved.

"These guys could give beauty lessons," was Yvonne's assessment.

"Seriously cutie-patootie," Dee agreed.

As soon as the music began, they were stunned into silence. It was haunting and exquisite. Finvarra played the fiddle like a gypsy king with searing abandon and awesome virtuosity. Findabhair sang in high thrilling notes like a lark. When his voice entwined with hers, it was a low dark stream running through the light that danced across the water.

Traveller, do not tarry
For the moon shines so bright

Traveller, be not wary
For the Old Ones call tonight.

Weirdly and subtly, other instruments joined the fiddle. The tingling tintinnabulation of the Celtic harp. The rapid-fire reverberation of a throng of *bodhran* drums. The full-bodied skirl of the uillean pipes, a hive of honeyed sound. The audience looked around briefly for the other musicians, but returned their focus to the stage when they couldn't find them.

Dee and Yvonne raised their eyebrows at each other.

"Where is the path my feet must tread?" sang Findabhair.

"Beyond the dark your heart doth dread," sang Finvarra.

In between the tunes and airs, the pair onstage took turns speaking. The lilt of Findabhair's Irish accent was evident, as was Finvarra's, but his speech was different from hers. Though peppered with modern words, it was also quaintly formal.

As the first set progressed, something struck the two aunts. They nudged each other. Being artists themselves, they were sensitive to nuances of thought and feeling. Both caught the undertone of sorrow in the music, the dark grief that tore at its heart. At times the jagged edge of lament resounded with a bitterness that bordered on rage. It was potent stuff.

"Grab your spear," Yvonne murmured.

"Look alive," Dee said suddenly. "I think he's scanning for us!"

Deirdre was right. Finvarra's keen eyes were surveying the room. When his glance settled on them, she gave him a little wave while Yvonne nodded. Finvarra's look changed to a piercing gaze. Both stepped backwards instantaneously. Then his eyes looked away.

"Whoa!" Dee muttered. "What was that?"

"Magic," said Yvonne.

They could feel the electricity still shivering through them.

As soon as the set was over, both members of The Fair Folk came directly to the bar.

"Is one of you Dana?" Findabhair asked.

"We are well met," said Finvarra.

Despite his words, neither he nor his wife was smiling. Their features were stiff. Their eyes veiled.

Surprised by the lack of real welcome, the aunts were unsettled.

"No," they said together, "we're—" They stopped, flustered.

"You talk," Dee urged Yvonne, "you're the firstborn."

"We're Dana's aunts," Yvonne explained. "She's back at the hotel. She's only thirteen. No amount of make-up was going to get her in here."

"*Thirteen?*" Findabhair looked at her husband, horrified. "She's only a kid!"

"She is no ordinary child," he insisted quietly. "She is the Light-Bearer's daughter. She has power of her own."

The bartender brought the Fair Folk their drinks. Findabhair was given a ginger ale, while a pint of Guinness with two shots of whiskey were placed in front of Finvarra. As he downed the whiskey in successive gulps, his wife frowned.

Yvonne and Dee exchanged glances.

"Do you know my cousin Gwen?" Findabhair asked them.

She saw the expressions on their faces before they could answer. She went pale.

"Is she all right?!"

"I'm afraid she isn't," Yvonne said with sympathy. "She disappeared over a week ago. Dana suspects she was taken by some enemy who's been after her since this whole thing began. Gwen's friend Laurel is also missing."

Findabhair gripped the counter. She looked ill.

"Why didn't you tell me?" she demanded of Finvarra. "You must have felt something! You felt it when the others were hit."

His eyes darkened. "I felt the doom of Faerie, not the fall of our companions. I am as blind as you."

"Oh God, I should've joined her," Findabhair said. Her voice rang with guilt. "She needed us and we abandoned her!"

Embarrassed by the tension between the couple, Yvonne spoke up. "Dana says you're Companions of Faerie? And you're the ex-High King?" she added to Finvarra. "She wants you to find Gwen and Laurel. In my opinion, you should join her quest as well."

"That's why we're here," Deirdre said bluntly. "To get your help."

"We must rescue Gwen!" Findabhair agreed.

Finvarra signalled to the barman to bring him more whiskey. He brooded over his drink without looking up.

"The blood of Faerie flows in Dana's veins. She is more than any of you can ever imagine. It is her destiny to complete this task. The rescue of Fairyland is in her hands, as is the fate of our comrades who have fallen."

Even Findabhair looked astounded by his pronouncement.

"You can't expect Dana to do everything!" Yvonne objected.

"She's still a kid no matter what you say," said Dee.

The aunts were furious with Finvarra. But even as they glared at him, they couldn't help feeling a little awed. Here was a former High King of Faerie. One who had lived in the world when the earth was young, before humanity was born. They recalled the power of his music and the keenness of his glance. Was that all that was left of his former glory?

"What's wrong with you?" Yvonne said. "What's your problem?"

"Aside from the fact that you drink too much?" Dee added.

Findabhair flinched at their words and was about to defend her husband when he cut her off.

"I do not expect you to understand," he said, looking up from his drink. In the fierce gaze of his eyes, they saw the anguish they had heard in the music. "The nature of my grief runs deep. I could not have known what I would have to bear until my exile came upon me. To be banished forever from the Kingdom is to suffer a torment that eats away at my soul." He reached out to clasp his wife's hand. Her eyes filled with tears. "I do not regret the sacrifice I made for my Beloved. Were I to face it again, I would make the same choice. Still, it grieves my heart sore to live in the shadowlands that are not my home and to endure an existence that is not my own."

Yvonne's glare had softened to sympathy. Findabhair leaned against her husband in silent support.

Deirdre was not so easily hooked.

"Hey you made your bed, you lie in it. It's not as if you've ended up in demonville. There are worse things than living in this world. It has a lot going for it. You've got a genius for music, not to mention a gorgeous wife who needs to read *Women Who Love Too Much*. Your music alone could sustain you if you let it, trust me, as one tormented artist to another. It's time you bit the bullet and stopped whining."

Yvonne gaped at her sister with admiration.

"Let's go," said Dee. "They're no use to Dana!"

As they left the club together, Yvonne showered Dee with praise.

"You were amazing! I was completely sucked in by the sad sack routine."

"That's because you're an old softie. You'd never make a film director."

Outside the tavern, they stood in the dark street and looked around for a taxi. It had begun to rain. As the initial impulse to storm out on high horses wore off, they were attacked by second thoughts.

"Dana's going to be very disappointed," Yvonne sighed.

"It's not as if they were offering to help," Dee said defensively.

"My dress is ruined," her sister groaned.

The quick shower had drenched the soft fabric and it clung to her skin.

"I'm like a wet teabag!"

"I told you to wear a coat," Dee replied crossly. "Are there no bloody cabs in this place?"

They were well into one of their usual spats when a tall figure approached them. At first they saw only the long coat and grey hat, but as he stepped in front of them, the outside lights of the bar lit up his face. They drew back involuntarily. In the flickering neon, the scars looked even more gruesome. But it was the eyes that truly shocked them. The burning hatred.

"Where is the child?"

His voice was chilling, inhuman. It grated on their nerves like a jagged knife.

Their first reaction was to freeze in terror.

Their second was to run.

They managed only a few steps before he caught them. With terrible force he threw them backwards into the alley beside the tavern. The passage was dark and dank and smelled of garbage. They opened their mouths to scream but he cut them off. Long bony fingers gripped each by the throat.

They almost fainted with horror as his shape changed in front of them. His features melted to a writhing mist. His hands transformed to viscous tentacles. A sickening vapour filled the air. His grip tightened. Their veins began to swell.

From the club windows above pumped the sound of Celtic rock. Any hope that The Fair Folk might have followed them died. There would be no rescue.

Slowly the monster lifted them into the air.

"Where is the child?" he repeated in a dead remorseless tone.

They managed to catch each other's eyes, wide and terrified. Their strangled features were turning blue. Each saw the message in the other's look. They would say nothing of their niece and they would die. In that last glance of farewell, they sent each other praise and courage. *Hang tough, sis. You're a hero.*

It was enough to encourage a final throe. With a surge of fury, they thrust out their limbs to break his hold.

Caught off guard, Grimstone dropped them.

They jumped to their feet. Gasping for breath, they backed against the wall. Yvonne pulled off her stiletto high heels and held them like weapons. Now Dee waded in, kicking ferociously, glad of her boots. Yvonne joined her, jabbing with her heels. At the same time, they screamed for help in yells that also served as war cries.

There was a moment when it looked as if they might succeed, when they drove the monster back. They had really surprised him. They were not as weak nor as easily cowed as most humans he had encountered. Still, he would kill them. It would just take more effort.

It wasn't long before the aunts began to sense what Grimstone knew. That their struggle was hopeless. He was far stronger than they were. But they continued to resist, kicking, punching, screaming, scratching. They wouldn't go down without a fight.

Now the tentacles gripped their throats once more, lifting them off their feet. Now the darkness dimmed their sight as he cut off their breath.

Losing consciousness, they weren't aware of the blast of wind that rushed through the alley, carrying with it an eddy of leaves. But they did feel the thump when they hit the ground again. Grimstone had released them once more. Reeling and coughing, unable to get up, they saw a blur of shadows attack the monster.

The battle was quick and deadly. Was that the gleam of swords? Who was singing? Were they wearing bright cloaks?

Yvonne and Dee blinked dizzily.

Grimstone howled with rage.

"I'll find her no matter where you hide her!"

Then he fled away in a trail of mist.

Yvonne rose shakily to her feet and leaned against the wall. She was willing herself not to faint from the pain. Her wounds were bleeding badly.

Dee was still sprawled on the ground, bruised and battered. Every time she struggled to get up, she fell back down. Something was broken.

Hands reached out to help her to her feet.

"You fought well, Lady. We were tracking the beast and heard your cries. We came as swiftly as we could."

His voice alone revived her, echoing as it did of forest and mountain.

"I . . . not a lady . . . really," Dee stuttered, still in shock.

As the aunts steadied up and their vision cleared, they got a good look at their rescuers.

The two men were striking, with earth-brown skin and flashing dark eyes. Their chestnut hair was tied back in ponytails. They looked like brothers, possibly twins. But where were their cloaks and swords? They both wore denim jeans with knives tucked into their belts. Despite the cold night they had no jackets, only T-shirts displaying bare muscled arms. The alley seemed less dirty and noisome in their presence. The scent of cedar lingered in the air.

Before the aunts could recover enough to thank them, the men took their leave.

"We gotta go now," said the one who hadn't spoken.

He lifted Yvonne's hand and kissed it gently.

The other did the same to Dee.

"Hope to see ya again, warrior gal," he said with a wink.

A gust of wind blew through the alley, kicking up debris.

The men were gone.

Yvonne recovered first.

"Dana!"

CHAPTER THIRTY

A<small>FTER HER AUNTS LEFT, DANA</small> paced the floor of the hotel room. There was no question of her sitting back and watching television, room service or no. While she was disappointed she couldn't meet Findabhair and Finvarra that night, they weren't the chief reason for her coming west. There was something else she had to do here. *What was it?* She had followed Grandfather's advice and the promise she had made him to travel across the land in the four directions. Reflecting back on her quest, she could see the wisdom of the path he had set her on.

It is important to encounter and acknowledge the life of the land. From such encounters come power.

With each adventure in the land, she had met its spirits, learning from them and gaining strength and power.

To what purpose? she asked herself.

Her pacing increased. The design in the puzzle was tantalizingly close.

The land won't yield its secrets to a stranger.

In her hotel room in Vancouver, gazing out at the night, Dana glimpsed the truth. The spirits of the land knew all about *The Book of Dreams.* They knew what it was and where it could be found. Hadn't Grandfather said as much? But they would not reveal the secret to an outsider.

She would have to convince them, somehow, that she belonged. That she was no stranger.

Dana didn't stop to write a note. She had to go quickly. They were waiting for her. She threw on her coat and left the room.

It was a balmy evening, much warmer than Toronto at that time of year. Dana walked determinedly along the boardwalk. It was less crowded than it had been earlier, but there were still a few strollers. Behind her rose the city towers. Ahead, the green shadows of Stanley Park. The sun had set over English Bay to drown in the waters of the Strait of Georgia. A flock of white gulls bobbed sleepily on the waves. Clouds moved in the sky to reveal a clear moon with a silver corona.

Traveller, do not tarry
For the moon shines so bright

The song was drifting on the breeze, whispered by the trees that bordered the path, leaves whispering and singing like dark tongues in the night. The farther she walked, the fewer people she passed. Alarm bells sounded in the back of her mind but she ignored them. There was no question of turning back. She had business there that night.

Traveller, be not wary
For the Old Ones call tonight.

She saw the forest ahead. Hurrying towards it, she plunged into the trees. The darkness inside was warm and inviting. A hush had fallen over the greenery. Slowly things began to move around her, to slip out of place, to shift and change. Colours appeared to compete with the darkness. Various shapes seemed to creep in her direction, then scurry away as if too shy to meet.

"Who's there?" she whispered into the shadows.

The forest replied with a susurrus of sound; the crinkle of leaves, the crackle of twigs, the snap of branches. The night pressed against her ears like a sea-shell, whispering and sighing. She heard the scuttle of small creatures in the undergrowth and the rustle of wings in the boughs overhead. Her eyes darted here and there to catch sight of what moved. They were quick as a heartbeat! Everything was in motion yet somehow invisible.

She walked quietly, carefully, stalking her prey. Deep in the Canadian woods that night, she was hunting the answer.

A while inside the park, Dana reached a clearing. Before her rose a stand of totem poles. Even in the darkness the carved features were striking; yellow beaks, white wings, black eyes and red lips. She was able to distinguish the different animal beings, Raven, Eagle and Bear, looking proud and lonely. As she gazed upon them, she heard a loud crack on the wind. A moment later, she knew they were moving.

There was no time to feel fear. It was Raven who flew down from the top of the pole, no longer painted wood but flesh and bone. His wings closed around her in a flurry of black feathers. She heard the sound of a rattle and the distant beating of drums, then a voice raised in song. There was something familiar in Raven's look, the wisdom and kindness that shone in his eyes.

"Grandfather!"

Like a child she reached out to accept his embrace, to be lifted upwards. He didn't hold her for long. She had no sooner been raised from the ground to the uppermost height of the totem than Raven flung her into the sky and far away. She flew through the night. The stars hurtled above her. Speeding beyond the forest, over gorge and narrow passage, she crossed the North Shore mountains and the craggy coast. Below, the great islands slid away to the west as she journeyed deep into the interior of British Columbia.

A little dazed but excited, she landed on her feet in another forest. The size of the trees was overwhelming, so too the sense of their age. Arboreal giants centuries old. The air was rich with the scents of red cedar, Douglas fir, sitka spruce and hemlock. It wasn't night here. Viridescent light filtered through the lace of leaves. This forest was greener than any woods she had known in Ireland, more emerald than the Emerald Isle. Massive draperies of green leafage cascaded from the boughs. The great trunks were shrouded with ivy and moss. Underfoot was a thick mat of old leaves, wood chips, needles and bracts laid down in layers over countless seasons.

Was this a forest in Canada or a primeval wood? The First Forest that begat all forests? It had an air of innocence, of paradise. A sense that no man had ever walked there. Black crows cawed from high in the tree tops. Grey squirrels scrabbled in their dreys. A great spotted slug crawled over a leaf. As raccoons and skunks ambled past, some stopped to sniff her as if in greeting. They showed no fear. A black-tailed deer let her stroke its flank. In the distance came the outrageous laugh of a coyote.

She could hardly describe how she felt in that forest; very old and yet incredibly young, new upon the earth though she had always been there. For as long as life existed so too had she, yet it seemed she was seeing it for the first time with new eyes.

Dana was attempting to orient herself when something rushed out of the trees to grab her. Though her mind cried "bear," she knew it wasn't. She had glimpsed features in the hairy face just before it threw her over its shoulders. The flat nose and lipless mouth were simian, like a gorilla or an orangutan. Over eight feet tall, with shaggy reddish-brown hair, it had broad shoulders, a barrel chest and no visible neck. Against the first stab of terror, she had caught the apologetic look in its eyes.

With the ease of one who dwelled in the forest, the furry giant carried her along paths through the greenery. It moved with quiet purpose, apparently with a destination in mind. When they reached a wide clearing beside a river Dana was set down.

It was a camp full of the same creatures. Makeshift huts surrounded a large fire. The structures of leaves and branches had the temporary look of nomadic shelters. While the adults went about their work, gathering water from the river or tending the fire, children of all ages played nearby. They appeared to be a quiet and peaceful race. Dana could hear in their low murmurings a snuffling kind of language that involved grunts and snorts. As they glanced at her with big curious eyes, she found herself hoping they weren't carnivorous. Was she on the menu? There were no pots or cooking utensils to be seen.

Her captor had left her sitting on a rock. No one approached her. She wondered whether she should try to escape. A quick glance at the huge forest that crouched around her discouraged the thought. Where would she go? She breathed a sigh of relief when more of the creatures entered the camp with baskets of roots, greens, nuts and berries. Herbivores, she assured herself.

One of the children ran towards her to drop a bunch of wild strawberries into her lap. Caught off guard, Dana let out a yelp that sent her benefactress scampering away.

"Oh sorry, sorry," she called out, too late.

The longer Dana remained in the camp, the more relaxed she grew. She could see that the creatures were friendly if shy. They showed no signs of aggression, either against her or amongst themselves. She noticed they kept looking into the trees. After a while she realized they were waiting for someone.

When he arrived at last, Dana thought she might faint with fear.

The ground trembled beneath him as he strode into the clearing. Even stooped with age he was much bigger than the others, at least twelve feet tall. There was no doubt he was ancient, the

Elder of the tribe. Where the others had abundant red or brown fur, his hair was white and thin and bald in patches. As he drew near, Dana caught the faint whiff of decay. His face was wrinkled like a dried riverbed. The dark eyes were wet and rheumy. Yet he was still terrifying, far more so than the others. For where they appeared to be domesticated, he was utterly untamed. A wild man of the woods.

He did not sit down. His manner was brusque and impatient, like a king or a politician. He had apparently come to fulfil a task and would leave again as soon as it was done.

He stood in front of Dana and pointed to the others around the fire.

"*Saskehavas.*"

Dana stared at him dumbly. Her mouth was dry. She fought against her fear to pay attention. He was trying to tell her something, but what?

He made a sweeping gesture that took in the forest all around them.

"*Klahanie.*"

Dana shook her head.

The others had gathered around and were watching curiously.

Now he made a drinking motion followed by feigned laughter and an exaggerated look of merriment.

"*Hootchinoo,*" he said, repeating the drinking gesture.

Their furry audience burst into loud laughter, startling Dana. What madness was this?

"Hootch—?" Dana tried.

Another explosion of laughter. Dana was growing more confused by the minute.

Several more words were directed at her, each sounding so different from the last that she finally guessed what was going on. He was trying out various languages on her.

"I speak English," she said, "and Irish. Also a bit of French."

The exasperated look on his face was comical. Had the situation not been so bizarre she would have laughed.

"Why did you not say so?" he returned in a deep rumbling voice.

"I . . . I . . . didn't think—"

"Your kind never do," he said with a grunt.

He indicated the others who were looking pleased and excited now that Dana and the Elder were talking.

"They called me here to speak with you. Do you know of the Sasquatch?"

Dana frowned. Didn't Fingal say something about them?

"I haven't been very long in this country," she told him. "I've only begun to learn—"

"Bigfoot is another name your people use."

"Oh yes! I know that one! You mean the North American version of the Abominable Snowman, the Yeti?"

"Tibetan cousins," the Elder nodded.

"Are you Sasquatch as well?" Dana asked, amazed.

"I am of the Firstborn. That is why I can speak with you. We have all the languages that are upon the Earth. There are only a few of us and we are solitaries. We live alone in the mountains. The Bigfoot, our descendants, are more sociable. They like to live in tribes, but they are also clannish. They shun human company and speak only their own language."

Dana smiled at the others who smiled back shyly. Some still looked a little nervous of her. How could she have been afraid of them?

"Why did they bring me here?" she asked.

"They want to help you. Know this, even as the evil which has entered the land gathers allies to its cause, so those who oppose the darkness are called to your light."

"Like an army?" Dana said worriedly. "I don't want to drag people into a battle."

"There is no neutral ground in this war," the Elder said. "Battles must be fought, within and without, both big and small. You have been brought here for a reason. It is time for your initiation."

A rush of fear swept through Dana, but she fought it down. Wasn't this why she had set out that night?

"What must I do?" she asked the Elder.

"You will go into the forest. The Sasquatch will prepare you. You must seek out the Old Ones to ask their blessing."

Again Dana fought a wave of anxiety. What if she failed? She steeled herself. She was at the heart of her quest, the core of her mission. If she proved her worth to the spirits of the land, she would find *The Book of Dreams*. It was up to her how she faced this test. As a coward or a hero.

"Is there something I should bring?" she asked calmly. "A gift or offering of some sort?"

The dark eyes assessed her.

"You are the gift," was his reply.

The Elder's visit was over. With a grunt of farewell to Dana and the others, he stalked out of the camp without looking back.

As soon as he left, the preparations for Dana's initiation began. The female Sasquatch led her to the river where they indicated she was to undress and bathe. The water was icy cold and took her breath away, but by the time she climbed out she felt invigorated. Her skin tingled, her blood sang. Clothes were laid out for her once she was dry. The deerskin shirt and leggings were soft and supple. Neatly stitched, they were embroidered with white quills and blue beads. A cedar bark apron went around her waist and fell to her knees. Her feet were shorn with high moccasin boots. When she returned to the fire, a younger female braided Dana's hair in a single plait down her back. Then an older male painted her face with ochre. Two last things were given to her, a short cape of black feathers and a tall staff of carved pine.

When they were finished and Dana was ready, the Bigfoot pressed around her with gentle noises of encouragement. For a moment she felt as if the trees were closing in, tall shaggy trees with red-brown bark. She understood that they were saying goodbye and wishing her luck.

"I don't know how to say thank you in your language," she said sadly.

She gazed into their features which no longer seemed alien. She saw the kindness and intelligence in their eyes. With sudden inspiration, she placed the staff on the ground to free her hands. First she bowed with respect and thanks, then she placed her palms together till the light welled up. The flow was far stronger than at any time before and it poured out of her hands in a stream of gold.

They were neither afraid nor surprised, but they were obviously delighted. All beamed big smiles at her as they bowed in return.

It was the first time Dana really understood the phrase she had been hearing since her quest began.

"Yes, I see," she said softly, smiling back through her tears. *"We are all family."*

As soon as Dana was back in the woods, she wished some of the Sasquatch had come with her for company. She knew, of course, it wasn't possible. This was her initiation and she had to do it alone. The forest was immense, a deep green country. While she had originally thought her staff was ceremonial, she soon discovered it wasn't. Without it, she would not have been able to make her way through the undergrowth that blocked her path. Again and again she had to beat back the sea of bracken, sallal, wild rose and blackberry. At times the woods threatened to engulf her, the dank smells, the mystery, the untrammelled growth, the clouds of insects, the density of trees. She could feel the weight of the massive greenery bearing down on all sides, creaking, sighing, muttering, groaning.

Hour after hour, she continued her hike through gigantic spreads of pine and cedar, rotting logs and forest debris, roots and stumps, toadstools and slugs, fallen branches and clumps of fern. Sometimes she stumbled into dips and hollows. Other times she waded through shallow streams. The forest soon left its mark on her. Her face and hands were scratched by briars, her clothes were caked in mud. Twigs and leaves clung to her hair. She was glad of the clothes the Sasquatch had given her. They had kept her dry and allowed her free movement. Her own jeans and coat would have long been destroyed.

Though the monotony of the trek began to wear her down, she didn't halt or rest. She was driven to fulfil her vision quest.

Then the Old Ones came.

She had already begun to sense Their presence. Something immense and profound in the forest itself. An impenetrable strength. An ancient secret.

Slowly but surely the truth seeped in. They were here. All around her.

The first sound she heard was high in the air, so far above her it could have come from heaven. A great sigh on the wind. Then came the rivers of light exuding from the trees themselves, ribbons and striations of colourful light that penetrated the green dimness like arrows and spears. They surged on the wind, a great movement through the forest, a force that sighed through every leaf and branch and blade of grass, surging through the undergrowth like the surge of the sea, a pacific force, urging the trees to explode into the sky, to swirl in spirals of green and yellow, terrible and rapturous, a great swell of light and movement and colour and presence, a vast overflowing, a hugeness of surging energy, all of it coalescing into a trembling luminosity that only the word *God* could come close to naming.

The Old Ones descended upon her.

She was caught up in that movement ascending, absorbed in one motion into the whole of infinity, the affinity of creation. She was part of all existence, the connectedness of all things, all growth, all space, all light, all energy, that cosmic energy that animates every particle of the universe, the one living weave stitched with the thread of *promise*.

How long Dana remained in that ecstatic embrace, she couldn't know. But there came a time when she struggled to emerge, rising to the surface of the ocean of being, white foam on the waves, an upsurge of consciousness, finally an infinitesimal mote of awareness that split her from the whole as she remembered who she was. *O nobly born, remember who you are.* And in that rising that was epic and glorious she knew that she, like all the others, like all other things existing in the universe, she knew that she was important. A hero of life.

That was the moment when she plummeted downwards
falling like a meteor
falling like a star
striking the ground with such force
she was embedded inside it.

She had landed in a bog and was buried beneath a tree. Sleeping there in the dark earth, inside the roots of the tree, she began to dream.

Where is the path my feet must tread?
Into the dark your heart doth dread.

CHAPTER THIRTY-ONE

LAUREL'S ORDEAL BEGAN AFTER DANA LEFT her on Brunswick Avenue. Once the girl was safely home, Laurel felt the full brunt of Gwen's disappearance. She had controlled her feelings in front of Dana but now she almost collapsed with distress. She should never have left Gwen! What could have happened to her? Where could she be? Was she imprisoned in some terrible place? Was she even alive? An old wound opened. The guilt of Honor's death. *It should have been me.* Her last arguments with Gwen came home to haunt her. The unkind words. Her impatience with Gwen's optimism and unquenchable good humour. Sick with despair, she stumbled down the street.

It was a short while after she had passed the old convent that Laurel sensed she was being followed. Turning quickly, she caught sight of a grey figure before he hid behind a tree. She was being stalked! Instinctively she reached for the protective charms in her pocket, then remembered she had none. She quickened her pace. It was late afternoon, still bright. She wasn't afraid. Yet. As she reached the busy thoroughfare of Bloor, she hurried to join the crowds. Would he dare to attack her in public?

Near the corner of Bloor and Spadina, a young Native man had set up a stall to sell dream-catchers and beadwork. In faded denim and a sky-blue shirt, he was dark-eyed and handsome with an easy-going smile. His raven-black hair was tied back in a ponytail. He wore snakeskin boots. Laurel stopped at the stall and feigned interest in the goods, then looked over her shoulder. There he was! A tall thin man, grey-haired, with a horribly disfigured face. As soon as she spied him he stepped into a doorway, but not before she saw the look of hatred in his eyes.

She was about to rush away when the Native seller stopped her.

"Take this," he said quietly. "Moonstone. Protects the female."

The necklace was plain, a leather string holding a smooth white pebble. He slipped it over her head.

Flustered, Laurel reached for her purse but he shook his head.

"The hunter teaches the prey to run. *Go,*" he urged her.

No need to be told twice. She raced down the street.

Rushing away, she didn't see her champion block Grimstone's path.

"See something you like?" said the seller, indicating his merchandise.

Grimstone's face twisted with fury. He spat out the words.

"Be gone, Ojibwa."

The young man's eyes flashed. His voice was like a roll of thunder.

"If you're gonna use names, Grey Man, try to get it right."

Grimstone jerked backwards as if struck by a blow.

Recognition passed between them like lightning before a storm.

"Nanabush!" hissed Grimstone.

"Yeah, that would do. Or Nanabozho. Or, well, there's a lot more but what do you care, eh?"

"I could crush you with—"

"I don't think so. You got no power over me or my people."

"I will call one who does."

"Go ahead. I'm in the mood for a fight. It's been a lousy day. No sales."

Grimstone looked as if he might explode with rage, then he realized what the other had done. Laurel was nowhere to be seen. With an exasperated cry, he dodged the young man and sped down the street.

Back in her rooms at Massey, Laurel moved quickly. She didn't know how much time she had. First she tried calling Dana to warn her, but the line was busy. *What should I do?* Frantically she rifled through her drawers and papers. Where was it? There! The tour itinerary of the Companions out west. Gwen had given her a copy to explain why the two had yet to join them. Well, regardless of their schedule, they were needed now. They were Dana's last hope if Laurel disappeared. Terror shot through her. She fought it down. Now she scribbled a note, doing her best to concentrate on the mission. Poor Dana! Would she be all right? Stuffing note and itinerary in the envelope of money, she ran to the porter.

"Could you keep this in my slot? If a young girl called Dana—Dana Faolan—comes asking for me, give it to her. I don't know when she'll come, today, tomorrow, whatever but just please remember to give it to her. It's very important. Okay?"

"Sure. No problem," the porter said, surprised by her vehemence but willing to be helpful. "I'll tell the night shift too."

As she left the porter's lodge, Laurel glanced through the gates. Her heart stopped. A black sedan with darkened windows was parked on the road. It looked sinister. She wasn't about to take any chances. There was a back door out of Massey leading onto a side street. She would escape that way. She rushed back to her room to grab her purse and some protective charms. She had no idea where she was going, she just knew she had to flee. When the telephone rang, she froze. Should she answer or not? It could be Dana. Or Granny or Dara.

She picked up the receiver.

"Laureelll."
The voice was oily. Hypnotic. Evil.

★   ★   ★

She was in a cavernous house built of cedar with one enormous open room. It was big enough to hold gigantic carvings of eagles with extended wings. The carvings dwarfed the inhabitants of the house, the chief and his family who lived there with their kin. Cradles hung from the rafters, rocking gently. When anyone passed by, they would give the cradles a push and the babies would laugh.

A storm was blowing outside the longhouse, but there were plenty of fires to keep the room warm. The air was smoky and scented with burning wood.

She left the house and wandered outside, oblivious to the wind and rain. Nearby was a rocky beach strewn with seaweed. Canoes lay upturned on the shore, elegant in shape and painted with bright patterns. Their bows curved dramatically like the crest of a wave.

Looking back, the village seemed to grow out of the green jungle of forest. The houses were low and flat with curled roofs. They were connected to each other but with separate entrances. Each door was fronted with a tall carved pole and anyone entering the house had to pass through the totem. The most common totem was Eagle with hooked beak and feathered wings. Another was Beaver with immense teeth and flat tail. The sacred animals towered over the village reaching as high as the great trees at their back.

When the rain stopped and the sky blazed with light, the village came to life. Hunters stalked into the forest. Women and children tended crops of vegetables, cured skins over fires, washed clothes on the shore.

She was drawn to steps leading up a high hill. More carved poles pointed to the sky, but these were crowned with wooden boxes that she recognized as coffins. A whisper told her they held the bones of the tribal ancestors. Beyond the totem poles was a different kind of house. When she looked up at the roof, she was blinded by light. Shielding her eyes with her hand, she saw a figure crouched there. A halo of feathers spiked from his head like the rays of the sun.

She was suddenly afraid. She didn't want to enter the house. It was not for the living. But something compelled her inside. She was instantly aware that the interior was crowded. As her eyes grew used to the dimness she was able to see, though she wished she couldn't. The bodies were piled on top of each other right up to the ceiling. They had all died horribly from diseases brought by the white traders and missionaries. Whole families had been wiped out, almost entire nations. She felt the grief and the anger in that House of the Dead.

When she returned to the village she found it abandoned. An oppressive silence hung over the empty buildings. The totems leaned precariously. The skeleton of an old canoe lay alone on the shore. In the distance came the sounds of clear-felling as great trees crashed to the ground.

She moved swiftly now along the coast, past glowering hills and driftwood on the beaches and too many ruins scattered like bones in the grasses. She found herself standing before a gargantuan carving of a woman holding a child. No passage of time, no splintering or wear, could despoil the tenderness of those big wooden hands, that mother's embrace.

We do not believe in beating children.

She stood in a cold and unfriendly building. With drab furnishings and old curtains, it had an institutional feel. A school or an orphanage. It was filled with Native children with sad silent faces filing through cold corridors or sitting at desks. The air was rank with the smell of misery, homesickness and fear. They had all been taken from their homes and families.

In the yard, a small girl was comforted by her brother. As he whispered the words in their own language, a smile crossed her face. Once upon a time Skokki the Spider travelled to the moon and learned from the Sky Dwellers how to weave. That is why the Salish people make baskets.

She was back in the forest at the heart of the darkness. Shadows blocked the light. Great curtains of foliage hung heavily around her. She was surrounded by totems all leaning towards her. She felt as if she were falling upwards into the sky, even as they fell earthwards towards her. She was lost in colours and shapes, faces and eyes, feathers and wings. Voices murmured in the air. Behind the voices came the steady beat of a drum and the hint of an eternal promise.

Not all that is gone is gone forever.

★   ★   ★

Mesmerized by Grimstone's voice on the telephone, Laurel left her room. He was waiting in the porter's lodge from where he had made the call. The porter looked pale and frightened.

Silently, obediently, she followed Grimstone out of the college and into his car.

He drove to the outskirts of the city and stopped near a deserted beach. She knew he was going to murder her, but there was nothing she could do. A dark cloud had fallen over her mind. Though she wanted to fight for her life, she had no will to do it. As he leaned towards her, she cringed with horror. His hands weren't human. Two cold tentacles gripped her.

There was a flash of white fire!

It came from the moonstone that hung from her neck. Grimstone sprang back with a screech of rage. He couldn't touch her. Furiously he tore at the air around her and she fell into the dark place that he had claimed for his own. The violence of the fall knocked her unconscious.

When Laurel woke, she had no idea where she was. As she scrambled to her feet, her head spun. She felt nauseous and dizzy. As far as she could see, she was in a bleak and blasted wasteland. The smell of rot and damp ashes choked the air. In front of her lay a bog that crawled with strangled trees. Beyond the bog rose a jagged ridge of ghylls and crags. Her heart sank. This was a dead place without hope or promise. She had been left here to die.

She felt like crying but it was against her nature. Instead, she surveyed the land. If she climbed the ridge she could get a better view. There might be a road on the other side leading to less hostile territory. At the least, she would escape the dreary bog. She made a map in her mind, noting the sluggish stream that crept past the trees. That meant swamp. There might be quicksand. She would have to be careful.

Once she had chosen a course of action, Laurel felt better. As the initial shock began to wear off, she considered her abduction. Could this be what had happened to Gwen? The thought gave her hope. She tried calling for Gwen, then stopped. The desolate echo of her voice was too awful to hear.

How long she wandered in the Brule, she had no idea. The view had been deceptive. Everything was farther away than it looked. She had yet to clear the bog. Though she wasn't thinking of food, she was already thirsty. The ashen air parched her throat. She took a detour towards the stream, but any hopes of a drink died as soon as she saw it. The creek trickled over a bed of slime. The water was fetid.

She stood transfixed on the bank of black mud, staring downwards. What was in the shadows beneath the surface? She leaned closer to look. The image was distorted, sickly white and bloated. A horror crept into her mind as she recognized what she saw. Herself drowned in the snye.

She tried to back away, but the water pulled her forward. She was about to tumble in when the leather necklace fell out of her shirt.

The moonstone swung wildly, spraying white light. Released from the stream's grip, Laurel teetered backwards. Her hand closed around the pendant. It felt cool to the touch. Her skin tingled. In that wondrous moment she felt clear and refreshed, as if she were standing inside a waterfall. With silent gratitude she thanked the young man who had given her the necklace.

Heartened by the moonstone, Laurel plunged back into the bog. Her progress was slow. When she wasn't tripping over roots or beating down briars she was pulling her feet from the thick dark gley. Someone less fit might have given up, but Laurel was an athlete who had kept in shape. Still, the ordeal was taking its toll. Her limbs ached and she was covered in scratches as well as foul-smelling muck. At last she broke from the bog and faced the ridge.

At first sight, the green lights seemed harmless. But as soon as Laurel headed for the ridge they swarmed like killer bees. As they charged towards her, she retreated to the trees. Quickly she looked around for a strong stick or branch. When she found one as hefty as a bat, she grinned. Softball was one of her favourite sports.

The lights flickered at the edge of the brake as if daring her to come out. Stealthily she moved towards them, gripping her stick. As soon as she stepped from the trees one shot at her. She batted it into the ridge where it exploded against the rock. The next she doused in the river and the one after that. Two more hit the rockface.

"Come on!" she yelled. "I'm just warming up! Batting practice! Let's go!"

The remaining few hovered in the air without moving.

"Hah!" she said. "Not so brave now, eh?"

She was about to make a run for the ridge when she stopped. More and more of the green lights were issuing from the ground to swell the ranks against her. No matter how well she batted, she couldn't take them all.

Gulping back sobs, she fled into the bog.

Don't give up, she urged herself, you just need more weapons. Plaited branches would make a shield. Soaked in water, they might be fire-proof. Dare she tackle that stream again?

Her foot was caught by a root. She pitched forward and fell into a ditch. The black ooze rose to smother her. She could sense its malevolence. *Don't bother to get up. It's hopeless. You may as well surrender.* She clutched the moonstone. It shimmered palely with a different message. *Get up, gal, get up. You're not beaten yet.*

"Yes," she gritted her teeth, "I'm not beaten yet."

She clawed her way up and out of the hollow. That's when she spied it, the small mound of soil heaped at the foot of a withered tree. It looked like a grave. There was a shape in the mound.

The hair on the back of Laurel's neck stood up. *Gwen?* Everything inside her cried out not to look. But she had to know. She approached the mound. A scream tore from her throat as she recognized the buried body.

*   *   *

Travelling over the Rockies, she delighted in the breathless freedom of flight. So many mountains, towering, glowering, some cloaked in snow, some covered in conifer, some brown, some blue, some barren rock, all shining like stone angels with limbs outstretched to embrace the clouds. Their presence, their very being was huge and overwhelming, such vast amassings of matter, such brooding souls, such strength and longevity. Guardians of the earth.

She dropped to the ground for a run on the plains. After the gravity of the mountains, it was a light-hearted experience to run with smaller creatures. Gophers popped up and down in the earth. Chipmunks somersaulted in the air as they leaped from tree to tree. Rattlesnakes slithered out of their holes. Coveys of prairie chickens clucked in the golden wheat. Meadowlarks sang from the top of fence posts. In the cleft of a coulee, a deer bedded down

near a patch of badger bush. Rabbits burrowed in the earth. On a high ledge
above, a golden eagle settled in her great nest of sticks. Across the river, a
muskrat scrambled through wolf willow and saskatoon.

Out on the prairie, she ran with the white-tailed deer and the ante-
lope across clear bright plains under endless blue sky. The tall grass
quivered with pheasant and grouse, prickly porcupines, tiny kangaroo
mice and long-eared jackrabbits as big as small dogs. From the distant
hills came the wild song of coyotes. Farther away still, the lonesome call
of the timber wolf.

Now she raced over country roads scored and rimed with frost, past the
brittle stubble of autumnal fields. The golden tips of the taller grasses
pushed above the poudrerie snow. A bitter wind blew from the north. The
last of the birds were flying south for the winter. The immensity of wings
resonated in the air.

She passed over ploughed fields, furrowed troughs, still dark sloughs
and tracks of wet gumbo turned to mud. In solitary treeless places rose the
stark dark shapes of hoodoos, eerie spirits of rock. As the starlit prairie fell
behind she fled into the north, into a boundless shroud of black spruce and
moose pasture and the broad sweep of muskeg sprayed with tamarack. At
last she sank exhausted into a bog, dreaming deeply and darkly of the
world of wild things.

★   ★   ★

Dana looked down at herself buried in black soil at the foot of a
tree. A dishevelled figure knelt beside her, sobbing wildly.

"This is very weird."

"Dana! What? How!"

Laurel spun around. Her grief and horror changed to shock.
She looked at the mound where Dana lay buried and then back
again at Dana who stood before her, alive and well, in Native
clothing.

"It's the quest," Dana said slowly. "I keep ending up in the strangest places." She looked around. "I think I'm here because I was worrying about you in the back of my mind. About you and Gwen."

"Gwen's not here. I've been alone the whole time except for these crazy fireball things. Are you really here? You look like a ghost."

Dana smiled faintly. There was a dreamy distant air about her.

"I'm not sure where I am. Even while I'm talking to you, I seem to be moving through time." Dana shivered. "I'm on the prairies and there's buffalo everywhere, thousands and thousands of them." Her voice echoed with wonder. "Now I'm running with them."

Laurel was stunned.

"Are you dreaming me? Am I dreaming this?"

"Yes. No. Maybe. Is life a dream?"

Dana looked confused, then she closed her eyes to listen. "Oh, I see." When she opened them again she looked clearer, more solid. "I'm windwalking in the west. But I'm also dreamspeaking with you. I've been sent to help you."

"Who were you talking to?"

"The wind. I think. I'm not sure. It's too hard to explain. This is what the Native peoples do, but we don't have words for it. It's a bit like fairy magic. The Old Ones are teaching me."

"You don't have to explain," Laurel said, touching the moonstone. "I'm just happy we're being helped. Things seem to be going from bad to worse."

Dana closed her eyes again.

"Things are bad, yes, but after the darkest hour comes dawn."

When she opened her eyes again, her voice was urgent.

"We've got to go. Grimstone doesn't know I'm here, but if he finds out he'll come back for you. You need to get over the ridge."

"I tried that already. The fireballs—"

"The *feux follets*," Dana nodded. "I've fought them before. Can you run fast?"

"That is definitely something I can do," said Laurel.

Despite her injuries and fatigue, Laurel was more than ready to try again. The nature of hope.

Dana cupped her hands together till the light spilled from her palms.

"Run behind me. Keep going no matter what happens. I don't know how long I'll be here."

It was a dash of hope and courage, Dana in front streaming her light like a banner, Laurel behind determined not to falter. The *feux follets* were taken by surprise, but they quickly recouped. Buzzing through the air like giant wasps they bombarded the runners. It was trickier this time, Dana saw. The *feux follets* had learned their lesson. Avoiding her light, they wove in and around her, darting and diving.

One struck her arm. She winced in anticipation of the pain and was surprised to feel nothing.

"I'm not really here," she told herself. "Once I get Laurel out, I'll wake up somewhere else."

Alas, it was not the same for Laurel. As fireballs hit her legs and back, she cried out in pain.

Dana had to do something. With all the effort she could muster she made more light, enough to cover the young woman with a golden shield.

The *feux follets* were incinerated like moths in a flame.

"Thank you!" Laurel panted.

They had cleared the bog and reached the ridge of jagged rock. Dana looked behind. Though she had destroyed the first barrage, more crazy fires were rising from the ground. They would soon attack.

Despite her injuries, Laurel attempted to scale the cliff. Her first efforts proved fruitless. The rock crumbled beneath her feet and she slid backwards to the ground. She leaned against the rock wall. Her face was white with pain.

"I . . . I need to rest a minute," she said. "If it gets bad, you've got to leave. Wake up or whatever."

"No," said Dana simply.

"Please," Laurel begged her. "The quest. It's more important."

"No," Dana said again. "You said that when Ms Woods disappeared and you were wrong. Everyone is important. We should have looked for her right away. If she's here—"

"Are you guys talking about me down there?"

High on the ridge above, Gwen peered down at them. Had she not seen immediately how bad Laurel was, she would have laughed at their expressions.

"Gwen! You're all right!" Laurel cried and she burst into tears.

"Yeah but you're not by the looks of things. If we throw down ropes can you climb?"

She called to someone behind her. The next minute two corded vines, heavy and strong, came tumbling down the cliff.

Laurel went to tie the rope around Dana.

"You first," said Dana. "They're about to attack. I'll fight them off till you're safe."

"Stop being a hero!" Laurel said angrily. "We'll go together. I'm older than you. I—"

"Age has nothing to do with it," Dana said firmly. "You're injured and you can't fight them. I can."

"Would you two stop arguing down there!" Gwen shouted. "Something's coming! *Move!*"

A shrill screech pierced the air as a phalanx of *feux follets* flew in their direction.

Even while she was arguing with Laurel, Dana had thought up a new line of defence. *Fight fire with fire.* As if making a snowball, she compacted the light in her hand into an orb. Then she hurled it at their attackers.

The globe of light hit the front line of crazy fire and blew them up. Dana let out a whoop. Gwen cheered from above.

"Go!" Dana shouted at Laurel, as she made another orb. "You're in my way!"

Laurel had no choice but to do what she was told. An experienced climber, she tied the ropes around her and started upwards. Despite her injuries, she moved steadily up the cliff-face. As Laurel climbed, Dana kept the *feux follets* back with fiery missiles.

When Laurel neared the top, Gwen reached down to pull her up.

"We came as soon as we could," Gwen said.

"We? Who—?"

But Gwen was leaning over the cliff to call down to Dana.

"Wait a minute! There's something I have to tell you! There's something you need to know!"

Too late, Dana was already fading away.

"Damn," said Gwen. But there was nothing she could do. She turned to hug Laurel, overjoyed to see her safe. "Strange as it may sound, you're about to wake up. And wait till you see! It's so wonderful, you won't believe it!"

★   ★   ★

She expected to wake in the forest where she had begun her journey, but it seemed there was another wind to walk, another dream to speak. As she flew through the sun-spangled sky, she heard a whisper.

This land is far more important than we are. To know it is to be young and ancient all at once.

She became the wind that blew through the tawny grasses, the sweet-smelling forbs, fescues and sedges. She touched them softly, lightly, lovingly, mothering Nature who cherished her children, gumbo primrose and buffalo bean, prairie sunflower and Canada thistle, snowberry, scarlet mallow and prickly pear cactus. Onward southerly wind she flew, into broad ranchland, cowboy country, to caress the juniper and dusky sage. In the brilliant clarity of landlocked light even the rocks blazed with colour, great boulders of rose-red, golden chert and orange.

The land rose to meet her. She found herself walking a deserted highway across moonlit plains. She walked beside time as if it were a river where the seasons flowed past. Sometimes the fields were awash with the gold of summery sunsets. Then they changed colour to charcoal grey and the white frost of winter.

She left the road to traverse the open prairie grassland. Buffalo grass crunched underfoot. Silver-leafed sage scented the air. She listened to the muted call of the nighthawk. In the distance came the caterwaul of coyotes. Something inside her howled back sorrowfully, knowing that the prairie wolf was extinct. All around her spread miles of yellow grass. Above her spread the radiant sky.

She spied a range of green hills ahead. As she crossed the stony field that lay before them, she discovered she wasn't alone. A woman walked there also, a rancher's wife dressed in jeans and jacket with a scarf on her head. The woman was lost in her own musings, gazing up at the sky.

"This star-ridden, green and scented universe," she murmured.

There was something about her that deserved attention. The way she walked with mindful grace, the way she touched the land as if it were precious, every blade of grass, every plant, every stone.

As she watched the woman walking her field, Dana was reminded of Skipper Tim. This woman moved on the land the way he moved on the water. Each belonged to their element, body and soul.

The woman turned at the sound of soft footfall.

Dana stood in the feathered light of sunset, bathed in rose-gold.

"Am I dreaming you?"

"I think I'm dreaming you."

They both laughed.

"You're a wise woman, I'm told," said Dana.

"Who said that?" she laughed shyly.

"The wind."

"What's your accent? It has a musical sound."

"I'm Irish," Dana said. Then she reconsidered. It didn't sound right. *"Irish Canadian."*

"Why are you here?"

"I'm looking for a book. It's somewhere in the land."

The woman smiled.

"Well that's a coincidence. I'm a writer. I write books about the land. I walk in this field and it whispers secrets to me."

"Because you belong here," Dana nodded, remembering Grandfather's words.

The land will not yield its secrets to a stranger.

"Actually, I'm pretty well a newcomer," she said to Dana's surprise. "But there's something a Crow Elder once said. 'If people stay somewhere long enough—even white people—the spirits will begin to speak to them.'"

"I want to stay here," Dana told her. "I want to belong to this land."

As soon as she spoke she was back with the wind, walking across the sky.

At first she thought she was looking at a vision, a mirage of infinity and timeless space. Then she realized she was looking at a country. She had grasped it in parts when she dreamed with the animals. Now she caught sight of something far grander. It was too vast even for the imagination, miles and miles and miles of great plain sweeping to the horizon at the edge of the world. A summer land that shimmered in waves of baked heat. A winter land blurred behind the white veil of blizzards.

Place names echoed in the air like spirits. Red Deer. Lonetree.

Ravenscrag. Medicine Hat. Qu'Appelle. The White Horse Plains. Portage la Prairie. *The geography of the wild heart of the West.*

From the four directions came the names of the Plains Nations winging on the wind. Gros Ventre. Shoshone. Siksika Blackfoot. Plains Ojibwa. Assiniboine. Lakota. Crowfoot. Crow Absaroke. Plains Cree. *She saw them in the wind, riding wild horses. Scorned by history, beloved of the land, they moved like bright shadows in the prairie sky.*

Wrapped in the vision of unbroken solitude, she mused to herself. What is the meaning of these images? This land? This journey?

At the heart of everything is spirit.

★   ★   ★

Dana began to wake. She was pulled away from the starlit prairies, back over the great mountains, deep into the green interior of British Columbia. There was a brief moment when she passed the Sasquatch camp and some of the Bigfoot looked up to see her. Then she was gone, flying over the painted totems in Stanley Park, and along the sandy shore of English Bay.

As gently as a leaf, she dropped onto the sidewalk in front of her hotel as a taxi pulled up.

Dana's aunts jumped out of the cab, faces white and frantic. As soon as they saw her, they rushed over.

"We thought you were dead!" Yvonne cried.

They smothered her in hugs, weeping with relief.

Dee stood back to regard her.

"Where did you get the cool gear?"

Only then did Dana see how bad they both looked.

CHAPTER THIRTY-TWO

"**Y**OU'RE HURT!" DANA CRIED WITH DISMAY.

"We're alive," Dee pointed out.

"Let's get inside," said Yvonne.

Ignoring the stares of the hotel staff and other residents, the three hurried through the lobby and up to their room. Yvonne immediately ran a hot bath, while Dee ordered room service.

"Tell me what happened," Dana asked them quietly.

She was the calmest of the three. Her aunts were moving around in fits and starts, taking off their clothes, donning bathrobes, checking their injuries. Both were badly cut and bruised. Their clothes were torn, spattered with dirt and blood. Some of their limbs looked wrong, twisted out of shape. There was a wild look in their eyes.

"We will," Yvonne assured her. "After we treat our shock."

"We've been here before," Dee surprised her. "A little rumble at our favourite club when it got raided by nasties. We had to hold our own till Toronto's finest arrived."

"This is a lot worse though," said Yvonne. Her voice trembled as she stared at a deep gash on her leg. "I think I might need a doctor."

"Me too," Dee admitted.

They both slumped on the edge of the bed. As the reality of the attack sunk in, they began to shiver. The dark thing that had touched them had left its mark. They called on all the liveliness of their personalities to rally against it, but it was too hard, too horrible. They looked defeated.

Dana walked over and took each by the hand.

"I'm really proud of you both," she said softly.

She gripped them firmly as she let the light flow. Like liquid gold, it seeped into their skin, slowly spreading throughout their bodies. As the light moved, it healed, not only the surface wounds but the ones deep inside. The terror and the horror of the evil they had faced.

When Dana let go of their hands, they were restored and refreshed and bursting with energy.

"Wow!" said Dee. "That was some hit!"

Yvonne had tears in her eyes.

"Thanks, sweetie. It feels lovely."

"Something I picked up in my travels," she said with a little smile. "I was taught about my power."

A knock on the door brought room service with the feast that Dee had ordered. They were now ready and able for it. There were several trays spilling over with food: grilled cheese, Westerns stuffed with peppers and ham, BLTs and double-decker clubs, plus a mountain of french fries. There were also vanilla, chocolate and strawberry milkshakes and a big pot of hot chocolate afloat with marshmallows.

"The grilled cheese is for you," Dee told Dana, "with fries of course."

As they ate they talked. Dana insisted on hearing their story first. She was disappointed by their descriptions of Findabhair and Finvarra.

"He's a lush," Dee concluded, "and she has co-dependency issues."

"Documentary on alcoholism," Yvonne explained to Dana, nodding towards her sister.

"I know what I know," Dee asserted.

"So they have nothing to offer us," Dana said quietly.

But it was the attack by Grimstone that truly upset her. She couldn't bear to think what might have happened to her aunts.

"The worst part was his tentacles," Yvonne shuddered.

"What?" said Dee.

"I said *tent*-acles."

"Oh."

"He couldn't find me," Dana murmured. "I was beyond his reach. That's why he went after you two."

They heard the guilt in her voice.

"We signed on for the whole kit and caboodle," Dee assured her.

"In for a penny, in for a pound," Yvonne agreed.

Dana shook her head.

"Not any more. It's too dangerous. What happened tonight was my fault. I should never have involved you."

"We'd take a hit for you any day," Dee declared and her sister agreed.

Dana was adamant.

"I'm not arguing about this. If you don't agree, I'll use a spell of forgetting on you both."

Her aunts looked shocked.

"That would be a violation of our basic human rights," Dee pointed out.

"I need to protect you from things that aren't human," Dana argued. "Please don't make me do this. I'd rather you agreed of your own free will."

Reluctantly, the aunts promised they would stay out of the quest. Neither said what had really convinced them, the thing they had noticed as soon as they met her. Their niece was different. She had an unmistakable air of power and knowledge.

She was more than a young girl, more than a fairy. She was a champion.

"I can't believe you're doing this to us," Dee said with admiration.

"She's right but," Yvonne sighed. "We'd only get in her way. You know the plot. We'd be captured and held hostage, weakening her position et cetera et cetera."

They were the picture of dejection. Dana almost relented.

"So you didn't get to meet any heroes, then?" she asked.

"We did!" Dee exclaimed suddenly.

She and Yvonne looked at each other, astonished.

"How could we forget them?" Yvonne wondered. "Shock?"

They described their rescuers to Dana.

"Native guys, I think," said Yvonne, "with knives."

"*Gorgeous* guys," Dee said, nodding. "I wonder what they were doing there?"

"The Old Ones must have sent them," Dana said.

It was her turn to tell her story. Her aunts listened awestruck as she described the Sasquatch and the vision quest they had sent her on, windwalking and dreamspeaking across the Great Plains. They were also amazed by the rescue of Laurel in the Brule. But as soon as Dana mentioned the woman in the field, they were on familiar ground.

"Well I'll be damned," said Dee. "You met Sharon Butala!"

"Who?"

"She's a writer, well, a mystic really," Yvonne explained. "She writes about the land. We've read her books. The best is *The Perfection of the Morning*."

"*Wild Stone Heart*," said Dee.

"The whole quest is about books," Dana said. "It goes with what Grandfather said, that we're all part of the Great Tale. And thanks to the Old Ones, the story is getting clearer. I know where I'm going now."

"Where?" asked Yvonne, quickly adding, "Not that we'll follow."

Her assurance was unnecessary. Dana's answer was simple.

"Home."

★   ★   ★

Dana and Jean sat together in the cafeteria, talking as usual in low voices. Dana was overjoyed that he was back. She was also happy to hear that *grand-père* was safe and on Cree lands again.

"I find him first in the Shaking Tent," Jean told her. "Then I track him with Roy. We find him near Labrador City." Jean's voice caught in his throat. "He try to go home."

"Oh, how sad," Dana murmured.

"It is necessary I visit him more," Jean said, determinedly. "He forget who he is and then he fight to remember."

Jean sat back a moment and stared at Dana. There was a puzzled look on his face.

"You are *différente*. I feel it. What happen?"

Dana's heart skipped a beat. This wasn't going to be easy, but she couldn't avoid it. She had thought long and hard while Jean was away. The same decision she had reached about her aunts applied to him also. Laurel was the one who had first argued the point, but now Dana herself was fully agreed.

"I went into the West," she said quietly, "and I met the Old Ones, the spirits of the land. They showed me that I have the power to complete my mission."

She saw him register that she had broken her promise to do nothing till he returned. His eyes flashed. His lips pressed closer together. Things would be worse by the time she was finished.

"I have to do the rest of this by myself, Jean. I'm sorry. Believe me, I appreciate everything you've done, but you can't stay on the quest. I'd be putting you in too much danger. If anything happened to you, it would be my fault. I couldn't live with that."

While she knew he would be angry, she wasn't prepared for the explosion that followed. He was already standing before she had finished and he was furious.

"*Tabernac,* you think you decide for me? Who you think you are, eh? You think I don't know for myself that I go to danger or not? *Maudit, câlisse.* I don't like this! I don't like *you!*"

Dana sat still as he stormed away, so still she might have been a statue. She was in shock. Devastated. Her insides were twisted into a knot. Her world had just collapsed around her.

"Boy trouble?" Georgia's voice was kind as she took the chair Jean had just vacated. "I caught the end of it. You look as if you've been hit with a ton of bricks."

"I . . . I have," Dana said. Tears pricked the corner of her eyes. She wanted to run away and hide, to cry herself to sleep. "Oh Georgia, I've done something really wrong. I've ruined everything!"

"Have you kissed another guy?" Georgia asked her directly.

"*No!* I don't even know any other boys!"

"Then you're okay. That's the only thing they won't forgive. Come on, we'll be late for class. Tell me what happened on the way."

Dana was already feeling a little better. Shamefaced, she realized she had barely said hello to Georgia once Jean was back.

"Where were you at lunch?" she asked guiltily.

"I sat with some other friends. Don't sweat it. You looked pretty intense. Two's company, three can be a crowd."

As they walked through the halls, Dana hurriedly explained that she had broken a promise—for very good reasons—and then tried to exclude Jean from something because she thought it was best for him.

"The situation sounds serious but not hopeless," Georgia said thoughtfully. "I recommend some damage control, grovelling and apologies. With regards to the broken promise, you owe him one. You need to restore his trust. As for you deciding what's best for him, have to say I'm on his side there. One look at that guy should tell you he's man enough to make his own decisions. Will I call you tonight?"

"Please," Dana said. "And thank you so much. You've saved my life!"

"What are friends for?" Georgia laughed.

When Dana left for home that afternoon, she was still grateful to Georgia. Jean had turned away when she tried to apologize and then ignored her all day, but Georgia kept meeting her between classes for pep talks. When the final bell rang, Jean disappeared without a backward glance, but Georgia's wave was encouraging.

"I'll call you after supper!"

Dana walked to the subway, half-sad, half-glad. While things couldn't be worse with Jean, her friendship with Georgia was heartening. At the same time, she knew she couldn't get bogged down in her personal life. She had work to do. During her time with the Old Ones, she had learned a lot, including the fact that *The Book of Dreams* would be found in the south, the final direction, somewhere near where she lived. It made sense, of course. The quest had brought her full circle. A journey was not completed until you returned home.

But she had to narrow the field. Where in southern Ontario? She would go hunting that night. She would journey into the land.

Lost in thought, Dana didn't notice the little bag lady right away. Seated on the bench in front of the subway station, the old woman was surrounded by plastic bags stuffed with clothes, bric-a-brac, dishes and blankets. All her worldly possessions. Dana immediately took out some money. She was always distressed to see homeless people, especially the elderly or the very young. The bag lady appeared to be napping. Her head rested on her chest and her eyes were closed. She wore a tatty coat of shiny black fur that looked like old feathers. There were laced boots on her feet and fingerless gloves on her hands. Wisps of grey hair escaped from a floppy wool hat. Her face was crinkled like a dried apple.

As Dana slipped the dollars into her hand, the old woman opened one eye to peep at her. A black beady eye.

"Stay out of the tunnels, dearie. There'll be a troll attack today."

"What! What did you say?"

The eye fluttered shut again and the bag lady tucked her chin into her shoulder, the way a bird tucks its head underwing.

Dana entered the TTC station and made her way through the turnstiles. Had she heard right? Was the old woman talking about "trolls" or "tolls"? On the train, Dana looked around with more attention than usual. Everything seemed normal. It was a new train, sleek and silver, with plush red seats and a grey-and-white speckled floor. As if to prove its worth and youthfulness, it hurtled through the tunnels at high speed. The metallic wheels squealed and scraped, the carriages tipped sideways as they careened around corners. The passengers looked normal, too, all ages and races, casually dressed as Canadians tended to be, some more muffled than others against the fall weather. The interior of the train was warm and cosy. Dana unbuttoned her jacket. Two kids ran up and down the aisle, swinging on the poles. Across from her, a young man petted the huge dog seated on the floor beside him. The animal had an intelligent face and was watching everyone closely. It gave Dana a particularly knowing look.

The train arrived in each station on a blast of wind and left the same way. After several stops with no surprises, Dana relaxed her guard. Lulled by the rocking motion of the carriage and the routine of the train as it stopped and started, doors swishing open, then closed, whistles blowing, automatic chimes—*The doors are now closing. Stand clear of the doors*—she fell into a doze. She was vaguely aware of St Patrick's station and shortly after, she woke with a start.

The train had come to a halt inside the tunnel.

Darkness pressed against the windows like black water. In a calm flat voice, the driver announced over the intercom that the delay was due to a mechanical fault. He asked for patience and would keep them informed.

The other passengers seemed unconcerned, continuing to do what they were doing to pass time in transit. Some read newspapers or books, others stared blindly at the floor or ceiling, a few read the ads for the umpteenth time, while one or two studied the other passengers surreptitiously. Most wore a look of patient boredom. A few were asleep.

Only Dana felt any anxiety. She knew something was wrong.

She was craning her neck to peer out the window, in an attempt to see down the track, when a familiar voice spoke behind her.

"Troll attack, eh? They're always causing delays on the subway. They get bored and up to mischief. Idle hands are the devil's work as my old mother used to say."

Dana spun round. The little brown man was grinning at her. He still had the Walkman and the dark glasses, but now he was dressed bizarrely in pink. A pink coat with padded shoulders and silver buttons matched pink baggy pants. He also sported a pink hat and pink gloves. Even his shoes were pink, pink running shoes with silver laces. Her jaw dropped as she gaped at his outfit.

"A secure man wears pink," he said.

"You! I've been so hoping to meet you again! I'm always looking out for you. I wanted to thank you for the advice about my friend. What's your name?"

"Trew," he said. "That's my name. What's yours?"

"Dana," she answered. "But I thought you would know that."

He peered over the edge of his sunglasses. The eyes were wide and innocent.

"How would I know your name? Aren't you a complete stranger to me?"

Dana was nonplussed. Were her suspicions wrong or was he being coy?

"We gotta go," he said. "They're comin' for ya."

She jumped up immediately. The warning sounded sincere as well as ominous. She didn't think to doubt him.

"Don't get me wrong. It's not that trolls are bad," he explained. "Most of the time they're harmless. They just get their kicks stallin' the trains. They like to watch people get all frustrated, lookin' at their watches, swearin' and whatnot." He did a good imitation of a harassed commuter and when Dana laughed he said, "See? Trolls find it even more hilarious."

All the time he was talking he led her through the train, opening the doors between carriages officially used by transit staff only. No one paid them any attention. Kids and teenagers were always walking between the cars. When they reached the last carriage, Trew opened the door at the end of the car and jumped onto the tracks. He offered his hand to help Dana down.

"Don't go anywhere near that bar on the side or you'll be electrocuted. 'Fire-fried' as the trolls say."

The tracks were caked with dirt, black as soot. In the fluorescent lighting, the tunnel glowed palely like an eerie labyrinth. The walls crawled with wires and cables. A musty wind blew down the passageway. Trains rumbled like thunder in the distance. Far ahead, at the end of the dark tunnel, the light of the next station flickered like a beacon.

Trew frowned as he looked up and down the track. Which way to go?

New sounds echoed through the tunnels. The boom of many drums. Big skin drums. Then came the heavy tramp of marchers. The sounds were threatening. The deep beat of the drums and the plodding trudge of ill intent.

Trew grabbed Dana's hand.

"As I was saying," he puffed, as they ran down the track away from the sounds, "usually the trolls are not much more than a big fat nuisance. But they're easily influenced. And right now the troll patrol are under a very bad influence indeed."

"Grimstone!" Dana swore.

The drums were drawing nearer. The feet were gaining fast. Whatever the trolls might be, they weren't slow. Luckily, Trew seemed to know the tunnels well. He rushed Dana around bends and twists, through workmen's doors and walkways, over tracks and through stations, till she was utterly lost.

Still the sounds followed.

"Drat!" said Trew. "We can't shake 'em. We'll have to take the TTT."

"I thought it was stalled!" said Dana, confused.

"I said *TTT* not TTC," he answered. "The Toronto Troll Transit."

Even as he spoke, Trew was searching the wall near them. Now he pushed against a large brick as if it were a button. A secret door swung open revealing steps that ran downwards.

"You're about to see the true meaning of 'rapid transit,'" he said.

As Trew hurried down the steps in front of her, Dana hesitated. The door had swung shut with a clang behind her. She could hardly see in the murk. She was about to make light with her hands when Trew's voice urged her down.

"Come on! A troll-tram's comin'! You'll be fine. It's brighter down here!"

Following him gingerly, she was amazed to find herself in an underground cavern as big as the subway station above. The walls and roof were of rock, covered with a phosphorescent lichen that glowed greenly in the dark. A maze of passages ran off in all directions. The ground was crisscrossed with tracks and cables that looked vaguely familiar.

"These tunnels are older than the human ones," Trew told her. "There was a lot of worry when the subway was being built. What if the workers dug deep enough to find the trollway? Rumours of war were rife. 'The trolls will protect their own' and so forth." Trew let out a laugh. "The only thing that happened was the TTT got an upgrade. They stole loads of material, let me tell ya. I heard that subway construction costs skyrocketed with everyone screamin' corruption and whatnot. You see, the trolls used to pull their own trams. Once they filched enough equipment from the TTC, they could tap the humans' electricity and fly along at great speed."

The ground trembled beneath them.

"Here it comes," Trew warned. "Get ready to jump. It slows down, but it don't stop for nobody."

"Won't we get caught?" Dana said, alarmed.

"I got tickets."

"I mean—"

Too late, a troll-tram hurtled towards them.

At first sight it looked like a giant tin can. A single open carriage with an awning for a roof, it was a heap of patched metal and scrap with wheels. The driver stood in the front amidst a snarl of levers and pulleys. A humped creature with belly-white skin and black lidless eyes, he wore a soot-covered TTC jacket and cap.

Trew let out a yell.

"Jump!"

Instinctively Dana followed him, throwing herself forward in time to land on the tram. It had slowed down ever so slightly as it entered the cavern, then immediately sped up again.

They darted out of the "station" and into a tunnel.

Clattering through the darkness at incredible speed, Dana understood why Trew wasn't worried that the other trolls might see them. It was like a ride she had enjoyed at the Exhibition, the one called "the Rocket." They were moving so fast they were pinned to the floor and couldn't hope to get up even if they tried. There were several trolls around them, also flattened and motionless. True commuters, no one looked their way.

"How do we get off?"

Dana managed to squeeze the words out in Trew's direction though her face was pressed to the floor.

"Don't worry, I know the stop," came the answer, equally compressed.

It wasn't the response Dana was looking for, but as the troll-tram entered the next cavern, she was glad to have heard it. With no distinguishing marks or signs, this station was identical to the one they had left.

"Trolls know tunnels like the back of their hand," Trew said, as if reading her mind. "The way you know the streets you live on."

As the tram slowed a little, they both sat up for a quick breath. Two passengers jumped off and a new one dived on. Trew shoved two tattered pieces of paper into a bucket beside the driver. He grunted his thanks without looking back.

"Where do they live?" Dana asked him.

"Deeper down," came the answer before they were thrown to the floor once more as the tram took off like a jet.

After what seemed like countless caverns, Trew finally warned her to prepare to exit. Having watched the other passengers,

Dana knew what to do. When the tram began to slow, she turned herself around and got ready to jump. As the train arrived in the station, she pushed herself off the minute Trew moved.

"That's much easier than it looks," she said, pleased with herself.

"And much faster than the subway," he pointed out.

"So where are we?"

"The east end. Scarberia."

There were no stone steps to take them upwards. Instead, they crawled through a long earthen burrow.

"Less amenities in the 'burbs as usual," Trew complained. "My suit is ruinated."

Sure enough, when they reached the top, his pink clothes were streaked with dirt.

They hurried along the tracks that led to the airy Warden station.

"You're safe now," said Trew, when they were outside.

Though it was late afternoon, the light seemed very bright after the dim tunnels.

"Stay out of the subway for the rest of the day," he warned her. "The troll patrol will soon tire of the chase, but not before they've thrown the whole system into mayhem."

"I don't really have any way of thanking you," Dana said. She rummaged through her pockets and found a chocolate bar. "Would you at least take this?"

He admired the shiny gold wrapping and was even more pleased as he bit into the chocolate.

"I love this stuff," he said, "big time."

"Can I ask you something?" She hesitated, not wanting to offend him. "Why are you helping me?"

He peered at her over his shades. The earth-brown eyes regarded her thoughtfully.

"Do you think this quest is just about you? You're not the only one who cares about dreams, eh? There's no neutral ground in this war. You sit on the fence, you get splinters in your bum. You know it's a sign of just how desperate your enemy's gettin' if he's callin' on the trolls. Scrapin' the bottom of the barrel now. You've got him rattled, girl, that's for sure."

"I think he has underestimated the people helping me," Dana nodded.

"I think he's underestimated *you*," said Trew. "Big time." Again he peered at her over his glasses. "In the subway, you weren't scared there for a minute, were ya?"

"No," Dana admitted. "I wasn't."

"I thought not. You got the power. Now there's somethin' I gotta tell you before I go. The thing you're lookin' for? It's near all right, but it ain't in Trawna. It's in a place called the Plain of the Great Heart."

"The what?" she said. "Where?"

"That's all I know," he shrugged. "A little birdie told me. I don't get out of the subway much."

He was shifting restlessly from foot to foot. Dana could see he was uncomfortable outdoors. Even with the dark glasses, he was squinting in the sunlight.

"That's Warden Woods," he said suddenly, pointing across the road.

Dana looked over at the small slope covered with trees.

"Your friend's in there. That's why I brought you here. Between you and me, a bit of advice. I see a lot ridin' the Red Rocket. The good, the bad and the ugly. He's good for you. Don't turn him away. Nobody said you gotta do this alone."

Dana shielded her eyes against the sun and stared into the trees. She couldn't see anyone.

"Do you mean Jean?" she turned to ask, only to find herself

talking to thin air.

She looked around quickly. No sign of Trew. *What was he?*

Well, whatever he was, she trusted him.

Dana hurried across the road and entered the woods. The ground was damp and fragrant from yesterday's rain. The October sun had set fire to the trees that still held their leaves. Red and gold flashes lit up the rusty brown of aspen and birch. The tamarack needles were a golden orange. Where many of the trees were already bare, the autumn sky shone through. Muffling the sounds of traffic without, the woods echoed with bird call and the scurry of squirrels.

She found him leaning against a tree, staring up at the sky. He wore a navy-blue scarf around his neck and his hands were plunged deep inside his coat pockets. Her heart beat quicker as she looked at him, the fall of dark hair over his eyes, the strong features. Every time she saw him she felt an ache in her heart, as if she hadn't seen him in ages.

He looked lost in thought. Deep sad thoughts.

A twig snapped underfoot as she walked towards him. He looked over, not really surprised. The wolf in him had caught her scent on the air.

Before he could speak, Dana slipped her arms around his waist and rested against him. Her tone was quiet but steady.

"I couldn't *not* go west, no matter what I promised you, and I didn't want to add to your worries by telling you. Things are moving so quickly, I'm just doing my best to keep up. Look, Jean, I have to do this, with or without your help. But I would prefer if you were with me. I'm sorry for trying to tell you what to do."

His features softened as he gazed at her. There was no anger in his look, only the same sadness she had noticed before.

"I'm sorry also," he said. "You take a lot on your back. I don't want to add to the problems. I want to help." He touched her hair lightly and kissed her forehead. "I'm angry that time because I'm not there with you. I have fear for you. This is *chauvin, non?* You are strong, but still I want to save you."

His smile was wry and she couldn't help but laugh. They both ended up laughing and then they stopped laughing so they could kiss.

"How do you know I'm here?" he asked her. They were walking through the woods, hand in hand. "This is a place I like to come when I am wolf."

She told him about Trew, about the attack on the subway and the trollway beneath the tunnels.

"There is so much we don't see, eh?" he said.

He put his arm around her. Her heart felt as if it might burst. It was so good not to be fighting, to be friends again.

As they couldn't take the subway home, they had to travel by a circuitous route of buses and streetcars. Dana didn't mind. It gave her more time with Jean. She was also able to catch him up on the quest and her western journey.

"But Ms Woods is not back at the school, *n'est-ce pas?* Where is she now? And this other one, Laurel?"

"I don't know," Dana said. "They must be with the Old Ones. There's something else," she told him. "Trew says *The Book of Dreams* is in a place called 'the Plain of the Great Heart.' Where that is exactly, he couldn't say, but it's not Toronto and yet it's somewhere near. Does the name sound familiar to you?"

Jean shook his head. "I think it sound like a Native name. I ask Roy and the Old Man."

When it was time for them to separate, Jean kissed her goodbye.

"I call you tonight," he said.

By the time Dana got home, dusk had fallen over the city and the street lights were on. She hurried in the door, all apologies.

"Don't tell me, I know," said Gabriel. "Radhi's just in ahead of you. It's all over the news. The subway's in chaos. Breakdowns everywhere. Were you hours in the tunnel?"

"It seemed like ages," Dana said truthfully.

"I've got a pot of ratatouille simmering. Grate me some cheese and set the table."

It was after supper, when Dana was doing her homework, that the telephone rang. Thinking it was Jean or Georgia, she raced to get it. Gran Gowan's voice came on the line.

"I'm getting in an early invite, what with you skipping out on my Thanksgiving dinner. Are you coming up to me for Hallowe'en? I won't have you trick-or-treating in Toronto. There are all kinds of bad people there who put razor blades in apples and rat poison in the candies."

Dana laughed.

"I don't go trick-or-treating any more, Gran. I'm too old for that."

Dana was thinking fast. She needed to dodge her grandmother's invitation. There was no time for a visit, especially on the day she had to restore the portals.

"You'll love how we celebrate it here," Gran Gowan was saying. "The whole village turns out. There are bonfires and plenty of hot chocolate to keep the kids warm. There's a haunted house for the youngsters and the Headless Horseman gallops down Mill Street."

"Gran, I don't think—" Dana tried to interrupt, but in vain.

"The King of Creemore does that. Puts on a great show. We like to do the whole kit and caboodle here in the place of 'the big heart.'"

Dana nearly dropped the receiver.

Why was the truth always so simple that you overlooked it? Why could one never see the forest for the trees? Despite all her questing and Grandfather's point about belonging to the land, she still hadn't seen it. The answer was right in front of her and in Irish to boot! There was a place in southern Ontario that she belonged to more than any other part of Canada. A place where her own family had stayed on the land for generations.

Creemore. *Crí mor*. Great Heart.

Dana's mind raced. Hallowe'en was two weeks away. If she could get up there earlier, it would give her more time to search for the book. Surely Creemore would yield the secret to one of its own? Once *The Book of Dreams* told her how to restore the portals, she would use her power to do it on the feast of *Oíche Shamhna*.

"Gran, could I come sooner? Maybe stay this weekend and then Hallowe'en too?"

"You know I'd love that!" Her grandmother was delighted. "We can make pumpkin pies. As long as your father agrees, of course."

"He won't mind," Dana assured her. "He and Radhi could do with some time together. With the baby coming, I'm sure—"

"The *baby*?"

The arch in Gran Gowan's voice crackled on the wire.

"Oops," said Dana.

"Put your father on this instant."

CHAPTER THIRTY-THREE

![decorative Celtic knot border]

Dana sat in the front seat of the bus to enjoy the view. In the midday light, the highway had a silver-grey sheen. On both sides of the road, the land stretched outwards like wings. The countryside seemed to be three-quarters sky, a vast blue space over a brown line of earth. When she first came to Canada she had asked her father, "Is the sky bigger here?" "Definitely," he had answered. Signposts marked her passage through southern Ontario. *Wildfield*. A flock of pigeons scattered from a white silo. The landscape rolled as gently as the highway. Tall grasses swayed on the verges. Rust-coloured barns, green barns and barns of grey weathered wood dotted the fields. Some fields were tilth, ploughed and ridged, others were bright with winter wheat. Flagpoles waved the red-and-white maple leaf flag. Farther north, the forests came to meet the highway. *Caledon Highlands*. Most of the maples and oaks had lost their finery, leaving a bare tree line streaked with evergreen. In the meadows, rolls of hay lay wrapped in opaque plastic. *Lemon Point*. The road was crammed with big trucks, tractor trailers as they were called in Canada, not the "articulated lorries" of Irish roads. A camper van lumbered in the slow lane with bicycles strapped on its back. A burnt-yellow school bus with antique black lettering beetled behind it. *Blue Church Road*. There was a little wooden church with a steeple painted blue. *Pink Lake*. There was a lake, but it wasn't pink.

Dana was pleased that she was travelling by herself. Gabe had put her on the bus in Toronto. There was a moment when he looked troubled.

"This is the second time you've left since we told you about the baby. Are you sure you're not upset?" he asked her earnestly.

"Da, I've already told you. I'm really happy about the baby. I like the idea of having a sister or brother. I just want to visit Gran. You know how much I love going to Creemore."

"She does spoil you rotten," Gabe nodded.

"So do you sometimes," she said. "Thanks for letting me go on my own."

"A few months back, I wouldn't have," he admitted, "but you're really growing up, kiddo."

He didn't say what else he was thinking, that he was a little in awe of the young woman she had become. All of a sudden his daughter had blossomed. Her poise, her quiet self-assurance, was impressive for her age. If she was a little secretive or evasive at times, he put it down to the fact that she was thirteen years old. A teenage girl could hardly be expected to confide in her father.

As Ontario farmland flew past the window, Dana allowed herself the luxury of daydreaming about Jean. The week had passed quickly and enjoyably. At school, she had introduced Georgia to Jean and they had both liked each other instantly. The three of them became a little gang, meeting between classes, sitting together at lunch. With Georgia there, they couldn't talk about the quest, but Dana didn't mind. She was glad to put it aside for a while. There was a moment when the three of them were fooling around in the cafeteria— Georgia had grabbed Jean's lunch and tossed it to Dana while Jean swore in French—when she realized she was perfectly happy. To have a best friend and a boyfriend was, for her, a dream come true.

As for the quest, she and Jean had made their plans by telephone. He would arrive in Creemore the following day and they would begin the search for *The Book of Dreams* together. She hoped he might be able to stay at her grandmother's house, but if all else failed he could go home at night by turning wolf. Dana grinned to herself. There were always more options when your boyfriend was a *loup-garou*.

Remembering the quest brought a flutter of panic. Time was running out. And even as she drew near to what she sought, the mystery deepened. Why was *The Book of Dreams* in Creemore? She had known from the beginning that she was connected to the book, but she had always assumed that the bond was through her fairy blood. After all, the book's secret would restore the portals of Faerie. But now her Canadian side appeared to be involved too. Why else would the book be near her family home? That couldn't be a coincidence.

There was another point to consider. The Canadian branch of her family originally came from Ireland. Creemore itself was founded as an Irish settlement. Did that mean that the three lands were involved in the book—Canada, Faerie and Ireland?

Looking back, she could see how her quest wove the three together in a web of tales like the circle of a dream-catcher. Was she the weaver of the dream's web?

She shook her head. The tales were far older than she was. The continuing story of Canada and Ireland was older than the emigrants who came to these shores. As she had discovered in the east, it went all the way back to Saint Brendan's time. The continuing story of Canada and Faerie was also far older than she had thought at first. Grandfather himself had told that tale. Long before her involvement or that of the other Canadian Companions, there had been commerce between the First Peoples and the Summer Land.

I'm not the weaver, Dana thought, but I'm definitely part of the web since I belong to all three countries. Does *The Book of Dreams* too?

By the time the bus stopped in Creemore, Dana had long given up trying to solve the puzzle and had returned instead to daydreaming about Jean.

"Look at you, smiling away!" her grandmother said as Dana stepped off the bus. "We're going to have great fun together!"

When they arrived at Gran Gowan's house, Dana saw that the rest of her day was scheduled. A heap of pumpkins spilled over the top of the kitchen table, surrounded by bags of flour, pie plates, rolling pins and spices.

"I got the pumpkins from the Hamilton Brothers since the Farmers' Market is shut. Won't be open again till May. You missed the big closing on Thanksgiving weekend."

Dana loved going to the Farmers' Market with her grand-mother on Saturday mornings. Stalls set up in the village square sold fresh produce from outlying farms and kitchen gardens. There would be bushels of corn cobs and rosy apples, all kinds of baked goods and preserves, homemade honey and jams, and hand-sewn items such as tea cosies and tablecloths. Gran would stop to gossip with her friends, especially those who lived outside the town whom she didn't meet as often. Whenever she introduced her granddaughter, Dana would be carefully scrutinized. Knowing they were wondering if she were anything like her aunts, Dana did her best to look well-behaved and innocent.

"Some of these will be jack-o'-lanterns," Gran said now, as she sorted out the biggest pumpkins. "If they don't get smashed to smithereens by hooligans, I'll make soup, scones and muffins out of them after Hallowe'en. It's a wicked waste to throw out a pumpkin without using it for something. But right now, we want to pick the best for pies."

Dana was delighted. Her grandmother had often promised to show her how to make pumpkin pie. Though Gabe was a good cook, pastry-making was in a league beyond him.

"Of all the cooking skills, this is the one you have to be taught," Gran insisted. "The battle is won from the start with technique and confidence."

Dana knew she was learning from the best.

"Pastry dough can tell if you're afraid of it," Gran continued, "and if you are, it'll play up! You're a Gowan. Stand strong. Show it you're the boss, but not with an iron hand. That never works, not in pastry nor politics. You've got to be subtle. The true sign of mastery is a light hand. Now, we start with good flour, none of that self-raising nonsense. There's something just plain wrong with flour that raises itself."

She sifted the flour from a height above the table and added a pinch of salt. Then the real work began.

"Everything must be cool, including yourself," said Gran. "Open the window if the room gets hot or steamy. Half margarine and half lard for the fat, pinch it in with your fingers. Softly. Softly. And speedily. The less you handle it the better."

Lost in a mist of flour, Gran sprinkled and stirred and made up the dough. Move for move, Dana matched her actions till each was wrapping her own bundle in foil.

"Let it rest for half an hour in the fridge while we prepare the pumpkins."

This piece of work was messy but fun. They cut off the tops of the pumpkins and scooped out the orange gloop clotted with seeds. Being an easier job, it didn't demand concentration and freed Gran Gowan to vent her mind.

"Of course I'm over the moon about it," she said. "Radhi will make a wonderful mother and it's about time they started on a family, those two. I just don't appreciate being the last to know."

"He planned to tell you at Thanksgiving, Gran, but then we didn't come. He wanted to tell you in person."

"Hmph."

The pumpkins were chopped into chunks and the leathery rind hacked away. Rough and malleable like turnip, the pale flesh was cut into cubes and boiled till soft. Then they mashed it into a mix with Gran Gowan's secret ingredients.

"Sweetened condensed milk, that's the trick," said Gran, "along with brown sugar, eggs, cinnamon, ginger, nutmeg and cloves. This is a melt-in-your-mouth recipe, a Gowan specialty."

It was time to roll out the pastry.

In warrior stance, Gran Gowan held her rolling pin like a sword. Beside her, the knight's page, Dana wielded the dredger.

"Use it liberally," Gran ordered, "on anything that looks like it's sticking. Not on the dough, mind you. Never on the dough! Shake it on the pin or the pastry board. Here, you do one. Roll gently, gently—yes! you've got the knack!—now roll it right onto the pin. Good, now unroll it on top of the tin and press it in."

They worked for hours. Pie after pie went into the oven till the kitchen was filled with the sweet musky scent of baked pumpkin.

"There has to be enough to go around," Gran explained. "We'll freeze a batch for Hallowe'en, then give the rest away. There's your family, the girls, Mrs Mumford up the road who's too blind to bake any more, Mr Nalty who just loves my pumpkin pie . . ."

At last they were sitting down, exhausted but pleased, with cups of tea and scones in front of them.

"So, I hear there's a boyfriend?"

When Dana didn't respond right away, Gran fixed her with a stare.

Dana knew the meaning of that look. She would have to surrender some information about Jean. She owed her grandmother. The Triumph Herald was once again in the driveway, shining like new since its restoration, paid for by Gabriel of course. Since the night it was damaged, not a word had been uttered about the incident. "Grandchildren are forgiven far more quickly than children," was her aunt Yvonne's assessment. But there was a price for everything, even forgiveness.

Dana mumbled.

"He's a . . . a friend . . . from school . . . a boy . . . friend."

Gran raised her eyebrow, noting the faint flush.

"Hmph. And your boy 'friend' is French, I believe?"

"*Oui.* I mean, yes."

"Roman Catholic, I suppose?"

"*Gran!*"

"Well they all are, aren't they? I'm just saying what I'm saying. No need to get all het up about it. I married one myself, didn't I? It's in your blood, that's all. The Faolan streak."

It was an ideal opportunity to mention Jean's arrival the next day, but Dana couldn't do it. She was so used to keeping everything about him a secret, she could hardly bear to mention his name out loud. It didn't help that her grandmother was not the most sensitive of confidantes.

"Tell me about Granda Faolan," Dana said instead, creating a diversion.

"That Irish charmer," Gran sighed. She took a sip of her tea, smiled to herself. "I was in trouble the moment I clapped eyes on him."

Dana grinned. As well as changing the subject, it was a story she loved to hear.

"I was thirty-two years old at the time. Though I was a beauty in my day if I do say so myself, it looked to be that I would stay a spinster. For one thing there wasn't a man in the town that had caught my eye except young John Giffen, and he died in a car crash along with any hopes I had of marrying him. I had pretty well accepted my lot in life and it wasn't a bad one. The family home was mine, even though it meant looking after Mother who was in her seventies and cantankerous as a bag of cats. Father had died five years before, being a lot older than her. My two brothers were gone, one to ranch in Alberta, the other out east in Halifax with the Navy. I had a close circle of friends, did a lot of charity work, and was active in the Daughters of the Eastern Star. Didn't have to work, as Father had invested wisely. You could say my life was proceeding in a pleasant and orderly fashion.

"Then he showed up. Like a tumbleweed blowing down the main street. A real spanner in the works, that handsome Irishman with a tongue like honey. He was a poet and a painter, pretty successful with portraits and could do a fine sign if you hired him to. 'Looking for a quiet place in the country,' he said, didn't like 'the urban milieu.' Had a real way with words, that man. He rented rooms in the boarding house where the book shop is now. He said the first day he walked up the street and looked around the town, he fell in love with it right away and told himself, 'I belong here. This is my home. I'm going to settle here.' Not long after that thought occurred to him—about five or ten minutes he always maintained—he spotted me across the street, coming out of my front door, and he said to himself, 'And there's the girl I'm going to marry.'"

Dana sighed. It was so romantic.

"He courted me shamelessly from that very day, starting right there on the sidewalk in front of this house, asking me questions, calling me 'darlin'.' What was my name? Did I have a beau? He just clean swept me off my feet with all his Irish charm and blarney.

"I knew he was a Roman Catholic, you can always tell by the look of them, though he didn't practise his religion. He was a Freethinker, as we'd say. There's been Irish Catholics in Creemore right from the start, but not a whole lot. We've always been a Protestant town. True blue Orange. Didn't the Hall go up before the church? Still, none of that mattered to me one whit. Lost the head altogether. He could have been a Hottentot for all I cared.

"The town was scandalized and I was coming close to disgracing the family entirely. The only way to end the scandal was to marry him. So I did. Once he promised we'd marry in my church and I wouldn't be raising any Romans. Mind you, I was to regret that decision years later. Your aunts could've done with a good strict convent school. They turn girls out like ladies, if the Dowlings and the Delaneys are anything to go by." She shook her head ruefully. "Might've put some manners on my two.

"Though the marriage was the talk of the town, the dust settled in time. He had married a daughter of one of the oldest and most respected families, they didn't have much choice but to accept him in the end. And he won over the last of the die-hards himself. He was devoted to the village, did a lot of good work, even helped me organize the Trillium picnics. A hard-working man," Gran sighed sadly. "He had a big heart, like Creemore itself, but not a strong one. When he died too young, too soon, the whole town turned out for his funeral."

Dana heard the sorrow that time made easier but would never heal. She reached out to touch her grandmother's hand. Across the years and the generations, they smiled at each other.

"He used to write me love poems," she said softly.

"So, the artists are on the Faolan side," Dana observed. "That's where Gabe and the aunts got it from?"

"I wouldn't say that entirely. Didn't your Great-great-grandfather Gowan write *The Book of Dreams*?"

She was so utterly dumbfounded that her grandmother noticed.

"Cat got your tongue?"

Dana could hardly think. She had to struggle to find her voice.

"What . . . what did you say about . . . the . . . *Book of Dreams*?"

"Your great-great-granddaddy wrote it. Thomas Gowan. Fancied himself a bit of an author, he did. A bit of a ne'er-do-well, more like, in his early days that is. Must've broken his mother's heart as he didn't settle down till after she died. He travelled all over the country in his youth, collecting stories, having adventures. Then he did settle, of course, and became one of the pillars of the early Creemore community."

Dana could hardly breathe.

"Was his book published?"

"Well not at first. He was writing it most of his life, from the time he was young. He emigrated from Ireland with the rest of his family when he was eighteen years old. They were cleared at Grosse Île, where so many died, and journeyed on to Ontario. That's how we came to be one of the first families in Creemore. Anyways, the book was his diary, his journal I guess you should call it, seeing as he was a man.

"He decided to publish it when he was seventy-three. Age meant nothing to my granddaddy. Didn't he build this house in 1901, when he was seventy-seven years old? He paid to have the book printed up at the offices of the *Mad River Star*. Limited edition, but it sold pretty well. They even did a second printing as there was a lot of people liked it. But it didn't go far outside the community. Truth is, he wasn't much of a writer. Just had a lot of good stories to tell."

At last Dana was able to ask the question.

"Do you have a copy?"

The suspense was dreadful. Hope hovered in the air like a hummingbird.

"Don't know about any copies," Gran Gowan shook her head. "They all got ruined or lost here and there."

The hummingbird darted away.

Of course not. That would be too easy.

"But we've got the original handwritten version right here in the house. His journal, that is. It was passed down along with the jewellery, china and linen. Precious heirlooms and family history, they go together. I thought maybe we should give it to the museum in Toronto, it being part of our pioneer history, but your great-grandfather, my father, was very strict about that. He said his father told him in no uncertain terms it wasn't to go outside the family. He wrote it for the ones to come. So, it's somewhere up there in the attic, all wrapped in tissue paper, safely stored away in a trunk."

It took all Dana's willpower not to race out of the kitchen and up the stairs to the little door on the top landing that led to the attic. How she managed to stay in her seat and finish her tea, she would never know. Her mind was reeling. Could it really be *The Book of Dreams,* the one she was looking for? The name could hardly be a coincidence! But how could it be a human thing? How could a book written by her mortal ancestor contain a fairy secret? She had to find it, to know the truth.

Gran Gowan saw the look on Dana's face and cut her off before she could open her mouth.

"Don't even think about it. Not at this hour. You can hunt it out tomorrow. Trying to find anything in that attic is like looking for a needle in a haystack, believe me. And it's already well past your bedtime."

Her grandmother was right. The hour was late. They had spent the entire evening baking pies and then cleaning up the kitchen. Though she could hardly bear the thought, she would have to be patient. And then she could tell Jean!

Dana kissed her grandmother goodnight and headed upstairs to her bedroom. There was a moment when she stood on the landing and considered sneaking up to the attic. She decided against it. She couldn't disobey her grandmother and risk getting caught, not after the Triumph fiasco. She would just have to wait until morning.

Despite her excitement about finding the book, Dana fell asleep easily in the big bed with the lilac quilt. Outside, the streets of Creemore were dim and quiet.

That night, she had a dream.

She stood amongst a crowd on a large ship, waiting to disembark. Everyone was dressed in old-fashioned clothes. She wore a long skirt of homespun fabric and a bonnet on her head. The passengers were being lowered into small boats and rowed ashore. Dana recognized the island she had seen from the flying canoe. Grosse Île! Didn't Gran Gowan say her ancestor had survived that terrible place? Immediately she looked around for her great-great-grandfather, Thomas Gowan. Would she be able to recognize him? Of course she could! He looked just like Gabriel when her dad was eighteen, with dark wavy hair and laughing eyes. Her grandmother always said that Gabe was a true Gowan.

Thomas looked tidy, if not prosperous. He stood with his family, waiting to be cleared by the medical officers. She could see by his face that the voyage had taken its toll on him. Yet despite the signs of hardship and suffering, there was something irrepressible about him. The jaunty smile and the good-natured demeanour overcame the sickly pallor and the shadows beneath his eyes. He was obviously overjoyed to find himself alive and well in the New World.

She elbowed her way through the crowd to meet him. That's when she saw it under his arm, a book shining with light. *The Book of Dreams*. She was about to call out to him when something else caught her eye. She stopped and stared around her. All the emigrants on the ship were carrying books and all the books shone with the light of their dreams!

Dana woke with a start. She was overcome with a sense of urgency. There was something she had lost. Something important she had forgotten. Silver light drifted through the lacy curtains. The moon was luminous, almost full. She slipped out of bed and padded barefoot through the hallway, up the narrow stairs to the little door at the top. Afraid to waken her grandmother, she left the light off and climbed the stairs in the dark.

Once inside the attic, Dana cupped her hands to make her own light. The task before her was monumental. The attic was the width and length of the house and every inch of it was covered with trunks and boxes. There was even baggage hanging from the rafters of the roof. But she was too excited to be daunted. Beginning with the nearest chest, she began her search.

An hour later, she was still making her way through antique dresses, hats and moth-eaten furs, albums and costume jewellery, samplers and old paintings. It was time to come up with a plan. Ignore anything but paper. At last she found a trunk bound with brass bands that was full of books and papers. There were ladies' diaries with jewelled clasps and flowers pressed between the pages, perfume-scented letters, and all kinds of books, dog-eared and yellowed with age. In the midst of that pile, like an egg in a nest, well-wrapped in tissue paper, she found her great-great-grandfather's journal.

The precious book was worn and well-travelled, with numerous stains and torn pages. At the same time it was strongly bound in leather and obviously meant to last. Slowly, reverently, she opened the book. On the first faded leaf, she was thrilled to see a big friendly scrawl.

The Book of Dreams by Thomas William Gowan.

Chapter Thirty-Four

On this the 21st day of June in the Year of Our Lord 1841, I, Thomas William Gowan, find myself on board the good ship Horsely Hill asail on the ocean of the great Atlantic. It is a big ship, three-masted, with a crew of eighteen hands, over three hundred steerage passengers and several families with cabins of their own amongst whom mine is included. We have come with lock, stock and barrel, my parents, my two brothers and sister, our maid-servant and myself, the firstborn at eighteen years of age.

It has been two weeks since we departed from the port of New Ross bound for Montreal in the land of Quebec. I stood on deck as we left the harbour and bade farewell to my native country that I shall see no more. Others stood with me weeping copiously as they cast last lingering looks at the beloved green shores of the Emerald Isle. I did not weep. I was too filled with the glorious joy of adventure. Here was I off to the New World to a new life and new freedom, to try my fortune in a land of promise where dreams might prove true.

I have yet to tell Father or Mother that I do not intend to settle on a farm in the backwoods of Canada. I am no hewer of wood or tiller of soil. Such is not the destiny I envisage for myself. There is a vast land to be explored from coast to coast. How could I be content to bide in one small part of *it when the whole cries out to enrich my knowledge and experience?*

The voyage out has been long and arduous. This ocean crossing will not be speedily made. There is much sea sickness amongst our fellow cabin passengers as we plough the heavy swell of the great Atlantic. Many stay indoors, lying abed, moaning and sickly. Truth to tell, the steerage passengers fare much worse. Some were already weak and ill from the trials and hardships of their life before they boarded. Fever and typhus rage amongst them. The majority are in bare feet and rags. Many are destitute and have only the most meagre of provisions. If the journey takes longer than predicted I fear they will suffer gravely from hunger and malnourishment. The very young and the very old are the most ill-affected. Only this morning we buried a small babe at sea still swaddled in her blanket. She was dropped most gently overboard while the Captain said prayers. The poor bereft mother had to be restrained from following her child into the Deep. It was a dreadful and piteous scene.

That was the moment when I decided to take pen and paper and write this journal. Observing the crowd of unhappy humanity so sorely distressed without minister or priest to assuage their pain, I saw the truth. Against the vagaries of Fate and suffering in this life, we have only our hopes and dreams to bolster us. It is they which keep us from drowning in the black mire of despair. It is they which fortify us with the assurety that we are God's children blessed with the gift of immortal souls. Thus I shall record here, for my own good and that of posterity, all the hopes and dreams that I shall so encounter on this journey of my life.

June 23, 1841. It is but two days since I last wrote in these pages. I have of late ventured below into steerage. The stench of unwashed bodies and sickness is most suffocating. I wonder why the Captain does not open more hatches to allow in fresh airs. Some of the more fastidious women have done their best to keep their quarters clean, constantly washing with buckets of sea water. However, they lack fresh straw to make new bedding. They tell me the crew mistreat them most cruelly often playing tricks on them and stealing their food. There are a few musicians amongst them who endeavour to keep up their spirits, a tin whistler, a fiddler and a lad with a skin drum. The three are of a most peculiar appearance which in itself brings laughter along with the merry jigs and reels. They sing a sweet ballad concerning the land we are bound for.

> Oh the green fields of Canada
> They daily are blooming
> It's there I'll put an end to my misery and strife.

The creaking and groaning of wood is more cacophonous in the bowels of the ship and the violence of movement more severe. One fears at times that the ocean might break us asunder. I can rarely stay long below decks and soon find myself yearning for the comfort of my cabin. The rolling and rocking makes me quite sick. How much worse off are these wretches who have no other refuge!

Here let me record some of the dreams of my fellow pilgrims on this voyage to a brave new world

Josephina McAtamney, 16 years, from Newry, County Antrim. I wish to find good employment in a nice house with a kindly mistress. Then later to marry a good man and have healthy children and my own wee home.

Seamus mac Mathuna, 25 years, from Bundoran, County Donegal. I shall work as a labourer and save the money to buy my own land. They say land comes cheap in the wilds of Canada. I will build my own cabin and raise horses and cattle.

Mrs Maggie Teed, Spanish Arch, 57 years, Galway Town, County Galway. I just want to survive this voyage in one piece, lad! That would be a dream come true!

I no longer note the day or hour of our passage as we are caught in a limbo of time and season. We were detained for weeks on the Banks of Newfoundland by heavy fog, stiff winds and the foulest of weathers. We are short of fresh water and provisions. What we have left must be meted out with the greatest of restraint. The steerage passengers are deathly ill and starving. I have heard that the Captain, a decent God-fearing Scotsman, has released food from the stores to feed those below deck. Alas there is little to go around. It must be said there are stories of other Captains who have let their passengers die without raising a hand to aid them.

Indeed we have had many deaths, all in steerage. Many men, women and children have gone into the sea. There were times when I wondered sadly would it not have been best that they stayed in their homeland? Yet they were driven from the misery of their lives to seek new hope and better their condition. They died for their dreams.

Canadian landfall. Never shall I forget that first glimpse of this magnificent country. I waited long and impatiently for the sight. The shores were shrouded by a fog of inclement weather and there was nothing to be seen for many hours though the scent of pine travelled on the air. Then the grey haze lifted and there they were, like giants stalking towards us, the high rugged mountains of breathtaking beauty! Cloud-capped and rocky, they were cloaked with the foliage of a dark-green forest. I could only gaze with awe upon the scene of an ancient paradise untouched by man.

At last we have traversed the great gulf of the Saint Lawrence to begin our journey up this mighty river. We are accompanied by ships of all nations flying their different flags. Many move under sail while others are steamers that shower the clear air with smoke and flame from their funnels. The waters are broken in many places with islands of all shapes and sizes. The shores to the south are low and rolling, while those to the north rise to lofty mountains. Along both shores are neat white-washed farmhouses, churches with tall spires and leafy orchards. This is country long settled by the French.

Our ship has cast anchor off Grosse Isle and we have been boarded by health-officers. They will determine who may continue the journey to Montreal and who must remain at the quarantine station on the island. There is no doubt that many will stay here, for the steerage passengers are rife with disease. We can only pray there is no cholera-plague aboard. Clothes

and bedding must be taken ashore to be scrubbed and washed. All of steerage have been ordered from the vessel to complete this task. The cabin passengers are not required to do so and we need only send our servants to clean what linen we have used. Apparently there are thousands of emigrants crowded onto the island. They say the sick are kept in sheds like cattle. God have mercy on them all. Though the island looks picturesque from this distance with its wooded shores and towering bluffs overhung with evergreen, I am glad not to visit.

A short voyage from Grosse Isle and we have passed Quebec high on its promontory. The fortress is encircled by majestic stone walls. The city stands on a precipitous cliff cradled by mountains. It is an impressive sight with the black waters below, the dark crags and the solemn stands of pine.

We have docked at last in the port of Montreal. Even with the grandeur of the mountain at its back, this city has not the pleasing aspect and beauty of Quebec. It is dirty and ill-paved. The open sewers, rendered thus to purify the place of pestilence, choke the air with intolerable stench. The streets are crowded with emigrants and the uproar of voices in so many tongues is a veritable Tower of Babel. There is no time to explore the many fine buildings and churches, for we are bound to travel westwards into Upper Canada.

It is a great discomfort to write in the failing light while suffering the jarring and jostling of the coach. However, I have asked my brother to hold the ink pot and for both of us this provides a diversion from the monotony and misery of our journey. We are closely packed into a narrow carriage. The wind whistles through the windows where design would have glass though it is lacking. The road is rough and plagued with a succession of mud-holes and corduroy bridges. This latter term is used to describe patches of ground on which logs are laid down over the boggy earth. Our teeth and our bones rattle as we traverse these dread patches.

The woods grow thick and dark on either side of the road. Giant pines rise to heights of over a hundred feet or more. Their trunks are surely six feet wide. This is bush country, gloomy with cedar and tamarack swamps, and infested with mosquitos that would try the patience of Job. We seldom see signs of habitation now. When we first travelled northwards from Toronto we passed many stone and wood frame houses with little gardens of vegetables and flowers. These stood near inns, mills or smithy forges. Such comfortable homesteads are long left behind us even as the number of clearings has greatly lessened. The few dwellings we spy through the dense growth of trees are no more than crude shanties befitting the occupation of cattle or pigs, not men. We have entered the backwoods of Ontario, the wilderness of Canada.

September 28, 1841. There has been no time to write these past several weeks. Each night I have fallen into my bed with a tiredness beyond any of my experience. I have done my part as a dutiful son and stayed with my family to help them settle

on the land. The work is hard and constant, clearing the trees to make a farm. The worst part of our labour is surely the stumps. What effort must be expended to remove each infernal one from its deep-rooted abode! I am more than proud to record that our cabin is built. It is a fine dwelling overlooking a lonely lake and a dark belt of pine. Summer has come to an end and while the days are still balmy, there is a chill of frost in the air at night. The rain is unlike that of Ireland where it falls soft and damp upon the green hills. Here it pours down in fierce torrents like the hammers of hell.

Do I regret this migration? Let me speak from the deep of my heart. I have been bewitched by this country. What words can properly describe its stern solitudes and beauties? How can I write of the dark forest, the deep lake, the sombre mountains? When I hear the call of the wild creatures nearby, the loon and the owl, the deer and the wolf, I swear I am hearing the voices of my soul. As for the peoples native to this country who come to trade and converse with us, they are most courteous and kind. Indeed they are more decent than many a settler we have crossed in our travels. The affection shown to their children by both men and women is a lesson to us all as is the respect they grant to their aged. They are honest and truthful in their dealings and they never forget a kindness done to them. Alas, they are too often ill-used and cheated by the Christians who have come to settle in their land. How much they have lost by our arrival! Will they survive this meeting of the races I wonder?

"I like this guy," Jean said.
"Me too," said Dana, proudly.

They took a break from the journal when their brunch arrived. The waitress set down plates of pancakes with maple syrup, along with a side order of peameal bacon for Jean. The two attacked their food with gusto.

Though Dana had dipped into the book the previous night, she had decided to wait for Jean before reading it properly. Tucking the prize safely under her pillow, she had fallen asleep satisfied. The next morning, she woke late to an empty house. A note to "sleepyhead" beside the cereal told her that her grandmother was out shopping and visiting friends. There was no time for breakfast. With the book in her hand, Dana grabbed her coat and raced out the door.

The bus had already arrived. The door swung open as she reached the stop. Jean disembarked to find her breathless from her run, hair wild, face flushed.

"Très jolie!" he said, putting his arm around her.

He was about to kiss her when she drew back in a panic.

"Small town!" she said quickly. "It's just like Ireland. Someone will see us and tell my Gran!"

"Okay okay," he said, hands in the air. He was amused but agreeable. Then he plunged his hands deep in his pockets as if to keep them restrained. "See? I am good."

Dana laughed at his antics. That was the wonderful thing about being apart, the excitement of meeting up again. Just to see him standing there, in his jeans and jacket, the dark hair falling over his forehead, the wintergreen eyes, thrilled her to the core. That he, in turn, looked so happy to see *her* made it all the more wonderful.

"Have you had lunch?" she asked him. "I'm starving. I got up late. I had a dream last night . . ."

By the time they were settled in the restaurant and their food was ordered, she had told him the story of her dream and her

410

great-great-grandfather's book. They had begun to read the entries together.

Everything Gran Gowan had mentioned was there and more besides. Not long after Thomas arrived in Canada, he had grown restless. He couldn't stay for long in the backwoods of Ontario. He was a dreamer, not a homesteader. Once he saw that his family was reasonably settled, he set off on his own to explore the country. The journal was sporadic, skipping months and even years at times. Often the entries lacked a date. They were a fascinating jumble of adventures, dreams, poems and reflections interspersed with descriptions of the countryside and the people he met. He told of his various jobs with the Hudson's Bay Company that brought him as far north as York Factory on Hudson Bay, then west to Fort Garry near the Red River Valley and west again to Fort Edmonton.

Though I hold these hunters and trappers in great esteem, for their bravery and resourcefulness knows no bounds, at the same time I cannot but be horrified at the ceaseless slaughter of wild animals. All summer long, brigades of boats and canoes arrive deep-laden with the skins and pelts of countless creatures. Surely this is greed beyond all necessity and comprehension.

"Oh I do like him so much," Dana murmured. "My dear great-great-granddaddy."

After their meal, they walked to the outskirts of Creemore and stopped on a bridge spanning the Mad River. The water was shallow, trickling slowly over a stony bottom. Trees lined the shore.

"The river got its name from one of the earliest settlers," Dana told him, remembering a story of her grandmother's. "Bridget Dowling was one of those tough Irish pioneers. She settled just north of here with her husband Matthew and loads of kids. One day she was coming back from the mill with a sack of flour on her back and a baby in her arms and she had to ford the river. It was wild and rushing. She said later she almost drowned in 'that mad river' and that's what everyone has called it ever since."

Jean smiled at the tale.

"It's kind of strange," Dana said, staring down into the water. "I know a lot of the old stories about Creemore and the early days, but I never felt they belonged to me. I mean, I've always thought of myself as Irish and I used to think of my family here as Irish too. Reading *The Book of Dreams,* I can really feel the connection to Canada. This country is part of my family history and my family is part of Canadian history."

They found a place to sit by the river and returned to Thomas's journal.

July 2, 1850. Eight years have passed since I last saw my family and today I am restored to them. It is to my shame and sorrow that I have not returned until this sad occasion, the untimely death of my beloved Mother. Father is broken-hearted and so too are my brothers and my dear sister. Despite Mother's goodly forbearance, I fear the hardship of life on a bush farm was too much for that brave woman. Father knew this too and I believe that is the reason he moved the family earlier in the year to the new settlement of Creemore. Alas, the move came too late for Mother's health. I shall bide here a while to help comfort the bereaved, though it is not my nature or inclination to linger long in one place.

I will write something of this settlement, for it is worthy of mention. Though it has not long been established, only five or a little more years, it is already a very promising village. A flour and saw mill have been built on the south side of the

*river, making good use of its strength. A school and church
have also been erected while there has been an Orange Hall
since early days. The street names demarcating the allotments
are that of Edward Webster's family, he being the distinguished
founder of the settlement. Though only a few houses have been
constructed as of yet, there are many families on outlying farms
who feel themselves to be members of the community. Most
hail from either Ireland or Scotland in this generation or the
one preceding.*

〜〜○

*Father and I had a mild but unhappy disagreement today. He
was not pleased when I introduced the notion of my departure.
While it grieves me to add to his pain, it is not in my tempera-
ment to settle. I am thinking of going east to Nova Scotia or
Cape Breton. Or perhaps I shall visit the lands of French
Canada. I know something of their language from my time
in the Red River.*

"That's odd." Dana stopped reading for a moment. "Gran said
he settled down after his mother's death. It doesn't sound like he
planned to."

"Something happen to make him stay?" Jean suggested. "Do
we come near to the secret?"

"I hope so," she said, flipping the last pages. "There's not
much left."

*July 12, 1850. This is the day so esteemed and respected by all
Orangemen everywhere no matter their station. In truth I do
not count myself among their number for I am not of like mind
with certain aspects of the society that would despise Roman*

Catholics. I have made many friends amongst Romish people in this country especially the Canadiens *as the French settlers do call themselves. Still, I would not like to offend my father or my brothers by disdaining their celebrations and I agreed to join them.*

There being not much of a main street in Creemore to make a parade, the good members of the Purple Hill Lodge determined that we should walk to the home of one of their group, Mr Edward Galloway. The Galloway farm is some distance outside of Creemore and thereby provided us with a worthy challenge. Both the Bowmore and Tory Hill Lodges joined the walk and we were all well rewarded when we reached our destination. What a feast awaited us! The fatted calf had duly been slain. Such well-laden tables as ever I saw stood amidst the trees. For our pleasure and consumption were dishes of venison, eel, legs of pork, roast chickens and ducks, fish of several kinds, and plentiful potatoes or "pritters" as they call them here. Most delicious and varied were the pies of pumpkin, raspberry, cherry, huckleberry, gooseberry and black-berry currant. Fresh loaves of bread were served with new butter and green cheese, maple molasses, preserves and pickled cucumbers. As is customary at these gatherings, a great deal of whiskey was provided along with the more sober beverages of tea and coffee. The latter is a favourite drink in this part of the world and some say it will replace our prized tea one day. I do not think so. It has a bitter taste and is only palatable when generously sweetened with sugar.

What trifles do I write here! It is done to calm the riotous state of my mind and emotions. Of all that happened on this day, I cannot bring myself to speak of the one event which lies at the heart of it.

"Come on, Thomas, you can do it," Dana murmured, turning the page.

July 13, 1851. There is a belief in the Old Country that "a year and a day" is the spell of time necessary for the working of a "cure" or the lifting of a curse. A year and a day have passed since that fateful occurrence in the forest near Galloway's farm. Still I tarry in this place, unwilling to leave. What happened has marked me. I am a changed man. I cannot but look back on that day with awe and wonder. Was it a dream? A madness or delusion brought on by too much sunshine and whiskey? Though doubt assails me, in my heart I choose to believe that the events were real. For if they were, then all hopes and dreams are real and to know this is to be the most fortunate of men.

Now Dana and Jean stared at the next entry in disbelief. Holding their breaths, heads bent so close to the page they might have dived in, they found themselves reading a series of poems. The rhyming couplets were short and sentimental, conveying old-fashioned notions of romance.

"*Câlisse!* What's this?" said Jean, exasperated.

The poems were followed by an entry dated in the year 1876.

"There is no fool like an old fool," my dear sister said to me today in a teasing but not unkind manner. I do not feel old though perhaps I do feel a little foolish. A suitor cannot help but feel so especially when he is courting a lady much younger than himself. Miss Harriet Steed has let me know that she is more than happy to encourage my attentions. I expect we shall be married before the year is out. I may be fifty-three years old, but truth to tell I feel as young as I did at thirty. I wonder

sometimes if this youthfulness might not have been a gift that
was bestowed upon me for the part I played that day.

Many years have passed since the Galloway picnic and I
have lived a life of quiet and contentment. It seems to me and
I do not believe I am being too fanciful, that whatever once
drove me in my ceaseless search for I know not what was satis-
fied that day in the Canadian woods. Peace of mind and heart
was granted to me. I have been blessed with good friends and
neighbours as well as my family and I have helped to build
this settlement into a thriving village. Whether big or small, we
each have our part to play in the history of this nation as it
unfolds in time. While I had thought to be a bachelor to my
dying day, leaving the Gowan name and posterity to that of
my brothers, it seems not to be. I look forward to raising a
family with my beloved Harriet.

Another poem followed called "Our Wedding Day." Dana
thought it was sweet and the best of the lot, but Jean snorted
with impatience. They continued to read.

The shivaree for my beloved Harriet and myself went not as
badly as I had feared. The usual ruffians were strangely absent.
Those who sang so sweetly beyond our window had the voices
of angels. While it may have been my own imagining, I
thought I also heard the sound of silver bells, like those one
hears on sleighs in the wintertime. Truly we both felt blessed
that night.

"What's a shivaree?" Dana wondered.

"Charivari," Jean told her. "They make the word English.
When the peoples marry, their friends come outside the house
on that night and they make a lot noise. It can be not so good

416

if they drink too much. They do it still now in Québec in the countryside. It's an old thing, a *tradition*."

"This is it," said Dana. "We're coming to the last page."

Born March 17, 1878 William Patrick Gowan.

"That's Gran Gowan's dad," Dana said. "My great-grandfather."

Born April 1, 1880 Harriet Frances Gowan.

Born June 23, 1882 Caroline Maisy Gowan.

Born February 16, 1885 Thomas Robert Gowan.

"What?" Dana cried. She turned the page over and stared at the blank sheet. "There's got to be more! Where's the secret? What happened in the woods? What did he see?"

She wasn't sure if she wanted to scream or cry. How could they come so close and find nothing at all?

"Is this some joke?" said Jean, stunned. "This is *The Book of Dreams* we look for, *non?*"

"It must be," Dana said, trying to calm down. "Look, something happened to him that day in the forest. It made him stay in Creemore. Maybe even gave him youth and long life, as he said himself. The secret's here. Somewhere in this book. It's got to be!"

Frantically she rifled through the pages of the journal. Then she noticed that the endpaper at the back was thicker than that at the front.

"Hey wait a minute, what's this? Under the lining!"

"There *is* something there," said Jean, excited.

He took a penknife out of his pocket. At Dana's raised eyebrows, he shrugged. "In the bush it's good. In the city maybe too."

He slit the lining of the back cover and there they were, tucked away as if in an envelope, several sheets of folded paper.

The writing was still that of Thomas Gowan but it was scrawled and shaky, the hand of an old man.

In the Year of Our Lord 1901, I enclose this addendum to my Book of Dreams *for the sake of posterity, for the one in the future who will come to read this.*

"Oh," Dana shivered, "a goose just walked over my grave."

Before I set to paper the record of events which did happen on that day, I must duly confess. There have been times these past many years when I have doubted the substance and reality of that extraordinary day. Indeed I have often wondered if such fancies were not the inevitable result of plenteous sunshine and the imbibition of homemade liquor. The sun did shine gloriously upon that day and it must be said I had taken more than my usual glass of strong whiskey. Perhaps it was these doubts which stayed my hand from putting pen to paper till now. What then do I credit the peculiar reluctance I have suffered at each attempt to broach the matter with my dearest Harriet? For not one small part of my life save this have I kept privy from my beloved helpmeet. In truth I am more inclined to believe that the thing itself has commanded my silence through the years, even as now it insists that I write.

I remember that day as if it were but yesterday. It has a place in my memory as rich and as vivid as anything that has happened to me before or since. I have called my journal The Book of Dreams *in honour of all that has brightened my life. Herein lies the tale of the brightest dream of all.*

It was the 12th day of July in the Year of Our Lord 1850,

that day when Orangemen everywhere celebrate the Battle of the Boyne. I was not a member of the Purple Hill Lodge nor had I any interest in it, but I was happy to walk through the forest with my father and brothers to the Galloway farm.

There we feasted and drank well into the day. What was it that called me away from my companions and into the woods? There was something in the quality of the light that I remember. It was not yet twilight but I had noticed a change, a faint glimmering in the trees that impressed my eye. Then I heard the drumming, low and quick like a heartbeat. I turned to my brother seated beside me and asked him, "Do you hear the drums?" He laughed and did accuse me of consuming too much whiskey. I had taken a few glasses but not as many as the others. It was soon apparent to me that no one could hear the drums but I.

Here I will explain why it was with no great surprise or difficulty that I answered the call from the woods. In my childhood back home in Ireland, there were times when I heard a sweet music rise from the old spinney behind our house. I would follow the high piping sounds into the tangle of trees and there I would see swift darting shapes dance amongst the leaves. I knew better than to remark upon these strange occurrences and I accepted them as part of my own converse with Nature. Such moments came to me also in my new land. One time I stood on the shore of a dark lake far in the northern woods of Ontario and I heard a loon cry my name. No matter where I have travelled, wherever I have gone, be it deep in the forests or high on the mountains and out on the windy plains, I have heard the Voice which speaks in a tongue above that of mortal men.

So it was on this day that I recognized the call and I left the picnic and walked into the woods. The talk and laughter of

419

my companions fell quickly behind me. I was soon lost in the forest of ancient white pine. The trees were like pillars in a great cathedral. The surge of wind in the branches was like the blast of the organ. I saw a deer leap ahead of me through the trees. Ravens cawed in the boughs overhead. When I heard the cry of wolves I grew anxious but still I continued on my way, following the drums.

It wasn't a wolf that awaited me on the forest path but an old Indian. He was a Chief, I knew, for he wore a fine blanket over his shoulders. At that time the Ojibway tribe still made their summer camp on the ridge south of Cashtown Corners. His blanket was a crimson red with various designs in black depicting wolf and raven. His countenance was noble, but I knew by his pallor and the dullness of his eyes that a sickness was upon him. I sensed that he had not long to live.

Unlike many of my race, I am not repelled or frightened by the natives of this land. They are a proud and decent people laid low by their encounter with us. It is the tragedy of human history that whenever two races meet, it must inevitably mean the downfall of one. The curse of Cain and Abel. Will we never meet as brothers and share the Earth?

I bowed my head to honour him, for he was a leader amongst his people and deserving of my respect.

"I do not speak your language," I said to him with regret. "I know words of some of the northern and western tongues, but I have not dwelled long in these parts."

The Chief raised his hand to end my apologia and replied in perfect and mellifluous English.

"I know your language. I have come a long way to meet you. You must undertake a task for one of your family who is to come."

On mature reflection, I remark with what readiness I accepted his words. No doubt or contest entered my mind for deep in my heart I knew he spoke the truth. A profound silence had fallen over the woods as if the moment were of such gravity it weighed upon the very trees. In that holy quiet there came to me a sudden and steadfast belief that it was not by chance or without purpose that I was born into the world. Whatever else I may have done or yet might do in the course of my life, this day would be the cornerstone. I had no doubt that it was ordained in that other Existence of which I speak from time to time, that I was meant to meet this man and to do his bidding.

I nodded my head to show my assent for I seemed to have lost the power of speech. The Chief opened his arms wide to enfold me in his blanket. To my utter astonishment and by some miracle or magic, his cloak had sprouted feathers to become the dark wings of a raven. How it came to be I cannot know, but we were then of a sudden transported from that place. Indeed we flew through the air as witches are said to do and it took all my concentration not to swoon with terror. Happily we did not traverse any great distance and soon alighted in a field.

Despite my wonderment and the weak state of my mind, I recognized the place to which I was brought. I knew it at first glance to be one of Edward Webster's allotments. On a low rise of land, it overlooked the hills that surrounded Creemore. Yet at the same time it was not his place, for upon it lay the shadow of something greater, a wide plain that shone with the lustrous light of the gloaming. At the heart of this plain stood the greatest marvel of all, a stone monument of stern grandeur. I had never seen its like in this country before, though they are numerous in my homeland. Yet not even the Old Country

*could boast one of this colossal stature. With its awesome
pillars and capstone overhead, it looked for all the world like a
giantish doorway.*

*"I had a dream," the old Chief said to me. "Listen, for
this is sacred. With your blood you will seal the door today so
that only one of your kin may ever open it again."*

*I do confess I was quite fearful when he produced a knife.
I steeled myself for some dreadful sacrifice, but his eyes were
mild and he looked kindly upon me. In the most gentlest of
tones, he bade me make a cut in my finger and mark the stone.*

This I did with little pain to myself.

*There was a moment before I touched the stone doorway
that I peered into its depths. What words could I use to describe
what I saw? Only those from the Holy Book could do the
scene justice. A fountain of gardens. A well of living
waters. In that brightest of moments I stood at the threshold
of a world so beauteous that it awoke in me the highest
emotions of reverence and delight. Here was a Kingdom that
revived the spirits and nourished the soul.*

*Alas, it was but a glimpse that I caught of that Land for
I had no sooner placed my hand upon the monument than the
whole disappeared from sight.*

*Once more the old Chief wrapped his blanket around me
and I was again engulfed in the softness of wings. When at last
he set me back down in the Galloway woods, these were his
parting words.*

*"There is one who will come many years from now,
blood of your blood and blood of the Summer Country. She
will follow your trail across the land. She will look in many
places to find this secret and she will gain in knowledge and
power. If she proves true, the spirits will speak to her and
they will give her many teachings. She will be a windwalker,*

a dreamspeaker and the key to the door. All this you will tell her and a final message. On the Plain of the Great Heart, where the living meet the dead, she will find the portal that leads to the Summer Land."

Dazed and confounded, I made my way back to the picnic but soon left for home. At first I repeated in my mind all that I had seen and heard lest I forget. For no matter how often I attempted to record the events on paper, I proved unable to do so. As time passed my mind rested easy as I came to understand that there was no fear of my forgetting. That day was burned upon my memory for all eternity. Now here at last, as I sense its permission, I do make my record for the one to come.

As a final note, I will add that before I took my leave of the Chief, I could not restrain myself from asking a question. He had come far to meet me despite his grave illness. Why would he make such an effort to help my descendant when we were not of his tribe or his people? Again I was struck by the kindness in his eyes and I found his response most touching.

"We are all family."

Thomas William Gowan
July 12, 1901

By the time they had finished reading, both Dana and Jean were dumbstruck.

Jean let out a low whistle.

"The Old Man! *C'est certain!*"

Dana nodded mutely. She couldn't find her voice. Yet it wasn't Grandfather's presence in the past that left her speechless, but the meaning of his visit to her ancestor and the message he had left.

There was a portal that the Enemy hadn't destroyed, a portal only she could open—and it was right here in Creemore!

CHAPTER THIRTY-FIVE

"A PORTAL IN CREEMORE!"

Dana was in a daze. She and Jean had left the Mad River and were wandering aimlessly through the village. She was still struggling to absorb the news. To think that her ancestor had kept the secret for her, all those years ago! The thought made her dizzy. Who was weaving the web? Whose dream was this? *We are all part of the Great Tale,* Grandfather had said.

"Why don't the Old Man tell us?" Jean wondered.

"Maybe he doesn't know in this life," Dana reflected. "It was all done in the past to keep the secret safe. Plus he did say to Thomas that I had to travel and get to know the land. That wouldn't have happened if he had told me where it was."

Jean nodded his agreement.

"These things are a *mystère, n'est-ce pas*? I can hear him say, 'It's best I don't tell you and you learn for yourself.'"

They both laughed.

"It *is* a mystery," Dana agreed, "but we're very close to solving it. Where do you think 'the living would meet the dead' in Creemore?"

They looked at each other and answered the question together.

"The graveyard!"

The cemetery was just south of the village, in a hilly wooded area at the end of Collingwood Street. It didn't take them long to get there. The site was sheltered on all sides by bosky growth and stands of tall pine. A bone-white pathway meandered through the wide scattering of graves. Granite tombstones of pink and white dotted the short grass. The view from the gently rolling height took in the hills that cupped the valley in which Creemore nestled.

Well out of sight of anyone, Jean put his arm around Dana and gave her a kiss.

"That's the hello I don't get at the bus."

She laughed. Everything seemed suddenly brighter.

"I missed you," she said, "even though it was only a day."

"Do you tell your *grand-mère* I come?" he asked.

"I didn't get the chance. I . . . ," she winced at his steady look and was driven to confess, "I chickened out."

"*C'est* okay," he laughed. "I go home as wolf."

Hand in hand, they strolled through the cemetery with only half a mind on the quest and the reason they were there.

Dana began to notice how many Gowans there were. *Separation is our sorrow, to meet again our hope.* Granda Faolan was buried amongst them. *Gabriel Patrick Faolan 1931–1981. Till the day break and the shadows flee away.* He was fifty when he died, a terrible tragedy for his wife and children. Poor Gabe, Dana thought, he was only her age when he lost his dad, while her aunts were just eleven and nine. It must have been so hard for them. *Yea, though I walk through the valley of the shadow of death, I shall fear no evil, for thou art with me.*

As she stood amidst her ancestral clan, something nagged at the back of Dana's mind. A clue she was overlooking. Her great-great-grandfather had recognized the place where the portal stood, but he didn't call it a graveyard. He said it was land belonging to Edward Webster, the village founder. Perhaps it hadn't yet become a cemetery? But when it did, wouldn't Thomas have chosen his own burial site?

"Look for his grave!" she exclaimed to Jean. "Where Thomas is buried! That's where the portal will be!"

Excited, she broke away to search through the tombstones. She began checking the dates. According to Gran Gowan, Thomas had lived to a ripe old age. After building his new house in 1901 at the age of seventy-seven, he had enjoyed it for more than a decade, dying at eighty-nine in 1913. Moving quickly through the graves, Dana passed the oldest names in the district, the pioneer families whose descendants still lived in the village. Along with the many Gowans were Giffens, Galloways, Kellys, Hoggs, Caseys, McDonalds and Langtrys. The moment she reached her great-great-grandfather's grave, she knew she was right.

His memorial was unusual, quite unlike the others. Instead of the customary rectangular shape, the obelisk of white marble was crowned with a sculpted bird in flight. Words from Psalm 91 were carved on the stone in curlicued lettering. *He shall cover thee with his feathers and under his wings shalt thou trust.* Simple inscriptions followed beneath, with the names of Thomas Gowan and his beloved Harriet, as well as some of their children and grandchildren who were buried there.

Dana stood at Thomas's graveside, remembering his life as he had described it in his journal. Here lay the man who had sailed to Canada, recording the dreams of his fellow emigrants, who had travelled across the country in search of his own dreams, and who had settled in the backwoods of Ontario once his dream was fulfilled. For here lay the man who had been given a glimpse of that other Existence he had sought all his life. Dana was proud to be his kin.

And as she stood there, her hunch was confirmed. Thomas had kept faith with that other world even unto death. The space around the grave crackled and sparked like static electricity. Her skin was tingling. With no effort on her part, her hands shed light. The portal was here.

She stared at the bird on top of the tombstone. Had Thomas been thinking of the raven who first carried him here? Fashioned of marble, it was white as snow. A soul-bird of Faerie? A great longing for home came over her. Her heart felt as if it might burst. Faerie was near, just beyond the veil.

She moved her hands to pour light over her ancestor's grave. But though she felt the portal's presence, it didn't appear. Something was wrong.

"It's here!" she called to Jean, turning around, "but I can't reach it! I think—"

Intent on her find, Dana hadn't noticed how far away Jean had gone. Nor had she noticed the shadow creeping out of the trees.

From the time they had entered the cemetery, Jean had been keeping a wary eye on the woods. The wolf in him was keenly on guard. When Dana ran off to find Thomas's grave, he decided to patrol the perimeter of the graveyard. The place was an ideal spot for an ambush. Surrounded by trees and shrubs on all sides, it was isolated and well-hidden by a rampart of greenery. There were too many nooks and crannies, too many places to hide. As he scanned the woods, they seemed to darken before his eyes. Neither he nor Dana had considered the possibility of an attack in broad daylight. He suddenly realized how foolish that was.

He called out to Dana to suggest they leave.

Deep in the gloom of the woods, something dark was watching. Called by an evil greater than itself, it had come down from the midnight lands of the North. Its ravening hunger craved human flesh and it knew the name of its prey.

Dana heard a whisper on the wind and felt suddenly cold. She had already turned around before Jean called out. The air had darkened as if night were falling. She stared into the trees, feeling bleak and lonely. What spell was being cast from the dark heart of the woods? A disturbing odour crept through the air, pungent and penetrating. With the smell came a low mournful sound, like the soughing of wind, both seductive and chilling. She stirred as if in sleep.

Daaa-naaa.

There was a cry in the voice, tortured and desolate, unbearable to hear, yet also of some abominable power.

The wind through the trees, the sigh of a restless soul, the waves of the waters are the unquiet spirits. The white man asks "what is that sound?" We who know the answer cry, "the We-ti-ko."

Dana knew nothing of the myths of the Canadian North, knew nothing of the spirits who roamed the taiga and the tundra. Though Grandfather had spoken the name of the We-ti-ko, she didn't know the giant cannibal whose heart was of ice. Its hands were gnarled with crooked fingers and nails like claws. Its feet had long pointed heels and a single toe. The face was the most dreadful to behold, black with frostbite and lips gnawed raw. The yellow eyes rolled in sockets of blood. Through jagged teeth it hissed and whistled before letting out screeches and blood-curdling yowls. Worse was the voice when it chose to speak. Nothing could be more awful than to hear it call your name.

Daaa-naaa.

Dana didn't know what was coming to kill her, but Jean did.

Though the We-ti-ko moved with a celerity beyond human ken, it could not evade a *loup-garou*. As soon as the monster broke from the trees, Jean was after it.

Only in those last minutes did they realize the extent of their foolhardiness. They had come to the heart of the quest with no preparation or defence. It was too late for plans, too late even for regrets. As catastrophe struck, both reached immediately for what made them strong.

When she saw the demon bearing down on her, Dana raised her hands to call on the light. She knew she could use it as shield and weapon. With Thomas's tombstone at her back for support, she stood her ground on her ancestor's grave. Though she quailed at the horror that raced towards her, she would not run. She had faith in her power.

Jean's decision was instant. It was the second time he had faced this moment and once again he suffered no doubt. It was his nature to act this way and his love for Dana simply made it easier. Still, the sacrifice was a bitter one, for he knew what it meant and what he would lose forever. Even as the midday sun beat down, he willed the change to come upon him.

Dana hurled her first fireball at the creature. It screamed with pain, but didn't slow down. She was about to throw another when she spotted Jean. By the time she had opened her mouth to cry— NO!—he had turned.

The great black wolf bounded towards her and cut off her attacker.

The We-ti-ko was an abomination of winter, an evil spirit that stalked the frozen lands of the North. It liked to grip its prey by the head or feet and lift it from the ground, high into the air. Horrified witnesses would describe in dismay how the victim's cries grew muted by distance, a melancholy wail that disappeared in the night. Then hidden away in the farthest wilds, in a foul lair fashioned of human bones, the demon would devour its prey alive.

But if the We-ti-ko had otherworldly power and strength, so too did the *loup-garou*. And the wolf was wild with rage, insane with the knowledge that he had lost his humanity, that he would never again take the form of his own kind, the form that matched his beloved's. Till the day he died he would be separate and different. He raged against fate, against the Enemy who had called up the creature, against the demon itself who had forced him to turn. Ears flattened, hair bristling, eyes glowing, he leaped at the We-ti-ko. Deadly fangs and claws tore through flesh and bone. In a matter of moments, he had ripped the demon to pieces. His sacrifice was not in vain. The We-ti-ko lay dead.

There was no time to celebrate, no time to mourn. Other things were coming out of the forest, spectral and malevolent. Dana and the wolf fled down the hill and out of the cemetery into the woods that bordered the Mad River.

Like a pack of hounds after the fox, the dark things bayed in pursuit. Wicked and grotesque, they moved like shadows, hiding behind the trees, calling out to each other. As the evil cries echoed throughout the forest, more joined the hunt. They slithered through the undergrowth. They leaped from branch to branch.

Dana's heart beat wildly. Their enemies were increasing in speed and number, running her and Jean to ground. Even as she ran, she ached inside, anguished by the enormity of a loss she had yet to absorb, a grief that threatened to defeat her before death had the chance.

In the wild flight and the fear and the anguish of her heart, she was the Hunted One and so too was he, the great black wolf that ran beside her.

Neither she nor Jean saw the arrows that rained behind them. Arrows that flew with uncanny speed and unerring marksmanship. Arrows that struck with silent and deadly purpose. Arrows tipped with burning light. Nor did they see their enemies fall.

Deeper and deeper into the woods they ran, till they reached the heart of the oldest trees. The ancient white pine stood tall and majestic, oiling the air with resinous scent. Green boughs reached downward as if to embrace them. Shafts of light fell like gentle caresses. At last they realized they were no longer being pursued.

As the trees thinned out, they stepped into a clearing. Dana looked around her. She knew this place. It was the same glade to which the deer had led her the night she journeyed in the Medicine Lodge. There was even a ring of stones and ashes where she remembered the campfire.

As the stillness and peace came dropping slow, she knew this was *sanctuary*.

Dana sank to the ground beside the black wolf and put her arms around him. Then she threw back her head and howled.

★   ★   ★

Even when she could cry no more, she still embraced him.

"You shouldn't have done it," she whispered. "I could have fought it. And even if I lost, I would rather have died."

Her heart was broken. She saw the tragic look in his eyes, but he shook his great head to show his dissent.

There in the glade, they leaned against each other, silently grieving, a girl who was almost a woman with her arms around a wolf. They knelt on a mat of red and gold leaves. The soft light of the day illumined their sorrow.

Out of respect for their pain, the others came quietly, on gentle footfall barely touching the ground. They had arrived too late at the Plain of the Great Heart. Having hastened there to the aid of the Light, they could have turned the tide. They had the power. But before they could loose their burning arrows, the *loup-garou* had turned, turned in the daylight to fight for his love.

It was a tragic sacrifice, for this they mourned, but it was also a noble one.

They drew near to the wolf. They wished to honour him, a trueheart, a braveheart, for his pure act of heroism. They began to sing, to praise him and to tell his tale, to set his name amongst the constellations, his story to be told as long as they lived.

And they lived forever.

It was some time before Dana heard the song and grew aware of the circle that had gathered around them. She stiffened in alarm, ready to flee, but the wolf didn't growl. These were not enemies.

The voices were melodious, like the whisper of rain falling on leaves, or the plash of water over pebbles on the seashore. The song was a glossolalic air, a medley of languages. Dana heard the tongues she knew best, Irish and English, while Jean heard French and Cree. In all the languages, the words were the same. It was a love song and a paean, a song of praise for a young man who had lost his humanity for the love of a young woman. A song of heroism, romance and sacrifice.

As she listened to the song, her arms around the wolf, Dana recognized the honour that Jean had bestowed upon her. She accepted the gift of his sacrifice and his love.

He himself held his head proudly, having no doubt about what he had done. He was content that his beloved was safe beside him.

Dana looked around at the singers. Her vision was blurred by her tears. She saw flickering flashes and columns of light. They kept shifting and changing like cascading water. She wiped at her tears. She wanted to see. There was something here. She was overcome with a sense of familiarity. Again she remembered the glade in her journey in the Medicine Lodge and the vague forms around the campfire, like trails of mist in the morning. She had almost understood the message then, the secret of their existence, but the moment had been fleeting. As soon as she had reached out to grasp the knowledge, it had swiftly eluded her. Even now, she was struggling to accept what she saw, for she knew them and yet she didn't know them.

There were several tall males with reddish-brown skin and a brush of green hair like feathered needles. Whenever she blinked,

Dana found herself looking at a stand of red pine. Beside the men were equally tall women of a silver colouring with bristles of fine hair. Long elegant cones dangled from their ear lobes. When the wind blew, they shivered like white pine. What were the ones with the wrinkled skin? They were greyish-brown with a tint of purple and their hair was shiny green. Eastern hemlock! There were others she slowly began to recognize: a fair-skinned lissome birch, three shy and trembling aspens, many sweet-smiling maples with scarlet locks. Their clothes were woven of wild daisies, black-eyed Susans and white trilliums. Some had large birds perched on their shoulders or wrists, a glossy black raven, a golden eagle, a blue jay. Smaller fox sparrows and woodpeckers nestled in their hair. At times they rustled and whispered like a small wood in the wind. Then they would return to a state of deep repose, like sleeping trees. As well as birds, there was a host of wild animals who sat or lay beside them: a beaver, a badger, a great black bear, several families of squirrels, a raccoon and a white-tailed deer.

Though the animals were unperturbed by Dana's scrutiny, the tree people appeared to be caught fast in her gaze. *Human struck.*

Dana continued to struggle with the huge fact of their being. She found herself comparing them to the ones she knew in Ireland. Like their Irish counterparts, they reflected the landscape in which they dwelled. They had a stern beauty that spoke of deep forests, cold lakes and high mountains, vast plains. They were incredibly old and wild and free.

When Dana finally accepted the truth, it was shattering, a shock that reverberated through her heart, mind and soul.

"You're fairies!" she cried out. *"Canadian fairies!"*

Chapter Thirty-Six

THE GLORIOUS CREATURES WERE BOTH wary and shy as they suffered her gaze. Though they knew something of Dana and her half-fairy nature, it wasn't easy to be so visible to her. Dana, in turn, was still reeling from the fact of their existence. The eyes that stared back at her were a luminous green, like stars from Ireland.

"You're *beautiful*!" she breathed at last.

A ripple ran through them. They looked happy, pleased, proud. Eased by her tone, they diminished to human height. Some shrank smaller still, as this was their preference.

One of the pine women stepped forward to speak. A daisy chain crowned her long green hair. Her skin was silver.

"I'm Daisy Greenleaf of the Clan Creemore. Pleased to meet you, Light-Bearer's daughter."

More came forward to greet her, some bowing, some shaking her hand. Others timidly stated their names before scurrying off. There were those too shy to do even that and they slipped away into the woods like bright shadows. But it wasn't long before a little circle of the brave were seated on the grass around her. Tall and lithe, Stanley Moon had eyes that flashed with mischief. He looked like Pan with his pointed ears and evergreen skin. His arm was draped lazily around Daisy's shoulders. They were obviously a pair. Fern Moon, Stanley's sister, was the same green colour with a head of bushy dark hair. She was quiet where her brother was brazen. Brown as an oak, Big James Tweed was robust and kindly. Flora Bird was blue, tiny and quick-witted, flitting here and there. Honeywood was a beauty with long yellow hair and dreamy eyes. Her voice was mellifluous, her movements languid like boughs in a warm breeze. Round and stout, John Trout liked to shout. He was a moody fellow, one minute cranky, the next full of laughter. Lavender was pale mauve, so small she could have been a flower petal blown by a breeze. She was the only one who had chosen to wear wings and she fluttered around Dana like a lilac butterfly.

The more at ease they became, the more the fairies shape-shifted at will, from creatures of light to earthly guise to various animal forms. The divisions of nature meant nothing to them.

While the fairies were introducing themselves, the *loup-garou* stayed by Dana's side. There were other animals present and he was at ease in their company. Flora Bird brushed his coat with a golden comb. A family of ravens, ever friend to the wolf, had settled beside him and were preening their feathers.

"I've been here for over two years," Dana said, astonishment ringing in her voice. "Why have I not seen you? Nor even sensed you!"

They looked at each other, then at her.

"You know the rules," Daisy said. "You can't see what you don't believe in."

"I believe in fairies!" she said indignantly.

"*Canadian* fairies?" they chimed.

Her huff deflated.

A thousand questions buzzed in Dana's mind like bees, but before she could ask them John Trout let out a shout.

"If we talk, we eat! Where's the feast?"

"Yeah! Bring it on!" the others clamoured while the animals hooted, barked, chirped and cawed.

Daisy, evidently the leader, burst out laughing and clapped her hands. In the blink of an eye, they were surrounded by a cornucopia of treats. Baskets of birch bark, spruce root and black ash spilled over with fruits: rosy apples, blueberries, fat gooseberries, cranberries, wild cherries and currants. There were hot dishes of roasted corn on the cob, sweet squash, toasted pumpkin and yams. These were followed by cold dishes of desserts: sugar cakes dripping with dark molasses, long pulls of sticky taffy, and every kind of maple confection, fudge and syrup, mousse and tart. The favourite drinks were raspberry cordials and spiced white wine.

Dana and the wolf joined in the feast while keeping a watchful eye on the forest. Big James Tweed noticed their wariness.

"You needn't worry. These woods are safe. This is the rath of *Dun Crí Mor,* our fairy fort. No minions of the Enemy can get in here."

As the picnic got underway, they told her about themselves.

"We emigrated with the Irish," Daisy said. "We couldn't bear to see our good neighbours leave without us."

"We're scattered across the land," Stanley Moon declared. "Wherever the Irish went, we went too."

"At first we were homesick," said Honeywood in her sweet golden voice. "Like the settlers themselves, we pined for the hills and woods of Ireland. And then, just like them, we grew to love our new country. That's when we took on the colours and shapes of the land."

"The B.C. clans are huge!" Lavender piped up. "Rainforest fairies!"

"They went west with the Guinness family," Fern added.

"In time, many of us forgot about the Old Country," Daisy said. "By that I mean Faerie. Some ran off into the bush or into the Far North, never to be seen again. None of us has gone back in over a century. We've all gone native. This is our home."

"I guess that's why I never heard of you," Dana murmured. She let out a sigh. "But then, there's so much about Faerie that I don't know. I was really surprised to hear about the queen who brought summer to Canada. Did she come through the portal here in Creemore?"

"Oh no," said Daisy. "She came through the oldest of them all, the one that stood in Newfoundland at the heart of the Rock. There were gateways in every corner of the land, before the Enemy destroyed them. They're all gone now."

"'cept for ours!" John Trout shouted proudly.

"Ours stood strong," Daisy nodded. "When the Enemy struck in the other world, it couldn't touch our gateway. For the portal of *Magh Crí Mor*, the Plain of the Great Heart, was sealed on this side."

"Thanks to the Old Ones," Flora Bird chirped up.

They were suddenly solemn.

"You know the Old Ones," Dana said.

"How could we not?" said Daisy. "All of Turtle Island—what you call North America—belongs to them. They are the spirits known to the First Peoples of this land."

Dana saw the looks that passed between the fairies. Their faces were difficult to read, but shame and sadness seemed uppermost.

"They've been helping me," Dana told them.

Daisy nodded. "Since long before you were born. They were the ones who sealed our portal, though we didn't know why at the time. It was all kept secret. We were simply happy to do their bidding. At their request, we called your ancestor to meet with the Chief Druid—"

"You mean Grandfather? The Old Man?"

"He has many names," Daisy said. "In the language of the Old Ones he is Magician-King-Holy One. He is not an Old One, but they speak through him. He has great power."

"He could see us," Stanley Moon said, "from the time we got here. That's how we knew he was a Druid. He said he was going to die soon but that his soul would migrate to another body. We brought your great-great-grandfather to meet him, here in our rath."

"We drummed till Thomas followed us!" Lavender said. "He was a man with a big heart."

"We blessed him for that," said Big James Tweed.

"We sang at his shivaree," chirped Flora Bird, "and we blessed his children and their children and their children . . ."

Dana reflected that it was no wonder her father ended up marrying a fairywoman.

"We are the guardians of *Magh Crí Mor*," Daisy said. "Though we knew nothing of the portentous days ahead, we have always kept watch on the Plain of the Great Heart."

"We're the ones who got Edward Webster to donate the site for a graveyard," Stanley Moon explained with a little grin. "He had a dream that the land should be secluded and peaceful."

"A good neighbour he was," Fern said with a sigh. "I cried buckets when he went away. It was so sad that he lost all his money and had to sell everything. We tried to help as best we could, but in the end mortals got to live their own lives."

"The other humans should've stopped him from goin'," John Trout asserted loudly. "After all what he did for them and their village. It was a disgrace, him dying far away in Americay. A darn shame!"

The other fairies vociferously agreed. Regardless of the passage of time, this was obviously a matter that still upset them. Dana was trying to get them back to the subject of the portal, when a small party broke from the trees.

"Ms Woods!" she cried. "Laurel!"

The young women rushed over to hug her. They looked like forest-dwellers, two Maid Marians in mottled clothing of green

438

and brown, with leaves caught in their hair. They were escorted by more of the Creemore troop. Alf Branch was like Daisy, a natural leader, short and stocky with an air of command. Weatherup was fat and jolly while Gaelyn Tree-Top was tall and dignified. Christy Pines looked half-girl, half-hedgehog with a mane of spiny bristles. Like the other fairies, they wore clothes woven of fern, bark and wildflowers.

They settled down in the circle and joined the feast.

"Isn't it wonderful?" Gwen said to Dana. "Fairies in Canada and we didn't even know!"

"How could we?" Laurel pointed out. "They didn't know about the Companions and they've been hiding for years."

"Some of them are so shy they still won't come near us," Gwen added.

"It's our nature to be elusive," Alf Branch said. "And it's not like Ireland here. The people are modern and don't believe in fairies."

"That's not true!" Gwen argued. "I keep telling you. More and more of us believe. If you showed yourselves a bit that would help the cause."

"I hate to tell you, but Ireland has changed since you left," Dana said. "It's just as modern. Everyone has gone mad making money. They're paving the green spaces for roads and dumping rubbish in the hills."

"Humans!" snorted Christy Pines. Her hair bristled angrily. "When will they ever learn?"

"How did you find them?" Dana asked Gwen.

"Actually they found me."

Alf Branch told the story of how the Creemore fairies saved Gwen from Grimstone.

"The day the portals went down, we all got a shock. Though we hadn't gone home in a hundred years we felt the cutting of the cord and it hurt, I can tell you. In that burning moment we understood why our gateway was sealed so long ago. It was the only one left standing. We were slow to act, I'll admit that now. In our defence, we knew nothing about what happened between Thomas and the Chief. All we knew was that they shut the door between them.

"I guess we were waiting for someone or something to come to us. Then rumours and strange tidings started to drift in. Dark things creeping through the countryside. Bad things happening in the city. By the time we got wind of your quest, you were already on the move. Once we heard you were a Gowan of Creemore, we put two and two together. It was time to end our isolation, not to mention our procrastination. We knew we had to go into the city to find you."

Alf Branch stopped and shuddered visibly.

"We'd rather go into battle than into Toronto!" Big James Tweed stated with conviction.

The others echoed his sentiment.

"We're woodland fairies, you see," Alf Branch explained. "The Big City is just too big. The crowded streets and the traffic and the noise."

He shuddered again.

"You should've seen us cringing around the corners of those skyscrapers," Honeywood breathed with soft horror.

"Unfortunately we don't know any urban fairies," Al Branch went on. "They hide even better than we do. But thanks to the city pigeons and squirrels we finally got our bearings. They told us about an evil thing squatting in an empty building on once holy ground. By no coincidence, it was near to a house protected by a Sacred One. We knew we were on the right trail. And not a moment too soon! We were in the area when we heard the cry. Gwen's spell of succour brought us to her in an instant."

"Poor girl, she was near dead," Lavender said gently.

"He was about to deal the fatal blow," Alf Branch said grimly. "We got right in there and lathered him good till he fled the scene. Then we took her back here as fast as we could."

"We thought she was you," Daisy told Dana. "Her wounds were terrible and she was close to death. It took all our healing skills and many long days before she was able to speak. Only then did we discover who she was and she told us about you and Laurel."

"We hurried back to the city," Alf Branch said, "but we couldn't find hide nor hair of either of you."

"I thought you were both dead for sure," Gwen said, recalling the nightmare of that time.

"I would have been," Laurel put in, "if one of the Old Ones hadn't acted to save me. I didn't know who he was then, but I realized it later. He gave me an amulet that stopped Grimstone from killing me. That's when I ended up in the burnt place."

"The Brule," Dana nodded. "I was in the West with the Old Ones and they sent me to you."

"We were over the moon to find you both there," Gwen said. "Messengers had been sent out everywhere to look for you, birds of the air and swift-footed creatures as well as the fairies. Laurel's body was found on a deserted beach. That was a bad moment. Then we saw she wasn't dead, but her spirit was absent. We had to find it."

"It wasn't too hard," Stanley Moon said. "We recognized the Grey Man when we rescued Gwen. He's an Irish elemental, very powerful but also predictable. It was only a matter of searching the shadows to find his lair."

"And that's when you came for me," Laurel nodded.

"We saw you were with the Old Ones," Daisy told Dana, "and we saw you had power. We figured you were safe. We were busy doing things to protect the portal, but we should have come to you, we know that now. We were caught off guard when we heard you were in Creemore and under attack."

"What!" said Gwen and Laurel together.

It was Dana's turn to tell her story. When she came to the part where Jean lost his humanity, Gwen wept openly while Laurel looked stricken. Dana didn't cry herself, she had no tears left.

"I haven't lost hope," she said firmly. "Faerie is the Land of Dreams and Promise. We just need to get there! I found the portal at my ancestor's grave, but it was beyond my reach."

"It's out of alignment," Gwen explained. "As I mentioned in my note, the worlds have been drifting apart without the gateways to bridge them. When they cross again on Hallowe'en, the portal will appear. That's your chance to open it."

Gwen looked as if she might say more. It was Laurel who finished what had to be said.

"Your one and only chance. If the door isn't opened, when the worlds drift again it will be forever."

Dana winced, but she preferred to know the truth.

"*The Book of Dreams* described how my great-great-grandfather sealed the gateway with a drop of his blood. Only the blood of his family can open it again. I'll just do what he did. That's easy enough."

They all looked at her. She felt the weight of their silence. There was something huge she was overlooking.

"It won't be easy at all," Daisy said at last.

"When the portal appears," Alf Branch said, "an army will stand between you and the door."

The wolf growled low in his throat.

Dana looked back at them, stunned. Of course she expected a battle of some kind, between herself and Grimstone, but she hadn't imagined anything bigger.

"The secret of the portal was well-kept through the years," Alf Branch pointed out, "but even as you uncovered the truth, so too did the Enemy's servant. Having failed to kill you, he has called dark forces to stand between you and what you seek. They are closing on Creemore. Many are already here, as you know yourself."

"You have allies also," Daisy assured her quickly. "We've been gathering our own army far and wide. That's why we were away and didn't know of your peril. You will be happy to know that you have made many friends on your travels across Canada. You passed many tests, received many blessings. Word of your quest and your cause has spread. Stories are being told about you. Even as the dark forces draw together, so too do the bright hosts who will stand against them. You are not alone."

Dana was steadied by Daisy's words. Her arm tightened around the wolf's neck. She would do what she had to do to open the door.

"So now, your report," Daisy said to the latecomers. "What's the news?"

"We steered clear of Creemore," Laurel told her. "As Alf Branch said, the dark is rising there. We went to Collingwood. We were told about a great hosting at Algonquin Park. They're coming from as far as Fort Severn and Lake of the Woods. All the northern Ontario troops will march down together on Hallowe'en."

"Excellent," said Daisy.

"There's good news from Ireland too," Gwen told her. "We rang from town. The Enemy's hold on our Irish Companions is broken. All are restored to health and ready to help. They'll gather in a sacred place on the eve of *Samhain* and send us power."

"Good news indeed," Daisy nodded. "And I can report that at the Grand Council held today on White Island, there were heralds from every province and territory. All will send troops to join the battle."

A lively cheer rose up from the circle.

"The giants are in," Gaelyn Tree-Top announced. He was a quiet man who rarely spoke, but when he did everyone listened. "Fingal has called them."

"The trolls too," Weatherup declared.

"Really?" Dana said, surprised. "They'll fight for us?"

"Natch," said Weatherup. "They're not bad, you know, just thick. Their king says he's a friend of yours? Little fella, half-troll, half-leprechaun?"

"Trew!" said Dana, even more surprised. "He's the King of the Trolls?"

"Will the dragons come?" Lavender asked. "They fly so beautifully."

"Lots of power too," said Big James Tweed.

"Would they want to join us?" Fern wondered. "After what happened?"

A shamed silence fell over the group.

Stanley Moon let out a sigh.

"What is it?" asked Dana.

"The Irish and the Chinese built the railways together," Stanley Moon said, "right across Canada. They got along most of the time, except when the Irish took to the drink on their days off. Then they thought it was funny to cut off the pigtails of the Chinese workers."

"Dreadful behaviour," said Fern, shaking her head.

"We used to pinch the blackguards black and blue," said Christy Pines, "but it made no difference. They just thought they fell over when they were drunk."

Dana frowned. History was a terrible thing. *The sins of the father.* It had an awful habit of coming back at you.

"None of you sounds Irish," she pointed out. "You've all got Canadian accents."

"Will we approach them as Canadians, then?" Alf Branch suggested.

"Yes and no," she decided. "We must be honest. Say I belong to both Ireland and Canada. That's the truth."

Even without the dragons, the tally was looking good.

"What about the Old Ones?" Laurel suggested. "They've helped us already."

The fairies frowned. Dana sensed their reluctance and something else she couldn't quite grasp.

"They seldom intervene in human affairs," Daisy said quietly. "When they do, it's on their own terms and not at anyone's request. They see a bigger picture, a Grand Design beyond our comprehension."

Even before Daisy had spoken, Dana had already decided against the notion.

"We won't ask them," she said. "It wouldn't be right. Why should they fight our battles? They've already been more than generous."

Flora Bird looked as if she might speak, so too did Gaelyn Tree-Top, but Alf and Daisy both shook their heads to say *keep quiet.*

"We will leave that decision for now," Daisy told them, then she turned to Dana. "When you travelled in the west, did you receive a blessing?"

"I . . . I don't know," Dana said. "They took me many places and taught me many things. Most of all, they gave me a sense of my own power. What do you mean exactly?"

"Was there any mention of a gift or ransom?" asked Alf.

"Oh yes!" said Dana. "The Sasquatch Elder told me. He said *I* was the gift."

Some of the fairies went pale at this. All looked deeply sad. They couldn't meet her eyes. Again, their leaders shook their heads. *Say nothing.*

"So be it," said Daisy, "but it may not come to that and we shall do our best to ensure it doesn't. Whether big or small, we all have a part to play."

★   ★   ★

The wolf stood alone at the edge of the forest, unable to deny himself one last look. The amber eyes were dark with grief as he gazed on the one he loved. Her black hair shone in the afternoon light. Her eyes were like blue stars. Despite the burden that weighed upon her, she had never looked so radiant or so strong. Her hands rested in her lap, glowing faintly. She had found her people. She was safe amongst them. It was time he returned to his.

He had heard the battle plans and decided the part he should play. He would head north to Roy and *grand-père,* and most of all to the Old Man. He would ask them to help Dana.

He was about to set out when she was suddenly there, blocking his path.

"Did you really think you could go without saying goodbye?"

Her face was streaked with tears, but her voice was steady.

"No use trying to spare me pain, Jean. It hurts either way and all the time."

She stooped to put her arms around him. He rested his great head against hers. She could hear his thoughts.

"Farewell, *mon amour.* I will return as soon as I can."

"Don't give up," she said, sobbing. "There's still hope for us. If I can open the portal, we have a chance. Faerie is the Land of Enchantment. It could free you of yours."

"Stay alive," he told her. *"Je t'aime."*

"Take care. I love you too," she whispered back.

When she returned to the camp, the fairies were singing.

> *She's like the swallow that flies so high,*
> *She's like the river that never runs dry,*
> *She's like the sunshine on the lee shore,*
> *She loves her love forever more.*

"I've got to go," she told them. "It's getting late. My Gran will be worried."

"Not a good idea," Gwen said. "Creemore is crawling with creepies."

"I'm going home," Dana insisted quietly. "I've got seven days till the battle and I'm going to spend it with my family. I'm not afraid of Grimstone. I can protect myself."

Both Laurel and Gwen were about to argue, but Daisy held up her hand.

"The Light-Bearer's daughter has power of her own."

Alf Branch agreed. "He won't risk attacking her now. She's too strong. He'll wait till he's surrounded by his army. The Enemy's servants are always cowards."

Dana took her leave of the fairy troop of Clan Creemore.

"Till we meet again on the battlefield," Daisy Greenleaf said, kissing her on the forehead.

"See you next week," was Dana's response.

As she left the camp, guided through the forest by Alf and Christy, she heard them singing behind her.

> *She's like the swallow that flies so high.*

CHAPTER THIRTY-SEVEN

"IS OUR GARÇON A HOPELESS TRUANT OR what?"

Georgia plunked herself down and took out her chopsticks. She glanced at Dana's lunch untouched on the table. Then she saw her friend's eyes.

"What's wrong!"

Dana didn't feel like lying or dodging the question.

"Something bad has happened to him."

"Not again," said her friend, dismayed. "Another mugging?"

"Worse."

Georgia frowned. She looked around the cafeteria. Everyone was busy eating or talking. No busybodies nearby.

"Can't your magic help him?"

Dana was hurting too much to ward off the question. She had hoped her normal routine would distract her from the ordeal ahead, but it wasn't working. As soon as she had arrived at school, Jean's empty seat was a painful reminder of what she had lost before the battle began. Reverting to her withdrawn and defensive self, she had avoided Georgia all morning. But her new friend was not easily put off and here she was, challenging Dana at the worst possible time.

Dana was about to leave the table when Georgia spoke hurriedly.

"Look, I haven't bugged you about it since the day it happened, but something's come up. It's important we talk and

I mean talk." Again Georgia took a quick look around. She leaned towards Dana and lowered her voice. "It's my great-granny. She's special. The way I figure you are too? She talks to dragons. She says they're all over the place but no one can see them because we're too modern and scientific. She's been telling me stories about them since I was a little girl. I believe her and I don't care what anyone else thinks. She's the smartest person I've ever known."

Dana could hear the tremor in Georgia's voice. It was obvious she had never spoken about this to anyone else. Dana was honoured. She knew what a risk it was to admit such things.

"Your great-grandmother's right," Dana said. "There *are* dragons. I've seen them too."

Tears welled in Georgia's eyes. Her voice rang with gladness.

"I knew there was a reason I wanted to be your friend! It felt so right! Here's the thing. The dragons told my great-granny about a girl from Ireland who's facing a big battle. They've been asked to fly to Creemore to help her. As soon as Granny told me the story I suspected it was you. It is, isn't it?"

There was no use hiding the truth. They were well past that point. Dana was surprised and happy. It was a true sign of their friendship that the deepest secrets could be so easily revealed.

Georgia was waiting for her answer with bated breath.

Dana nodded, expecting to be hit with a barrage of questions. There was only one. Again, a sign of their friendship.

"Will you be all right?"

"I don't know," said Dana, truthfully. "I hope so. Did the dragons say they would come?"

"They're still debating the matter. They asked my great-granny what she thought they should do. Seems something happened awhile ago? Between the Chinese and the Irish?" Dana sensed that Georgia was being diplomatic. "Dragons have long lives and long memories. Do you know much about them?"

"Not a lot," Dana admitted. "I never met one. The dragons in Faerie live in the sun with their cousins, the salamanders. They don't come out that often. From what I can tell from the fairy tales, it's just as well. They can be wild and destructive, breathing fire and burning towns and villages."

"Eastern dragons aren't like that," Georgia said. "For one thing, they're water spirits. Only a few of them breathe fire. In our stories, they're always noble and friendly, peaceful and wise. And they bring good luck. In China and Japan, they've got their own temples."

"They sound wonderful," said Dana. "I hope they'll join us."

That was all Georgia needed to hear.

"I want you to come meet my great-granny. If you impress her, I'm sure she'll put in a good word with the dragons. They respect her opinion."

Dana felt a stab of anxiety. What if Georgia's great-granny didn't like her?

Georgia saw the worried look.

"Hey, no sweat. You'll pass. You're good people."

Dana laughed. She was feeling better already. With her appetite returned, she started on her lunch. As best she could, she gave Georgia a summary of the quest.

"What a fabulous story!" said Georgia, enthralled. "It's like the *Hsi Yu Chi*! That's a legend my great-granny's been telling me since I was small. It's all about Hsuan Chuang and his pilgrimage to the Western Paradise to find the Buddhist scriptures for the Emperor of China. It's a long chronicle full of demons, ghosts and fairies."

A shiver ran through Dana, a thrill of recognition. She caught a glimpse of a truth so profound it left her breathless. She was one of the People of the Great Journey. There were so many of them in so many stories.

"What about our missing buddy?" Georgia prodded her. "I notice you left him out of the story, but I have a feeling he's in it? I could tell he was special too, you know. You've both got the same thing around you that my great-granny has. Some kind of aura, I guess, without getting too New Agey about it. What's happened to him?"

Dana hesitated. She really wanted to tell. They could both comfort each other. After all, Jean was Georgia's friend as well.

"I can't say," she said at last. "That's his stuff. I'm sure he'll tell you himself if—*when*—we get through this. But I can't do it for him. I'm sorry, I really am."

"Don't worry about it," Georgia said, "I'm not pushing you. I'm just glad you could tell me your side. I'd like to help if I can in my own little way."

"You've helped me a lot by being my friend," Dana said and she meant it. She felt less lonely and more hopeful now.

"Well, maybe I can do a bit more. I'll call you tonight about my great-granny."

That night, Georgia rang Dana with the news.

"It's all set. We're to meet her on Wednesday first thing after school. We're going to *yum cha* in her favourite restaurant."

"We're going to what?"

"*Yum cha.* Drink tea. You'll love it. If we hurry, we'll be in time for *dim sum.* Have you had that before?"

"No."

"You'll love it!" Georgia said again.

On Wednesday, Dana and Georgia left school together and headed for the old Chinatown on Spadina Avenue. They hurried through the bustling streets past outdoor stands of exotic fruits and vegetables, small shops cluttered with porcelain statues, paper parasols, dishes and woks, clothing stores with their wares displayed on rails on the sidewalk, and butchers with barbecued pork and duck hanging from hooks in the windows. The air was pungent with an aromatic mélange of incense, raw fish, cooked meats and spices.

"This is it," said Georgia.

The Dragon Palace was a grand old establishment near an Asian mall. Two stone lions guarded the doorway. A silken banner above the lintel displayed a golden dragon with Chinese lettering.

"*Lung tik chuan ren.* 'Children of the dragon,'" Georgia translated. "That's what Chinese people call themselves."

A wide red-carpeted stairway led upwards into a cavernous dining room decorated with tasselled lanterns and delicately painted screens. The music of a two-stringed lute, *baa-u,* flute and hand bell chimed behind the tumult of voices. The restaurant was packed to the brim with round tables seating whole families and other groups. Amidst the diners, waitresses wearing embroidered cheongsams pushed handcarts of food. From bamboo steamers and kettles of boiling water, they served the small delicacies that comprised *dim sum.* As they moved between the tables, they called out the dishes in Chinese and English. *Ha gao!* Shrimp dumpling! *Nor mai gai!* Sticky rice in lotus leaf! *Sui mai!* Pork dumpling! *Wu gok!* Taro cake!

Georgia and Dana hovered in the entranceway till a beautiful hostess glided towards them. When Georgia spoke to her in Chinese, Dana noticed the change in the young woman's expression. The gracious smile faltered. Was that a trace of fear in her eyes?

She led them down a corridor lined with paintings of dragons.

"I should warn you," Georgia whispered to Dana. "If you see anything strange, it isn't your imagination. There's two of her."

"What!"

"You'll see. Maybe. Just remember I told you and don't freak out. Oh, and she doesn't speak English, so I'll be your interpreter."

At the end of the hall was a doorway draped with a heavy red curtain. The hostess drew the curtain aside and ushered them in, then hurried away with visible relief.

In contrast to the noisy restaurant, the private compartment was dim and hushed. The rich furnishings were of mahogany inlaid with ivory. A thick red-and-gold carpet covered the floor. Images of the dragon were everywhere, in carved red wood, bright ceramics, green jade and pale porcelain. Against the back wall was an altar with joss sticks in brass holders. A musky incense smoked the air. In the centre of the room was a lone dining table with high-backed chairs. Seated at the table was a tiny wizened woman.

Dana was surprised. After the edginess of the hostess and Georgia's warnings, she was expecting someone fierce. The little old lady beaming at them was the picture of a beloved great-granny. She wore a high-collared trouser suit of a flowered pattern, with buttons and toggles. Her wispy grey hair was pulled back in a bun. Except for gold earrings, she wore no jewellery. When Georgia ran to hug her, she cackled with delight.

Georgia waved Dana over to be introduced. Relaxed and smiling, Dana put out her hand. In that moment, she became aware of the other.

As the shock ran through her, Dana was glad of Georgia's warning. It stopped her from crying out. For there behind the little great-granny, like a ghostly shadow, stood an imperious figure. Her features were haughty, her gaze cold and stern. She was formally dressed in the sumptuous robes of a noblewoman, padded silk and brocade finely worked with gold-wrapped thread. Her shining black hair was bound up with jewelled combs. Her throat and ears dripped with pearls.

Instinctively, Dana bowed towards her.

Georgia's great-granny responded quickly in Chinese.

"Good move there, girl," Georgia said to Dana. "She says you have good manners. But you needn't address the Dragon Lady again. Don't worry, you're not being disrespectful. She's the secret part of great-granny. I figured you might be able to see her. I can only do it when great-granny sleeps. No one else can, but they sense her sometimes. That's what scares them, eh?"

The two girls sat down as various waitresses arrived, wheeling carts. Dana could see how nervous they were and how they avoided coming too close. Yet none looked directly at the Dragon Lady.

The little great-granny herself bantered away in Chinese as she chose different foods, while Georgia did her best to guide Dana.

Before she had even looked at the dishes of food on the carts, Dana was stumped by the plethora of small bowls, cups, chopsticks and china spoons set in front of her.

"There's actually a method to *dim sum*," Georgia explained. "It means 'light heart' or 'touch the heart.' You start with the steamed stuff, then you move on to the more exotic, like the chicken feet— no?—then the deep-fried and finally the dessert."

Dana's heart sank as she studied the portions of chicken, pork, shrimp and beef.

"I'm vegetarian."

"No sweat," Georgia assured her, "there's lots of things you can eat here."

Soon Dana was tasting turnip croquettes, red bean cake, water chestnut and taro root dumplings, sesame seed balls and crispy egg tartlets. All went down happily with tiny cups of tea.

"This is delicious!"

As they ate, Georgia kept up a stream of conversation and translation between her great-granny and her friend. Like the little dishes of food, the talk was light and varied, centring on Dana's family and background. Mindful of the Dragon Lady's ever-watchful eye, Dana did her best to be truthful. Neither Georgia nor her great-granny showed any surprise when she told them of her fairy mother.

"Great-granny's like you," Georgia said. "She's the daughter of a human woman and a Dragon King. That's how come she's the way she is and why she's able to talk to dragons. She said everyone in the olden days could, but it's different now."

By the time they had finished their dessert of almond pudding, Georgia's great-granny was looking sleepy. Her eyes kept closing, then fluttering open again, till finally they stayed shut. Her breath came in low whistles.

Georgia sat up straighter. There was an expectant look on her face, mingled with awe. Now she bowed her head towards the Dragon Lady.

Dana knew it was time for the other to speak.

The Dragon Lady didn't move from behind the chair, yet it seemed as if she had stepped out of the shadows. Her silken robes rustled. Small white hands appeared from inside her wide sleeves. Dana stared at the long red fingernails. When the Dragon Lady spoke, her voice was cool and aloof. Her language sounded different from the little great-granny's, more formal somehow.

"She's speaking Mandarin," Georgia told Dana. "We were speaking Cantonese before. She has only one question for you. It's not a trick or anything, so just answer as honestly as you can."

"Work away," said Dana, as her stomach tightened.

"She wants to know," Georgia said carefully, "do you respect your ancestors?"

Though Dana found the question odd, it wasn't difficult to answer. She thought immediately of Thomas Gowan, the story of his life, and *The Book of Dreams*. She liked what she had read, what he had written, how he had thought, and she was proud to be descended from him. She thought also of his "beloved Harriet" and their children from whom Gran Gowan had come. On the other side of her family was her mother, Edane, the Light-Bearer, a *spéirbhean* and a queen in Faerie. Behind her was the fairy ancestress of whom Edane had spoken, the White Lady of the Waters.

"I'm very proud of my people," Dana said. "I hope to do them honour when I face my destiny."

Georgia looked delighted even before she translated the answer.

The Dragon Lady's response was immediate. From deep in her sleeve, she produced three bronze coins. They had square holes in the centre and were inscribed on one side. She handed them to Dana.

"Keep throwing them on the table till she tells you to stop," Georgia said.

As Dana obeyed, the Dragon Lady watched the falling coins with keen eyes. After the sixth throw, she raised her hand and retrieved the coins. She went to the altar and stayed there awhile, writing on sheets of gold paper.

"Have you heard of the *I Ching*?" Georgia asked Dana, who shook her head. "*The Book of Changes*. It's so old some people say it was the first book. They also say it has a soul of its own and when you throw the coins, you're asking questions of that soul."

"A book with a soul!" Dana breathed. "But how can you talk to it?"

"It's kind of complicated. Do you believe in coincidence?"

"There's no such thing as coincidence," Dana said automatically. "That's what they say in Faerie."

Georgia nodded. "That's what the *I Ching* says too. When you throw the coins, there are patterns in the way they fall. The heads and tails are lines of yin and yang. You throw six times to make a hexagram. The book describes the sixty-four hexagrams that three coins can make. The patterns you throw mean something specific to you. Not a fluke or coincidence, but something true and important."

"I should have asked a question!" Dana said, disappointed.

"The Dragon Lady already did." Georgia spoke in a low tone.

"What did she ask?" whispered Dana.

Before Georgia could answer, the Dragon Lady returned. She handed Georgia a piece of paper and went on at some length. Georgia interpreted for Dana, attempting to explain the notes and lines.

"The reading's good! You get two with the moving lines. They're the changes. I'll explain that later if you want the details. The first pattern is Hexagram 10, called *Lu,* meaning 'Treading.' The small and cheerful *Tui* here—that's the Lake— treads upon the large and strong *Ch'ien*—that's Heaven. It shows a very difficult situation ahead but the message says 'For the weak to take a stand against the strong is not dangerous here because it happens in good humour.'"

Dana looked skeptical.

"I can't imagine there'll be anything to laugh at in this battle."

Georgia caught her mood and wavered uncertainly.

"You said there's another one?" Dana prompted, not wanting to discourage her friend.

"Yes, the first one changed to this, Hexagram 64. *Wei Chi.* 'Before Completion.' Now this is amazing," Georgia insisted, hoping to convince her. "It's the last pattern, the one that ends *The Book of Changes.* That's auspicious in itself. But see how the two parts mirror each other? Fire and water. *K'an* over *Li.* The message says there is order inside chaos regardless of how bad things look. That's the step 'Before Completion'—get it?"

"The darkest hour is before the dawn?"

"More or less. *The Book of Changes* ends with the promise of new beginnings and that's the message it's giving to you."

"I like it," Dana nodded. "Sounds more probable than the first one. So, do you think the readings will affect what she says to the dragons?"

457

Georgia glanced askance at the Dragon Lady who had resumed her position behind the great-granny's chair.

"You want to ask her?"

"Nope," said Dana. "You?"

"No way."

"Chicken."

"Steamed chicken feet."

Dana took a deep breath and was about to ask the question when the little great-granny yawned. She was waking from her afternoon nap.

The Dragon Lady withdrew into the shadows.

"Time to go," said Georgia.

Before the girls left, the little great-granny gave each a fortune cookie. On their way down the stairs, they broke open the cookies to extract the slips of paper.

"You first," said Georgia, popping the crisp biscuit into her mouth.

"*O nobly born, remember who you are.*" Dana felt a little shiver. "I keep hearing that all the time! What is it?"

"A saying from the Buddha," Georgia shrugged. "Everybody knows that."

Dana's mouth dropped open.

"You've got brains to burn. What does yours say?"

Georgia's eyes widened as she read her fortune, then she burst out laughing and nearly choked on her cookie.

"I don't believe it! From the sublime to the ridiculous. Just my luck!"

"Come on. Tell."

"*May your life be as long and useful as a roll of toilet paper.*"

They laughed all the way to the subway.

CHAPTER THIRTY-EIGHT

SHE WOKE THAT MORNING CALLING JEAN'S name. Though her eyes were open, the last trails of the nightmare lingered in her mind. *A great wolf running through a forest in the mountains. Hounds in pursuit. The hunter raises his gun. As the shot rings out, the wolf somersaults violently in the air.*

Dana lay in bed weighed down with grief. It was a dream, of course, but the reality was no less painful. A tear trickled down her cheek. The only one she allowed herself. Today was the day of her destiny. The day she would succeed in restoring the portals or die in the attempt. She would do this for Faerie, for Ireland, for Canada and most of all, she would do this for Jean. It was hardly a task for a young girl to shoulder, but she was more than a girl. Half-fairy, half-human, windwalker, dreamspeaker, she had the power to do it.

By the time Dana got out of bed, she had wrestled the last of her fears to the ground. She was ready. With quiet purpose, she dressed and headed down for breakfast.

"Hey sleepyhead!" her aunt Yvonne greeted her.

Dee was also there, popping up waffles from the toaster and whipping them across the table as if they were Frisbees.

"We're better than you," she sang, exultant. "Those who rise first are morally superior. It's a universal law."

"What are you doing here?" Dana demanded, immediately suspicious.

"We got in late last night," said Yvonne. "As soon as we heard you were in Creemore for Hallowe'en we knew something was up."

Dee sat down to attack her plate of waffles and burst into song.

> But the night is Hallowe'en, lady
> The morn is Hallowday
> Then win me, win me, an ye will
> For weel I wat ye may.

"You promised to stay out of this," Dana accused them.

"Like we keep our promises," Deirdre said, her mouth full.

"We thought about it," Yvonne admitted, "but it's against our nature to stay out of trouble. You can't leave us out," she added quietly. "It wouldn't be fair. Not after Vancouver."

"Especially since we're skipping a hot party to be here," Dee put in.

Dana sat down at the table and helped herself to some breakfast. She had mixed feelings about her aunts' presence. She loved being in their company, they would cheer up a corpse, but she didn't want them in danger.

"And you're not to worry about our safety," Yvonne said, as if reading her mind. "We're old enough and ugly enough to look after ourselves, as your Gran would say."

"Just accept the fact," said Dee, reaching for more waffles. "We're in this with you, whether you like it or not. We intend to shadow you all day. You're not going anywhere without us."

"All right already, I give in!" Dana said, laughing.

Her aunts exchanged looks of triumph. Despite her misgivings, Dana too was happy with the pronouncement. The dark cloud that hung over her brightened a little.

She caught them up with the latest developments. As usual they heard the good news and glossed over the bad.

"Fairies in Canada!" Dee cried. "Hurrah!"

"Our own great-granddaddy at the heart of it," Yvonne sighed. "No wonder we're crackers. And there's Mom trying to blame it all on the Catholic side. Hah!"

"I've got to see that book," Dee said, "I feel a doc about families coming on."

She didn't tell them about Jean. Even now, in the final hours, she protected his secret. No matter what happened, she would never let him down.

At lunch time, Gabriel and Radhi arrived from Toronto. They had planned to join Gran and Dana for Hallowe'en and were delighted to see the two aunts as well. After salads and quiche, the pumpkin pies were presented with fanfare and fresh cream.

"Dana was as much the baker as I," Gran announced to the table.

"Her talents know no bounds," said Dee, knowingly.

Yvonne threw her a look.

"I'm glad we're all together today," said Gran, as she sat down at the head of the table. "Besides Hallowe'en, we should also consider this a celebration of the new member of the family on its way to join us."

"The gang's all here, the gang's all here," sang Dee.

"I'm so glad you're into having kids," Yvonne confided to Radhi. "Dee and I have decided to girl it out to the end. We do love being aunties, however," she added, winking at Dana.

Dana sat happily between her father and stepmother, drinking in the warmth and security of her family circle. It was just like the old stories, she reflected, when the warriors were fêted and pampered before going into battle. As it was then, so it was now, she felt strengthened by the feast.

"You are very quiet," Radhi said.

"I'm just glad to be here," she answered.

The day itself had been dreary since morning, with a steely grey sky and fits of cold rain. Dana knew it was Grimstone working his ill will with the elements, but as the afternoon waned, other forces came into play. A southerly wind blew warm and strong, sweeping the clouds away.

Outside on the streets, in the last hour before dark, the smallest children set out for their Hallowe'en trick-or-treats. Dana thought of how the night was celebrated in Ireland. *Oíche Shamhna*. First there would be potatoes and colcannon for supper, followed by apples and nuts and a barn-brack cake with a gold ring inside. Once the night grew dark, there would be bonfires on the streets and fireworks. In the Faerie world, it was a bigger festival still, one of the special feast days when the two worlds collided and mingled in full. There would be feasting and frolic along with sorties into the Earthworld to cause mischief and mayhem. It was a time of great power when anything could happen, for good or ill.

As twilight drew near, Dana went to her room to change. She had brought the clothes the Sasquatch had given her: the deerskin shirt and leggings embroidered with white quills and blue beads, the cedar bark apron that fell to her knees, and the high moccasin boots. The short cape of black feathers felt reassuring around her shoulders. *Under his wings shalt thou trust.* The staff of peeled pine was suddenly more than something she could use to beat back the underbrush. It was a weapon. Even as the Bigfoot females had braided her hair in a single plait down her back, she did the same now. Finally, she took the white feather the soul-bird had shed in the north and tied it to her braid.

A quick knock on the door and her aunts barged in without waiting for permission.

"Whoa, I love it!" said Dee. "Seriously shamanic."

Yvonne eyed the clothes thoughtfully.

"How about costumes for us?" she asked her niece.

"Yeah, come on, do some magic," said Dee, more directly. "We want to be fairies. Not little pixie things. The gorgeous naughty kind."

To the same tune she sang at breakfast, she added more lines.

> *Just at the mirk and midnight hour*
> *The fairy folk will ride.*

Dana frowned. She was about to tell them it wasn't a game when she stopped. Behind their irrepressible humour, she sensed something else. Her aunts were using jokes to ease the tension, to face the danger. And they were clever enough to ask for magical garb. It would give them an edge, something extra besides their courage.

As for working a spell on them, it wouldn't be difficult. The quest had given Dana confidence in her gifts and abilities. Fairy glamour was a simple matter.

"Any particular colours?"

"You have to ask?" said Dee, dressed as usual in black.

"Fire and brimstone for me!" was Yvonne's request.

In the blink of an eye and a spray of starry dust, the two were transformed. Dee was swathed in midnight satin filigreed with silver. Yvonne was a silken sunset that shimmered as she moved, from rose to orange to crimson and back again.

"I'm wearing a Tequila Sunrise!"

"This is fairy glamour," Dana explained. "It isn't real. You could be wearing tatty old rags or nothing at all."

The two aunts raised their eyebrows at that thought.

"Who cares? We're gorgeous!" cried Dee, twirling in front of the mirror. "But what's at the back?"

She twisted her neck to see. Yvonne did the same. Both gasped as they caught sight of the leaf-thin pale-veined wings that fluttered from their shoulders.

"Are they real?" Yvonne asked breathlessly. "Can we—?"

"Not in public," Dana warned, "and only till the stroke of twelve."

"When we turn into pumpkins," Dee nodded.

With squeals of delight, they slowly achieved lift-off. Their wings were like another pair of limbs, but it wasn't easy to co-ordinate movement along with direction. Bumping in midair, they got all tangled up and landed on the floor with a thump. Their screeches of laughter bordered on hysteria.

Gran Gowan shouted up the stairs.

"What's all the racket up there?"

Snorting and hooting, they disentangled themselves and smoothed their dresses.

Dana was holding her stomach from laughing so hard.

"Come on, we're dressed to kill," Dee announced. "Let's blow this popstand."

The sun was setting below the horizon. A dusky light suffused the air. Along the main road, fires burned in steel barrels to provide heat and light. The streets of Creemore were crowded with witches, goblins, vampires, fairies, princesses and warriors, all troop-ing from house to house to collect their treats. Jack-o'-lanterns flickered with orange light on every porch. Paper skeletons dangled in the windows. Shrieks and howls rang through the night. There were plenty of adults in costume too. The first full moon on Hallowe'en in fifty years was due to rise. Everyone felt the magic.

Only Dana was aware that not all the creatures who moved through the crowds were in fancy dress. She could see them slith-ering in the shadows, peering around corners, hurrying through the streets. Knurled and grotesque, toothed and clawed, some with tails or leathery wings, distorted bodies and malevolent stares, they belonged to the Enemy. They had been called to this place to increase the darkness, to join the battle. All were moving in the same direction, towards the cemetery.

Dana knew it was time to go. She would have to hurry. It was already twilight. Despite her agreement with her aunts, she still hoped to escape them. She didn't want them in danger. She looked around impatiently for her grandmother. She needed a distraction. At last Gran Gowan arrived with Gabe and Aradhana, bearing cups of hot chocolate. They admired the costumes of Dana and her aunts.

"We'll stop here," Gran commanded. "This is a good spot. There's something special on the way."

Surrounded by her family, Dana felt a pang of regret. She would have to leave them soon. What if she didn't return? She had tried to write a note. But there was nothing she could say to explain the situation or to make things easier. As she sipped her hot chocolate and listened to their banter, she wished for a moment that she could forget the whole thing. Oh to be an ordinary girl enjoying Hallowe'en with her family! Then an image of Jean flashed through her mind and the fantasy died. He was out there in the night, lost to humanity, because of her. She had to do what she could to bring him back.

A church bell tolled sonorously as if for a funeral.

"Is he coming?" said Dee, craning to see down the road.

"Ssh!" said Gran.

The main street was lined with people waiting expectantly. A hush of suspense fell over the crowd. Now a sound broke the night.

Hooves striking the road at a gallop!

He came from the north, charging down to the south, a tall dark rider on a great black horse. Children screamed. Adults cheered. Everyone applauded. For the horseman carried his head in the crook of his arm.

"He's the local carpenter," Gran was saying to Aradhana, "the King of Creemore for Oktoberfest."

Remembering the real Headless Horseman she had seen in the east, Dana joined the applause. She was already inching away from the others. They were all entranced by the spectacle. It was an ideal time to slip away. But now as the rider approached, Dana felt suddenly ill. A cold chill knifed through her. She almost fainted. As the horseman paused on the road nearby, her legs buckled under her.

The dark horse reared up, eyes white and maddened. The cheers of the crowd swelled.

Weak and dizzy, Dana could hardly move. It was as if she had been seized in an iron grip. That's when she knew. The rider was no Creemore man. This was the Dullahan, an ally of the Enemy!

Everyone's eyes were on the horseman. They had all been mesmerized. It was only when Dana staggered against her aunt's wing that Yvonne turned around. Her reaction was instant. Catching Dana in mid-fall, she nudged her sister. Between them, they supported their niece and moved her back from the crowd.

The Dullahan's horse reared again with a high-pitched screech.

"We must get away," Dana gasped.

"I can see that," Yvonne said grimly. "Let's take her home," she said to Dee.

"No! The cemetery!" Dana ordered, though she still felt weak. "There are others there. I must join them!"

They hurried down the street. The horseman followed, shadowing their movements from the road.

"Short cut to the graveyard," Dee said to her sister. "Remember?"

"You read my mind," Yvonne answered shortly.

They were still holding Dana between them, but she was steadier now and they broke into a run. With the echo of hooves behind them, they raced down Mill Street and onto Edward. It was only when they reached Collingwood, not far from the cemetery, that they dared turn around.

Terror gorged in their throats.

Head back on his shoulders, the Dullahan had found them and was gaining fast. Before they could escape again, he bore down on top of them. With sharp blows he knocked the aunts aside and grabbed at Dana to haul her onto his horse. She kicked out wildly to fend him off. As Yvonne and Dee recovered, they flew at him like harpies.

The Dullahan was shocked by the ferocity of their defence. He was used to striking terror in the minds of humans and fairies alike, but here were three not easily cowed. Dee gave him a swift kick in midair that sent his head rolling, even as Yvonne pulled Dana away from the horse.

Half-running, half-flying, they ducked down a narrow lane nearby. This was the short cut that the aunts knew led directly to the graveyard. But when they came out at the other end, their hearts sank. There in front of the cemetery gates stood horse and rider. The Dullahan's eyes blazed as he watched the road.

"Damn," said Dee, catching her breath.

"What will we do?" said Yvonne.

The three huddled in the shadows.

"We'll have to fight our way past him," Dana told them.

Her strength was returning. She had been caught off guard, but it wouldn't happen again. She was rubbing her hands to make a fireball when shouts erupted on the street.

Two lithe figures raced into sight. With shining swords drawn, they charged at the Dullahan.

"Hey, it's The Fair Folk," Dee said with approval, "arriving like the cavalry."

"Class act," Yvonne agreed. "They're off my black list."

The horseman fled without stopping to fight.

Dana and the aunts ran across the road.

"Didn't expect to see you two again," said Dee with a grin.

"Not that we're not glad," Yvonne added.

Findabhair grinned back.

"Let's just say the royal bollocking was effective. Tough talk can work sometimes. You're both looking gorgeous."

"Fairy glamour," Yvonne said airily.

"The admiration's mutual," said Dee. "You're seriously Xena."

Both Findabhair and Finvarra were dressed in black. With silver chain mail, helmets and swords, they glittered like stars in the night.

Neither Finvarra nor Dana had spoken. They stared at each other, blood calling to blood, as they acknowledged their kinship. In the formal manner of Faerie *courteisie,* Finvarra bowed.

"Greetings, Light-Bearer's daughter. We are well met. Late is the hour that I come to thee, yet I do place my sword at thy command."

Dana bowed her head in turn. She had spent enough time in Faerie to know the protocol.

"I am more than honoured to be served by a High King. Let it be the time of your own choosing, Sire."

"No more a High King," Finvarra said, with a wry shake of his head, "but a mortal who is prepared to die in your cause."

"Once a king in Faerie, always a king," Dana said.

"We must go," said Findabhair, looking around.

"To *Magh Crí Mor,*" Finvarra nodded, "to the Plain of the Great Heart."

As they stepped through the iron gates of the graveyard, Dee sang under her breath.

Gloomy gloomy was the night
And eerie was the way . . .

"Would you stop with the *Tam Lin* already," Yvonne hissed.

"I love that song. Besides, it's very appropriate. Music heightens the atmosphere in an action scene."

"This is not a movie!"

Seconds later, the two stopped dead in their tracks.

Creemore cemetery was gone.

In the twilight of the Eve of All Hallows, in the crossing of time and the collision of worlds, *Magh Crí Mor*, the Plain of the Great Heart, had descended upon the site. An immense level plain of moonlit grass, it was surrounded on all sides by primeval forest. A bluish mist whispered over the ground. Yet it wasn't the eerie beauty of the plain that shocked them, but the sight of the great megalith that brooded there.

Stone upon stone it stood, a massive dolmen, two colossal standing stones with a giant capstone overhead. Stark and silent, it arched against the sky, dwarfing the muted shapes and shadows around it. Though fashioned of granite, it gleamed with a dark metallic sheen that reinforced the impression it was a gigantic doorway.

"It looks so near," Dana said softly. "A quick run across the meadow."

"Before this night is done," Finvarra said gravely, "that meadow will be a battlefield. Come. We must join our friends before we are joined by our enemies."

They hurried into the ancient woods that bordered the plain. When they arrived at the rath of the Creemore fairies, Dana found it utterly changed. No longer a secluded clearing, it was the stronghold of an army.

Stretching away into the distance, throughout the great forest, were tents and leafy shelters on the ground and in the trees. Stores of arms were piled in gleaming heaps of swords, spears, shields and axes. A great assembly had gathered there, with more troops arriving every minute. Heralds rushed from tent to tent. Parleys were called and meetings held, as the various leaders debated the battle plan.

Findabhair let out a cry when she spotted Gwen outside a pavilion. The cousins ran to greet each other with tearful hugs.

"I was so afraid you were dead!" Findabhair said. "I only heard the good news a short while ago."

"I'm over the moon you've come," said Gwen. "What do you think of the Canadian fairies? Here all the time and we never knew!"

"Finvarra did," said her cousin. "Of course they all disappeared over a century ago and he had completely forgotten about them. Why is it that fairies are always going missing and no one seems to notice?"

"They're not like us," Gwen sighed.

"Tell me about it," said Findabhair, rolling her eyes. "I was glad to hear Dara and the others are well too. I only wish they could be here."

Gwen agreed heartily.

"We could do with the Company of Seven right now."

Even as the cousins chatted, another reunion was taking place. The fairies of Clan Creemore were clustered around Finvarra, kissing his hand and murmuring their affection. As more of the Canadian troops caught sight of him, they swelled the throng. The last time all of them had been in Faerie, he was their High King.

Daisy Greenleaf threw her arms around him.

"Sire, your people are overjoyed to see you again!"

"Far out!" shouted John Trout.

As the warmth of their welcome touched Finvarra's heart, the bitter years of his exile fell away like withered leaves.

"I am no longer your king, dear hearts," he told them gently. "No longer immortal. As I lost all for love, I am sure you approve."

"Whatever you be, our regard for you will never lessen," said Daisy. "We got the story from Gwen," she added with a grin, "and of course we approve. It's a good one!"

Finvarra let out a laugh.

"Ever the romantic, dear Daisy. Are you still with that mad Midsummer Moon?"

"He's called 'Stanley Moon' now. Says it's more Canadian. Some of the others have changed their names too. And, yes, we're still a couple. He still makes me laugh."

Finvarra was impressed.

"That's two millennia now? And your own troop as well, I see. Well done. You've kept the fairy faith."

Daisy shook her head.

"I share the captaincy with Alf Branch, the one you knew as *Craoibhín Ruadh*. Things are less hierarchical in this land."

Hovering on the sidelines, Yvonne and Dee were drinking in the scene with wide-eyed enchantment. It was as if every fantasy they had ever read had come to life around them! At the same time, they felt a little awkward and out of place.

Till the clans of British Columbia arrived.

The B.C. fairies were huge, the height of the great trees in which they dwelled: the giant red cedar, Douglas fir and western hemlock. Beside them strode their furry neighbours, the Sasquatch Nation. All shyness cast aside, the Bigfoot were armed to the teeth and fearsome.

"Hey, it's our heroes!" Dee cried suddenly.

There in the troop from British Columbia were the two young men who had come to their aid in Vancouver. No longer clad in T-shirts and denim, they wore hide leggings and forest-green cloaks. Quivers of arrows hung at their backs and they carried tall bows. Swords fell at their sides. At first they appeared gigantic, then they diminished to human size as they entered the camp.

Dee and Yvonne wasted no time in running to greet them.

"We meet again, fair maiden," said the one who liked Dee. His dark eyes flashed as he bowed to kiss her hand.

Yvonne snorted. "Maiden?"

But now his companion bowed to her and kissed her hand also.

"I am Andariel and he is Tomariel, my brother. There is surely joy in battle when it brings such beauties to our side."

"Za za zoom," said Dee.

"Are you kin to us?" asked Tomariel, glancing at their wings with surprise.

"Nope. We're only queens for a day," Yvonne said ruefully.

"Pumpkins the rest of the time," Dee sighed.

The two fairy-men looked baffled.

"Fully human and fully alive," Yvonne confessed.

They expected their heroes to be disappointed, but the brothers exchanged grins of delight.

"It has been long since we made merry with mortal women," said Andariel.

"We used to have great sport and play," his brother agreed.

"We're into sport," said Dee, brightening.

"And play," Yvonne added.

At the same time the aunts found their admirers, Dana was reunited with friends of her own. She had recognized the beat of the big skin drums long before Trew marched into sight leading a battalion of trolls.

She joined his side as he dismissed his troops.

"Build yourselves hootchies, boys," he commanded. "Use good strong branches with plenty of leaves, in case it rains. I'll go get the chocolate."

The pale faces of the trolls lit up at his promise and they let out a cheer. All were kitted out in TTC uniforms with gruesome-looking weapons slung over their shoulders. Trew himself was uncharacteristically sombre in the grey jacket of an inspector, but the peaked cap was set at a jaunty angle and he still wore his shades.

"You're the King of the Trolls!" Dana said. "And you didn't even tell me!"

"Means nothin' in the subways," he said with a laugh. "Half the time they don't remember. But as long as they get plenty of chocolate they'll do what I say. Who's the quartermaster round here?"

"Daisy Greenleaf is the one who claps for treats," she said, pointing out the Creemore chief.

"Sounds like the one I want," Trew nodded. "See you in a tick after I get these guys settled."

The ground trembled underfoot as a corps of giants arrived, led by Fingal.

"There you be, little one!" he roared happily. Reaching down, he scooped Dana into his palm. "Where's the boyfriend?"

The big smile died on his face as she told him.

"Oh that's bad," he boomed, scratching his bald head with concern. "But we'll get him back for ye, hen. Just see if we don't!"

As more and more troops and clans arrived, the ache in Dana's heart increased to anguish. How many would die before the night was through?

For as surely as these gathered to defend the Light and the Land of Dreams, so too another army was massing. On the far side of the plain, a gloom hung over the ragged tree tops. A sickly vapour seeped from the ground. Through the air came strange cries and moans, shrieks and growls. The wind carried a foul stench in its wake. There on the opposite side of *Magh Crí Mor* were the servants of the Enemy, those who shared its hatred of life and light.

And in the centre of the plain stood the prize to be won, the great portal, alone and shining at the heart of the battlefield.

Dana was called to the pavilion where the leaders were holding their Council of War. Dee and Yvonne followed her in.

There was a long table spread with a feast, but the food was untouched and the goblets brimmed full. Everyone was standing. They looked stern and grave. Gwen and Laurel were there beside Finvarra and Findabhair.

Daisy Greenleaf's voice was cool like a stream as she told Dana the battle plan.

"There is no need for complicated stratagems or tactics. The plan is simple. The army is here for one purpose only: to hold back the tide while you go forward to reach the portal. Step by step, inch by inch, you must make your way towards it, even if that means climbing over us, injured or dead. You are the key. Only you can open the door. You must not be distracted by what happens around you. We have come this day to defend our dreams. We gladly offer our lives for the sake of the cause. Even as we do play our part, so must you."

Weighed down by the thought of what lay ahead, Dana couldn't speak. She simply nodded to show her agreement.

"Wait a minute," said Yvonne. "You mean you guys can be harmed? What about your magic? Your immortality?"

Alf Branch waved in the direction of the Enemy forces.

"They're immortal too and they've got their own magics. Truth is, we can maim and kill each other . . . and we will."

Both the aunts paled. They were beginning to realize the true nature of the situation. This was no gossamer fantasy or playful daydream. This was real and dangerous. If the fairies could be hurt or killed, then horrible things could happen to them also. Each faced the stark fact they might die that night.

They looked at their niece with sudden regret.

"We should have stopped you from coming," said Yvonne.

"We were being selfish," Dee agreed. "Chasing the fun as usual and hang the consequences."

Dana's voice was firm.

"You couldn't have stopped me. This is my place, my destiny. I'm the one who's been selfish. I shouldn't have brought you here. You must go now, both of you."

There were murmurs of agreement around the table.

Dana's aunts were furious. Yvonne reacted first.

"You think we're going to desert our niece like two big cowards?"

"We're the fairy's godmothers. We stick by her," Dee declared. "And don't try whisking us away. We've got wings till midnight. We'll come back." She surveyed her silken clothes with a grimace. "I just wish I had my boots."

In the blink of an eye they were there, her heavy black boots with the nails in the toes. The ones that made her feel safe when she walked home late at night through the streets of Toronto. The same ones that had done her proud against Grimstone in Vancouver. Scuffed and battered, they were an interesting contrast to the shimmering gown.

"I like it," she said, hitching up her dress to admire them.

"Be careful what you wish for," Gwen said quickly. "Everything is awry around the fairies. Time and space mingle. Reality is fluid. Anything can happen."

The aunts had to clamp down on all the wishes that suddenly clamoured in their heads.

"Russell Crowe begone," Yvonne muttered.

"You are not warriors," Alf Branch tried again, "nor have you any powers or abilities."

"Hey, we fought Grimstone and the Headless Horseman," Dee argued.

"We don't have powers or abilities," Yvonne said quietly, "but we do have courage. Not the fearless kind—we are both afraid, very afraid—but the kind that goes ahead anyway regardless of the fear. No matter what you say, we won't abandon our niece."

Findabhair smiled with approval at the two aunts. So too did Gwen and Laurel.

"The Companions of Faerie are mortal," Laurel pointed out in their favour. "If they choose to stay, I say let them."

"I'd be proud to fight by their side," Gwen agreed. She turned to the fairy leaders. "Humans have always rescued Fairyland. It's our mission, our duty. And it's our battle too, since our dreams are tied up with Faerie. This very day, across the ocean, four Companions will add their strength to ours. Sadly, the Enemy knew what it was doing when it struck them down in Ireland. Together, a Company of Seven can wield great power. Still, if we—"

"Excuse me," Yvonne interrupted, putting up her hand. "Sorry to butt in but, while I realize we don't know a lot about this stuff, I can definitely count. It seems to me there are seven of us here. Seven mortals, I mean. Am I right or am I right?"

A shiver ran through the company as the head count was made.

Dana. Gwen. Laurel. Findabhair. Finvarra. Yvonne. Deirdre.

Seven.

Finvarra's voice rose with excitement.

"She will not cross the plain alone. Six of us will make a queen's guard and the seventh herself can march at the centre. The Light who is the key to the portal."

Now Gwen's voice rang out with authority. The original leader of the first Company of Seven, she spoke the words to bless their fellowship.

"*Seven were the days of Genesis. Seven are the pillars of life. Seven will be the fires of the Apocalypse. No better number can ride the storm. As a Company of Seven we will forge our destiny.*"

It was at that moment that Gaelyn Tree-Top entered the tent with a face like thunder.

"It has begun."

CHAPTER THIRTY-NINE

BEHOLD A TEMPEST RAGED UPON THE EARTH
*and throughout the heavens. As above, so below. All elements, visible and
invisible, and every creature seen and unseen, were provoked into a murderous frenzy. Earth, air, fire and water clashed together, broke open, erupted.
Lightning flashed across the sky. Thunderous explosions wreaked death
and destruction. Mountains collapsed, forests burned, seas boiled and the
air was choked with noisome gases.*

From the moment the Battle for *Magh Crí Mor* began, Dana
understood the nature of the conflagration. Here was yet another
skirmish in the titanic struggle at the heart of the world. The
never-ending war of the spirit between darkness and light, good
and evil, between that which loved life and chose to nourish it,
and that which hated life and worked to destroy it.

*There were voices and thunderings and lightnings and an earthquake.
There followed hail and fire mingled with blood. The third part of the trees
was burnt up and the green grass was ashen. A great mountain burning
with fire was cast into the sea and the third part of the sea turned to
vapour. An angel flying across the firmament cried out with terrible
voice—Woe! Woe! Woe to all!*

Grotesque hordes, monstrous and terrifying, poured from the
dark forest and onto the plain. In the murk of twilight, they
carried flaming torches or spat fire themselves. Some moved with
slow and mindless ill will. Others darted here and there with swift

malevolence. There were many Dana recognized, denizens from the dark side of Faerie, known to the Scottish, Welsh and Irish. They too had migrated across the sea. The Redcaps were a goblin clan who normally lived in the ruins of old castles. A brutal tribe, they got their name from the habit of bathing their caps in the blood of their victims. Small and swarthy, they came with all their kith and kin, Redcombs, Bloody Caps, Dunters and Powries. Across the dim skies flew the wraiths of the Unseelie Court, night shades of evil that inhabited the air. A pestilence, an ill wind that did no good, their screeches joined company with the green and ghastly Banshees. A fang-toothed Black Annis stood shoulder to shoulder with the west coast behemoth called D'Sonoqua. Both cannibal, both ravenous, they had come to feed on the living and the dead. Swarms of hags and spectres, gargoyles and demons marched alongside other nightmarish beings Dana had never seen or known. With a sinking heart, she realized what they were. *Les esprits du mal* of whom Grandfather spoke, the dark spirits that plagued the First Peoples of the land. The Enemy had servants in every part of the world.

They were met on the battlefield by an army of light. All creatures bright and beautiful, they had come to fight for the cause of hopes and dreams. In the first onslaught of the conflict, in the first charge and engagement, it seemed the two sides were evenly matched. Whether fighting on the ground or in the air, neither side made headway either forward or back. The initial clash was a draw. The battle raged on.

Where was Grimstone? Dana wondered. The Enemy's general, he was strangely absent from the field. What deception was this?

The Company of Seven was called together. Dana stood in the centre of the phalanx that would be her guard. On her right, just ahead of her, Gwen took up position. No longer the plump and pleasant Ms Woods, she was armed and armoured like a warrior-queen. Though years had passed since she had fought the Great Worm as Captain of the first Company of Seven, she could feel the old courage rising. As it was then, so was it now, she was ready to fight for the Land of Dreams.

On Dana's left, again just ahead of her, was Finvarra. Once High King in Faerie, he had honed his skills at *Bruíon Amhra,* the Wonderful Strife, the game of war the fairies played. Now he would use those skills in a war that was no game.

In the middle ranks, on either side of Dana, were Yvonne and Deirdre. Breathing deeply to swallow their terror, they exchanged looks with each other. *I'm dying here. Me too. Can we do this? We're about to find out.* Like the others, they wore chain mail and were armed with shields and weapons.

The rearguard was composed of Findabhair and Laurel, both experienced in fairy warfare. They would defend Dana's back.

Once more Gwen called out the Company's blessing.

"Seven were the days of Genesis. Seven are the pillars of life. Seven will be the fires of the Apocalypse. No better number can ride the storm. As a Company of Seven we will forge our destiny."

At the centre of the Seven, at the eye of the storm, Dana was calm. She could feel the strength she had gained in her travels, the courage she had garnered from her quest. She could feel her power. As the light surged from her hands, she threw it over the Company like a golden cloak.

Moving as a unit, they stepped onto the battlefield, but before they could go forward, Trew came running to report. His face was ashen.

"Something's not right at Ground Zero. I've lost half my gang. Whenever we get near the portal, it's always the same. Screams of pain, bad burns. We can't see who or what's doing it, but something's there!"

"An invisible enemy!" Gwen said, dismayed.

Before they could act on the news, a cry went up at the edge of the forest. It came from the ford where the Mad River flowed, wider and deeper on *Magh Crí Mor.*

"Now what?" said Laurel, impatient to join the battle.

White sails shone in the dimness as a leather boat glided up the river. Lanterns hung from the masts, illuminating the great emblem of the Celtic Cross.

"It's Brendan!" cried Dana.

Breaking out of formation, she raced down to the river bank. A plank was lowered from the boat to allow the abbot ashore. He rested his hand gently on Dana's head in greeting.

"We have been at sea for many months since I last saw you," he told her. "We sailed down a river as wide as an ocean, then a number of freshwater seas. For the past seven days we have been lost in a fog. Only now as we made our way up this passage did the mist begin to clear."

Brendan gazed upon the Plain of the Great Heart, at the horrific scene of war and apocalypse. His face darkened. This was the most sinister marvel he had yet to witness. The Second Sight seeped into his eyes, bringing him knowledge.

"This is the end of my pilgrimage," he said, "even as it is the end of yours. *Tír Tairngire* is near. I see what was written in *The Book of Wonders.* The Land of Promise is behind a rampart of fire. An eldritch fire that cannot be quenched."

Though she wasn't sure what he meant, Dana was inspired by the saint's words. Lifting her hands to the night sky, she sent her light forward like a shooting star. It swept in a great arc across the plain, shedding its rays onto the battlefield. The ranks of dark creatures shrank back with dismay. As the golden light rained down, it exposed the invisible wall that surrounded the portal.

An inferno of hellfire.

"My brother monks and I shall join the battle," Brendan declared. "The dream I seek is on the other side of that fire."

"But . . . you're clergy!" Dana said, surprised.

The saint's smile was rueful.

"Do you not know of the warrior-monks of Ireland? Often we have to defend our monasteries. We can acquit ourselves in battle. If there are fiends to be fought, then we shall fight them."

Leaving Brendan to assemble his crew, Dana rejoined her guard. She arrived in time to see the battle take a turn for the worst.

Swarms of Bag o' Bones were flying from the tree tops and descending on the plain. Screeching and chattering, they dove like hawks. As they snatched up their victims in bony claws, they carried them to the fire and flung them in. The stench of burnt flesh choked the air. The cries of torment were wrenching. Against the malevolent magic of the flames, the children of Faerie had no defence. It murdered them slowly without remorse or pity.

The fairy response was swift. All over the plain, bright-winged creatures took to the air to fight off the skeletons. The battle raged on high. The fairy defence was brave and furious, but the Bag o' Bones were not beaten back. Their initial success had made them daring and despite their losses they continued to prey. Many had gone into the fire. Many more would be added.

Sick with horror, Dana looked around wildly. Trew was missing, so too was Honeywood, and where were the Sasquatch? Not a single member of that furry nation could be seen on the field.

"We've got to do something!" she cried. "We've got to rescue them!"

Triumphant and gloating, the Enemy's forces surged forward.

It was a moment of dark defeat.

"We must move now," Gwen said quietly to Finvarra, "before the battle is lost."

"Heads up!" Fingal shouted.

A ragged cheer followed the cry.

There in the sky, passing the moon like winged shadows, flew a vast squadron of dragons.

Beneficent beings, life-giving and valiant, chief of the three-hundred-and-sixty scaled reptiles, father of the emperors of ancient times, their numbers were astounding. Every dragon clan had sent a troop. There were *Tien-Lung,* celestial dragons who protected the heavens and the mansions of the gods; *Shen-Lung,* spiritual dragons who caused the wind to blow and the rain to fall; *Ti-Lung,* earth dragons who directed the course of rivers and streams; and *Fut's-Lung,* underworld dragons who guarded the hidden treasures of precious metals and gems. They came in every shape and size, from hundreds of feet long to as small as a silkworm. Their sinuous bodies had the head of a horse, the tail of a snake and the claws of an eagle. Some had horns and antlers, others long whiskers trailing from their snouts. Many flew by the grace of great wings. Many more were airborne by their own power. Their glittering skin was scaled in all colours, golden, purple, aquamarine, ruby-red and emerald green. Their eyes shone with humour and intelligence.

As they swooped to attack the Bag o' Bones, the fairy hosts cheered.

"Thank you, Georgia," Dana whispered. "Thank you, Georgia's great-granny."

The rout was swift and sharp. Dragon talons ripped the skeletons apart and scattered their bones on the wind. In a short space of time, the skies were won.

Now the Dragon Commander hovered over the firewall to assess the situation. Chien-Tang, from the city of Winnipeg, had blood-red scales and a fiery mane. With sorrowful eyes, he regarded the suffering of those trapped in the flames. Then he made his decision.

Dropping out of the sky, he flew into the fire.

A gasp rose up from the fairy army and from his own troops as well.

A cloud of steam burst around the Commander, obscuring him from sight. It seemed an eternity before he appeared again. His flanks were scorched as he flew out of the flames, but he held his head high. In his claws he clasped a small bundle, the unconscious body of Trew.

"Go," he commanded the other dragons. "Free the prisoners."

Before long, everyone in the hellfire had been taken to safety.

Now Chien-Tang ordered his troops to surround the firewall. In a spectacular display of elemental power, they unleashed torrents of rain, black clouds of storm, and thunder and lightning.

To no avail. There was nothing they could do to quench the flames. The Enemy's holocaust withstood their magic.

Unable to break the impasse, the Dragon Commander returned with his squadron to guard the skies and fight from the air.

The battle continued to seethe back and forth with each side winning or losing by turns. There was no break or lull or cease-fire in the fighting. The Enemy forces were unrelenting, their onslaught merciless. They didn't stop to tend their wounded or dead, but left them on the battlefield if they didn't devour them.

The Company of Seven conferred amongst themselves.

"We need another plan," Laurel pointed out. "There's no use reaching the wall and getting stuck there."

"It would be suicide," Findabhair agreed. "There's no hope of success as long as the fire burns."

Even as they wavered, with Gwen looking lost and Finvarra uncertain, Dana left them once more. Many of her friends had been rescued by the dragons. She had to know if they survived or if she could help them.

When she found Trew in one of the healing tents, she almost cried out. He was so badly burned, she hardly recognized him. His small body was livid with blisters that bubbled on his skin. Despite fairy ministrations, he was delirious with pain. The malignant magic that had caused his wounds was not easily countered.

"Oh Trew, *mo chara, mo stór*," wept Dana, lapsing into Irish in her grief.

He was too raw to touch, so she held her hands above him. The light showered him gently. Though the burns seemed unchanged, he brightened visibly and was able to speak.

"Was that the Old Tongue?" he whispered. "Can't say I know it. I'm a new kid on the block. Born in Trawna."

She smiled through her tears.

"I called you 'my dear one' and 'my treasure.'"

"You goin' sweet on me?" He tried to smile back. "I must be bad, eh? No more riding the Red Rocket?"

Their eyes met. Both acknowledged he was dying.

Dazed with sorrow, Dana looked around at the slain and injured. She knew there were many more tents like this.

"Too many," she said, soul-sickened.

Daisy Greenleaf entered along with Alf Branch. They had obviously come looking for her. One glance at their faces told her the truth.

They were losing the battle.

"What should we do?" Dana demanded.

Before Daisy or Alf could answer, Trew signalled to her. Dana bent over as he struggled to say the words.

"You gotta call in the Canadians."

She straightened up, surprised, and turned to the others.

"He says we have to call in the Canadians?" Her voice echoed her confusion. She waved towards the battlefield. "We're already here."

"We're new Canadians," Alf pointed out. "Trew means the ones who have always been here. That's what he calls them, though the name's not right. He means the Firstborn. The Old Ones."

Dana frowned.

"I thought we agreed. This is not their battle. We are not their people. We don't have the right to ask them. We can't expect—"

"They will come," Alf said.

He looked to Daisy for support.

She took Dana's hand.

"We *are* their people. Everyone and everything that lives in this land belongs to them. It's up to us to acknowledge that. To open our hearts and allow them in."

Her words echoed in Dana's mind, reminding her of what others had said.

Your gods are all around you, child of Faerie, you need but open your heart to them.

The land, the plants, the animals and the people all have spirit. It is important to encounter and acknowledge the life of the land. From such encounters come power. The power of the spirits rises up from the land.

If people stay somewhere long enough—even white people—the spirits will speak to them.

"They'll come for you," Alf Branch said quietly. "You have their blessing."

Suddenly Dana knew. It was like a sunburst in her head. *You are the gift. You are the ransom.* Again and again she had heard the others say that they were willing to offer their lives for the cause. She had thought about dying, but not very much. Now she understood. A ransom had to be paid for Faerie. A gift had to be offered to keep the dream alive.

The other members of the Company arrived.

"We must do what we set out to do," she told them. "We must reach the portal. A gift will be offered. A sacrifice will be made. Once the hellfire is destroyed, I can open the door."

There were several in the Company who knew immediately what she meant. Findabhair had once offered herself as the sacrifice and Gwen had fought against that decision. Finvarra was the one who finally paid the ransom with his immortality and the High Kingship of Faerie. Though these three looked stricken, they didn't argue the point. They knew all too well the universal law. *For every dream to exist, there must be a sacrifice.* And no matter how much they wanted to, they couldn't take Dana's place. She was the key. The only one who could open the door.

Along with Laurel, the aunts weren't certain what Dana meant, but they suspected the worst.

"Wait a minute," Yvonne began.

"What's going on?" Dee demanded.

"Don't," said Dana.

There was no time for explanations or disagreements. Too many were dying. She had to go now.

"You should have told me sooner," was all she said to Alf and Daisy.

They shook their heads, eyes wet with tears.

"We couldn't, dear heart," Daisy said. "We were all agreed on that. We have lived long upon the earth. We would rather have sacrificed ourselves instead."

Gently Dana kissed each of them goodbye. Then she turned to hug her aunts. They were both in shock, hoping against hope that what was happening in front of them was not actually happening.

"No," said Dee. "No."

"Yes," said Dana firmly

As she left the tent, the others followed.

For the third and last time, the Company of Seven fell into formation. Dana was about to cast her shield of light when Gwen raised her hand.

"Wait! Can you feel it?"

Images flickered across their minds.

A high green hill in the north of Ireland. A grey stone wall rims the peak like a crown. The Grianan of Ailech. The ancient fort overlooks the Donegal mountains and the wide bay of Lough Swiligh that empties into the sea. Four figures stand upon the ramparts. Matt, the businessman, has parked his Mercedes at the base of the hill. Katie, the farmer, rode her motorbike all the way from County Clare. Dara, the young King of Inch, supports Granny Harte, the fairy doctress who will lead the ritual. Stooped with age and weariness, she is still recovering from the Enemy's attack. But where the grey hair sweeps over her face in the wind, her eyes are keen with an indomitable will.

"Four is the sacred number of Turtle Island," she says. "We will forge a chain of power to cross the ocean."

Each takes up a position in the four sacred directions, North, South, East and West. They raise their arms to the midday sun, knowing it is evening on the other side of the Atlantic.

As Granny begins the incantations, power rises from the earth and swirls around them.

Even as the circle was formed in Ireland, another four met in northern Canada.

A full moon shines on a forest of tall spruce and pine. A newly built Medicine Lodge stands in a clearing. Inside the tent, tobacco smoke curls with sweetgrass and sage. Roy beats the drum as the Old Man rattles to the four directions. Two great wolves complete the circle, the silver-grey and the black.

As Grandfather begins to sing and chant, power rises from the earth and swirls around them.

"They're sending us power!" Gwen cried. "Stand ready to receive it!"

Like a blast of wind, the power surged through the Company of Seven, clearing away all doubts and fears. They were buoyant with a sense of strength and purpose, with the confirmation of their role in life, the knowledge of their place in the cosmos. Suddenly they were taller, stronger, and shining with light.

Imbued with new courage and battle skills, Yvonne and Deirdre felt like Amazons. They threw each other a look of triumph. *We can do this.*

At the centre of the phalanx, Dana felt the surge of power bolstering her guard. She was pleased for their sake. It would help them bear what lay ahead. No more power had come to her, for she had enough. She was ready to do what she had come to do. She was ready to forge her destiny.

A cheer rose up from the fairy hosts as the Company of Seven moved onto the field. The last battle for the Plain of the Great Heart had begun.

CHAPTER FORTY

LIKE A GREAT GOLDEN BEETLE they inched across the plain, shielded by the carapace of Dana's light. But though they were protected from black magic and spells, they still came under attack. The fairy forces thronged to their side to increase the guard, but the outer circle was soon overwhelmed by a ferocious onslaught. The news had spread through enemy lines. *The key has entered the field.* As a ground swell of animosity seethed against the phalanx, they were pressed on all sides.

Dana's guard fought tooth and nail to hold their places around her. There was no time to think or feel. All acted on instinct, the will to survive. The din of battle was deafening. The fog of war was red. Their swords and spears flashed in the dimness.

With all her strength, Dana upheld the shield of light. She could feel the force that strove to break it, a relentless malice emanating from the firewall.

Slowly but steadily, the shining Company cut a swath across the plain. After an interminable span of murder and mayhem, they reached the rampart.

Immediately their spirits flagged. The flames gave off a deadly cold as well as intense heat. The cruel extremes worked to disturb and disarm. The golden shield wavered, then dispelled. The moment their defences fell, they were struck full force by an overpowering enmity.

They couldn't hold their ranks. They broke apart. It took all their effort not to fall to the ground.

"Go now," Dana ordered her guard. "There's no time for farewells. May we meet again when the Kingdom is restored."

Her hands were shaking, but she made enough light to surround herself.

The others had backed away from the wall.

"The light will protect you from the fire, right?" her aunt Yvonne insisted.

Dana didn't answer.

Gwen and Findabhair were crying openly. Laurel and Finvarra looked ashen.

"What is it?" demanded Dee. "Isn't she safe with her light?"

There was no point in lying when one battled for the truth.

"The light may protect her," Laurel said. "That's our only hope. But we can't know if it will."

"We should go with her!" cried Yvonne. "We're her guard!"

Finvarra moved quickly to hold her back even as the others grabbed Dee.

"She's only a kid!" screamed Deirdre, struggling against them. "She can't go alone!"

"There's nothing we can do to help her," Gwen said. Her voice was hollow.

"Don't you think we would if we could?" Laurel said in the same tone.

The aunts knew in their hearts they had no choice. The die had been cast. The decision had been made. Only one could go into the fire. Their niece had turned her back on them, so she couldn't see their pain. Weeping out loud, they were led away from the wall and were soon fighting for their lives on the battlefield.

Though she heard her aunts' distress, Dana didn't look back. She couldn't. She needed all her strength for the contest ahead.

From the moment she had stepped on the battlefield, she had known who lurked in the fire. Now as she stood before the flames, she sensed his presence. This was what she had dreaded for so long, the confrontation with her adversary, when she would face him alone. The time had come.

"So this is where you're hiding, Grimstone? You're a typical general, Grey Man. Safe in the back while your soldiers die. Doing the Enemy's dirty work as usual. I see you couldn't touch the portal."

There, just beyond the fiery wall, on an island of green grass, stood the gateway, pristine and intact.

Dana knew what she had to do to reach it. Without stopping to think, she stepped into the flames.

As soon as Dana was inside the wall, she saw Grimstone's face. It leered at her with grotesque glee. As the first stabs of pain pierced her armour of light, she felt his triumph, his belief that he had won even as he was killing her.

His voice crawled into her mind like a worm.

"Idiot! What good is a door without a key? Once I've destroyed you, it can stand there forever. Sealed and useless. The Earthworld on one side and Faerie on the other, never the twain to meet."

The peals of cold laughter tolled like a funeral bell. The flames seared Dana's skin. As her human body suffered the pain and her immortal self struggled to bear it, Dana realized the truth. Her light would keep her fairy self safe, but her humanity could not withstand the fire.

It was the final irony of the quest. Before she had begun her journey, Dana would not have mourned this loss so deeply. She would only have regretted leaving her family behind. But now she grieved the end of a life she had only begun to live, her new country, her new friends. Sadly, she bade farewell in her mind to so many, Georgia, Trew, Roy, Grandfather, Gwen and Laurel, Findabhair and Finvarra, Clan Creemore and all the Canadian fairies, and most of all, her beloved Jean. Heartsore, she lamented what she and he had lost, all the time they should have had together.

And even as her mortality slowly burned away, Dana's fairy self moved inexorably towards the portal. The flames seemed to stretch for an eternity. A fiery plain to traverse. An endless gauntlet to run. It was important that Grimstone believe this was her sole intent. He mustn't know the part he himself would play in the sacrifice. Not yet.

She was drawing near to the heart of the matter, near to the malevolent heart of her adversary. She could sense the endless depths of hatred, the mindless imperative to maim and destroy. This was not the imaginary evil so often depicted in the world as epic and exciting. This was barren and monotonous and utterly dismal. *The banality of evil.* There was nothing lively or imaginative about it, for it worked always to kill liveliness and the imagination.

Dana's mind strained under the onslaught, the murder of her body and spirit. She could feel herself falling, falling into the abyss, overwhelmed by an inertia she couldn't resist.

Revelling in his victory, Grimstone was merciless. He bombarded her with images to feed her despair. She saw how evil ruled the Earthworld, how it triumphed continually in every corner both big and small: the greed of the powerful who squandered their riches while so many starved; land and air polluted by industry; forests felled and waters poisoned; animals tortured for human gain; women and children enslaved; racism and murder; war and war and war. Everywhere she saw the face of the Enemy, the murderous shadow that dogged mankind. *There is no respect for life in the shadow of the Enemy.*

In a lightning flash, she saw the true nature of the war being waged, ancient and never-ending, in humanity's history. The battle fought on the Plain of the Great Heart was the battle fought in the hearts of all men and women. The monstrous forces pitted against the Land of Dreams were shadows and projections, misshapen creations of the human mind. Fairy tale versions of the real evil in the world that came from humanity, not gods or spirits.

"We are the enemy," Dana whispered, "and we are the battlefield."

There is no neutral ground in this war. You are either on the side of life or you have fallen to the Enemy and serve its cause. These are the End Days. The last days of this phase of human life. This is a time of critical metamorphosis. The forces of darkness and light gather within and without. Either we transform our world into something better or we all die in the flames of our own destruction. Change or die. The cosmic law of evolution. There is no neutral ground in this war. Either you choose to cherish life and protect it, or you choose to hurt it for your own profit and power. Evil is a choice, a series of choices. Decisions are made for right or wrong. You can determine if you are good or evil by looking at yourself and at what you do.

"You don't even know who you are," Grimstone hissed.

Infinitely weary, weighed down by the eternal and incessant struggle, Dana searched in her heart for a reply to his charge. Deep in her mind an image flickered against the darkness. It was faint at first, but as she strained to see it the image grew stronger. A beautiful woman, tall and pale and as luminous as the stars. She rode a white horse that trod upon shining waters and she carried a spear. Dana knew who she was though she had never met her. *You belong to that tribe who herd the stars across the heavens, who have light in their veins, who are descended from the White Lady of the Waters.* The Lady was her forebear, her fairy ancestress. But though Dana was inspired by the image, it wasn't enough. Drowning in the darkness that was human despair, she needed more than a distant ideal to cling to. She needed something real. The image wavered and was overlaid by another.

There before her was Gran Gowan, steady as a rock, a staunch Protestant who had married a Catholic for love. With the raw courage of the pioneers that ran in her veins, she had walked a broader path than many. Dana could see the lines in her grandmother's face, the hardship she had suffered, left to rear her children when her husband died young. Despite adversity she had lived undefeated, a woman proud of her life. As she smiled at Dana, she wielded a rolling pin as if it were a spear. *Pastry dough can tell if you're afraid of it. You're a Gowan. Stand strong!*

Dana burst out laughing.

And the laugh echoed like music, like freedom, like light.

If there's one thing evil cannot bear to hear, it's the sweet sound of light-hearted laughter. As the flames shrank back and Grimstone cowered, Dana spoke her truth against the darkness.

"I know who I am. I am the ransom. I am the sacrifice. I am the key to the door."

She reached out to grasp Grimstone and drew him to herself. He no longer wore the form he had taken for his mission, but had returned to his elemental nature. Incorporeal, he was all the more deadly. As she clasped him against her, Dana embraced the evil that he was and the evil he had shown her. There was a moment when she was overwhelmed by his presence. A thick cloying stench enveloped her. She sensed him in her mind like a malignant tumour. Worse than the physical revulsion was the mental anguish that came with the true knowledge of evil. She struggled to contain its reality without despairing, without falling prey to the darkness itself. *Truth shall be thy shield and buckler.* Acknowledging that evil existed in the world, she held to the truth of the struggle for good. Good existed and that was the truth and as long as good existed the war was not lost.

Slowly and steadily, Dana smothered the evil within her heart.

Only now did Grimstone realize the depth of his failure. Though he raged and clawed and screamed against it, he was assailed by that truth which evil hides from itself. The truth at the heart of the universe. *Evil is but a small and passing thing. The true nature of all is Good.* Unable to bear the blinding light of that truth, he dispersed like a ragged mist in the morning.

As Grimstone faded away, Dana collapsed with relief. The flames still burned and she still clung to her light, but everything was different. Like perfume in the air, she caught the scent of *promise*. Vague figures moved around her. Some looked human, others appeared as animals, and there were those who seemed a mixture of both. Human heads on animal bodies. Animal heads on human bodies. The bright shadows increased in number till they were a shining assembly, multitudinous, living, glorious. The murmur of Voices rose up. They were speaking amongst themselves. She sensed a debate that involved her quest but she also caught a glimpse of something much bigger. A Great Tale. A Grand Design. Something so immense it was beyond her comprehension.

When at last they addressed her, she could feel their good will. It was like a great sigh of wind rushing through the trees of a giant forest.

The gift is accepted.

Dana was filled with joy. She had defeated Grimstone, but the hellfire was beyond her. It had to be dealt with by powers greater than herself. She had done her part. She had brought a gift. And now she knew They would come.

The world was fading around her. The sounds of battle on the plain were receding like the tide. As she released the last shreds of her humanity like a torn garment discarded, she heard a howl on the wind. A cry to her heart.

She looked back for a moment into the red night of battle. High in the air, the spirit boat flew past the full moon. Grandfather and Roy paddled the canoe. Two wolves sat between them. They had come in the last hour for one reason only. They had come for Dana.

She could hear Jean's cry inside the wolf call.

Stay alive. I love you.

Suddenly the ground trembled beneath her feet. The beat of drums sounded over the plain. Deep and loud, reverberating through the air, the pounding drowned the din of war.

O for a voice like thunder, and a tongue
To drown the throat of War!

The drumming quickened like a thousand heartbeats, call-notes throbbing, pulsing louder and louder. Then came the Voices. The song was carried by the wind and all heard the song before they saw the Singers.

> *O Siem*
> *We are all family.*

Chapter Forty-One

$\diamond$Over the rim of the horizon they came, rising up from the earth. Bounteous, multitudinous, living, glorious. The Old Ones of Turtle Island. The gods and spirits of the land.

The beat of innumerable drums reverberated through the air. The cadence of countless rattles rained down from the sky.

Some came in human form, tall and noble. Others wore the magnificent shapes of animals. As they descended upon the Plain of the Great Heart, they danced and they sang.

> *O Siem*
> *We are all family*

There was Old Man Coyote, Trickster of the Great Plains. He howled at the moon to announce his arrival. Beside him ran Grandmother Spider along with Fox, Hare and Possum. Through the night air flew Raven of the Pacific Tsimshian, Raven who made the western waves flow free by tricking the Old Woman who held onto the tide line. And with Raven came Crow of the Tagish-Tlingit who cast sand on the Earth when it was flooded with water.

"Become the land!" Crow had cried.

One of the Singers was We'sa-ka-cha'k, Hero of the Cree, he who created the Sun Dance as a prayer for all the people.

Mischievous and quick-witted, he was always getting into scrapes that made the others laugh. One day he was walking through the land when he heard the sound of singing and the beating of drums. Always one to enjoy celebrations, he painted his face with vermilion and hurried to the great encampment where a lodge had been built. Inside the huge tent were many dancers, men and women, all dressed in their best garments with beadwork and feathers. They were grave and solemn in their dance, blowing little whistles as they advanced towards a buffalo skull clothed in a finely stitched robe. They prayed for health and peace as they danced. We'sa-ka-cha'k watched the dance for a long time until he fell asleep. When he woke up, his head was stuck inside a buffalo skull with hundreds of ants biting him. He fell around the place, yelling, till the skull smashed on a stone. He knew, then, that his vision was true and he gave the Sun Dance to the people.

> *O Siem*
> *We're all the same*

Tall and beautiful, White Buffalo Calf Woman walked so lightly that her feet hardly touched the ground. It was she who gave the gift of the Sacred Pipe to the people so they would know the unity of all things. The bowl of the Pipe was fashioned of red stone, the colour of the flesh and blood of mammals. The wooden stem spoke of trees and plants and all things green and growing. The smoke from the Pipe was the sacred wind, the breath that carries prayers to Wakan Tanka, the Creator. It was White Buffalo Calf Woman who taught the people to offer the Pipe to Earth and Sky and the Four Directions. As she walked on the plain, she rolled once upon the ground. When she stood up, she had taken the form of a black buffalo. Now she rolled again and became a brown buffalo. Then another roll and there stood a red buffalo. With the final roll, she became a white buffalo and then resumed her shape as White Buffalo Calf Woman.

O Siem
The fires of freedom

In the sky above, the night was shadowed by an immense winged shape. It was Pe-ya-siw—Thunderbird—Lord of the Heavens. His plumage gleamed with the colours of the rainbow. His eyes flashed lightning. His voice rumbled thunder.

Below on the plain stepped the hump-backed Flute-player. He was the one who brought the seasons and gifted the people with the seeds of plants. Beside him walked Fisher the Hunter who dwelled in the sky amidst the stars of the Big Dipper. Once upon a time, he broke into Skyland with his friends Otter, Lynx and Wolverine. They released all the birds who now flew in the world.

Sacred to the Plains Lakota and Sioux was Tunka-Shila, Grandfather Rock. First of the Firstborn, he is remembered at the heart of every sweat lodge. For when the Earth was but a vast body of water, a burning Rock rose to the surface. The steam became clouds and the Rock itself, dry land.

Strong winds came sweeping over the plain. White Bear, the north wind, brought the cold breath of ice and snow. Moose, the east wind, shook rain from his antlers. Gentle Fawn, the south wind, blew warm sweet air while Panther, the west wind, struck with sudden force.

Dance in the burning flame.

Glooskap, he who was also called Koluscap and Gluscabi, was dressed for war. Fierce and robust, he had painted his face

499

half-black, half-white. He rode upon a stallion that was also black-and-white. In his hands were a shield and spear of the same colours. A great eagle perched on his shoulder. Glooskap lived in a tent with Woodchuck, his Grandmother. Another of his names was Odzihozo, "the One who made Himself." For after Tabaldak made human beings of dust, there was one last bit that got sprinkled on the Earth. Gluscabi took form from that bit and sat up and looked around.

"Well here I am," he said.

It is the Mi'kmaq in the east who tell the story of the time Glooskap went to the Summer Land. When he came up with the plan, he told his friend Loon.

"There is a land where the sun shines throughout the year and it is always summer. I must go there and meet its queen. Maybe she can help us deal with Old Man Winter."

"Good idea," said Loon. "Try singing her a song. Women like that."

> *Siem o siyeya*
> *All people of the world*

There also came one whom Laurel recognized, the one who had helped her in her hour of need. Nanabush, Trickster-Hero of the Anishinabe Ojibwa. It was he who brought the gift of fire to his people. After he stole it from the Fire-Keeper, he ran fast and far in a great relay with Cougar, Fox, Squirrel, Antelope and Frog. He was the son of the West Wind and he had many powers. When he was a child, he lived with his Grandmother Nokomis. One day he was so hungry he turned himself into a rabbit so that he could eat the grass. Nokomis cradled him in her arms and called him Nanabozho, her "little rabbit."

Siem o siyeya
It's time to make the turn

These were but some of the Old Ones who arrived on the plain, invincible, laughing, fearless, joyful. As they crossed the battlefield, singing all the while, the dark army fled before them. The Old Ones who were warriors smote the baneful creatures down. Those who were animals swallowed them up. Everywhere the servants of the Enemy were thrown into turmoil and despair, for here was beauty and light they could not withstand.

The Old Ones continued to sing as they vanquished the dark till no trace of the foul army was left on the plain. Now the Singers advanced on the fiery rampart. Without pausing their song, they walked into the fire that was a mere mirage, the illusion of evil. And they danced and they sang at the heart of the flames.

Siem o siyeya
A chance to share your heart

The song they sang within the flames was one of pain and loss. They sang of the wounded side of humanity, of the many peoples who walked the trail of tears upon the Earth. For the most powerful songs and the most enduring are those that rise to defeat despair, to overcome adversity, to survive and prevail. They sang the song of the Risen People.

Siem o siyeya
To make a brand new start

And as they sang they quenched the fire till there was nothing but ashes that blew away in the wind.

And watch the walls come tumbling down.

Their song finished, their work done, the Old Ones left the plain.

And so the battle was over that night. The claps of thunder and the winds and the storms had ceased their disturbance. The uproar of the elements and the sky and the land had been stilled. A great peace and harmony settled over everything. For all had been cleansed and healed and whatever was foul had been banished. There arose the greatest tranquillity to play its part in the Divine Plan.

Dana lay on the grass in front of the portal. She hadn't the strength to move, let alone pass through the doorway. Vaguely she sensed those who reached out to help her; her guard, the black wolf that was Jean, the fairies of Clan Creemore. But they couldn't touch her. She was already beyond them. She heard their calls, heard the wolf's howl, but there was nothing she could do. They were in the Land of the Living. She had gone into the Dreaming.

Only Grandfather was calm. He stood on *Magh Crí Mor,* but he was also in the cemetery beside Thomas Gowan's grave. A brief smile crossed his lips as he remembered that good man and their meeting long ago. He touched the white bird carved on Thomas's tombstone. It flew into the air with a rush of pale wings. Flying high like a lark, it let out a call-note of sobbing and joy.

From the great forest around the plain, the cry was echoed a hundredfold. Up from the trees, in a blur of white flight in the moonlight, rose the soul-birds of Faerie. The night resounded with the sibilance of wings. Feathery voices rang through the air. Swooping down on the plain, the birds flew towards Dana and lifted her into their midst. Without substance or weight, she was as light as a feather. As they carried her to the portal they sang a Homecoming song, for her whom they bore and for the end of their exile. With melodious voices, unearthly and sweet, they sang of her quest, of her mission and her sacrifice.

Lost in the daze of her dying, Dana saw that her companions no longer had the heads of birds. Instead they bore the faces of those she knew, both human and fairy, her family, her friends, and all who had helped her. Jean was there beside her. Grandfather was the one who led their flight. Everyone she had ever loved was in that shining flock. That's when she knew they were a vision to accompany her death. She accepted the honour with gladness, for it showed the wealth of her life however brief.

Half-human, half-fairy, half-Irish, half-Canadian, once upon a time she was the light to bridge the darkness. Now she was the key to open the door.

As the soul-birds of Faerie bore her through the portal of the Great Heart, Dana sensed an infinity of doors opening everywhere, in minds and hearts, in distant lands, on distant worlds, all bursting open like flowers as she went Home.

Chapter Forty-Two

Dana was walking in a green and radiant garden. The scent of flowers sweetened the air. Butterflies flitted around her. Her mother, Edane, was with her as well as Honor, the High Queen of Faerie. They linked her arms as they walked beside her, speaking gently as if to coax her awake. She felt light and airy, like a puff of thistledown drifting on the breeze. Her mother's voice rang with gladness but Honor's seemed tinged with regret. Words and phrases floated in her mind. They were explaining her new reality, the new nature of her being. Her human self had died. She was purely fairy.

Of course she could visit the Earthworld now that she had restored the portals. She could even dwell there if she chose. But she would do so as a fairy, like those of Clan Creemore, and not as a mortal. She could no longer live amongst humans the way she had done when she was part of their race.

Dana felt the protests rising inside her but she couldn't speak. She was trembling all over. What was going on? Where was she? She pulled away from the fairy-women. Though she was weak and dizzy, she struggled in her mind to call up the portal. She needed to get away, to go back.

The portal took shape, responding to her command. She lurched towards it. In the shadow of the great arch, she could see the Plain of the Great Heart. It was still night. Bonfires lit up the darkness. The battle was over. The wounded were being carried from the field to the healing tents. The dead were being taken away to be mourned. She could see the luminous face of the full moon and the spray of white stars in a Canadian sky.

Behind her lay the summer meadows of Faerie, the Many-Coloured Land of dreams and enchantment. On a high hill a golden palace gleamed. Banners flew from every pinnacle. A great crowd was gathered there, calling her name. The celebration awaited the guest of honour. She had rescued Fairyland.

Dana was devastated. This was not how she had imagined the end of her quest. This was not what she had hoped for, not what she had dreamed.

She pleaded with her mother and the High Queen.

"I thought if I got back to Faerie everything would end happily! Isn't that how fairy tales are supposed to end? I thought I would get Jean's humanity back and we would be together. This is supposed to be the Land of Dreams, where everything is possible. I don't want things to end this way. This isn't my dream! It's a nightmare!"

Edane was bewildered by her daughter's reaction.

"But you were unhappy in the Earthworld! You fled to us constantly and did not want to return. It was your humanity that pulled you back. Now that it is gone, you can stay with us always!"

Honor, however, understood. When she died as a human to become the High Queen, she had to leave the world of her twin and her parents behind. *For any dream to exist, there must be a sacrifice.* Her voice was full of sympathy.

"We cannot restore your mortal life, Dana. It is beyond our power."

"I don't accept this!" Dana cried. "This is not my dream!"

Now Dana found herself in a different place. A small island floating like a lily on the waves of a warm sea. The light was astonishingly bright. A short distance away, on the rim of the horizon, shone the giant face of the Faerie sun. She was standing on a green hillock at the foot of a great tree. The tree was bare of leaf or flower, but its branches were covered with countless birds. White birds like blossoms. Fast asleep, their heads were tucked under their wings.

"The soul-birds of Faerie!" said Dana, breathless.

Though Edane had vanished, Honor was still beside her. The High Queen gazed upwards.

"I didn't really know what I was doing when I woke them. All I knew for certain was that they would change things. Everything looked hopeless. It was the only way I could think of helping you. Desperate times—"

"Call for desperate measures," Dana nodded, remembering the High Queen's motto. "But what are they? What do they mean?"

Honor frowned. "I don't quite understand myself. They're something very old. A part of Old Magic."

"There were soul-birds in the Earthworld, too, different from these ones. I met them on the ocean."

"There are soul-birds in every world. They are being born all the time, but they were also there before the worlds began. They are part of what made the worlds come into being." Honor shook her head. "I'm saying this all wrong." She sighed. "There are things that have no limits—they are boundless—and as soon as you put words on them, the description is wrong because it contains them, like putting something that should fly into a cage." She tried again, holding herself upright as she donned the mantle of sovereignty that brought her wisdom. "The soul-birds are fleeting like thoughts yet their power is immeasurable. They are the dreams of the Creator, they are the hopes of the Old Ones, they are the hopes and dreams of everything that exists. They are the utterances that make things come into existence and that hold things together, but they are also what change things. They are the unravellers, the undoings, the unmakings . . ." Her shoulders slumped. She gave Dana a rueful grimace. "It's all that 'life, the universe and everything' stuff that gives me a royal headache."

Dana smiled sympathetically, but in fact she understood. These were echoes of the teachings she was given when she was windwalking and dreamspeaking.

"I know why the soul-birds of the Earthworld suffer," she said softly. "Life is difficult there. Hopes and dreams go astray all the time. The soul-birds of Faerie rest easy in the Land of Dreams."

"Not if you wake them," Honor pointed out, "which is why no one does, as my husband has reminded me. I knew I was taking a huge risk. By sending them to you, I started a chain of events with no guarantee that things would get better. Change is change. Hope can be a burden. And people die for their dreams." She looked at Dana sadly. "It's my fault you died."

Dana was about to respond when something caught her eye. She stared up at the sleeping birds. There was something wrong. Something was missing. She touched her hair where she had tied the white feather when she dressed for battle. It still hung from her braid.

"It's not here," she said. "The bird who gave me this feather. It's still in the Earthworld."

"Ah," said the High Queen, catching her breath, "hope is still on the wing."

★　　★　　★

Word had reached the Fairy Court that Dana would attend the celebrations later that night. The news was met with joy, and the revels commenced in earnest.

Music filled the air as the bright lords and ladies twirled on floors of jade and marble. The hall blazed with the light of a thousand candles. Green garlands draped the walls and pillars. Long tables covered with snowy lace groaned beneath the weight of a fabulous feast. Gold and silver dishes offered every kind of sweetmeat and savoury, delicacy and dainty. Fountains bubbled with champagne.

Many who had fought on the Plain of the Great Heart came to enjoy the victory ball. The Canadian fairies were greeted with a tumultuous welcome. Time had passed in both worlds since they were last seen in Faerie. Friends and family embraced them with open arms. When a troop of Chinese dragons arrived, they were hailed as heroes. Stories and songs were already being composed to praise their part in the battle. The trolls of Toronto were led to their own table where a mountain of chocolate treats awaited them.

Dana's aunts were brought to the palace by Daisy Greenleaf. They had acquitted themselves well on the battlefield, suffering only minor wounds. Colouring the air with curses as they fought back to back, they had proved both skilful and lucky at war.

"We can't go to the ball like this!" Yvonne said with dismay.

"Cinderellasville," Dee agreed.

Their finery had disappeared at midnight and their own clothes were in tatters.

Daisy waved her hand over them. Now Yvonne was a party girl in sparkling red flounces while Deirdre wore sleek black satin with silver stars.

Once they were told they would see their niece later, they were ready to celebrate. Eagerly they looked around the hall.

"There's Andy and Tom!" said Dee.

The handsome brothers were also scanning the crowd. As soon as they spotted the two women, they hurried towards them.

"Sport?" said Dee, raising her eyebrow.

"Play," Yvonne nodded.

There was one of Dana's guard who couldn't come to the feast. When the battle ended, Gwen was discovered deep in enemy lines, badly wounded and unconscious. Brought to a healing tent, she finally woke to find Dara leaning over her.

"Are you really here or have I died, beloved?" she asked.

His eyes darkened as he relived the terror of that moment when he came through the portal and couldn't find her.

"No, you haven't died, *mo stór,*" he said gently. "You're made of stronger stuff than that."

His Irish accent fell like soft rain. She smiled to hear it. He took her hand in his.

"I've been watching over you," he said quietly, "and I've been thinking hard. It's time you and I were married. No more nonsense about it. We can sort the rest out as we go along. What do you say to that?"

Her smile widened.

"Yes, of course. Yes! What else could I say?"

Despite the pain that wracked her body, she managed a small laugh.

"You have a brilliant laugh," he murmured.

When Laurel entered the fairy hall, she did so with a divided heart. Surveying the bright company, she wasn't sure whom she hoped to see first, Honor or Ian. As it turned out, the High Queen had gone missing along with Dana, which left Laurel to deal with Ian first.

He came to her as the Summer King, resplendent in a crimson mantle. A golden circlet bound his raven-black hair. The blue eyes of Faerie stared into hers.

"Art thou well, Lady?"

She was dressed in a blue gown seeded with pearls. Her long

fair hair fell to her shoulders. Though one of her arms still bore a bandage, most of her wounds had been healed.

"I'm feeling a lot better, thanks. My friend Gwen got the worst of it rescuing a little fairy called Lavender. But they're both recovering. We're lucky we survived the battle. It was worse than the one you and I were in."

She managed to appear calm as she spoke, but it wasn't easy. She was so overjoyed to see him, she wanted to throw her arms around him. But she knew he had every reason to reject her. She was the one who had ended their relationship despite his pleas.

"All the time the worlds were divided, I thought of you," he said quietly. "I knew there would be a great battle and that you, being you, would be caught up in it somehow."

Remembering her refusal to join the mission at first, Laurel's smile was wry.

"It wasn't my quest, but I played my part."

He hesitated before taking his leave. His pride insisted that he go. After all, she was the one who had rejected him.

She saw that he was about to leave. She knew she had to put aside her pride and take the risk. It was now or never. Either she reached for her dream or lost all hope of getting it.

The words came tumbling out.

"When I thought you were dead or injured . . . It hurt so badly. My heart was broken. The thought of never seeing you again . . . It was the reason I took the mission. When I went into battle, it was *you* I was fighting for."

For a moment he looked as if he couldn't believe what he was hearing. She had never spoken so directly, so ardently to him. He searched her features. She was different somehow. There was a lightness about her, as if she had finally let something go.

"Come dance with me, Lady," he said, catching her hand.

*   *   *

A hush fell over the great hall as soon as Dana entered. Everyone knew that something was amiss. It was known before she arrived that she was not joining the feast. She had come only to seek an audience with Midir, the High King. Though there had been a lot of whispering and speculation, only her mother looked upset. Refusing to eat or drink in Faerie was the customary sign that one didn't want to stay.

Dana made her way across the marble floor towards the dais where the High Majesties were enthroned. She didn't wear shining raiment nor was she bedecked in jewels. Instead, she wore the clothes the Sasquatch had given her, her battle-dress. The black feathered cape folded like wings over the deerskin shirt and leggings. The cedar bark apron fell to her knees. On her feet were moccasin boots. In her hand, she carried her staff of carved pine. Her hair was braided, draped with the feather of the soul-bird still on the wing. On either side of her loped two great wolves, the silver-grey that was *grand-père* and the black that was Jean.

A ripple of shock ran through the assembly. The Canadian clans grinned their approval. She didn't look like an Irish fairy. She looked like a *man-i-tou,* a spirit of Turtle Island.

When she called out her challenge, her voice was steady.

"I have rescued Fairyland. I request a boon."

The High King frowned. His red-gold hair fell in a mane to his shoulders. His eyes were solemn. Though he wore no crown, a star shone on his forehead to mark his sovereignty. On his left stood Edane, regarding her daughter anxiously. On his right was Honor, his wife. The High Queen sat stiffly as she controlled her features, but her eyes sparkled with mischief. This was just the best yet.

Midir's frown was not directed at Dana, but rather at the wolves.

"This enchantment is not of Ireland or Faerie."

"It's a French-Canadian thing," said Dana.

"We have no power over magics that are not our own," he told her.

"The High Queen is or was Canadian," Dana pointed out succinctly.

The Canadian fairies let out a cheer. Honor barely managed to stifle a giggle.

"Also, as I've recently discovered," Dana continued, "there has long been commerce between Turtle Island and Faerie. This isn't entirely beyond your jurisdiction."

Dana thought she saw amusement and admiration in Midir's look. He nodded his head, an encouraging sign. After what seemed an eternity, he answered.

"I will take counsel with the Old Ones of Ireland: the Salmon of Assaroe, the Old Woman of Beare, Blackfoot the Elk of Ben Gulban, the White Lady of the Waters and Laheen, the Golden Eagle, King of the Birds. The Five Ancients came before Faerie and the new magic of our realm. They will know if the spell can be broken."

Dana was overjoyed. This was definitely a "maybe" as opposed to a "no." They were in with a chance.

"Just a minute," she said quickly. "I haven't stated my request. There's three parts to it. I'm asking not only that Jean and *grand-père*'s humanity be restored, but mine too."

Before Midir could accuse her of asking too much, the High Queen spoke up.

"Three is the sacred number of the Summer Land. It befits the boon requested, my Lord."

Midir glanced at his wife with sudden suspicion. She made an admirable effort at returning his look with some semblance of innocence. He had to stop himself from laughing out loud. Like his subjects, he took great delight in the way the High Queen flaunted the rules. She was more impish than the best of them. Still, the matter was grave.

"You agreed to be the gift. The sacrifice."

"And I died willingly," Dana agreed. "But there is another law in the universe. *Love is as strong as death.*"

Midir was impressed by her words.

"So be it," he declared. "The three-fold boon will be put to the Ancients. You shall have your answer before the night is done."

*　　*　　*

Dana didn't feel like joining the ball. The suspense was too great. Instead, she sat by a fountain in the palace gardens with the two wolves at her side. Gazing into the falling water, she could only wonder—what did Fate hold in store for them?

One by one, the others came to express their support.

"We'll raise blue murder if you don't get what you want," Dee told her. "Nothing short of a happy ending is acceptable."

"Being a fairy is all very well, but we'd rather have you in our world," Yvonne agreed. "They say even the gods want to be human."

"'They' say a lot of stuff, don't they?" Dee remarked.

When Laurel arrived with Ian, Dana noticed the two were holding hands. She also noticed the change in the young woman. Laurel looked more like her sister now, light-hearted and happy.

The Summer King bowed to Dana.

"May you be restored to your beloved, as I have been to mine."

A shout from John Trout heralded the arrival of Clan Creemore. In a blast of wind they appeared around her.

"It's our wish that you return home with us," said Daisy Greenleaf.

"Home to Creemore," Alf Branch added, "where Gowans belong."

When Trew came hurrying towards her, she almost lifted him off the ground to hug him.

"You didn't die!" she cried.

"Almost. Close call. It took them this long to get me off my back and on my feet. I missed the grub, but at least I'm here for the party!"

"What is that colour?" Dana demanded, laughing.

He was outrageously dressed in a yellowish-green suit of frills and fripperies.

"Chartreuse," he told her. "Preferable to puce, eh?"

Brendan came to wish her well before he set sail for home. As he sat down beside her, he clasped her hands.

"I have prayed that your intentions be granted," he said, "that *your* book ends as joyfully as mine."

"So *The Book of Wonders* is finished?"

Dana was pleased for the saint. Brendan nodded happily.

"As soon as I stepped through the portal into this wondrous land, a rider approached me on a white horse. She wore a purple mantle and gold-embroidered gloves and her feet were shod with sandals of white bronze. In her hand she carried a silver branch with three golden apples. I bowed before her.

"'You are the Queen of *Tír Tairngire,* the Land of Promise,' spake I, 'as described in the book that I am restoring.'

"'Indeed that name belongs to me,' she said in her melodious voice. 'I have come to tell you that your work is done. Your pilgrimage is fulfilled and you may return home.'"

Dana smiled to herself as she imagined Honor enjoying that task.

Gwen had requested to be brought to Dana though the healers had yet to release her. Still pale and weak, she was carried on a silken palanquin supported by her friends from Ireland. Her eyes shone with happiness as she introduced Dara and the other members of the first Company of Seven. Dana thanked them for their help with her mission.

"We all had our part to play, whether big or small," said Granny, the fairy doctress. Her visit to Faerie had restored her health. She looked younger and livelier.

"I was glad to do more than throw money at the problem," Matt stated.

"Thank God we woke up in time to do something!" were Katie's heartfelt words. "We nearly slept the whole thing out!"

Gwen leaned over to Dana and spoke quietly just to her.

"It was an honour to be your guard in battle, but you know what? I'd rather be standing in front of you in class, with Jean there as well. Would that be too dull for you?"

"It's one of my dreams," said Dana and she meant it.

It was almost dawn in Faerie when their Royal Majesties returned. The festivities had waned but no one would leave. All had remained in solidarity with the Light-Bearer's daughter for whom they wished only happiness.

Dana saw immediately that the news wasn't good. The faces of the High King and High Queen were sorrowful. Edane was with them, looking distraught.

Silence gripped the hall. The air crackled with tension. Dana went down on one knee to put her arms around the wolves.

"The humanities of the three may be restored."

As soon as he made his announcement, Midir raised his hand to stay the applause.

"Here comes the 'but,'" Dee muttered.

"However, it is not a simple matter. The boon requires both High Magic and Old Magic. As it has been since time began, High Magic calls for a noble sacrifice. Old Magic calls for a death."

Dana's hold on the wolves tightened. Jean and *grand-père* bared their teeth.

"What must be done?" she asked steadily.

"The three of you will go beyond the Black Gates of Faerie to meet Crom Cruac. The Great Worm is the guardian of the balance between the worlds. He will preside over the death and the sacrifice. The death is twofold. The wolves must die to allow the men to live. They will be fully human and *loup-garou* no more."

The High King's eyes grew darker. It was obvious that what he had to say next caused him great pain.

"The noble sacrifice is the act of an immortal. To regain your humanity, you must offer up your fairy self."

Now she knew why her mother looked stricken.

Dana was stunned. Having steeled herself for a straight yes or no, she wasn't prepared for complications. She was staggered by the proposal, the price to be paid. How could she give up her birthright? Her glorious inheritance! And yet she yearned to be human, to live out her life, to be reunited with Jean and her family and friends.

For every dream to exist there must be a sacrifice.

As difficult as it was for her, so too it would be for Jean and *grand-père*. They would lose a part of their souls to become human again. All the wildness and freedom of the *loup-garou*.

Kneeling beside the two wolves, Dana bowed her head against theirs. All three were shaken to the core of their being.

The High King of Faerie gazed upon them with compassion.

"Each of you is free to choose your own destiny. One decision is not bound by the others. But choose you must, between your magical self and your humanity."

CHAPTER FORTY-THREE

It was still Hallowe'en in the Earthworld, for both the Plain of the Great Heart and the Land of Faerie were outside time. Gabriel was still standing beside his wife on the dark streets of Creemore, laughing with the crowd as the Headless Horseman galloped down the road. Suddenly he found himself elsewhere, in a place he knew well. He was in a forest in Ireland, in the Wicklow Mountains, on a high ridge overlooking a road. The trees were a tangle of old oak and holly. It was springtime. The air was green with sunlight filtered through leaves. He was sitting on a fallen tree trunk, his silver flute in his hand.

Bewildered, he looked around him. Was this a dream? Then she stepped out of the trees and walked towards him. Her gown was pale silk, her feet and arms were bare, and her head was wreathed with a crown of white blossoms. For a moment he thought she was Edane, his first wife, but her long hair was dark. Then he realized with a shock that the glimmering girl was his daughter.

"Gabe . . . Da . . . I'm so sorry."

Her voice echoed with sadness.

He felt an ache in his heart. Despite his confusion, he knew what this meant, the thing he had always secretly dreaded. She was going to leave him, his fairy daughter, even as her mother had.

As Dana reached out to him, her hands spilled golden light.

"This is what I am, Gabe, and I can't hide it any more. I can't protect you from the truth. I'm going away for a while. Something has happened and I'm no longer able to live in both worlds. I've got to choose one or the other. I need to think about it, but I promise to return and let you know my decision. I don't want to hurt you, but it's my life and I have to choose for myself. I'm more than a kid. I think you know that already."

Gabriel dropped the flute from his hands. His heart was breaking. Yet even as he looked at her with love and awe, he knew her words were true. She was more than a child.

"Take care of yourself, Da, and Radhi and the new baby."

With tears in his eyes he held her tightly, hoping it wasn't for the last time.

"You'll always be my baby," he murmured, "my firstborn."

★   ★   ★

By the time Dana caught up with Findabhair and Finvarra, they were at their hotel in Toronto. Finvarra had taken off his shirt so that his wife could change the dressings on his wounds. The room was filled with the sweet scent of fairy herbs.

"You should've stayed in the healing tent," she chided him, but her voice was gentle as was her touch.

"You have power of your own," he smiled. "And it is best we go back onstage as soon as possible. Our honour must be restored. We broke our pledge with the tour."

"The show must go on," Findabhair agreed. "A make-up concert should fix things. We're not the first musicians to go astray. *All's well that ends well.*"

Neither looked surprised when Dana appeared beside them, but both were saddened by her news.

"You must know the full consequences if you choose human-ity," Finvarra told her. "You will be banished from the Land of Faerie. Once you lose your immortality, you cannot return."

This was the reason she had come to see them. She needed to talk with someone who understood her dilemma.

"But I'll still be able to see fairies, won't I? If they show them-selves to me? Like Clan Creemore? And my mother will visit me and show up in my dreams?"

"That's the theory," said Findabhair.

She and her husband exchanged glances.

"I need to know the truth," said Dana, "to help me make the right choice."

Findabhair sighed.

"The bottom line? Fairies are flighty. You know that yourself. Life is a game for them, feasting and frolic, music and dancing. They never grow old and I'd say they never grow up. And that's another thing. Time. Because of their immortality, they don't notice it passing in their world or ours. They don't mean to forget to visit, but years can pass before they remember. You need to understand, Dana, that if you choose to be human, you're not in for a penny, you're in for a pound. Faerie will play a very small part in your life. It may even disappear from it altogether."

Dana's eyes filled with tears. This was her worst fear.

"But the others, like Gwen and—"

"It is a different thing for the Companions of Faerie," Finvarra explained. "They have right of passage to the other realm and are ever a part of it. For you and me and any other immortal who falls out of the Great Time, the door is closed. We are exiles in this world."

Life is a peregrination through a foreign land.

"Is it forever?" Dana asked, catching her breath.

She saw the first glimmer of promise in their eyes.

"Actually, that's something we don't know," Findabhair said. "Immortals who have fallen face death as a mystery."

"Hope is still on the wing," Dana murmured, releasing her breath.

★   ★   ★

Georgia was asleep when Dana arrived at her house. Instead of waking her, Dana slipped into her dreams. She found herself outside a ruined building in a darkened city near a river. Georgia crouched nearby with a gun in her hand. As shots rang out, she stood up to fire back, then hunkered down again. She didn't look surprised to see Dana. After all, it was a dream.

"What on earth is going on here?" Dana hissed at her.

Explosions sounded across the river.

"Don't you dream you're on secret missions fighting some mysterious enemy?" said Georgia. "No wait, that's your real life."

She stood up to let off another round but she had run out of ammunition. Crouching again, she reloaded.

"According to dream books, I'm fighting the dark side of myself," she commented. "So far we're even."

Dana snickered. Even in her dreams, Georgia was a card.

"Could we go somewhere quiet?" she asked her friend. "I need to talk to you."

Now Dana found herself perched beside Georgia on a high wall overlooking a hilly countryside. The sun shone on their faces. Their legs dangled over the warm stone. The wall stretched away on both sides as far as the eye could see, rising and falling with the roll of the land. There was no sign of habitation or people or animals, only brown soil and green bushes and the wall going on forever.

"Wow," Dana said, "is this the Great Wall of China?"

"Yeah," said Georgia, banging her heels off the stone. "Isn't it neat? I love this place, but I can't always get here. Lucid dreaming is tricky."

"I'm really here," Dana told her. "You're not actually dreaming me."

Georgia sat up. Her look was serious.

"Is it all over then, the battle and everything?"

Dana nodded.

"Great-granny said the dragons went, but they didn't come back yet to tell us what happened."

"They were brilliant. They saved a lot of our army."

"That's great! So how come you're not keeping this news to brighten an otherwise boring day at school?"

Dana saw the worried look in her friend's eyes. Georgia might be a card, but she was also very bright. Dana hesitated. In that pause, Georgia's worry turned to fear.

"Did you die? Is that why you're here?"

Dana hesitated again, then nodded.

Georgia's eyes filled with tears.

"I'm still alive as a fairy," Dana hurried to say.

"It's not the same!" Georgia burst out. "I thought we were going to do the best friend thing. You know, graduate together, go to university, be each other's bridesmaids, all that corny stuff."

She started to cry. Dana did her best to comfort her, explaining the situation and the choice she faced.

"That's easy," Georgia sniffled, recovering quickly. "I vote you take the human option."

"Then I won't be special any more," Dana pointed out. "Isn't that why you picked me for a friend in the first place? Because I was like your great-granny?"

"Yes and no," Georgia argued. "I just wanted someone I could talk to about magic. Someone my own age. It's lonely having a secret you can't share. I can still do that with you as a human."

"This is really hard," Dana sighed. She stared down at the ground far below her and found herself thinking of Humpty Dumpty. "I'll lose so much and what do I get in return? Old age, sickness, death . . ."

"Hey, Ms Glass-Is-Half-Empty, don't forget the other things. Friendship and love and," Georgia waved her hand over the vast expanse of wall, "all the wonders you can find in our world."

Dana smiled. "I knew you'd help."

"Speaking of love, how's our *garçon*?"

Dana was about to answer when she stiffened.

"I've got to go. You're waking up."

"Whatever you decide, don't forget me!" Georgia cried.

The two girls hugged goodbye on the Great Wall of China.

★   ★   ★

Laurel went to the High Queen's solar. It was an airy chamber high in the palace, overlooking a green garden and sparkling fountains. Honor was reclining on an embroidered couch. Beside her was a small lacquered table with a china tea set and a plate of seedcakes and red berries. The High Queen nibbled restlessly on the tidbits as she gazed out the window. When Laurel entered the bower, she jumped up with delight.

"Here you are at last!"

The twins embraced joyfully.

"I was looking for you, but I couldn't find you," Laurel told her.

"I was out and about with royal duties. It's not all party-party no matter how it looks. Will you have some supper?"

Honor regarded her sister proudly as she poured the tea.

"I knew you wouldn't abandon us."

Laurel sighed. "It seems you can take the girl out of Faerie but you can't take Faerie out of the girl."

Honor laughed. "Did I see you walking in the garden with the Summer King?"

Her sister wasn't ready to touch that subject yet.

"What do you think Dana will do?" Laurel asked instead.

Honor's face clouded. "I was dwelling on that matter just before you arrived. She has so much to gain and so much to lose. My heart goes out to her."

"Can't you help her decide? You more than anyone else can understand her position."

Honor disagreed. "It was different for me. I didn't have a choice. In truth, I'm glad I didn't. How can one choose between two homes?"

★   ★   ★

On Iynu lands in northern Quebec, where the snow lay white and glistening in the dark of night, they waited for Dana in Grandfather's kitchen. Roy leaned against the wall, too restless to sit. The great black wolf that was Jean lay in front of the stove. On either side of him sat the two old men, smoking their pipes. *Grand-père* was a stately gentleman with short grey hair and the same wintergreen eyes as his grandson. He wore a thick woollen sweater over his trousers. From time to time he looked at Grandfather and they would nod their heads through the curl of tobacco smoke. Grandfather was wrapped in his black-and-red blanket. All of them stayed silent in the stoic manner of men who didn't need to talk when there was nothing to say.

Outside in the cold night, high in the clear starry sky, Dana was playing with her mother in the Northern Lights. *Aqsarniit,* soccer trails, was what the Baffin Islanders called the shimmering strands. One moment the lights were swirls of milky silver, the next sheets of green and lilac rippling like veils. The sky was the playing field for a great game of soccer in which thousands of spirits were taking part. Breathless and barefoot, with stars in her hair, Dana ran amongst them, kicking at the ball and shouting to Edane. All the time she played, the questions rang through her mind.

Are you or are you not? Have you the taste of your existence or do you not? Are you within the country or on the border? Are you mortal or immortal?

When the game was over, she parted from her mother with the same words she had said to Gabe.

"I promise to return and let you know my decision."

Falling to earth, Dana landed in the snow near Grandfather's house. Being a fairy, she didn't feel the cold as she walked in her bare feet towards the door. It was early in the morning, the darkest hour before dawn. If anyone had looked, they would only have seen a pale wisp of light.

With every step she took, Dana felt the weight of her decision. How could she embrace humanity? To grow up in the mortal world, she would have to accept so much pain and sorrow, failed dreams and lost hopes, inevitable change and inevitable tragedy. There would be so many things she couldn't control, both in herself and in life.

On the other hand, there was so much to gain, all the joys and wonders of being alive, of human friendship and love, of the great mystery of life, when you can never really know what might happen next.

She stopped before she reached the door. She knew what to do. She turned and ran from the settlement. With the ease of a shape-shifter, she dropped to the ground and took the form of a wolf. Now she let out a howl, high and wild, that woke all the dogs for miles around and set them barking furiously.

The door of Grandfather's house opened. Light spilled onto the snow. Out bounded the black wolf in a rush to join her. When he reached her side, they touched noses in greeting. Then they played together for a while, chasing each other in circles in the snow, dashing back and forth around the trees, snapping and barking in fun. After a time, without a backward glance, they ran into the north.

*   *   *

That evening, the two old men sat drinking tea by the stove. It was dark outside the window but the moon glittered on the snow. The Northern Lights were swirling across the sky. Heads close together in easy companionship, the men talked in a mixture of French and Cree. A jeep pulled up in front of the house and footsteps drew near. Roy came in the door, stomping the snow from his boots. He looked sad and a little resigned.

"I tracked them as far as Lac à l'Eau Claire."

Grandfather and *grand-père* regarded him with sympathy.

"They came up to me. There was plenty of jumping and barking and they let me hug them, but they didn't change back. Then they ran off. Is that their choice, do you think?" he asked worriedly.

The old men exchanged glances.

"They'll always be your friend whatever they do," said *grand-père*.

"Give them time," Grandfather added. "Some things can't be decided right away."

*   *   *

Far in the north, on a promontory overlooking the vast lonely tundra, two wolves howled at the moon. Across the clear sky, the Aurora Borealis illumined the night with multicoloured lights.

Les chèvres dansantes, the French Canadians called them. *The dancing goats.*

The two wolves exulted in the wild beauty of the night, the wild freedom of their nature, the wild magic of the land. And even as they howled, they asked themselves the same questions.

Are you or are you not? Have you the taste of your existence or do you not? Are you within the country or on the border? Are you mortal or immortal?

*   *   *

Farther north again, beyond the Northern Lights, in a place some Native legends called Skyland, the High King and High Queen of Faerie arrived. They bowed before the Old Ones, the Firstborn of Turtle Island.

"Because of you, the Battle of the Great Heart was won," Midir said.

"We are here to express our gratitude," said Honor.

"There is no need," came the reply.

We are all family.

POSTSCRIPT

A YEAR AND A DAY later, Roy went to bed at midnight, having failed as usual to talk his grandfather into doing the same. The Old Man sat at the stove, smoking his pipe and drinking tea. The wise dark eyes gazed out the window at the night beyond.

"We can't wait forever," Roy had said quietly, more to himself than to Grandfather. "They made their choice. Let them go in peace."

It was later, much later, close to dawn, when Roy woke up. Surfacing from a dream of wolves and goats playing soccer in the sky, he heard feet crunching in the snow outside. Then came the sound of familiar voices, talking and laughing. He jumped out of bed, pulled on his jeans and ran barefoot to the door, yelling.

GLOSSARY

Qué yo no vuelva jamás a sentirme el dolor. (Spanish) — May I never know the pain again.

Fado, fado (Irish) — long ago. Usually found at the beginning of a fairy tale, as in "once upon a time."

Tabernac (Canadian French) — swear word referring to "tabernacle." Many French-Canadian curses refer to the Roman Catholic Church. Also used in the book are *câlisse* for *calice* (chalice), and *maudit* (damned).

Monsieur (French) — mister

Un peu (French) — a little

Oui (French) — yes

Mais peut-être (French) — but perhaps

Excus'-moi (French) — excuse me, sorry (informal of *excusez-moi*)

S'il te plaît (French) — please (informal of *s'il vous plaît*)

Merci beaucoup (French) — thank you very much

Ce n'est rien (French) — It's nothing. Used as "you're welcome" in reply to "thank you."

Dis-moi (Canadian French) — tell me (informal of *dites-moi*)

Irlandaise! Magnifique! C'est un très beau pays, l'Irlande. (French) — You're Irish! Great! Ireland is a beautiful country.

Dangereux (French) — dangerous

Prends garde. (French) — Take care/be on your guard.

Mea culpa. (Latin) — (It's) my fault.

Ouvre la porte! Vite! (French) — Open the door! Quick!

Qu'est-ce que tu fais? (French) — What are you doing?

Oíche Shamhna (Irish) — Hallowe'en

Craic agus ceol (Irish) — crack and music — Crack means great fun, as in "having the crack."

Āyā (Hindi) — anglicized to "ayah." A nursemaid or governess.

Sādhu (Sanskrit) — literally meaning "good." The name given to a Hindu holy man or woman who wanders throughout India. They have renounced material life and live in a state of perpetual pilgrimage.

Gurū (Hindi) — A Hindu or Sikh spiritual leader or teacher. While the term has taken on derogatory connotations in Western society, it is one of great respect in India. From the Sanskrit *guruh,* meaning "weighty."

Le Brûlé (Canadian French) — "The burnt place." Anglicized to the Brule. A patch of wasteland or swamp created by a forest fire.

C'est bon. (French) — This is good.

Alors (French) — then, in that case

Bravo! (French) — Good work! Well done!

Qu'est-ce qui se passe? (French) — What's happening?

Mon ami (French) — my friend

Tabula rasa (Latin) — blank/clean slate

Comment ça va? (French) — How's it going? (How are you?)

C'est incroyable! (French) — It's incredible!

Aventure (French) — adventure

C'est vrai? (French) — It's true?

C'est ça. (French) — That's it.

Maintenant (French) — now

Bon (French) — good

Mais non (French) — of course not

Mon grand-père (French) — my grandfather

Je pense (French) — I think

Mais oui (French) — (but) of course

Famille (French) — family

C'était merveilleux! (French) — It was wonderful!

C'était très beau (French) — It was very beautiful.

Toujours (French) — always

Anamchara (Irish) — soul-friend

Chercher une aiguille dans un botte de foin (French) — to look for a needle in a haystack

Chez toi (French) — (at) your house

Gentille (French) — nice

D'accord (French) — agreed, okay

Jongleur (Canadian French) — Native medicine man/shaman *(sorcier indien)*. Also used in the book is *jongleuse* — Native medicine woman/shaman *(sorcière indienne)*.

Irlandais (French) — Irish

Beaucoup de magie (French) — lots of magic

Alors, regarde, chérie (French) — Then look, my darlin'

Bí ar d'fhaichill ar an strainséir. (Irish) — Beware the stranger!

Le canot (French) — boat

La chasse-galerie (Canadian French) — Often directly translated into English as "witch canoe" or "spirit boat," but this is incorrect. *La chasse-galerie* is the process of flying a canoe. One "runs *la chasse-*

530

galerie" (courir la chasse-galerie), but there is no direct translation for the term itself. The boat is *canot* or *canot d'écorce*—see below.

Allons-nous! (French) — Let's go!

Vitement (French) — quickly

Sensible (French) — sensitive

Je m'excuse. (French) — I'm sorry.

Diablotin (Canadian French) — demon

Comment dit-on? (French) — How do you say?

Comprends-tu? (French) — Do you understand?

Nous sommes ici! (French) — Here we are!

Nous risquons de vendre nos âmes au diable! (French) — We risk selling our souls to the devil!

Canot d'écorce qui vole, qui vole! (French) — The bark canoe/boat that flies, that flies!

Canot d'écorce qui va voler! (French) — The bark canoe/boat that is going to fly!

Fais-nous voyager par-dessus les montagnes! (French) — Let's journey over the mountains!

À gauche! À gauche! (French) — To the left! The left!

Dans l'bois! (Canadian French of *dans les bois*) — Head for the trees!

Pas de problème (French) — no problem

Âme soeur (French) — Like the Irish term *anamchara*, this means soul-friend. It tends to be translated as "soul-mate" but it transcends romantic connotations though it may include these. As a Québécois friend explains, it refers to *"une grande amitié, une forte relation amicale et très respecteuse."*

L'histoire (French) — history, story

Loup! Enfin! Ça va? (French) — Wolf! At last! How are you?

Salut (Canadian French) — Hi

Bienvenue, Loup (French) — Welcome, Wolf.

C'est le combat éternel entre les forces du Mal et les forces du Bien. (French) — It is the eternal struggle between the forces of evil and the forces of good.

Je comprends. (French) — I understand.

Moi aussi. (French) — Me too.

Je suis ancien, pas invalide. (French) — I'm an old man, not an invalid.

Son nom? (French) — His name?

Fatigué (French) — tired, weary

Esprit du mal (Canadian French) — evil spirit

Roth Mór an tSaoil (Irish) — The Great Wheel of Life (Note: this is the Irish title of Micheal MacGowan's book about his adventures in the Yukon's gold rush called in English *The Hard Road to Klondike.*)

Voyageur canadien (Canadian French) — woodsman, guide, trapper, boatman, explorer. Literally "Canadian traveller."

Qu'est-ce que c'est? (French) — What is it?

Attention! (French) — Watch out!

Qu'est-ce que c'est que ça? — What's that?

Dehcho (Dene) — The Big River (the original name for the MacKenzie River in the Northwest Territories)

Caribou (Canadian French of Algonkian origin) — large deer in Arctic regions of North America. Both male and female have antlers. The same deer in Asia and Europe is called reindeer.

Les lutins (French) — goblins

Les fantômes (French) — ghosts

Le Diable (French) — the Devil

À bientôt. (French) — See you soon.

J'ai peur (French) — I'm afraid

Mon frère (French) — my brother

N'est-ce pas? (French) — Isn't it? Another way of saying "eh?"

Allons! Allez! — Let's go! Go ahead!

Abú (Irish) — Forever! Hurrah!

Je n'sais pas. (French) — I don't know (short for *je ne sais pas*).

Oui. Bien. Très bien. (French) — Yes. Fine. Very well.

Go raibh maith agaibh. (Irish) — Thank you (plural).

Oui, je connais. (French) — Yes, I know/recognize it.

Buíochas le Dia. (Irish) — Thank God.

Biens le temps (French) — plenty of time

Et toi? (French) — And you?

Ma grand-mère (French) — my grandmother

Le Diable, beau danseur (French) — the Devil, a great dancer and handsome too

Une chanson irlandaise (French) — an Irish song

Oui, c'est ça! Exactement! (French) — Yes, that's it exactly!

Regarde, chérie, regarde mon pays. (French) — Look, sweetheart, see my country.

Seigneurs (French) — lords, landowners

Habitants (French) — tenant-farmers

Tourtières (Canadian French) — French-Canadian meat pies consisting especially of ground pork.

Les cabanes à sucre (Canadian French) — cabins used at maple sugar time

Vite! Rapidement! (French) — Quick! Hurry!

Complainte (French) — lament, sad song

Naturellement. (French) — Of course/naturally.

Catholique (French) — Catholic, as in Roman Catholic

Cailleach Beinne Bric (Scots Gaelic) — The Hag of the Speckled Company

Conte merveilleux (French) — wonder tale, fairy tale

'S FOSGAIL AN DORUS 'S LEIG A 'STIGH SINN! (Scots Gaelic) — Open the door and let us in!

Ceann groppi (Scots Gaelic) — stuffed cod head. A Cape Breton delicacy. The cod head is stuffed with cod livers mashed with corn meal, flour and rolled oats, then boiled or steamed. Yum.

Cat sith (Scots Gaelic) — fairy cat

Omadhaun (Irish) — anglicized version of *amadán,* meaning "fool."

Saltair na Rann (Mediaeval Irish) — *Psalter of Verse,* a tenth-century manuscript containing songs and poems about "life, the universe and everything."

Cara Mia (Latin) — My dear/beloved lady

Cá bhfuill Naomh Bhreandán? (Irish) — Where is Saint Brendan?

Perigrinni (Mediaeval Latin) — pilgrims

La Pèlerine (French) — the female pilgrim

Navigatio Sancti Brendani Abbatis (Latin) — *The Voyage of Saint Brendan the Abbot.* Written in Latin around A.D. 800, it tells the story of the sixth-century Irish monk who set sail for the Island of Paradise on the other side of the ocean. It was a "bestseller" in mediaeval Europe.

Dia duilech (Old Irish) — God of the Elements

Coimdiu na nduile (Old Irish) — Lord of Creation

Ban martre (Old Irish) — white martyrdom

Glas martre (Old Irish) — green martyrdom

Derc martre (Old Irish) — red martyrdom

Is scith mo chrob on scribainn. (Old Irish) — My hand is weary with writing. (Found in the margin of an old manuscript, mediaeval monkish graffiti.)

Tria digita scribunt, totus corpora laborat. (Mediaeval Latin) — Three fingers write, (but) the whole body labours. (More graffiti written by another monk long ago.)

Na péistí. Ansin! (Irish) — Sea monsters! Over there!

Liber Monstrorum (Latin) — *Book of Marvellous Creatures*. Probably written in England (they don't know for sure) early seventh century, but maybe earlier.

Physiologus (Latin) — *Natural Science (book of)*. Originally a Greek work of late antiquity about the natural world. Popular in the Middle Ages in Latin. Icelandic version written later.

Angakuk (Inuktitut) — shaman, medicine man/woman

Nunatak — Anglicized version of *nunataq* (Inuktitut) — an isolated peak of rock projecting above a surface of inland ice or snow.

Le Nord (French) — the North

Nunavut (Inuktitut) — "our land." Canada's new territory, which officially came into being April 1, 1999.

Mal de raquette (Canadian French) — leg strain caused by heavy snowshoeing

Umiak (Inuktitut) — skin boat

Ogham (Middle Irish) — ancient lettering of the Celtic peoples based on straight lines drawn perpendicular or at an angle to another (long) straight line. Usually found on stones or carved on wood. Related to the God Ogma, inventor of the alphabet.

Inummariit (Inuktitut) — "the real people," those who live on the land in the manner of their ancestors

Innunguaq (Inuktitut) — This is the proper term for the human-shaped stone figures (*innunguait,* plural) most of us call *inuksuk* (*inuksuit,* plural). *Innunguaq* means "in the likeness of a human." The *inuksuk* comes in many shapes. It means "acting in the capacity of a human," e.g., as a navigational aid, marker to hunting grounds, indicator of food caches, doorway to the spiritual world.

Grand-père est disparu. (French) — Grandfather has disappeared.

Fais attention (French) — be careful

Chauvin (French) — chauvinistic

Saskehavas (Coast Salish) — Sasquatch in Canada, Bigfoot in the US, and in Tibet, the Yeti, or Abominable Snowman

Klahanie (Chinook jargon, a Native-based trade language used west of the Rockies and as far north as the Yukon) — the great outdoors

Hootchinoo (Tlingit) — distilled liquor, shortened to "hooch" and now North American slang for liquor, particularly illegally distilled

Poudrerie (Canadian French) — drifting or powdery snow

C'est certain! (French) — For certain! It's definite!

Mystère (French) — mystery

Magh Crí Mor (Irish) — the Plain of the Great Heart

Mon amour (French) — my love, beloved

Je t'aime. (French) — I love you.

Garçon (French) — boy

Craoibhín Ruadh (Irish) — Little Red-haired Branch

Mo chara (Irish) — my dear one

Mo stór (Irish) — my treasure

Man-i-tou (Algonkian) — spirit of the land, sacred force

Aqsarniit (Inuktitut) — soccer trails, the name used by Baffin Islanders for the Northern Lights. Another Inuktitut name for the Lights is *Aqsalijaat* meaning "the trail of those playing soccer."

COPYRIGHT ACKNOWLEDGMENTS

Other works:

Throughout the book, there are quotes from other sources such as the Bible, Shakespeare, Farid ud-din Attar's *Parliament of the Birds,* Hildegard of Bingen (as translated by Matthew Fox), Hannah Arendt, Scott Peck, and Henry David Thoreau, and poets including Rainer Maria Rilke, Gerard Manley Hopkins, Samuel Coleridge, William Blake and Wallace Stevens. These are usually in italics.

Most of Grandfather's statements are teachings of Elders given to me or found on record. His words concerning the land are from the written brief *In the Spirit of the Land: Statement of the Gitskan and Wet'suwet'en Hereditary Chiefs in the Supreme Court of British Columbia, 1987–1990.*

Quotes from the *I Ching* or *Book of Changes* are taken from the Richard Wilhelm translation rendered into English by Cary F. Baynes (Penguin Arkana).

Lyrics from *"Vive la Canadienne!"* and "She's Like the Swallow" are found in *The Penguin Book of Canadian Folk Songs* compiled by Edith Fowke (Penguin Books, 1973).